THE SHOES COME FIRST

A JENNIFER CLOUD NOVEL

JANET LEIGH

Enjoy,
Janet Leigh

JANET LEIGH BOOKS

PROLOGUE

May 2004, Monaco

The old man leaned against the wall of the garage. His unobstructed view of the track as the drivers finished their test runs for the day made him smile. The cars whizzed by, blurring into a mosaic of colors. Rolling his cigar between his fingers, the old man waited patiently. He knew smoking was prohibited this close to the cars, but a few puffs of his favorite Cuban eased the tension that showed in the deep crevices on his forehead.

The red Formula One race car slowed as it pulled into the pit. As the car came to a final stop, its roaring engine ceased, and the driver was assisted out by his team. Marco Ferrari smiled as his teammate, Enzio, walked over and gave him a high five.

"*Fantastico*, Marco. That's your best time today."

Marco laughed as he pulled off his helmet, exposing his blond curls, coiled tight with sweat, to the cool air. "Thanks. Just don't beat it tomorrow in that overdecorated junk heap of yours."

"I'll have you know, my friend, I get paid a lot of euro by my sponsors."

"Yeah, but I can hardly see the color of your sled for all the advertisements."

"Would you like to make a wager?"

Marco raised an unnaturally dark eyebrow at his friend. "Does this wager involve women or alcohol?"

"Maybe a little of both."

"Then I'll pass. The last time I made a bet with you, I couldn't drive for three days from the massive hangover. Not even a golf cart."

The crew moved Marco's race car to the garage. After signing off on his test times for the day, he walked over to double-check his car. The setting sun blinded him to the figure leaning against the garage wall. As he moved closer, the familiar scent of a Cuban cigar met his nose, and he smiled. Only his grandfather indulged this close to the track.

Giorgio Ferrari was extremely proud Marco chose to follow in his footsteps, not only as a Formula One driver but as a time traveler as well. Only the lucky inherited the gene that made time travel possible, and his grandson was blessed with the gift.

The day he passed his key to Marco was one of the happiest in his life. Now he must ask for it back. Only temporarily, of course, but Marco used his key to drive his time vessel, his Formula One race car. He only used the key when necessary, but that was Marco. He wanted to win using his skill, not his magic, and he wouldn't give his key or his car up easily.

"Nonno," Marco said as he approached with open arms to embrace his grandfather.

Giorgio placed the cigar in his mouth and returned the hug.

"Did you come to watch me win the race tomorrow?" Marco asked.

"No, I am sorry, Marco, but I need a favor," his grandfather answered in his thick Italian accent.

"What do you need, Nonno?" Giorgio knew Marco preferred to speak English, and a small smile tugged at the corners of his mouth as Marco quickly made the change to Italian out of respect for his grandfather.

"Let's go inside." Giorgio motioned to the garage. A few remaining members of the pit crew completed the final cleanup on Marco's car. Giorgio motioned for them to leave, and they obeyed as they had in the years when they had been in his service. "She looks good."

"You know there is no smoking in here, Nonno." Marco hung his helmet on the equipment rack and turned to face his grandfather.

Giorgio paused and studied his grandson. Marco was mature for his eighteen years, and he had earned the same respect Giorgio commanded from others. Giorgio extinguished the cigar and moved closer to the car. He ran his fingers down the rear wing of the vehicle as if he were caressing the cheek of a small child.

"I need the key," he said raising his dark eyes to meet Marco's light ones.

"You know I can't race tomorrow without my car."

"Elma's in trouble. She transported with her new defender yesterday, and he came back a short time ago barely alive. He hasn't regained consciousness. I need to help her."

"You gave your key to me. Your relationship with Elma caused nothing but heartache for my nonna." Marco crossed his arms over his chest and planted his feet firmly on the ground.

"Your grandmother and I have an understanding that doesn't concern you."

"I need my key and my car tomorrow."

"Marco, this is important. I wouldn't ask otherwise." He moved around the car and laid a hand gently on Marco's shoulder. "Besides, you know I will return in just a matter of hours."

Marco knew he would give in. How could he deny his grandfather? While his parents flitted around the world attending parties, his grandparents cared for Marco and his sister. Giorgio refused to allow them to be raised by the slew of servants his parents left behind.

"Fine...take it." Marco peeled the zipper of his racing suit down, revealing a stone medallion suspended by a silver chain. The stone glowed slightly as he touched the ancient heirloom that hung from his neck, the key to his time travel vessel and his most prized possession, his race car. He reached behind his neck to remove the key, a feat only *his* hands could do unless he was dead. He handed it over to his grandfather, and a small electrical tingle shot up his arm when they touched.

Giorgio hastily secured it around his throat. He placed his hand on Marco's arm.

"Thanks, Marco. You are a good boy." Giorgio climbed into the car. "Now, stand aside."

"Nonno, what are you doing? You can't transport in here. There isn't enough room." But the roar of the motor drowned out his words. Marco shielded his face from the exhaust. A sharp crack sounded followed by a flash of light. In an instant, the car and his grandfather vanished.

Marco stood in the empty space, alone and concerned about the trouble that Elma woman brought his family. She helped his grandfather capture criminals. It should be a job and no more. Nonno had a family, a wife.

Marco showered and changed out of his gear. In his clothes of choice, he appeared more like a high school student than a Grand Prix driver. He wore a faded T-shirt and jeans, an outfit that brought a frown to his mother's face and caused his sister to refer to him as a "tool." He liked the artistic drawings imprinted on his Archaic shirt, and he prized his favorite jeans, a pair of broken-in Diesels.

Thanks to private tutors, Marco completed high school two years early, allowing him more time to race. He put college on the back burner. His father wished for him to attend Harvard and obtain a business degree, but Marco didn't see the point. He was happy racing and didn't need to climb the corporate ladder.

Marco moved outside and locked the garage. Digging in his pocket, he found a half-smoked cigarette. He dropped his backpack on the ground and lit up, leaning against the wall the same way he found his grandfather earlier. He would have to forfeit the race tomorrow if Giorgio didn't return with his car and his key. Marco took a long drag on his smoke and studied the moon. It had just begun to wane; possibly a day would be all the time remaining to return safely.

A loud crack broke the silence. Marco pulled away from the wall. Had his grandfather already returned with that Elma woman? The sound came from a field behind the garage. A huge oak tree held court in the center of the field. Marco's race car waited under the vast expanse of its branches. He flicked his cigarette to the ground, smashing it with his shoe as he proceeded to the vessel.

An empty car greeted him. A few minutes later, Elma's vessel appeared almost on top of him. He dodged out of the way. Elma stumbled and almost fell out of her vessel, holding up a semiconscious Giorgio.

"Marco," she sobbed "I tried to save him, but there were too many of them." Marco's heart froze as he helped Elma lay his grandfather down on the ground.

A pool of blood spread slowly across the center of Giorgio's chest, staining his white shirt a deep crimson. He opened his eyes for a brief second and ran the backs of his fingers across Marco's cheek.

"I'm sorry." He strained to speak. "We found it, you know."

"Hold on, Nonno, I'm going to call for help." Marco searched his pockets for his phone. He had left it in his backpack. Elma shook her head and wiped the tears from her aged face as she held Giorgio's hand in hers.

"Marco, you are such a good boy," Giorgio whispered as his eyes went empty and he died in Marco's arms.

Elma's arm was badly injured, but she removed the key from around

Giorgio's neck and, reaching up, removed her own. Using her uninjured arm, she pulled Marco to his feet, and secured his key around his neck. She placed her key in his palm and closed his fingers around it with her own. Marco wiped away his tears.

"What happen—," Marco started, but Elma cut him off.

"There's no time now." She looked around nervously. "Move your car to the garage and wash the blood from your hands." She looked helplessly at Giorgio. "He didn't want me to take him to headquarters. He wanted to see you."

Marco stood rooted to the ground.

"Do it now, boy; we don't have much time." She looked at him with damp eyes the color of the sea. "Marco, you must protect the gift. I need you to give my key to my great-niece, Jennifer Cloud."

"Your niece?" Marco stared down at her with a bewildered expression. "But she can't have the gift."

"Promise me you will do as I ask. It's imperative for the future of my gift." She gave him a little push. "Go now—get your vessel safe."

CHAPTER 1

July 2013

I bent over to secure the strap on my new pair of Steve Stone metallic snake sling-backs. They'd set me back a few hundred dollars but were worth every penny. I sat upright to finish my makeup and complete my morning routine.

The round mirror on my antique dressing table reflected that a few random strands of my blond hair had escaped from my updo of the day. I secured them with a few bobby pins and plastered on the hairspray like all good Texas girls do. After applying the finishing touches on my eyeliner, I swiped some mascara across my lashes, and voilà, I was ready for my day at the best job ever.

I sighed as I relished my good fortune of landing the perfect job. Jennifer Cloud, assistant merchandiser for Steve Stone Shoes. The sound of it made my heart dance.

Steve Stone Shoes was a specialty shoe store in Dallas that sold tons of designer shoes. It was in the most exclusive mall in Texas and it was my dream job. I had the luxury of being the first one to preview the new spring lines, not to mention I received a fabulous discount. A substantial portion of my paycheck was left behind to pay for my purchases, but I had cute shoes, shiny shoes, shoes in every color, shoes for wet days, and shoes for hot summers when I didn't even wear shoes. I was a lucky girl.

My face smiled back at me in the mirror. The silver chain around my neck sparkled in the light. Tiny blue gems in the shape of stars encircled a piece of stone that resembled a crescent moon. My great-aunt Elma Jean Cloud gave me the necklace in her will. I ran my fingers across the smooth medallion and remembered the first time I laid eyes on it.

~

I WAS nine when I first saw the gift. It was August, one of the bake-your-ass-off months in Texas. My family's Ford Explorer rattled along the asphalt roads looking for the nearest place to have its radiator overheat. The air conditioning was on high and the car radio on low. My mom didn't like country music, and my dad didn't like our hip-hop tunes. So we proceeded on with the soft drone of Elvis Presley in the background.

Dad squinted into the afternoon sun, cursing the fact he had forgotten his sunglasses. His Comanche Indian ancestry showed in his smooth, bronze skin and jet-black hair. He was named after the famous cowboy actor John Wayne, but he went by JW just to rule out any confusion. Pointing the car in the direction of east Texas, he entered the highway. Mom insisted he was the only one with enough patience to navigate the backwoods of his birthplace.

Mom relaxed in the passenger seat next to him, working on a cross-word puzzle and looking very chic in her oversized straw hat and sleek Chanel sunglasses.

We occupied the backseat. My thirteen-year-old sister, Melody, sat to my right. She was the spitting image of my dad. Her big brown eyes focused on the *Tiger Beat* magazine she held in her hands. The blast from the air conditioner blew the layers of her dark-brown hair, cut in the latest Jennifer Aniston hairstyle. She demanded a window seat because she was older than me. So unfair, in my opinion—birth order should not determine car placement.

My brother, Eli, sat on the other side of me, also with a window seat. Two years older than me, he donned the same thick, black hair as my dad and a lighter version of our mom's sea-blue eyes. He stared out the window through his John Lennon glasses. The headphones connecting to the CD player in his lap were latched onto his head, excluding him from my constant questioning about the end of our trip.

I was stuck in the middle—Jennifer Cloud, doomed to ride without a window. I didn't inherit my dad's thick, dark hair or my mom's beautiful blond locks. Instead, I had what Mom called dishwater-blond. Why would anyone name a hair color after dishwater? Go figure. I did, however, have her deep blue eyes. My long hair was pulled back into pigtails and braided with yellow bows at the ends to match my dress. This gave Eli something to tug when he teased me.

"Where are we going?" I asked for the fifth time.

"I told you," Mom replied, "to Aunt Elma's house in Mount Vernon, Texas."

"It's not *aunt*," said Dad. "It's Aint Elma." Mom laughed but probably would not succumb to Dad's East Texas drawl. "Everyone down here has aints and pappies, mawmaws and pawpaws, and most of the boys are just called junior."

My mom, Mary, was an editor for a well-known publishing house. She specialized in cookbooks. Her prim and proper style from being born and raised in Upstate New York threatened to take the twang out of our accents by overenunciating everything.

"We are going to Aunt Elma's birthday party; the entire family will be there," Mom said, tucking the pencil she was using in her crossword book and closing it. "It's kind of a family reunion and a birthday all in one."

"How old is she?" I leaned forward placing my forearms on the front seat.

"No one knows; she won't tell," Dad said, looking at me in the rearview mirror.

"How do we know how many candles to put on the cake?" This was very important to a nine-year-old.

"Duh, when a person gets to fifty years old, you just put one candle for every ten years the person lived," explained Eli.

I guess he can hear under those headphones after all.

Melody saw an opportunity to put in her two cents. "That's the dumbest thing I've ever heard. What if they are fifty-two?"

"You would round up to the next decade. So that would be six candles. But you stop at eight candles." Eli held up eight fingers.

"Why would you stop at eight?" Melody pursed her lips. Making conversation with Eli took extra effort on her part.

"Jeez, Melody, everyone knows old people can't blow out more than eight candles in one blow."

"You're making that up," Melody accused.

"Am not!"

"Are too!"

"Brace face!" Eli shouted, showing off his set of perfectly straight white teeth.

"Shut up, Eli!" Melody screamed through clenched, metal-encased teeth.

"Shut up, Eli." He mocked his interpretation of Melody's voice.

"Settle down, kids. We're almost there." Dad sighed as he exited the highway and turned down a narrow dirt road. Tall live oak trees lined both sides of the pothole-ridden road. Cedar trees and wild brush gathered among the tree trunks like soldiers on the front lines daring anyone to break through.

The vast canopies of the live oaks came together above us, forming a tree tunnel that provided relief from the harsh summer sun. We bounced along for about ten minutes until a few homesteads began to appear sporadically along our route.

Aunt Elma lived in a small, white frame house surrounded on either side by a cluster of deep-rooted oak trees with the occasional red-leaf maple thrown in for color. Her tiny house sat back a ways, barely visible from the road. Today her front yard resembled a used car lot. People parked haphazardly wherever they stopped.

"Good gracious, what a mess," Mom said. "I hope Aunt Elma's yard survives all these cars."

"Honey, don't worry, the only kind of grass that grows out here is crab-grass, and even your cooking wouldn't kill it," Dad said. A small smile tugged at the corners of his mouth.

"That's real cute, JW." Mom pulled her sunglasses down her nose to give Dad the evil eye. He loved my mom's cooking but teased her anyway just to get a rise out of her.

My parents met at a food convention in Las Vegas. Dad had just opened his own health-food store (which was actually a glorified feed store) and had traveled to Vegas to give a lecture on healthy foods and vitamins. Mom had been working as a grunt at a publishing house and was tagging along with the assistant editor in hopes of meeting some of the up-and-coming chefs, so she could edit their future cookbooks.

It was love at first sight. The way my dad tells the story, Mom was crossing the conference room when she accidentally tripped on Dad's outstretched cowboy boot and landed face down in his lap. They married the following week in the Chapel of Love, and since Dad owned the store, Mom moved to Texas and hasn't worn her pearls since.

As we climbed out of the car, the dust rose to meet us. An old tire swing hung from one of the giant oak trees. Melody complained about the dirt, and Eli took off toward the tire swing. The more dirt, the better, in his opinion.

Dad and I unpacked the gifts we had brought for Aint Elma. Melody helped Mom get her homemade chicken casserole out of the car. Apparently, when you go to a family reunion, you're required to bring a covered dish. My mom told me most people bring a casserole since they are easy to carry. I hoped someone brought cake, 'cause I wasn't too big a fan of casseroles.

Today was August 13th. "That's kinda neat that Aint Elma has the same birthday as me, except mine is in June," I said to Dad.

"Actually," he said bending close as if to tell me a secret. "Her birthday is really on December twenty-fifth."

"On Christmas Day? Why are we having a party today?"

"She never has a real birthday party because everyone is busy celebrating Christmas with their families. This year we decided to give her a special party day."

"I like that idea. A special day, just for Aint Elma to celebrate her birthday."

Dad placed his hand on my shoulder. "You haven't seen Aint Elma in a long time, but I know you'll like her. She used to tell me fun stories when I was a boy. All us kids would pile up in her old, wrought iron feather bed. The bed was so fluffy, I sank into it as if I fell into a jar full of cotton. She would sit in the old rocking chair that creaked when she rocked and spin stories about far-off places. My favorite was the story of the Old West."

"Did she travel a lot?" I asked.

"Only in her mind. She had a great imagination, and even though she only finished eighth grade in her education, she loved to read. We couldn't afford to travel. She never had any kids of her own, so she kept us when Mamma worked late. That is until Mamma Bea got the job in the sewing factory, and we moved to Dallas. But Aint Elma wanted to stay right here in the country."

"Did you visit her?"

"After we moved, I didn't see her much." He sighed with a faraway look in his eyes. "But I sure did love her stories about the cowboys and Indians. The way she told those stories, it was almost as if she had actually been there."

I patted my hand over my mouth making a woo-woo sound.

He reached out, making guns with his index fingers and thumbs, and pointed them at me. "Bang."

I grabbed my chest and fell to the ground. Mom gave me a dirty look that I interpreted to mean, "If you get that dress dirty, you are in big trouble." I stood, and my dad handed me a package to carry into the house. He shut the back to the SUV and tickled me in the ribs as we walked toward the porch.

The front porch wrapped all the way around the house like two arms hugging the small frame structure into its bosom. Three wooden steps took us to the screen door, which was propped open by an old milk jug, allowing people and flies to come in at random.

A man hollered at us from a rocking chair on the porch.

"Go on in," Dad told me. "I'll be along in a minute."

I entered the front room. A long floral sofa held several adults. Straight-backed kitchen chairs had been moved into the room, providing additional seating. The room smelled stale. I wrinkled my nose at the décor. Several plastic flower arrangements crammed into glass Coke bottles lined the windowsill. A large birdcage sat on top of an old console TV. A bouquet of fake pansies adorned the inside of the birdcage. All eyes turned toward me as I entered the room.

"Where's the bird?" I asked, pointing at the flower-filled cage.

"Isn't that cute," said a hefty older lady. Her bountiful body was stuffed like a sausage into an easy chair. "The little angel asked where's the bird. How darlin' is that?"

"Where's what?" asked the old man sitting next to her. He leaned over like he was trying to hear a secret.

"Never you mind, Earl," she told him. She leaned closer to me and whispered, "He's a little deaf from the war."

My dad stepped in behind me. "Howdy, Uncle Earl, Aint Mable."

"Well, land sakes, it's JW." She clapped her hands together and then squeezed out of the easy chair. Waddling over to my dad, she opened her arms to hug him, smashing me in the middle.

"I haven't seen you for years," she said.

I hadn't met many of my relatives. Family get-togethers were few and far between. We enjoyed living close to the city of Dallas, often referred to as "Big D." The rest of the family lived here in Mount Vernon, except Mamma Bea. The scent of her White Shoulders perfume reached me before I heard her voice.

"Mamma Bea!" I squeezed out from the Aint Mable hug.

"You come on over here, darlin'," she said with her arms open.

I ran into her arms and she pulled me in tight. She had Dolly Parton hair stacked high on her head and dangling sunflower earrings.

Dad was born and raised in the Texas oil fields. Literally, that is where Mamma Bea gave birth. There was no time to get back to the house, she had explained to me one afternoon after she had a few sweet teas. I later found out Mamma Bea liked to spike her sweet tea with a little Johnnie Walker Red Label.

We were greeted by various "aint thises" and "uncle thats." Mamma Bea took our gifts and told my mom to put her casserole in the kitchen. Adjacent to the kitchen was a long, pine dining table covered in casseroles. There were green ones, yellow ones, brown ones covered with cheese, some with potato chips on the top, and others with green beans sticking out.

"Gross!" I said in my outdoor voice.

"Jen," Mom said in her ventriloquist-style indoor voice. Whenever my mom said something she didn't want anyone else to hear, she partially closed her mouth, clenched her teeth, and said without moving her lips the dreaded words she could not speak. "Go outside and look for your cousin Gertrude."

Gertrude is the daughter of my dad's cousin Trish. They live in a town called Mount Pleasant, but my mom told us it wasn't pleasant 'cause they lived in a trailer. Dad told me a trailer was a house on wheels. I thought this was practical and efficient.

I wanted to know where Gertrude's dad lived. My mom told me Cousin Trish was divorced and it was a good thing too, 'cause he ended up in prison (she said this through clenched teeth).

I made my way to the backyard, where many cousins, second cousins, nephews, and nieces were sitting in fold-out lawn chairs. Babies played on quilts spread out in the brown grass, which would have been green except for the massive drought that was scouring the Texas landscape.

My dad told me I'd played with Gertie as a toddler. I stood awkwardly fidgeting with my braid and scouted for a girl my age. I hoped Gertie would make an appearance soon because Aunt Mabel had waddled to the back porch and was heading my way.

At the back of the yard, a tall row of shrubs formed a wall like a sentry standing guard. I later learned these bushes are called Photinia. An old white picket fence peeked out from behind the red-tipped bushes.

A flash of something metal caught my eye, and I went to investigate. I pushed the long branch of the bush out of the way, revealing a short, round-top gate. Hanging by a rusty nail centered on the gate was a small, hand-painted metal sign that read "Elma's garden—enter at your own risk." What did that mean? How dangerous could a garden be? I was adventurous, right? Maybe she had a child-eating plant or a monster rabbit. I peeked into the garden, but several large trees casting protective shadows prevented me from seeing farther.

Sometimes Eli, Melody, and I would play superheroes. I would be SuperJen, the marvelous hero. I wore my bright-green dance leotard and a big paper *S* drawn in crayon taped to my chest. A blue towel tied around my neck formed my supercape, and a black Zorro mask left over from Halloween disguised my face.

Eli would be my archenemy, Evil Eli. Dressed entirely in black, he would tie Melody up, and I would rescue her from certain demise. Before every rescue I would sing my mantra, "I'm spunky and I'm fierce and I'm smarter than most men. Bad guys run and hide 'cause here comes SuperJen."

After mentally reciting my theme song, I proceeded through the gate and into the shadows. Rows of beautiful flowers soon surrounded me. As I walked down the dirt path, I touched the soft petals of American Beauty roses. My mom loved growing roses. Although our backyard was small, we had several rose bushes lining our fence. I even did a report on the types of roses for my fourth-grade science class.

I proceeded down the path, stopping to admire the tulips, bluebonnets, and flowers whose names I couldn't recall. I bent down to one of the roses and inhaled. The sweet scent tickled my nose. Why didn't Aint Elma put these in her house? Why did it smell so old and stuffy when she had all these lovely flowers? And why was this beautiful garden hidden behind a tall hedge?

I meandered a bit further and came upon the heart of the garden—the vegetables. There were rows of corn, tomato plants, bushels of strawberries, blueberries, and various other vegetables sprouting from the earth. The watermelons were the biggest melons I had ever seen. Who would have thought all this could grow in a dust bowl of heat? How did the old lady take care of this entire garden? Maybe there was a neighbor who helped her out. Go figure.

I wove around a row of tall cornstalks and came to a halt. A huge willow tree grew in the back corner of the garden. The branches hung to the ground like a cascading waterfall. Under the willow sat an odd-looking house. It was about ten feet tall and built from wood that had aged the color of gray skies right before a nasty storm. Someone had tried to paint it green at one time, but most of the paint had chipped off, leaving the building looking worn and tired. The roof was pointed like a doghouse, and the door hung slightly off its hinges.

Carved in the wood above the door, a crescent moon hung, with small stars forming a circle around it. The house was about the size of one of the portable toilets that we use at the state fair. The entire structure was covered in lush green vines that trailed down the sides and out into the garden. This was truly the greenest part of the garden.

I moved closer and was surprised to find Blue Moon roses growing around the base of the little house. I had never seen a blue rose, and as I reached out to touch one, a twig snapped behind me. *Oh Lord, was this the danger the sign had warned me about? Was I about to meet my doom?*

As I contemplated my fate, the rows of corn parted, and out stepped a girl about my age. We were the same height. She was a little plump around the middle and had hair the same color as Ronald McDonald. Her unkept hair accentuated her blue eyes and pale complexion. As she moved closer to me the scent of stale marshmallows emanated from her clothing. Her blue jeans were torn at the knee, and she wore bright-red cowboy boots. At least the boots matched her hair. Her green tank top was a size too small and had a grape-jelly stain down the front.

We faced each other. She stared, assembling her own judgements about me.

"Hi," she said, "I'm Gertie. You must be Jennifer. I think we're second or third cousins, but my mom says it don't matter 'cause blood is blood, no matter how thin."

"It's Jen." I stifled the scream I'd almost set free a moment earlier.

"Wouldja look at that!" Gertie bounced up and down on her toes.

"What is it?" I asked.

Gertie laughed. "You've never seen an outhouse before?"

I shook my head.

"City folk." Gertie giggled. "Well, a long time ago, I think when George Washington was alive, they used them fer the bathroom."

"No way?"

"Yes way. See..." She stepped toward the outhouse. The door gave a loud creak as she pulled it open. Sure enough, there were two round holes side by side cut into a long bench. There was even a small wooden rod for toilet paper. "You jus' poop right in them holes, and it drops down into the dirt. That's why it's so green back here, on accounta all the poop fertilizes them plants."

It smelled kinda funny, and there were two holes. How could anyone do their business with someone sitting right next to them?

A noise came from behind the bushes.

"Quick, get in," Gertie said. Before I knew it, she grabbed my arm and pulled me into the outhouse.

I started to protest, but Gertie put her finger to her lips. "Shush, they're gonna hear us."

"Who's going to hear us?" I asked.

"Them garden gnomes. They're mean little buggers."

Now I might only have been nine, but garden gnomes? Get real. As I sat there, the smell of potties past and Gertie's marshmallow mildew burned my nose.

Gertie whispered, "Do you think it's safe?"

Before I could answer, the ground started to shake.

"What's happening?" I asked.

"It's one of them earthquakes," she said. The walls began to creak and rattle. The door flew open, and we were thrown out into the dirt, both screaming like we were on some scary carnival ride. I skinned both knees, and Gertie had snot running down her face.

"Boy, are you gonna get a butt whoopin'!" A voice laced with anticipation called out above me.

"Butt whoopin' fer sure," said another voice. I looked up to find two small boys with skin the color of Milk Duds. They had on matching Hulk Hogan T-shirts and high-top tennis shoes that lit up when they walked.

"What ch'all doin' back here?" Gertie asked in her outdoor voice.

"Mamma said you gots to come, on accounta Aint Elma's gonna open her gif's." One of the boys was missing front teeth, and the other one had only lost one front tooth

Good, I stood and brushed off the dirt, *I can tell them apart.*

"This here's Cousin Jen." Gertie made introductions, oblivious to the dirt clinging to her clothes. "These are my half brothers from my mom's second husband. He was a wrestler."

"Oh, like Hulk Hogan?" I asked, pointing to their shirts.

"No, a cattle wrastler," she replied. "He got caught stealing some cattle, and the judge said he had to work off his badness far away from here in some town called Penitentiary. I ain't never been there, but Mamma went up once. Mamma said she couldn't handle him bein' so far away, so she got a deevorce, and now she can kiss whomever she wants."

The boys gathered around me to get a closer look. "My momma said your momma is a damn Yankee bitch," Two Teeth said.

"Yeah," One Tooth chimed in, then they started to dance around me chanting, "Yankee bitch, Yankee bitch."

Gertie raised her fists like a prizefighter. "Y'all better stop right now, or I'm gonna knock out the rest of your teeth." I'm not sure if this was how they lost the first teeth, but it shut them up.

"I'm gonna tell Mom," cried Two Teeth, and they took off toward the house.

Gertie charged after the twins. I looked down at my pretty yellow dress, now covered in dirt splotches. I sighed and slowly made my way back to the house.

I found my mom standing on the back porch with her hands on her hips.

"There you are, Jen," she said, then did a double take. "What on earth happened to you?"

I couldn't tell her I had been vomited up by an outhouse. "I fell," was my only reply.

"Aunt Elma has been asking to see you, and now your hair is a mess, and your dress is torn."

I hadn't noticed the tear in my dress. Mom frowned and brushed at the dirt on my dress with her fingers. She prided herself on the fact that our clothes were always name brand and usually came from the Saks Fifth Avenue clearance rack. She told me it reminded her of New York, where the finer clothes were worn.

We walked into the house through the back door, passed through the casserole kitchen, and ended in the living room. The wilted-rose aroma was back, along with mothballs and bleach. My nose began to run immediately.

Aunt Elma was sitting in a floral wingback chair surrounded by gifts and discarded wrapping paper. Her snow white hair was pulled back in a tight bun that rested at the nape of her neck. Her frail bones barely held the housedress she wore, and a pair of knobby knees poked out from under her skirt hem. She was the oldest person I had ever seen. Her wrinkles had wrinkles, and they were everywhere. Someone had put a crown on her head that blinked "Happy Birthday."

"Come here, dear, so I can get a better look at you."

The wolf said the very same thing to Little Red Riding Hood right before he tried to eat her. I looked down at her furry house slippers. They had bunny ears on them. I guessed that anyone who wore bunny slippers couldn't be all that bad. I wiped my runny nose with the back of my hand and moved closer to her.

The interesting necklace she wore caught my eye. A silver chain hung around her neck, and a medallion peeked out from the open buttons at the collar of her dress. The round piece made from a smooth stone rested in the hollow at her throat. The medallion was engraved like the carving I remembered from the outhouse.

She smiled at me, and I thought the necklace twinkled a bit. I gazed into her watery blue eyes. Aint Elma reached out and put her bony hands on either side of my face. At first, I felt a warm, tingling feeling on my cheeks. The warmth moved down my neck and began spreading into my arms.

"You have the gift," she said, pulling her hands away from my face and clasping them together.

"The what?" I asked.

"The gift, the gift!" Her voice grew louder and enthusiastic.

"She wants you to hand her a gift, dorkface," said One Tooth, who was now standing next to me.

I reached for the nearest package.

"Here you go." I placed a gift wrapped in blue polka-dotted paper into her hands.

She smiled at me, and I made a quick retreat.

CHAPTER 2

Six years later and one week before my sixteenth birthday, a knock sounded on the front door.

"Eli, get the door," yelled Mom. "I'm on the phone with Rachel Ray's people."

As I bent to pick up my book bag for school, I overheard the deliveryman tell Eli he had a package for Miss Jennifer Cloud.

"That's me," I said, coming up behind Eli in the doorway. The deliveryman stated it was a pretty big package and asked us where we wanted him to unload. Eli gave him directions to the back of the house and asked him to park under the carport.

The deliveryman gave Eli a thumbs-up and turned to move his truck around back. I adjusted the backpack on my shoulder. *Cool, who would be sending me a package?* Maybe it was a car. Maybe Mom and Dad were going to surprise me with a new car. They said money was tight and I needed to wait until Eli graduated next spring, but maybe it was all just a plan to surprise me.

"Hooray, I'm getting a car!" I cried out as I ran past Eli.

"In your dreams," Eli said, running after me. But when we arrived out back, there was no car. Instead, there was a huge crate being unloaded by the deliveryman; his name tag read Frank. Apparently, Frank was the deliverer not of new cars but of large crates.

"Where do you want it?" Frank asked, scratching his large beer belly.

The buttons down the front of his brown shirt threatened to pop off from the strain of holding his shirt closed.

"I guess you could put it in the backyard." I pointed to the gate.

Frank gave a grunt as he wheeled the crate to the backyard. I signed the paperwork, and he handed me a copy. "It's all yours. Oh yeah, this also goes with it." He placed a padded envelope in my hand—the kind that are stuffed so the contents don't get squashed during shipping. There was no return address. I figured the envelope had my name on it, so what the heck. I tore it open and read the letter inside.

Dear Miss Cloud,

Before the death of your great-aunt Elma Jean Cloud, she bequeathed the items below to you in her will.

1. Outhouse from her garden passed from several generations of Clouds

2. Antique necklace given to her by her mother

Regards,

Mr. Nolan Smythe, Executor

ELI WAS busy trying to pry the crate open with the back end of a hammer. "Got it," he said, and all four sides of the crate fell open simultaneously, revealing the outhouse.

"Whoa!" Eli jumped back out of the way. He regained his balance and slowly walked around until he was standing in front of the structure. "What's that?"

"It's an outhouse," I answered matter-of-factly.

"Someone gave you a toilet?" Eli said with a mischievous grin spreading across his face.

My mom appeared in the back doorway holding her black binder she used to schedule her clients. "What is that?" she asked, waving her empty hand at the outhouse.

"Someone gave Jen a toilet." Eli was now holding his sides and laughing hysterically.

"What on earth? Who would give you such a thing?"

"It's all in the letter," I said, handing my mom the letter from the deliveryman.

"Oh my goodness, I'll have to let your father handle this one," she said, pressing her lips together in a firm line. This normally meant she knew something but didn't know if she should explain it to the children. I got the same look from her when I was younger and asked where babies came from, and what happened to Cousin Trish's second husband.

"Children, you go on to school." Mom tucked the letter in her binder, turned back toward the house, and gave us a wave.

"What are you going to do with it?" Eli wrinkled his nose. "It smells weird."

"Not any worse than your gym socks." The thing kinda creeped me out. I walked around it trying to decide why Aint Elma wanted to give me the scary old outhouse. *Maybe there is a treasure inside,* my inner voice suggested. *I am definitely not sharing the treasure with Eli.* My inner voice agreed. I tried the door. It must have been nailed shut because it wouldn't budge.

"The outhouse looks kinda rustic; we could plant a garden around it."

That freaked Eli out—this was the end of his junior year, and he had better things to do than help his little sister plant a garden around some old shed.

Eli paused at the door. "Sorry, Jen, I won't be able to help you. This is the last week of school before summer break, and I have to prepare for my senior year. I'm working at the store all summer. There will be football practice and SAT preparation and, um, everything else. My senior year is a real busy time, you know?"

Yes, I knew this, because he told me at least a dozen times in the last week. "You don't say."

"I have to make the grades, so I'll be accepted into a good college. I can't waste time digging in the dirt if I want to become a doctor." He disappeared into the house to retrieve his backpack.

Geesh, Eli's obsession with himself was exhausting. I had forgotten about the envelope still in my hands. I turned it upside down, and out fell the necklace Aint Elma had been wearing on her birthday. Well, at least I got some jewelry out of the deal. It was the moon hung on a silver chain.

The medallion itself was made from some kind of rock inlaid on metal. The crescent moon was engraved in the stone. Tiny stars inset with twinkling blue and white stones were dancing around the moon.

"Are these real diamonds?" I asked no one in particular. The necklace was beautiful but a little eclectic for my taste.

"Get a move on, kids!" Mom shouted from the kitchen. I dropped the necklace in my book bag and headed off to school.

We lived in a rural suburb of Dallas, Texas, called Sunnyside. Most of the people in my town were farmers or drove the twenty-minute commute to Dallas to work behind a desk. Although most of the houses in Sunnyside sat on a few acres, there was a small section of town that consisted of a neighborhood with single-family brick houses and two streets of townhouses. I lived on Rollingwood Court in one of the townhouses.

I considered our town nostalgically attractive. Others said it was undeveloped country. There was a Baptist church, Dad's feed store, and an Exxon gas station out by the highway. We had an elementary and middle school but didn't have a high school. Eli and I drove ten miles into the neighboring city of Mesquite to attend school. Mesquite was mostly a blue-collar town famous for the rodeo. Cowboys came from across the nation to compete at the Resistol Arena, made famous by rodeo clown, Neal Gay.

Going from a small country school to the jam-packed halls of my high school was a huge adjustment. Luckily Eli was the quarterback of the football team. This earned me a little respect from a few of the bullies and immediate friendships with popular girls trying to climb the social ladder by dating Eli. My older sister, Melody, was a talented dancer, so she had a scholarship to an arts magnet school in Dallas and didn't have to put up with the riffraff from my high school. She graduated last year and went on to study dance at what my relatives referred to as "some fancy-schmancy school in New York City."

Eli spent his summers working in Dad's store and saved enough money to buy a car. He had just turned eighteen, and I thought he was full of himself, but I loved his car, a 1992 dark-blue Ford Mustang GT.

The Mustang had originally belonged to Mr. Schwartz, who lived down the street. Mr. Schwartz had been saving the car for his son, Zach. However, Zach marched to the beat of his own drum. He dropped out of high school, joined a rock band, and drove a rusted 1972 Volkswagen bus that was missing the back door and had floor-to-ceiling purple shag carpet. Zach told his dad Mustangs were for pussies and took off with his band for LA.

Mr. Schwartz upgraded to a new Mercedes and sold the Mustang to my brother. The car oozed coolness. Eli replaced the radio and the muffler. The speakers thumped so hard, the bass felt like it was beating right through your heart and coming out your ears.

We listened to U2 on the way to school. My brother's choice of music was fine with me. We both thought the old rock was good, and we agreed on most top-forty hits. Eli practiced football after school, so I usually rode home with my best friend, Jake.

Jacob McCoy was tall, and lean from running track, and he had big, brown puppy-dog eyes. His sandy-brown hair hung low over one eye. He had huge dimples, and all the girls thought he was "*sooo cute!*" I thought he was "just Jake."

In fourth grade he asked if I stuffed my bra, and I politely socked him in the nose. Both of us were sent to the principal's office and served detention for a week together. We became fast friends. He told me he thought I had a great right hook. I thought he didn't want his friends to know he was taken down by a girl. Besides, all the other boys threw rocks at me, so it was nice having one on my team.

Jake drove a black Jeep Wrangler, which only enhanced his status as a chick magnet. Every day after school, I had to walk through a nest of cheerleaders to find my ride.

"Honestly, Jake, why don't you just pick one?" I would ask him on a daily basis.

"I like keeping my options open," would be his response. "If one is busy, I can just call another." *Like any one of them would be too busy for Jake.*

I told Jake about my gift on the way home. He parked in front of my townhouse. Our house was connected on either side by an adjoining townhouse. The entire neighborhood was made up of rows of four townhouses joined together. Every three years there was a meeting to decide what color to paint the houses so they would all match. Mom called this "the battle of the bullshit." I overheard her tell Dad she would rather try to get Paula Dean to give up butter than argue with the neighbors.

This year we were painted a nice olive green. I thought it covered the ugly mustard yellow from the previous painting very well. As we walked in the front door and through the kitchen, the outhouse stood beyond the sliding-glass door and hovered over the small set of patio furniture on the back porch.

"Cool," Jake said as he grabbed an apple out of the fruit basket my dad kept on the counter in the kitchen. According to Dad, fruit should always be within arm's reach for times when we needed a "snack." What he didn't know was Mom hid a stash of Ding Dongs in the laundry room.

We went out the sliding door and into the backyard. "My great-grandma had one of these—we used to play hide-and-seek in it," Jake said as he opened the outhouse door. "Radical, two seats." He stepped inside.

"Jake, I wouldn't do that if I were you," I said cautiously.

"Oh, come on, it's kind of like being in a tree house." He grabbed my hand and pulled me inside. We sat down on the bench, being careful to straddle the holes. I noticed two small handles attached on either side of the seat. I didn't remember seeing them before, but I grabbed hold just in case the ground decided to have another quake. Jake closed the door.

"Jake, it's dark in here."

"Yeah," he said with a mouth full of apple and scooted closer to me. "Do you know what people do in the dark?" he whispered, dropping his voice an octave. But before I could figure out why he was acting so strangely, the ground began to rumble and the entire outhouse began to shake. The door flew open. I had a death grip on the handles.

Jake was catapulted across the yard. The apple he had been eating went flying from his hand like it was shot out of a twenty-two-barrel shotgun and smashed into the sliding-glass door. There was a loud crack, and the glass promptly shattered into a million tiny pieces.

"Oh damn, what happened?" Jake sputtered, choking out bits of apple.

I scrambled out of the outhouse. "Are you alright?" I helped Jake to his feet. We looked back at the outhouse. The door was once again shut, and I swear the little moon was smiling at us. My mom came running to the back door.

"Mother Mary Francis, what in God's name happened?" Mom, having been raised Catholic, always started calling out the saints when there was some excitement.

"Um, we had an accident?" I asked more than said, hoping not to get into trouble.

"With an apple," Jake added.

"Well, next time you are going to play baseball with an apple, do it in the front yard," Mom scolded.

Trying to explain what happened would have been unbelievable. Jake and I cleaned up the glass and promised to work at Dad's store to pay for the damage. Jake thought it must have been instability in the ground under the outhouse. I thought the thing was possessed, and I didn't want to go near it again.

After dinner, Dad called for a family meeting. We gathered around the glass-top kitchen table. Dad sat at the head of the table in a yellow padded cane chair, and the rest of us filed in around the table for our typical family meeting.

These meetings were held when there was a major crisis in the family, when a major decision needed to be voted on, or when someone died. I assumed this was about my gift because Mom made cookies. If someone had died, there would be pudding (a comfort dessert), and a major crisis got us chocolate cake.

Dad reached into his shirt pocket and pulled out the letter I had received that morning. "It seems Jennifer has been given a very special gift from Aint Elma."

"Yeah, a toilet." Eli laughed and made farting sounds with his armpit.

Dad cleared his throat and glared at Eli over the rim of his glasses. Eli went into sulk mode, and my dad sighed.

"I called Mamma Bea, and she said all Aint Elma could talk about the last month before she died was how important it was for Jennifer to have the outhouse if something were to happen to her." Dad looked me square in the eyes. "It was as if she knew her time was coming to an end."

I REMEMBERED THE FUNERAL. It was the middle of May in the tiny Baptist church in Mount Pleasant. The entire family was crowded into the small sanctuary, fanning themselves with the program adorned with a picture of a smiling Aunt Elma on the front. She seemed happy. For a woman of her age, she was quite spry, and her death was a mystery.

My family sat ass to elbows in the church pew listening to Uncle Durr speak of his late sister. He was mopping his brow with a handkerchief and pounding on the podium, ranting on about the unfairness of life. The service was closed casket, which raised my curiosity about my great-aunt's demise.

Uncle Durr revealed in his eulogy that Aint Elma had been on her roof fixing a leak when she fell off.

"Dad," I whispered, "how did Aint Elma fall off the roof?"

He looked down at me with glassy eyes and pulled me in close for a hug. "She just lost her grip and tumbled off. If it hadn't been for her broken arm, she might have lived."

"She broke her arm in the fall and died?"

"No," Dad said. "She was mowing the lawn a week earlier and tripped. She broke her arm, but the weight of the cast she was wearing kept her from grabbing on for support when she fell off the house. She landed on her head and broke her neck." *OK,* I thought, *this is scary—she was really old. What was an elderly lady doing on top of a house with a broken arm anyway?*

Mom leaned in from the other side of me, rattled off a few saints, and made the sign of the cross. "I feel terrible," she said, full of Catholic guilt. "She called every summer for the kids, especially you, Jennifer, to come stay with her. We always had so much going on, and I wasn't sure she could take care of you at her age. Now we're too late."

Dad reached behind me and squeezed my mother's shoulder. She rested her free hand on his and reached up to dab her eyes with a Kleenex.

After the funeral services, we drove to spread her ashes at the ancient burial grounds of the Indian tribe of her mother, Mahalo Jane.

"EARTH TO JEN." Eli waved his smelly armpit hands in front of my face.

"Why did Aint Elma leave Jen a toilet?" Eli asked Dad.

"It's an outhouse," I corrected him.

Dad shrugged. "I don't know, but she wanted her to have it, so we should make room in the backyard, maybe plant a garden around it."

Eli immediately remembered some homework he had forgotten to finish and left the room.

I didn't want to explain the strange things that happened when you went inside the outhouse. I had visions of my Uncle Buster coming by after a few drinks, using our outdoor facilities, and getting rocketed into the Blaylocks' yard three doors down. I agreed planting a garden around it was a good idea.

"We could set it way back in the corner and plant all around it. It could be like garden art," I suggested. Maybe the garden would keep people a stone's throw from the outhouse. Mom frowned at the idea of having an outhouse in her backyard, but dad promised to plant the herb garden she had been asking for, and it was a done deal.

Later in the week, Dad bought some herbs and tomato plants. We spent a weekend digging up the yard around the outhouse, and soon we had grown an amazing garden.

Mom used the herbs in her recipes, and life was good. When spring came the following year, flowers in all colors bloomed. And like in Aint

Elma's garden, the Blue Moon roses grew around the base of the little house.

Dad figured the seeds must have blown in from a neighbor's garden. I hated to tell him the only thing our neighbors had blooming was a wild honeysuckle vine on Mrs. Dombrowsky's fence.

CHAPTER 3

*E*li graduated high school and moved to Iowa to attend chiropractic school. I had never been to a chiropractor, but Dad took Eli once when he injured his shoulder in football practice. Mamma Bea told us those chiropractors were like witches laying their hands on your bones and making them go pop.

I devoted the next couple of years to enjoying high school. I never made grades as good as my siblings. My mom told me if I would put as much effort into my studies as I did on shopping for my next pair of shoes, I'd be a straight A student.

I spent the summers reading fashion magazines and lying around Jake's pool, talking about what we wanted to do after graduation. Jake had a scholarship to run track at Texas Tech University. This was great for him but several hours away from me. I didn't have a clue what I wanted to do. Probably I would pursue something in fashion. My parents suggested I attend the local junior college. I can't blame them. My grades wouldn't get me in a four-year school.

Once, I overheard Mamma Bea ask Dad, "The first two were so smart; what happened to that one?"

"Jennifer will figure things out in time." *Go, Dad!*

ONE SATURDAY AFTERNOON, in the first part of May, Jake and I floated around his pool. The early-summer sun provided us a day of eighty-degree weather. It was the perfect temperature for relaxing outside in Texas, because in a few weeks it would be escalating up to our summer boil. It was nearing the end of our senior year. A gaggle of girls had just left to go do whatever the cheerleaders normally do, leaving Jake and me alone.

Best friend Jake was an awesome person. We watched football together, we read comics, and he liked to shop. Boyfriend Jake was a totally different animal. He didn't have any patience with the girls he dated. I'd made it my mission to turn him into a guy even I might want to date.

"You know, Jake, the only reason you run so fast is because you always have so many girls chasing you," I said to him as he tossed a miniature basketball into the poolside goal. "If you would just pick one...I noticed you were paying special attention to Sarah Montgomery."

"If I picked one," he replied, "I wouldn't have to run fast. If I didn't run fast, I wouldn't have this great scholarship at this awesome school where I can meet even more girls to chase after me."

Casanova had returned. Just when I thought maybe he was ready to have a steady girlfriend, he pulled the snake card.

WE HAD DECIDED to go to prom together so Jake wouldn't have to break any hearts by picking just one girl, and I wasn't dating at the moment. Most of the boys at school were just plain old boring. I was looking for a guy who would make my toes curl.

My prom dress was from Neiman Marcus, a deep midnight blue. Mom told me it made my eyes look like the color of fresh blueberries. I guess that was a compliment from a food connoisseur.

Luckily for me, I was blessed with my mom's long legs and subtle curves. The dress hugged my frame in all the right places. The straps hooked around my neck halter fashion and pushed my boobs up an extra cup size. I was already a 34C—so, Barbie, eat your heart out.

My dishwater-blond hair was introduced to highlights, and I now felt more comfortable around Jake's cheerleaders. I even made friends with a few of them. I wore my hair up like Shania Twain on her Woman in Me CD and put on a pair of stunning drop earrings. I slid my freshly painted toes into some Jimmy Choo stilettos that I had saved for six months to buy off the clearance rack at Neiman's. I looked pretty good even without the fairy godmother. I mean, I was always stylish, but tonight I'd fit in with the cool crowd. My inner voice gave me a thumbs up.

I needed a necklace that would complete my ensemble. As I studied my reflection in the mirror, I noticed my old book bag hanging from the corner of my bedpost. Was it still there? How did I forget to put it away? I dumped the contents out on my bed: a roll of cherry lifesavers (my favorite), an old movie-ticket stub for Spider-Man 2 (I went with Jake), some bubblegum lip gloss, and three pennies. And there it was—the necklace from Aunt Elma. The tiny blue and white diamonds sparkled up at me. The moon was smiling; it was perfect. I secured the clasp and a warm, comforting sensation spread over my whole body.

A sexy whistle sounded from the doorway. "Wow, you look great!" Eli said stepping inside my room. I rushed over and hugged him.

"What are you doing here?" I asked. "I didn't know you were coming home."

"I came home to make sure your date is threatened properly."

"Don't worry, it's only Jake."

"I know, Mom told me, but even Jake needs to be warned occasionally." He frowned. "It does take all the fun away. Couldn't you get a date with a guy I could abuse?"

"Nope, I'm going with Jake. The prom will be more memorable going with a friend."

"Well, don't put too much faith in Jake. When he sees you in that dress, 'friend' may have a new meaning," Eli said, making air quotes with his fingers.

"You're so full of crap; I'm not Jake's type anyway."

"Whatever you say, sis." Eli shrugged slightly. A sly grin caused the dimple in his cheek to wink.

"I'm ready." I left my bedroom and headed toward the stairs. Eli jumped ahead of me, propped his hip on the banister, and slid down like he had many times when we were growing up. Jeez, boys!

"Doo-doo-do, announcing Miss Jennifer Cloud," Eli introduced me, making little piping gestures with his fingers.

Rolling my eyes heavenward, I went downstairs. Mom, Dad, and Jake waited at the bottom of the staircase. They stared at me with open mouths.

"What?" I asked, knowing full well I looked fabulous.

"You look beautiful, honey." Dad's eyes glistened, and he blinked rapidly to avoid shedding a tear in front of Jake.

Jake stood slack-jawed, holding a corsage in a plastic box. Eli was standing behind him, mouthing "told you so" to me.

"You look pretty," Jake stammered, thrusting the corsage box at me.

Dad patted Jake on the shoulder and took the box, holding it open for Jake to remove the corsage and slide it onto my wrist.

"Now, you kids be home by midnight," Mom said, snapping a picture. "I know what goes on at these so-called chaperoned dances, and I don't want you kids out so late, drunk drivers and all."

"Yes ma'am," Jake said, opening the door for me. I walked outside to a black stretch limousine waiting at the curb.

"Oh my God! Jake, you rented a limo? This is so perfect." Best friend Jake didn't pull any punches on this date.

"This is senior prom—we should do it right." He grinned.

"You're the best, Jake." I gave him a quick peck on the cheek.

"I know, I rock." He put his elbow out for me, and I slid my hand through. Mom took a few more pictures, and we were off.

Prom was held every year at the Four Seasons hotel. The high coffered ceilings and sparkling gold chandeliers added an aura of sophistication to our date. We ate the catered food, talked with our friends about college plans, and danced our hearts out to Bon Jovi.

The DJ announced the next song would be the last slow dance of the evening. I started back to my seat, knowing there would be a long line of girls begging to dance with Jake. Suddenly he grabbed my hand and pulled me close.

"Jake?" I raised my eyebrows, questioning his choice of partners.

"Let's just dance this last one together." He wrapped his arm around my waist and placed his cheek against mine. His embrace felt warm, cozy, and he was the perfect height for my head to rest on his shoulder. I inhaled his Abercrombie cologne and relaxed into the safety of his arms.

Madonna's eighties hit "Crazy for You" played in the background as we swayed together. The heads of envious girls whipped around to have a better view of us dancing around the ballroom, but I didn't care. Jake was comfortable, like my favorite pair of boots. The fit was perfect, they looked great, and I could wear them for hours without getting a blister.

As the music relaxed into the final chorus, Madonna reminded me I was crazy for you, and then Jake, my best friend since fourth grade, did the unexpected. He kissed me. Not one of those short, brotherly kisses, but a long kiss. The shock took a moment to sink in and then...I kissed him back. There were bemused gasps from the girls around me. When we broke, the song ended. I looked up at him, confused by his actions.

The room was dim, lit only by soft side lights and the disco ball hanging over the dance floor, but I could have sworn Jake was blushing. We stared at each other, then he seemed to snap out of the dream world that held him prisoner.

I saw Jake's football buddies pointing at us from across the room. Jake looked around at the curious stares of the couples dancing close to us. He cleared his throat and announced, "That was pretty good. If I had known you could kiss like that, I would have made my move on you sooner."

The music changed, and an electropop song blared from the speakers. One of Jake's track buddies danced over to us and gave Jake a fist bump. "Way to go, my man," he said as he danced off with his date.

Jake, aware of the attention we were drawing, said, "Maybe we should get a room here."

My eyes widened. Crap, the womanizing snake had appeared. "If I had known you were going to treat me like one of your real dates, I would have brought some condoms!"

I stormed off the dance floor and avoided Jake for the rest of the evening. We didn't talk on the way home. Jake tried to apologize when we got into the limo, but he fumbled for the words, and I wasn't in the mood to hear them.

I fumed silently all the way home. How could he ruin our friendship by thinking I would just put out on prom night? Part of me wanted to remind him of my right hook he had seen in fourth grade, but the other part was secretly having an egotistical moment glorying in the fact that Jake wanted to be with me. Is this the way the other girls feel when he gives them a smidgen of attention? I pushed the thought away and focused on the anger bubbling up in my throat.

My parents, having already had many prom experiences with my sister and brother, would leave the back door unlocked for me. The limo pulled up to the back of my house. I got out and slammed the door behind me. I marched with purpose, opening the gate to our backyard and letting it bang shut. Jake caught up with me before I made it to the back door.

"Jen, wait," he said. I stopped and turned to meet his gaze. His eyes held mine and his carefree smile transformed into his serious face. The same one that told Butchie Weston in sixth grade if he didn't quit talking about my hooters, he would knock his block off.

"I'm sorry." He shrugged, but his brown eyes never left mine. "I don't want to lose my best friend. But these past few months, the thought of not seeing you every day has scared me. Maybe the reason I haven't picked one girl is because the one I want to be with is you."

"C'mon, Jake," I said moving toward him. "We've been friends forever. How can we do the girlfriend-boyfriend thing?"

"Does that mean you might be interested?" His mouth turned up into an almost smile, and his dimples winked out at me.

"What about all your other girlfriends?"

"When I saw you tonight, I didn't think about any other girl," he said. "Let's try, OK?" And then he leaned in and kissed me. His lips were warm and gentle. I knew this would be a huge deal between us, but maybe he was the one. I looked at my toes—did they curl? My heart raced a mile a minute and butterflies tickled my insides.

"You know you're not very good at the boyfriend thing."

"Maybe you can teach me."

"OK," I finally agreed, "let's give it a go."

He smiled down at me. The full moon shone brightly behind him, forming a halo around his head. His lips brushed mine, and we embraced each other in a different way than we had in the past. A tingle of excitement sent sparks to my nerve endings, like the feeling from my childhood of an early Christmas morning when I would rush downstairs to see what presents Santa left under the tree.

"I'd better go; the driver has to be back by one o'clock." He leaned in and gave me one last good-night kiss. "This was a good prom. Have sweet dreams, Jen." The back gate creaked softly as it shut behind him.

CHAPTER 4

$\mathcal{W}$as I dreaming? Could my best friend be my one and only true love? Was he my happily ever after and forevermore? I floated around my backyard. Before I realized what I had done, I found myself in the outhouse, sitting sideways, hugging my knees to my chest, humming the melody to "Crazy for You."

My insides tingled, a warm and happy sensation like after eating a slice of homemade chocolate cake. The outhouse door hung open slightly. Had I opened it? I couldn't remember.

My fingers brushed across my necklace; I now considered it my good luck charm. A perfect sliver of moonlight reflected off my necklace and illuminated the wall of the outhouse, revealing several markings carved into the wall. I didn't recall seeing those before, but then again, I hadn't spent any time inside the outhouse. My legs unfolded, and I scooted in for a closer look. A few cobwebs had found their way inside, along with a light coat of dust. I brushed the dust away, revealing what appeared to be a word. I could barely read the primitive carving.

"Hanhepi," I said the word aloud. Suddenly, my necklace began to glow. I looked down at the round stone. "What is this?" I asked myself. "What's happening?" Then it happened. The outhouse door slammed shut. I sprang to my feet. My heart started pounding along with my fists against the weathered wood as I tried to open the door.

The ground began to shake. I braced myself as the outhouse began to sway. Wind swam around me like a tornado and sucker-punched me in the gut. I couldn't breathe. I saw a bright light, and then I think I heard myself scream.

With a loud crack of thunder, the outhouse landed on a hard surface. The door flung open and I was launched out of the damn outhouse onto the ground. My hands scraped across stone. The soft, green grass of my garden had changed to gravel. My body ached as if I had been in a car wreck.

"Am I dead?" I asked out loud. "Is it my heart? I try to eat healthy. I only put mayonnaise on my French fries sometimes."

I looked down. Gone were my beautiful blue gown from Neiman's and my Jimmy Choo shoes, and in their place, well, it looked like my aunt Agnes's tablecloth. My mother's sister, Agnes, indulged joyfully in her Scottish heritage. She had all kinds of things made from plaid: curtains, pillows, placemats, and even little outfits for her Scottie dog.

I struggled to stand. I was wearing a pleated plaid skirt and a high-necked, ruffled white shirt overlaid with a matching corset and bound together by plaid ribbons down the front. White wool stockings scratched at my legs, and—*gross!*—loafers. Not a cute Sperry-style shoe but an ugly, brown, square thing had replaced my Choos. My feet had never been in loafers before. A wool scarf was choking me around the neck, and I was sure I didn't have on any panties. The necklace hidden under the frilly white top glowed briefly, then went dark.

What did I do to deserve to be here? Was kissing Jake the reason? I reached up, and on top of my head was a wool hat pulled down over my Shania Twain hairdo. *Damn, that's going to be a mess to comb out.*

"God," I called as I struggled to walk down the rock-strewn road, searching for any signs of life. I didn't see any houses in the vast farmland surrounding me, but the enormous full moon hung on the horizon like a beacon of hope.

The moonlight glistened off the gravel, making each pebble sparkle like a bed of pearls. The glow lit the entire area, allowing me to get my footing and scope out the surroundings. I slowly made my way down the road. With each step the gravel crunched under my loafers, echoing loudly in the quiet, dark countryside.

The road turned into a small dirt trail, and the comforting crunch of stones under my feet dissolved into a ghostly quiet. I was in some sort of field. There was a line of ash and pine trees to my left. In front of me, the shadowy profile of a large hill resembled an old man's face with a big crooked nose and pointed chin.

"Where am I?" I yelled out into the creepy calm. As I was about to sit down and cry, the sound of running horses thundered in the distance.

"Hello!" I shouted and moved closer to the trees toward the sound of the horses. A hand clamped over my mouth, and someone grabbed hold of me from behind. I tried to scream and kicked hard, fighting my captor.

"Quiet, lassie!" a voice commanded in my ear, "or they will hear you." The voice didn't sound like a rapist or the devil. But since I had never personally encountered either one, what did I know? There was a slight lilt in his accent, but his words were smooth and his tone was firm, yet soothing. It was a sexy voice, deep with a kind of arrogance that comes from being confident. I struggled, jabbing my elbow into his ribs.

"Oof," he responded but didn't release his firm hold on me. A sharp pain stung the side of my neck. He pressed a knife against my jugular, and I stiffened in response. "Be a good lassie and I willnae slice yer pretty throat."

He pulled me back in the shadows of the trees, and we peered at a clearing through the branches. An old-fashioned water well sat in the middle of the space. The riders came into the moonlight about thirty yards in front of us. There were four of them, two women and two men. They stopped and dismounted.

The women wore long, flowing gowns. The first woman turned away from me to assist the other woman. A dark braid descended out from her white bonnet and continued halfway down her back. Her simple blue dress had a white pinafore covering the front, tied at the waist and neck.

The second woman was dressed in a beautiful deep-burgundy satin gown with exquisite gold trim and beads that sparkled in the moonlight as she moved. She took off her hat and shook her head of reddish-blond curls as if they had been suffocated by the cap for far too long.

The two men dressed in old-fashioned riding clothes scouted the area as if searching for my captor. All four of them looked like they had just stepped out of the pages of my English literature book. I couldn't wrap my head around why these people rode horses and dressed in elaborate costumes. *They must have come from a costume party,* I speculated loosely.

I wasn't sure what to make of the horses, but rich people in Dallas often went out of their way to be authentic. In fact, last year I read in the *Dallas Observer* that one of the Maverick basketball players showed up at the owner, Mark Cuban's, Halloween bash dressed as Prince Charming in a horse-drawn carriage identical to Cinderella's and proceeded to escort his high-priced call girl, dressed as slutty Cinderella, into the Cubans' mansion. The reason it made the paper was slutty Cinderella tried to steal a set of sterling-silver candlesticks that belonged to Mark's grandmother. She was promptly thrown out, glass stilettos and all.

I struggled to get free. Maybe these people could help me find the way home.

"Not yet," my captor purred in my ear with a firm grasp over my mouth. His body leaned against mine, pinning me to the sappy bark of an aging pine tree. His other hand had a secure grip on the handle of the knife at my neck.

"You will ruin everything," he whispered.

The woman in blue drew water from a nearby well. The crank squeaked as it raised the bucket to the top. *They must be in trouble with the law. Why else would they drink well water? It's polluted.*

One of the male riders said, "Excuse us, Your Highness, we seek privy in the woods."

The woman in burgundy nodded her head, and the two of them turned their backs as the men headed in my direction. I could tell this was a dilemma for my captor because he froze solid as a stone statue.

I considered making noise to reveal our hiding place when one of the men stood directly opposite me and dropped his drawers, exposing me and my captor to his rather large penis. He grabbed it in his small hand and proceeded to relieve himself on the tree trunk. The other man waited with his back to me, keeping his eye on the two women.

"Do ye think they will catch us?" The exposed man lowered his voice as he spoke to his companion.

"No, I think naught. We have gained serious ground on them today. But I am worried for our queen. France has shunned her, and I fear her cousin will naugh be kind."

"Weel they execute us if we are caught?" he asked, shaking his member and securing the beast back in his pants.

They changed positions, and the other man watered the tree. Thankfully, his penis was blocked from view by a large bush.

"I dinna ken, we would surely be worthy of a trial first and imprisonment for certain. No worries, lad, we are not in the Dark Ages. 'Tis the year of our Lord 1568."

The year 1568. My head began to swim, and I felt faint. My captor must have sensed my weakness, because he hissed into my ear, "Shhhh."

The men returned to the well. After they had each taken a drink from the water, one of the male riders said, "We must go, Yer Highness."

"But I am so tired. Can't we rest here?" asked the woman in the beautiful gown.

"No, My Queen," said the male. "We must get to the other side of the loch before dawn."

He called her queen, and their accents were so strange. Where on earth did that dumb outhouse bring me? I was contemplating a time continuum like in *Land of the Lost* and was secretly relieved I wouldn't be chased by giant dinosaurs but concerned that maybe I was being held by Jack the Ripper.

I assumed my clothes had changed to blend in; maybe I should copy the accent until I figured out where I was and if my captor was friend or foe. I had taken four years of drama. It was a blow-off class, but I loved the acting. If I could just channel a little Mrs. Doubtfire, maybe I could buy some time with this creep.

The voice in my ear said, "Please, I beg ye. Just a few minutes more, and I weel release you." He secured his grasp on my mouth, pulling me into him. His deep masculine scent engulfed me—a combination of the fresh smell of pine and a hint of cinnamon. Although I was being held against my will, as I stood there, I sensed I was witnessing something magical.

The woman gathered her skirts and was assisted onto her horse by the other male. They rode off into the night.

I should have made more noise—that was probably my only way home —but once again a sexy male voice played with my sanity.

"Now," the voice said, "I'm going to let ye go, but dinnae scream, aye?" His hand remained over my mouth contemplating my release. "Because if ye do, you will alert the scoundrels." He paused a moment. "Ye promise?"

I nodded my head yes and said, "I promise" into the hand. But I had my fingers crossed just in case. He released his grip, and as I turned around, the most handsome face appeared in my line of vision. As he pulled back from me, I realized he was tall—about six foot three. He looked slightly older than me, maybe around Melody's age.

The moonlight illuminated his rugged features and the square angle of his jaw, which sported a day's stubble. He had dark hair that hung down to his collar in glorious waves. I couldn't make out the color of his eyes, but the dark, glistening pools reflected the moonlight. Unfortunately, little frown lines marked the crease between his eyebrows. His lips pressed together in a tight line.

"What the bloody hell are ye doing out here, alone in the Scottish countryside, at this wee hour?" A tinge of anger lined the edge of his voice.

"If I knew where the bloody hell here was, I would tell you," I stammered back, mimicking his accent.

"So, ye are lost?" he asked, raising one of his dark eyebrows in suspicion.

"Aye," I said, "I was walking and lost my way."

He sheathed the small knife he was holding in the pouch on the side of his calf and looked at me curiously. "Where were ye walking from?"

Panic overcame me. I couldn't remember a single town in Scotland, and would it exist in this time if I could recall one. I did the only thing I could think of. I fainted

He cursed, gathered me in his arms, and placed me gently down by the nearest tree. My ugly hat had fallen off, and loose tendrils of my hair were blowing in the small breeze. I kept my eyes tightly shut, hoping he would go away.

He reached over and brushed back a strand of hair that had fallen across my face, securing it behind my ear. *Wait, he wasn't acting like Jack the Ripper.* His started to remove my scarf. *Wait, what if he were a thief and stole my necklace?* I changed my strategy. Better to attack him with my eyes open.

I fluttered my eyes open, trying to look dazed, and swatted his arm away from my neck. Thankfully, the thick wool scarf and frilly top hid my necklace.

"Easy now. Are you unweel, lassie?" He placed his hands on my shoulder in a comforting gesture. A warm sensation spread down to my fingertips, and I had the feeling of annoyance combined with a tinge of attraction. He removed his hand and the feelings disappeared.

I shook my head, took a deep breath, and tried to figure out if I should tell this handsome stranger how I arrived in the year of our Lord 1568.

"Look, we dinnae have much time. I have a job to do, and then I will help ye find yer way home. But ye need to stay here in the shadows and keep veera still and veera quiet. Do ye understand?"

I nodded. He squatted beside me and decided I was going to live. The sound of another horse approaching caused him to put his finger to his lips, reminding me to be quiet. He pulled his hat onto his head and eased around the trees, leaving me alone.

The wind picked up and fat drops of rain splatted against my skin. Drawing my scarf close around me, I located my ugly hat and pulled it back down over my head. If this man took my necklace, I might not be able to return home. I slipped the necklace from around my neck and tucked it into the deep pocket of my skirt.

A horse whinnied and I stood, wondering where Mr. Sexy had gone. I peered around the tree and through the bushes. A man dressed in—I couldn't believe it, but he also had on Aunt Agnes's tablecloth and an official-looking jacket with a badge embroidered over the right breast. He went to the well and inspected it. He knelt and checked the ground as if tracking the direction of the previous riders. The man must be some kind of policeman. He might help me.

I took a step forward out of the shadows when—*wham*—Mr. Sexy hit the policeman over the head with a big rock. He went down like a sack of potatoes. I raced out of the bushes.

"What did you do that for?"

Mr. Sexy looked at me with a shocked expression on his face, almost as if he had forgotten I existed.

I heard horses in the distance. "Help me get 'em, lassie," he beckoned as he started to pull him toward the trees.

"I most certainly will not help you commit a crime!" I said, stomping my foot.

Mr. Sexy grabbed him by the arms. The man was shorter than Mr. Sexy, but his stocky frame probably outweighed him by thirty pounds. Mr. Sexy struggled to pull him into the trees. He propped the man against the tree's trunk, giving him shelter against the rain.

He returned to the well and took the rope off the basket used to gather the water. He tied the man's hands together behind his back and secured his legs.

"Give me your scarf," he demanded.

"No!" I said. The rain was coming down harder, and the sound of horse hoofs in the distance drew closer. He walked over to me and yanked my scarf from around my neck. He put it over the man's mouth, making a gag.

"Let's go," he said, then he proceeded to climb on the man's horse.

The rain was coming in buckets, and I was freezing. "I'm not g-g-getting up on that thing, and I'm not s-s-stealing a horse." My teeth chattered.

"C'mon, lassie, don't be like that—I cannae leave ye oot here; they will jail ye for crimes against the Queen."

Holy crap, that sounded bad. What were my choices? Get on the big horse with the extremely attractive guy, or wait to see if I would be put in jail? I held my hand out and put my foot in the stirrup. He pulled me up behind him onto the horse. I wrapped my arms around his waist. He was pleasantly warm, and I pulled myself in tight against his back.

"I haven't committed any c-c-crime," were my last words as we rode away into the soggy night.

I didn't speak during the ride. The rain had settled into a slow drizzle, making conversation difficult without yelling. I wasn't exactly sure how to explain where I came from, so silence seemed like the best choice. After a bit, the rain stopped, and the trail we were riding on narrowed and forced us to ride through a small wooded area. The vast number of trees and brush blocked the moonlight, enveloping us in the pitch-black night.

"Is this safe?" I asked. "I mean, riding in the dark like this?"

"Aye, the horse knows the way. They see better in the darkness than we do. Dinnae tell me ye have never ridden a horse before?"

"Oh, um, sure, lots of times," I lied. "I've never ridden in the dark."

"Where are ye from then, lassie?"

Here came the moment when I would have to try to explain myself. As I chewed over the best way to describe the twenty-first century to this common Scottish thief, or whatever he was, the trees closed in on us, causing the brush to scrape against my legs. The horse kept moving, and a buzzing noise sounded close to my ear. I swatted at the pesky insect, and a small light appeared in front of my eyes.

"A firefly," I said.

He made an "mm-hmm" sound of noninterest, but when we rounded a bend in the trail, the trees widened, emptying us into a space filled with the glowing creatures. Small bursts of light fluttered around us; it was like we were riding through a shower of lights.

"It's so beautiful," I said, laughing at a firefly that had settled on Mr. Sexy's shoulder.

"Aye, the ones on the leaves of the bushes there," he pointed to a cluster of brightly glowing leaves. "'Tis the females. They're brighter than the males."

"Why are they brighter?" The man's description of the tiny insects had me curious.

"To attract the males. The females cannae fly, so they attract the males' attention with their lights."

"Are you a biologist?"

"Noo, I'm a male." We both laughed, and the tension seemed to wash away with the rain.

As we came out of the woods, the rain began again, starting in a light drizzle and gradually increasing to a steady downpour. The trail began to widen and eventually turned into a country road. A small farm came into view over the crest of a hill. Mr. Sexy clicked his tongue, and the horse ambled over to a tree. I went to step off, except there wasn't a step, and I slipped off and landed with a hard thud right on my ass.

"Are ye all right then?" he asked.

I nodded, feeling a slight flush crawl up my face.

"Next time you should wait for me to help ye." He looked down at me; a slow, sexy smile spread across his amused face as the rain dripped off his hat.

I crab-walked backward out of the horse's way. Getting to my feet, I brushed the grass from my wet clothes. He dismounted and secured the horse to the tree. We crept closer to the house to get a better look. Apparently, the occupants were fast asleep because the house was completely dark.

"This way, sunshine," he said, grabbing my hand and pulling me behind him.

There was a barn behind the house, and he quietly pulled the door open and we slipped inside.

"This is a barn," I said.

"Aye, but you're out of the rain now."

He was right. My clothes were dripping wet, my nose was running, and my teeth were still chattering, but I was out of the rain. The full moon was forcing its way through the dark, cloudy sky and illuminated the barn from an opening above the hayloft. I could make out the empty animals' stalls, a pitchfork, and other equipment stacked neatly in the corner of the barn. He walked over to the supplies, picked up a horse blanket, and spread it over a pile of hay. He wrapped another one around me.

"This should keep ye warm, but you should take off yer wet clothes and let them dry." He removed his long riding jacket, revealing a black silk shirt that fastened up to his neck, black riding pants and boots. The shirt clung to his muscular body, and I bit my tongue to prevent it from rolling out of my mouth. I didn't have men like this in high school. He looked dry and warm. He kicked off his boots as I contemplated my next move. I was freezing, but I wasn't about to undress in front of a stranger.

"You need to turn around." I motioned for him to turn away from me.

"Are ye shy?" The corners of his mouth turned up in a wicked grin.

"No, but I don't know you." My fake accent quivered a little, and I reminded myself to keep it together.

"Here, let me introduce myself," he said as he came close. A small scar cut through the end of his right upper lip. Sexy. He pulled me into his arms and brought his lips to meet mine. His mouth was warm, and he tasted like cinnamon as he stroked my tongue with his own. His heavy-lidded eyes gazed into mine and my insides ignited. The cold was no longer a concern as I melted in his arms.

He lowered me to the hay. I couldn't speak as he peeled the stockings from my legs. My mind was saying no, but my body was saying yes *please!*

"Do ye want me to stop?" he asked.

"No," I heard myself say, and his mouth found mine

He drew away my wet skirt and tossed it aside. His taut, muscular body pressed against mine in the darkness. I decided I must be having one of those dreams that feel real and then you wake up and say, "I can't believe that wasn't real." If that was the case, then what the hell—it was my dream.

I responded to his kisses, allowing his tongue to caress mine and moving my hands around to his buttocks, pulling the silk shirt free from the back of his trousers and pushing them lower. He obliged and removed the pants, returning to cover me with his warm body. My fingers roamed under his shirt and across his bare back as I kissed the stubble on his chin, and down the masculine curve of his neck. I tried to unbind the ties on his shirt so I could run my tongue along the hollow beneath his sexy throat, but he pulled my hands away and pinned them to my sides as he worked his way down to my inner thighs.

The heat intensified as we explored each other. Streaks of fire soared up my arms and wrapped me in a cocoon of warmth. Pulling the ribbons loose from the corset, he worked his way upward, ripping my shirt open and discarding it. Raising my shift, he tasted me, and I cried out with pleasure.

He ran his tongue up my neck until he found my mouth, kissing me hard. His hands were roaming over my breasts, my stomach, my thighs. My heart was beating in time with his as he stroked me, increasing my hunger for him. I climbed higher and higher, until I reached the peak of the mountain, and seconds before I dove over the edge, he slid inside me. I felt a sharp pain, and then my whole body exploded in a frenzy of sexual need. I ran my hands through his thick hair, wrapped my arms around his neck, and matched his desire.

I woke the next morning feeling incredible. I rubbed the sleep from my eyes, and reality hit. My escapade from the night before wasn't a dream; it was real. I was lying on a bed of hay covered with a horse blanket. Where was Mr. Sexy?

My skirt rested in a heap next to me, and my stockings hung over the horse stall. I was still wearing the thin shift. I discovered my blouse haphazardly thrown over a nearby hay bale; however, a few of the bottom stays were missing, lost in passion and hay. How embarrassing—my first real love affair, and I wasn't even wearing my Victoria's Secret panties, but some kind of grandma nightgown.

Frantically, I searched my skirt and found my necklace still hidden in the pocket of the folds of the material. I blew out a sigh of relief and secured it around my neck. At least I could get home. Now to find the way.

My legs were saddle sore, and it took all my energy to pull on my stockings, blouse, and skirt. My hair was a disheveled mess, so I stretched the ugly toboggan down over the damage and waddled outside to figure out what had happened.

The horse was gone. Mr. Sexy was gone. I, however, was stuck. How was I going to get home? The rain had stopped, and the sun was peeking between the green hills. The surroundings were breathtaking. If I weren't in such a predicament, I might have enjoyed the lush grass glistening with morning dew or the pasture across the road filled with furry black sheep grazing lazily in the sunshine.

A rumbling sound drew me to my left and a hay wagon approached, captained by a weathered old man. A big gray donkey pulled the full cart of straw. As they drew closer, I waved a hand for them to stop and described the big hill from the previous night to the farmer.

He scratched his head and then said, "Oh, ye mean Bernardi Hill? I'm headin' in the direction. I could drop ye if ye like."

The wagon was a one-seater, so I climbed in the back of his wagon, and after about an hour of bumping along, my ass hurt and my legs were itching from the hay poking through my stockings, but we were back at the big hill.

I thanked him and hopped gingerly out of the wagon. The man looked around and then looked back at me. His eyes were questioning my choice of destination.

"Don't worry, I'm off to meet someone," I explained.

"Good day to ye, lass." He tipped the brim of his straw hat, gave the donkey a giddyup with the reins, and lumbered off down the path.

I made my way down the gravel road looking for the poor man Mr.

Sexy had confined in the night. No man was tied up in the trees; only the remnants of the rope remained. No Mr. Sexy was lurking about either.

"I can't believe I don't even know his name," I said out loud, mentally bitch slapping myself. "I am a careless little slut!" *I have wonderful Jake at home wanting to be my first real boyfriend, and what do I do? Roll in the hay with some arrogant asshole who leaves me stranded in the year of our Lord 1568.*

"Where is that Scottish bastard? Where is that damn outhouse?" As soon as I said the words, it appeared out of nowhere in the same spot it had abandoned me in the first place.

"Great!" I said. "You disappear and then you reappear. What kind of crappy magic toilet are you, anyway?" I got in, sat down, and held on for dear life.

"I just want to go home." I repeated the magic word, "Hanhepi." My necklace started to do its Care Bear thing, and off we went. The second trip wasn't so bad. I didn't get the wind knocked out of me, and when we landed, I didn't get thrown out the door.

I expected my parents to be frantic with worry, and the police would put out an APB for Jennifer Cloud. Poor Jake, he would be the clueless suspect, last seen with the missing person. But when I opened the outhouse door, it was dark outside; I was in my blue dress, not a single hair out of place. I looked down and almost cried—there on my feet were my Jimmy Choo stilettos. Life was good once again.

CHAPTER 5

eez. Snap out of it, Jen. I pushed away from the mirror and checked the clock. Crap, all this reminiscing had made me late. If I were lucky and didn't hit any traffic, I might make it to work on time.

I caught Interstate 635 and drove in to work, trying to avoid traffic accidents triggered by a recent downpour. Parking was always a chore at the mall, but I managed to find a spot outside Neiman's. Damn, due to the traffic, I was late.

My small red umbrella was tucked under my seat. I grabbed it and opened my door. The rain was coming down sideways and pelted me right in the face. I poked my umbrella out and pushed the automatic-open button. The umbrella opened in one swift motion and—*whoosh*—a big gust of wind carried it away. My umbrella went tumbling down the parking lot with me in hot pursuit. I tackled it an inch from the front door.

As I stepped inside, umbrella in hand, a puddle formed around my new Steve Stone heels. A woman covered head to toe in a yellow rain slicker came in after me. If I didn't know any better, I would say she escaped off the Morton's Salt box. I recognized her as a sales associate from the lingerie department in Neimans.

"Honey, you look like a drowned rat," she said removing her hat and shaking drops of water from its brim.

I caught my reflection in the glass door. Gads, she was right. My updo hung in a wilted mess, with pieces of hair falling free and clinging to my neck like depressed seaweed. I tried to wring out my wet hair.

"Are those new Steve Stone shoes?" She bent down to take a closer look at my shoes.

"Why, yes," I said proudly, holding my soggy foot out for inspection.

"Too bad Mr. Stone was such a crook; I loved that store."

"What do you mean *loved*?" I always figured he was a little sketchy in the law-abiding-citizen role, but the man was a genius when it came to shoes.

"Didn't you watch the news this morning?"

Like, no, I sleep until noon. I never watch the news. I shook my head.

"They took the guy out in handcuffs," she said, clicking her tongue while taking off her raincoat. "Yep, led him right through the food court... tax evasion or something."

Oh my God. Not Mr. Stone. Surely, she was mistaken. I sprinted off through the mall. Rain droplets flew off me as I passed nearby shoppers. By the time I arrived at the store, my clothes were almost dry from the run. My hair was sticking out like a troll's, and I was wheezing. I desperately needed an exercise program. There were people everywhere. I pushed through the crowd of onlookers and found Evelyn, the store manager, standing at the register crying into a hankie.

"Oh, Jen, did you hear? The feds came and took poor Mr. Stone to jail."

Men in gray uniforms were carrying boxes of shoes out of the store. Following them was a portly man with a commercial dolly wheeling out Mr. Stone's computer and filing cabinet.

"What are we gonna do?" I asked.

Evelyn dabbed at the mascara running down her face. "Mr. Stone said not to worry; he'd see us in five to ten."

"Years?" My shoulders slumped as I sunk down into the giant purple stiletto-shaped chair the customers used for trying on shoes. My chest ached, and my hair was frizzy. Could this day get any worse?

"Why don't you just go on home, dear?" Evelyn patted me on the back. "There's nothing more you can do here." And then she started to cry, again. "There's nothing more any of us can do."

I decided to pack my desk and go home. Maybe I could persuade my mom to make some of her pick-me-up brownies. She always made them when I was down in the dumps. I found an empty shoe box and put my few personal belongings inside. I attached the "I love my job" pin to my shirt and sneered at the feds as they checked off my contents. I hugged Evelyn good-bye and headed out the door to my new life.

I smelled the brownies as I entered my house. Mom must have seen the news. *Isn't it wonderful moms have that intuition when their children need comfort and comfort food?* I went upstairs to take a shower and wash my misery away.

The Steve Stone shoe store was closing. After my shower, I sat in the kitchen with my hair wrapped in a towel, wearing my pink fluffy robe and slippers.

"Why is this happening to me?" I wailed to Mom as I ate my third brownie.

"You'll find another job, dear," she said, patting my hand, completely aware of my over-the-top drama-queen attitude.

My dad came in through the back door. He kissed me on top of my toweled head. "I'm sorry about your job, sweet pea."

He came home early from work because he knew I lost my job. How thoughtful. I ate another brownie.

"Dad, you didn't have to leave work early." I gave him my sad-little-girl smile. The one that told him I appreciated the attention.

"That's not the only reason why I'm home early," he said, sitting down next to my mom at the table. He sighed, and they both looked at me. Something was up; they were double-teaming me.

"What?" I asked. They were about to tell me something important. I knew by the way Dad took Mom's hand and they looked at each other and then at me. What was wrong? Was somebody sick? *Just tell me and get it over with already.*

"Maybe now is not such a good time, JW," Mom said.

"No time like the present." Dad peered at me over the top of his glasses.

"But she lost her job today." Mom looked woefully at Dad.

"I'm right here, you guys!" I frowned. The little-girl sympathy was a ruse. They were harboring secrets. "Out with whatever it is."

"Well, Jen, we're moving," Mom said to me. The words sounded like the Charlie Brown cartoon's teacher—slow and muffled.

"Moving? But we have always lived in the townhouse. Where are we moving?" I asked.

"Well, dear, *weeee* are not moving, just Dad and me. All you kids are grown, and we would like to move into a retirement community, a place where JW could play golf and I could relax and write that cookbook I have always talked about."

"But you're not retired," I said.

"That's true," she said, "but these places are difficult to get into, and we need to strike while the iron's hot."

I sat staring at them in disbelief, my fifth brownie left half-eaten on my plate.

"I know this is bad timing, but there is a house available, and it's right on the golf course," Dad explained with a "please understand" expression. "We love it and want to put a contract on it before someone else snatches it up."

Although I was happy my parents wanted to improve their lifestyle, and the idea of having my own place was appealing, it was also a little scary. They had allowed me to live rent-free while I went to college and began my career.

"What about me?" I stuttered. "Where am I going to live?"

"We don't want to sell the townhouse; it will make a great rental property. So, we are going to rent it to you."

"Rent it to me? I can't afford a whole house. I just lost my job."

"Yes, we thought of that. Your brother has an opening at his new clinic. I called him when you went upstairs to change. He said you could work as a CA."

"What's a CA?" I asked.

"Chiropractic assistant," Mom responded with a satisfied smile. The same one she used when she scratched an item off her to-do list.

Go to the grocery store.

Pick up dry cleaning.

Get Jen a life.

Now, I knew I was too old to be acting like a teenager, and I should have been grateful my mom was helping, but I was feeling full of self-pity.

"Mom, I don't want to be a CA; I want to buy shoes."

"It's only temporary, and to help with the rent, your cousin Gertrude's moving in. She needs a place to live while she finishes college, so I told her she could come live here and pay half the rent. How great is that?"

My life was truly over. I no longer had an awesome job, my parents were deserting me, and my smelly cousin Gertrude was coming to live with me. How much more could a person take?

My parents left me alone in the kitchen to contemplate my future and eat the entire pan of brownies. I reached in the pocket of my robe for my cell phone and hit Jake's number. If anyone could make me feel better, it would be Jake.

Jake and I had seen each other on and off during college. On one of his rare visits home for a weekend, we would hang out just like old times, except there would be some kissing, and after I showed him what I learned in the barn with the Scottish creep, our relationship was way more exciting. As a bonus, Jake was very good at the extracurricular activities.

I still wondered about Mr. Sexy, occasionally. I never told anyone about the outhouse or the time travel, and I continued to wear the necklace as a daily reminder of what not to do. Sometimes at night I would wander out back and imagine myself sitting in the outhouse, going for another ride so I could tell him a thing or two. But I was scared. What if I didn't return? I needed answers, but I had no idea whom to ask.

Jake had graduated from college with a degree in criminal justice and returned to Dallas to work at the office of internal affairs. He traveled between Dallas and Washington, DC, but mainly he worked in Dallas. I'm not sure exactly what he did, but I knew he worked long hours and hoped to land a job with the CIA.

After taking our relationship to the next level in college, I decided we wouldn't work out as a steady couple. I knew there were girls he was seeing at school, and I didn't want to have the pressure of jealousy. Jake insisted we could work long distance, but I knew deep down he couldn't make the commitment, and it would tear our friendship apart. In the end we decided to date each other when he came home and keep it a "casual" relationship. Since he'd moved back home, we had been seeing more of each other as his work allowed.

Jake lived in a loft apartment off Main Street in Downtown Dallas. Once an industrial district, now it was the cool place to live. At night, Jake would open the windows and we would listen to the bands in Deep Ellum playing the divergent sounds of local musicians. I called to tell him of my plight, and he agreed to meet me at our favorite Mexican food place.

I chose to wear my favorite red sweater and black leather miniskirt with my red Escada pumps. I added some M.A.C. Brave Red lipstick and felt a little bit better. I pulled my hair back in a low ponytail, dumped the contents of my purse into my red Prada bag, and headed out the door.

When I was working at Steve Stone Shoes, I'd purchased a used Mustang convertible from Mrs. Peterson. Her husband had been having a midlife crisis, but after it was over, he was ready to go back to his pickup truck. \

The car was white with gray leather bucket seats, a custom Bose sound system, and chrome wheels. It had the faint odor of Old Spice, but I felt sexy driving it around town. The construction workers would whistle as I drove by; however, they also whistled at Ms. Martin down the street, and she drove a Cadillac—go figure.

I drove out of our neighborhood and hopped on the Lyndon Banes Johnson Freeway, which connected to Interstate 30, to take me downtown. Driving into Dallas always made me feel energized. The setting sun illuminated the skyline of tall buildings. I squinted to view the ball at the top of Reunion Tower. Its lights danced, begging you to come and have an expensive dinner in its rotating restaurant. As I turned east onto Main Street, the Deep Ellum arts and entertainment district came into view.

Deep Ellum was the renovated warehouse district about three blocks from downtown. Some creative genius had taken the decrepit, run-down industrial warehouse area of Dallas and turned it into a dwelling place for the eclectic. People who lived here marched to the beat of their own drum. Most were musicians and artists, but occasionally, mixed in with all the graffiti, you'd find a yuppie. I am not sure I would classify Jake as a yuppie, but he was somewhere in between. He dressed like one but had the heart of a guy who would rather be playing lead guitar for Van Halen.

Luckily, I found a parking place in the lot next to the Blind Lemon club and took the short walk to Monica's. Jake and I had discovered the small Tex-Mex restaurant shortly after he moved back to Dallas. It was charming and funky at the same time.

I ambled in past the brick walls that were painted with swirls of various shades of red and displayed bright, attention-grabbing art pieces done by local artists. There was a live band playing jazz in the corner. The tables were covered with red- and caramel-colored linen tablecloths, and the smell of homemade tortillas filled my nostrils, making them flare out and my mouth water.

Jake had arrived first and had commandeered a corner table. He sat drinking a Corona. I slid into the booth and kissed him hello. There were dark circles under his eyes. He was a great guy to meet me when he was obviously exhausted.

"Do you want a beer?" he asked and signaled the waiter.

"Sounds good. I've had quite a day."

"Me too," he said, but a sly smile crept at the corners of his mouth.

The server brought my Corona, and I squeezed the lime slice that rested on the mouth of the bottle down into the golden liquid. I took a long pull, and the tension eased in my neck.

Jake was watching me. Small frown lines formed between his

eyebrows. I knew he hated when I drank straight from the bottle. He thought a girl should drink a cocktail, and, heaven forbid, if she had a beer, she should at least ask for a glass to pour it in. This was one of the many pet peeves we argued about.

Jake wanted his girlfriends dainty and with manners that would make Martha Stewart proud. I had the style, but my manners were all Chelsea Handler. I could put on a good show, but I decided I wanted a man who didn't roll his eyes if I burped or drank from a bottle. Hence the fact we were friends with benefits.

"So, tell me what's up?" I asked.

"No, I would rather hear about your day first; mine is sort of confidential. I'd have to kill you if I told you."

"Wow, they're giving you some serious cases. Should I fear for your life?" I said it jokingly, but his eyes didn't laugh with me.

"I do have some good news, but first tell me what happened to make you dig out your favorite red sweater," Jake said, placing his hand on mine.

It was early in the wrong season for a sweater in Texas, but when tragedy struck, the red sweater was my comfort blankie. I told Jake about my terrible day, and he listened intently. He was always good at letting me vent and not providing any opinions that would make me pissy.

"What am I going to do?" I whined. "My life is a black cauldron swirling with the bowels of disappointment and despair."

"It can't be that bad. You have a new job, and you have shoes that will last you at least two seasons," Jake said, tweaking my cheek.

This was true; I could probably make do before they went out of style. Plus, after I spoke with Eli on the phone, he was going to pay me. Not as much as I was making at the shoe store, but a fair wage. Maybe working in a chiropractic office wouldn't be so bad. I was going to help sick people get well with my spunky spirit and appreciation of life. After a few Coronas, I was feeling a little better.

"So, what's your news?" I asked, turning my attention away from my miserable life.

"You are looking at the newest member of the CIA," he said, drumming his fingers on the table.

"Jake, that's wonderful." I gave him a big hug. "I know you have been working your butt off."

"Amen," he said as we tapped our beer bottles together in a toast.

We ate and listened to the band. Jake explained how impressed one of the directors had been with his work. He couldn't go into all the top-secret details, but I could tell he was excited to get a position in the CIA.

After dinner we walked hand in hand back to his apartment. We passed a tattoo shop, several bars, and a sushi restaurant before we came to a stop in front of his apartment building.

"Do you want to come up?" he asked.

"Sure," I said, feeling a little tipsy from the beers at dinner.

Jake lived in one of the converted warehouses. It was a little more upscale due to the fact it had a small reception area downstairs and a doorman. A few rich and famous young people lived in Jake's building. It was a mix of wealth and upwardly mobile executives trying to downplay their stuffed suits by living in an uber-cool neighborhood.

I had run into a pro hockey player on the elevator one day, and I knew a relative of Ross Perot lived in the penthouse. Jake's grandma Pearl had left him a small inheritance when she died—enough to allow Jake to pursue his dreams of becoming a CIA agent while living like a poor James Bond. Jake got stocks and bonds; I got an outhouse. Go figure.

"Good evening, Mr. McCoy," the doorman said to Jake, and tipped his hat at me.

"Hey, Mike, how are the Cowboys doing tonight?"

"Beating the Giants twenty-one to seven. It's the third quarter." He pointed to an earbud in his left ear.

"I'll catch it upstairs, thanks," Jake replied as we entered the elevator.

Jake's loft-style apartment used to be a warehouse. It was open and airy, and the windows were immense. Jake had left the windows tented open, and the jazzy music from the street below flowed inside. Huge pieces of art decorated the walls. My favorite hung over his brown leather sofa. It was a picture of the Beatles walking across Abbey Road.

I sank down in the soft leather and propped my feet on the rustic wood coffee table. Everywhere you looked, Jake's apartment shouted comfortable. All he needed was an old hound dog lounging around to complete the ambiance.

"Jake, you need a dog," I called to him from the sofa.

"I told you before, Jen, no pets," he said as he came into the room carrying two beers. Mine was poured conveniently in a glass.

"Are you are trying to get me drunk?" I arched an eyebrow at him.

"Maybe." He handed me the glass.

"Well, maaaybe I'm trying to get *you* drunk so you'll let me buy you a dog."

"I can't have a pet," Jake said, looking at me sternly. "I didn't want to tell you since you were already having such a terrible day, but I'm leaving in the morning. Jen, I'm going overseas."

"Overseas!" I sat up quickly, spilling my beer down the front of my sweater. Another reason I preferred drinking from the bottle. "Damn, that's cold," I said, placing my hand on my chest and pulling my sweater away from my skin. "Overseas, like Europe?"

"No." He handed me a towel he had retrieved from the kitchen. "I can't tell you where I'll be, because I'm getting a top-secret assignment."

I dabbed at the wet spot on the front of my sweater. "Jake, are you going somewhere dangerous?"

"Not exactly. I'm going to oversee a top-secret project that needs...sort of a babysitter."

"As long as you're the good guy and you aren't going into a war zone, I guess I'm OK with that, but I'll miss you." I took a drink of the remnants of my beer.

"Me too," he said. Removing the beer from my hand, he pulled me to my feet and gave me a long, deep kiss.

"Your sweater is all wet," he said, running his lips along the nape of my neck.

"I should probably take it off."

He agreed, pulling my sweater over my head.

"Well, since I'm the good guy..." He unhooked my bra with a flick of his finger. I leaned into his arms, wrapping my legs around his middle, and he walked me into the bedroom with his lips pressed to mine.

I woke the next morning in a tangle of sheets and nothing else. I heard noise in the kitchen, and the smell of coffee floated into the room. Jake walked in right behind it. He was showered and fully dressed in a suit and tie.

"Good morning, gorgeous," he said.

Jake had lost the Zac Efron hairstyle and boyish face of high school. What stood before me was lean and sexy, a combination of Brad Pitt and Ryan Seacrest. His hair was cut short and spiked in peaks across his forehead.

"Did I miss church?" I joked from under my sheet shield.

"Funny," he said. "I have an early flight."

"Jake!" I shot up, forgetting about my lack of clothes. The sheet dropped, and my girls spilled out, exposing me to the handsome CIA agent.

"Damn, Jen, why did you do that? Now I have to take another shower, a cold one." He laughed as I pulled the sheet over my chest.

Jake came and sat on the bed next to me. "As much as I would like to stay, my flight leaves in two hours, and if I'm not on that plane, I'm pretty sure my new position will belong to someone else."

"When will you be back?"

"Don't know, and I'm not sure what kind of contact I can make once I'm there.

"No phones, not even your cell?" I asked, frowning. "Are you going to Antarctica? Wait, I think they even have cellular service; I'll check my coverage."

"I'll know more once I'm there. I'll e-mail if I can, I promise." He leaned in and kissed me.

"I've really got to go. Do you still have your key?" he asked.

"Yes." I pouted.

"OK, there's coffee in the kitchen. You're on your own for food. I'll see you soon. Bye, Jen." And he was gone.

I stretched out like a cat, satisfied from a night of glorious sex but slightly depressed there wouldn't be any more of that for a while. I managed to get up and take a shower. Jake was gone, and I had to face a new job and a crazy new roommate.

I came out of the shower with a towel wrapped around me and one turbaned up in my hair. Jake's shirt from the night before was lying on the chair. I put it on and inhaled the scent of his cologne, which immediately made me feel better.

I strolled into the kitchen and replenished my coffee. I stripped the bed and put on new sheets, because I felt Jake's housekeeper shouldn't have to change the sex sheets. Another area Jake and I disagreed. As I was making the bed, the phone rang. The answering machine picked up, and Jake's voice let the caller know he was not in. I smiled; even the voice on his answering machine was that slow, warm Texas drawl. I could picture his dimples winking in and out as he said the words.

Due to the security level of his job, he was required to have a land line. I liked the fact Jake still preferred to use an answering machine, so old school. The machine beeped, and a woman's voice giggled.

"Hey, Jakee, it's me, Bambi. Sorry we couldn't get together last night, but maybe we could catch a quickie before you fly off to work. Love ya, call me."

Oosh! My blood was boiling. I knew Jake and I weren't exclusive, but jeez, Bambi? What kind of bimbo name was that? And she knew he was leaving town before I did. I dressed quickly, crumpled Jake's shirt into a ball, and threw it on the freshly made bed. Grabbing my red Prada bag, I stomped out past the guard in the foyer. It wasn't until I reached my car, I realized my hair was still wrapped in a turban on top of my head. Dang.

Two weeks later, I woke to a loud pounding on my front door. I hurried groggily down the stairs toward the cause of the ruckus. My cousin Gertrude had her face pressed against the glass window in the door, trying to see inside. I unlocked the door and pulled it open.

"Good morning," she said. Her voice a decibel above what I considered chipper.

"What time is it?" I rubbed my eyes.

"Six a.m.," she replied. "I'm supposed to move in today, right?"

"Yes, but my today doesn't usually start until ten on Saturday."

I looked past Gertie and saw a small moving van parked at the curb. I had run across Gertie at a few family functions, but it had been years since I had seen her. She was still shorter than me, but her Ronald McDonald hair had calmed down into a deep red and hung down her back in a thick braid. She wasn't the chubby girl I remembered from my childhood, but thick and curvy. She definitely came from the Cloud side of the family.

My parents had moved out the week before. Mom cried as she loaded the last box. Now they lived in a new house with all the amenities and a neighborhood full of senior citizens to keep them company.

I moved aside and let Gertie enter. She was followed by her two very large brothers carrying large boxes.

"You remember the twins, Billy Ray and Bobby Ray, don't cha?" asked Gertie.

"Y'all have, um, really grown," I said, and they both grinned widely. "And you guys have all your teeth, well, sort of..." Billy Ray had a gold cap on one of his front teeth.

"Yeah," he said, "knocked it out in football, but now I look like Mike Tyson."

"Absolutely," I agreed. *Not.*

Last time I had seen Gertie, she had a tongue ring and was sporting paint-on tattoos to irritate her newest stepdad. Gertie had removed the tongue ring. I guess the rebel attitude had worn out its effect on her step-dad. We helped Gertie move in and paid her brothers with pizza and beer. Six empty pizza boxes later, the twins left.

Gertie took my parents' old room. The space was bigger than mine, but

I had turned the spare room into a closet, and my room was comfortable and familiar. I would feel weird sleeping in the room where my parents "did it." I knew I should be more mature about such things, but, *ewww*, you never get over the thought.

Gertie and I were polar opposites. I liked designer things, and she liked pink and lots of it. Her bedspread was pink, along with her curtains and most of her clothing, and she had an oversized pink papasan chair that took up an entire corner of her room. When I first stuck my head in, I thought the Pepto-Bismol bottle had exploded.

"Whoa," I told her, "this is sooo pink."

"I know, my mom told me once I looked terrible in pink, so I made it my new favorite color."

Gertie and her mom had a love-hate relationship. Gertie was taking classes for her degree at Southern Methodist University. At night she worked part time in the library on campus. I wondered how someone with such a loud voice could work at a place where quiet was revered. Gertie told me she spent all her time catching the college students making out in the stacks.

When Cousin Trish married Vincent Gambino, things changed for Gertie. Vinnie and Trish moved to Manhattan. The next week Vinnie sent Gertie and her brothers off to Catholic school. Gertie explained the nuns had whacked that white-trash behavior right out of her. On the other hand, Billy Ray and Bobby Ray had given the nuns so much grief, they were expelled and sent off to military school.

After a few months, even the armed forces couldn't handle them. They were kicked out and moved back to Mount Vernon to live with Trish's mom, Aunt Azona. My dad says Aint Azona could make the devil sing the "Hallelujah Chorus," but she was heaven in the kitchen.

Gertie told me she loved to read. When she was sent away to school, she didn't have many friends, and one of the nuns encouraged her to read. Gertie's infatuation with history books led her to study for her bachelor's degree in history. She had a ton of books. The boxes filled the entire living room. Who would have thought the redheaded, freckle-faced, kick-your-ass cousin would be a book-reading nerd? Although I bet she could still kick some ass if you pushed the right buttons.

We decided to place Gertie's books on my dad's bookshelf in the living room. This way either of us could have access to them. I liked to read a book occasionally, while my nails dried.

Dad had cleared out his homeopathic medicine books, leaving me a few about medicinal herbs and vitamins in case I had an herbal emergency. I unpacked books on medieval history, ancient Roman history, American history, and various other countries' histories. I called to Gertie, who was in the kitchen. "Did you read all of these books?"

"Yes, I have what's called a photographic memory," she answered from behind the kitchen wall. "I can remember anything I have read at least once. Mamma Bea said I get that from the Cloud side of the family."

I couldn't recall the last book I had just put on the shelf, so I figured I had missed the photographic memory gene. If Gertie had a photographic memory, why did she need to keep all these books? Go figure.

I was reaching down for another book when a hiss came from below the box I was unpacking. Removing the box, I found a crate with a hinged metal front. Sticking through the bars was a gray paw. I bent down for a closer look, and a pair of bright green eyes squinted at me, followed by another hiss.

"Gertie!" I hollered. "What is this?"

Gertie rounded the corner with a bowl of ice cream. "Ooooooooh, cuddleumpkins!" She put her bowl of ice cream on top of the crate and opened the metal door. I backed up a few steps 'cause cuddleumpkins didn't look so happy to see Gertie. She reached in and pulled out a huge gray tabby cat, stuck him in the crook of her arm, and rocked him like a baby.

"No one said anything about a cat. I'm not sure we can have a cat." My older sister, Melody, had allergies, so we were never allowed any animals.

Gertie grimaced. "I already cleared it through your dad."

My dad loved animals; it was my mom who always put her foot down. Gertie had asked the right parent for permission. Maybe having a pet wouldn't be so bad. He would kill the bugs and any mice that might wander into the yard.

"This here's Smoke, my little cuddleumpkins." Gertie said the last part in baby talk as she kissed the cat on the head. "He's real friendly once you get to know him." She scratched under his chin, and he tilted his head up, rolled his eyes back into his head, and purred. I studied the creature.

Cats always acted pissed off. He looked at me upside down, his green eyes barely visible through the slit-like openings. He seemed harmless, so I stepped forward, extending my hand to pet Smoke on the head. He opened one eye, then performed a perfect backflip out of Gertie's arms, claws extended, and attached himself to my leg.

"Yikes, he's got me," I shrieked, running around the room with the cat stuck to my leg. "Get him off, get him off!"

"Hold still!" Gertie said, chasing after me. "He's nervous."

She plucked him off my leg, along with a chunk of my sweatpants.

"Nervous, my ass!"

"He just doesn't know you yet."

I bent over with my hands on my knees, panting. "Maybe cuddleumpkins should stay in your room."

"Okeydoke. Once you make friends, he won't jump you," she said, placing the cat in front of the bowl of ice cream, which he licked at victoriously.

"How long does that take?"

"Mmmm," Gertie said with a finger on her lips. "Oh, I'm not sure. He's never warmed up to anyone but me."

Great, not only am I sharing my space with a cousin, but now I also have a psycho cat. My life just keeps getting better. Jeez.

CHAPTER 6

*M*onday morning my alarm sounded, playing the sweet sound of Carlos Santana. Waking up with Carlos always put me in a good mood. I crawled out of bed to get ready for my job as a CA for my brother, Eli. After graduating from chiropractic school, he moved back to Dallas to open his own clinic. Owning your own business right out of college was cool. I wasn't sure how cool it would be for me to work for him.

After a two week break to help my parents move and sulk over my situation, I was ready to move on. I decided to wear my white Dior sweater and black slacks, subtle yet sophisticated. I pulled the sweater on over my favorite Victoria's Secret camisole. *Damn hanger titties.* These are the annoying little bumps that form when you leave your sweater on the hanger from the dry cleaners. I smoothed them away as best as possible, slid on my Jimmy Choo pumps with a slight mourning for my past employer, and I headed out the door. I hopped in my car and drove east toward what we call the country.

Sunnyside had a few farms, and I waved at the cows as I passed. My dad, being part Native American, told us if all the cows were standing in the same direction, it was going to rain. I had the top down, so I checked out the cow forecast, and about 30 percent of the cows were standing in the same direction, so my chances were good it wasn't going to rain today. You can never tell about the weather in Texas. It's as finicky as a woman going through menopause. One minute it's ninety degrees and sunny skies, the next you're in the middle of a downpour. I chose to go with the cows instead of the local meteorologist. More accurate.

Dad's health-food store—well, really it was a feed store that sold a lot of vitamins, but being so close to the farms, he sold more products for animals than humans—sat on the corner of Beltline Street and Main Street. The town of Sunnyside and the city of Mesquite intersected at my dad's corner. He got the farmers and the suburbanites all in one swoop. Dad's Ford truck was parked behind the store. He has always been a diehard Ford man. I beeped my horn as I passed the store and turned right on Beltline. I motored down Beltline, passed the high school, and took Highway 80 out of Mesquite.

Eli's clinic was in a small town called Coffee Creek, about twenty minutes east from my house. People in Coffee Creek didn't take any shit. They were hardworking, blue-collar people. Most of the locals worked on farms or at the ice-cream factory. The factory was the only big industry in the town.

I exited Highway 80 and made a beeline to the drive-through at the McDonald's on the corner. I needed a jolt of coffee to motivate me. The girl at the drive-through had a name tag that read "Marie." I wanted to tell Marie that she and I were going to be good friends because if I had to be at work every day by eight-thirty, I was going to have to start it off with a large mocha latte.

After I was properly caffeinated, I turned on Fourth Street and entered the downtown area of Coffee Creek. My brother's building was located on the downtown square. The big red courthouse stood tall and proud, identifying the center of the town. About twenty steps led up to the entry, lined with colonial-style columns across the front. It was a typical, small-town square with four intersections and one-way-only signs directing you around the courthouse. Eli's chiropractic office was bookended by a barber on the right and an empty building on the left. A nice courtyard stretched between his office and the empty building. On the other side of the vacant building was Busch Taxidermy. He had a sign in the window that read, "Get mounted cheap." Geesh.

I motored around the square and parked behind Eli's building in his employee-only parking. I tried the back door, but it was locked, so I walked through the courtyard and stood admiring the big plate-glass window that read "Cloud Chiropractic Center." I was proud of Eli but not so sure I was cut out to work in a medical office. I tried to watch CSI once and got queasy.

"You can do this until the great shoe-buying god finds your resume and calls for an interview," I said to myself as I took a deep breath and walked in the door.

The office wasn't open for business yet, and I took a minute to take it all in. The waiting room walls were painted a soft beige, and the deep blue carpeting gave the office a calm feeling. There was a TV turned on in the corner carrying on about your bones and how you should be taking care of them. I stood straighter and walked up to the sliding-glass window at the front counter. Voices resonated from the other side of the glass. The window slid open, and a gray-haired woman stuck her head out.

"We open in five; you can take a seat," she instructed.

To my left a door opened, and a cute girl who looked about sixteen came bouncing up to me.

"Hi, you must be Jennifer," she said with a perky smile.

"Yep, that's me." I extended my hand.

"I'm Paulina, Dr. Cloud's assistant," she explained as she grabbed my hand and pumped it up and down. "I'll show you around. We opened last month, and we're already super busy. On account of your brother is so cute. All the LOLs just love him."

"LOLs?" I asked.

"Yeah, little old ladies," she answered. "Your brother has a way with them."

The gray-haired woman chimed in, "Yep, they haven't had a hot doctor in this town since Dr. Evans moved in thirty years ago and gave away free gynecological exams with your first visit."

"Dr. Evans was a hottie?" Paulina looked over at me, making a face.

"Girl, that was back in the day."

"Must have been," giggled Paulina. "Now he looks like Gene Wilder in Dr. Frankenstein. This is Mary, by the way; she's our office manager." Paulina gestured toward the older woman.

"Proud to meet ya," Mary said. "Why don't you show Jennifer around the office? We have a few minutes before the morning appointments arrive."

Paulina showed me the front office where Mary worked, then took me down the hall, passing rooms that opened off the hallway where the chiropractic would take place. Beyond this was an open room where patients could exercise and receive physical therapy. Paulina explained this to me as we crossed the hall into a break room.

She also informed me she was twenty-two—could have fooled me—

and had a two-year-old daughter. Her husband worked at the ice-cream factory. I suddenly felt the hands of time around my throat, and my biological clock struck twelve, reminding me I had one. I swallowed hard, breaking the grasp, and tried to smile politely at Paulina. She poured a cup of coffee, and I followed her out of the break room and into an X-ray room.

My brother stood looking over a patient's X-rays. Paulina handed him the coffee and left, giving me a pat on the back. For the first time, I noticed my brother was no longer the big football jock. He was dressed in a white doctor's coat, dark pants, and a tie. Under the coat he had a blue shirt the color of his eyes. Every strand of his dark, short hair was held in place by some space-age gel. Eli had grown up.

"Hey, Jen," he said, embracing me in a bear hug.

"I like the tie, but I swear I remember a certain boy proclaiming he would never wear a tie when he went to work."

"Yeah, well, I guess Mom was right; it does look nice, and she bought it for me." He grinned and his cheek dimpled. "I get you don't know much about chiropractic, but you're friendly, determined, and I can teach you what you need to learn."

I took his coffee and drank a big gulp, wishing it had some Bailey's in it.

"I'm a little nervous. I've never been to the chiropractor. I have no idea what you do."

"Once you become familiar with the work and the way it helps people, you'll do a good job here." He reached for his coffee and took a sip. "You can assist me today. All you need to do is follow me around and write down the things I say." He handed me a clipboard.

"That's it?" I asked.

"For now," he said, "I want to start you off slow. You've never been to a chiropractor, and I want you to watch me work so you can understand what I do."

"No problemo," It sounded easy enough.

Paulina stuck her head in the doorway. "Dr. Cloud, Mr. Creedy is ready in room one."

"OK, thanks, Paulina," Eli said.

"What do I do?" I shifted so Eli could pass me and tried to calm the butterflies taking flight in my stomach.

"Follow me..." He rubbed his palms together and spoke in his best Mad Doctor voice.

I followed Eli to room one, and Mr. Creedy was lying face up on the table. He was about seventy years old and had equal amounts of wiry hair protruding from his ears and nose. His head was bald except for a small crown of gray hair. He was wearing tan coveralls with big, brown, work boots covered in the remnants of dried bird poop. He had his eyes closed. My brother bent down at the end of the table near the patient's head.

"How are you today, Mr. Creedy?" he asked in a loud voice.

"No need to yell, son, I can hear just fine."

"OK, Mr. Creedy," Eli responded with a smile.

"Whadya say?" Mr. Creedy asked.

Eli rolled his eyes and mouthed, "Hard of hearing," at me.

I couldn't help but smile at this comic routine. Eli asked how he was again, this time leaning toward the patient's right ear and giving me a wink.

"Not so good today," Mr. Creedy responded, eyes still closed. "My chickens got out last night, and I had to chase them all around the yard to shoo them back in the coop. I think I pulled something in my neck."

Eli turned to me. "Jennifer, write down Mr. Creedy says he has neck pain."

Mr. Creedy cracked open one eye and looked in my direction. I wrote it down. I watched my brother feel Mr. Creedy's neck. In one swift motion, Eli torqued Mr. Creedy's head to the right, making a loud crack.

I gasped, and then everything went dark. When I regained consciousness, my brother and Mr. Creedy were leaning over me. Eli was shining a light in my eyes.

"She's going to be fine."

"I don't know, Doc, she don't look so good to me...kinda green."

I opened my eyes, squinting at the light. "What happened?" I asked Eli, then turned to Mr. Creedy. "You're OK?"

"Yes sirree Bob!" he said. "Doc Cloud gives a good adjustment, fixes me right up."

"Mr. Creedy, this is Jen, my little sister. She witnessed her first adjustment today."

"Glad I could help out," he said and gave me a pat on the shoulder.

Eli helped me to my feet. "Are you sure you're OK?" He gave me that Cheshire cat smile.

"Very funny," I said. "You could have warned me. I didn't realize it was going to sound so loud."

"How about if you work the back desk with Elvira?" Eli asked, keeping a hand on my back.

I agreed. I was still a little queasy from my first adjustment experience.

Elvira, I found out, was a heavyset Caucasian lady who used to drive a truck. She had a cobra tattoo on her right leg directly above her ankle. Elvira oversaw the collections. This meant if people didn't pay their bills, she would call the deadbeats and persuade them to drag their butts in to make a payment. Apparently, my brother thought he needed this service before he opened his doors for business in this town. I watched Elvira make a few calls to verify what the insurance companies would pay. She threatened a lady at Blue Cross because she didn't like the way she gave Elvira the benefit information.

"Next time I call, you'd better say 'please' when you need to ask me somethin'. You don't just go demandin' personal information thatta way." She winked at me and wrote the info down. After she hung up, she said to me, "You just gotta let them know who's boss."

Elvira twisted her stringy brown hair into an alligator clip as if she were donning her battle armor. She activated the speaker on the phone, so I could listen to the next call. Learning on the job. The next call was to a Ms. Jones.

"I understand you're on social security, but you forgot to make your co-pay, and you can't just walk outta here and blame it on dementia." The patient on the phone apologized several times and promised to pay on her next visit. By the time Elvira was finished with her, the woman was promising to drop by at lunch with her cash payment.

I decided I would use the "kill 'em with kindness" approach instead of "Attila the Hun."

I verified a few insurances without the threats and answered a few phone calls. Around ten o'clock a girl named Su Le came in.

"She's the one who does the real torture, you know, needle sticker," Elvira told me. I thought I would save learning about Su Le's job for another day.

We saw several patients, and by lunchtime I had mastered the phones and made a few new friends. A nice man who worked for the ice-cream factory brought me a gallon of chocolate-chunk ice cream—yum—and another older man asked for my phone number. He might have been about eighty years old, but who am I to complain? Paulina breezed in and out of the front office, taking patients back to rooms and being very perky.

Around one o'clock, Eli came in carrying an armful of scrubs that Paulina had ordered for me. Most of them were brightly colored and covered with flowers, happy faces, or cartoon character. I scrunched my nose.

"SpongeBob, seriously?" I asked him.

Eli slung an arm around my neck. "The kids I treat love SpongeBob. He's the new Superman. Let's go grab some lunch."

I decided this job wasn't so bad and I could get some cute shoes to go with my SpongeBob scrubs. Maybe Nine West casuals or Manolo slides. Who knew the possibilities?

We ate at a little Italian-food place on the opposite side of the downtown square. The people were friendly, and the food was great. I was on my second piece of Canadian-bacon-and-pineapple pizza when Eli said, "I know this isn't what you want to do with your life but look at it as a temporary learning experience."

"I feel like everyone around me has a plan for the future except me."

"You'll figure it out. One day something will happen that will change your life, and you will know it's your destiny."

"Is that what happened to you?"

"Yeah, remember when I had that shoulder injury my junior year, and I couldn't throw the football?" I nodded, remembering how devastated Eli was because of his injury.

"I thought Johnny Stephens was going to take over my position. I was looking forward to playing my senior year."

"I remember you tried every type of medicine. The bottles were always crammed on the breakfast table blocking the saltshaker."

Eli laughed. "Yeah, then Dad took me to a chiropractor. The first time he adjusted me, I felt better immediately. After three weeks of care, I was playing again. That's when I knew I wanted to study chiropractic."

I sucked down the rest of my Coke through the straw. "I hope something like that happens to me. Don't get me wrong. I loved buying shoes, but I didn't feel like I was doing anything important. I did love the discount."

"Everyone needs shoes, and everyone also needs chiropractic, so let's get back to work before I have a line of angry patients." Eli pulled out his wallet and waved away my attempt to pay my part of the bill. "Today's on me, because I have half the Coffee Creek football team coming in for school physicals this afternoon. One look at you, and they'll be my patients for life." He grinned as he left a tip, and we headed toward the door.

CHAPTER 7

$\mathcal{G}$ertie and I lived in peace for a few months. She went to school during the day and worked at night in the library, and I worked during the day for my brother. Our paths didn't cross too often except coming and going. Jake had e-mailed a few times to let me know he was fine, and his new job was a little more trouble than he expected... something about difficult employees.

The summer turned into fall. A slow drizzle outside fogged up the windows and reminded me winter would be here soon. In Texas, fall came and went in the blink of an eye. Texans considered themselves lucky if we managed to get a couple of breezy days. The trees turn from bright green to naked in a matter of weeks. If you wanted to see the fall leaves, you needed to look down, because most of the fall color was on the ground.

Halloween was right around the corner, and the air was charged with the excitement that preceded costumes, parties, and trick-or-treating. Gertie invited me to a Halloween party on Saturday night at one of the fraternities on campus. Normally hanging out with college guys wasn't my scene, but my last date had been with Jake. I thought going might inspire me to start dating again.

I had just returned from my Friday-morning duty at the chiropractic office. Thankfully the clinic was only open half a day on Friday, saving me from a whole day of people complaining about their bad backs.

"Hey," I said to Gertie as I removed my raincoat and hung it on the coat rack next to the door.

"Hey yourself. That's a real nice outfit," she said. A wry smile winked dimples at me from her spot on the couch.

I was wearing my Friday scrubs, which were a baby-blue and had big yellow smiley faces all over the top.

I shrugged. "Eli likes us to match, and Paulina picked out scrubs for each day. She felt like the scrubs would put the patients in a good mood for the weekend."

"I'm feeling happier already," Gertie smirked. "The shoes are cool."

I had on my favorite Dr. Martens vintage floral flower boots. They were so awesome. Gertie was sitting cross-legged with a book open on her lap, eating a big bowl of popcorn. The rectangular coffee table was loaded down with Twizzlers, gum, M&M's, BBQ potato chips, and a giant Slurpee. All the basics needed for a midterm study session. An old Marlon Brando movie was playing on the TV. Attack cat lounged on the back of the couch behind Gertie's head, stretched the length of a sofa cushion. His green eyes focused on my every move.

"I love these old movies," she said. "They are so romantic; I want to meet me a Marlon Brando type."

"Marlon Brando was also the Godfather," I pointed out. "He killed people."

"Yes, but he was sexy when he gave the death order." She threw some popcorn in the air and caught it in her mouth. "So powerful and mysterious and shit, you know."

Not really, but I went along with it.

"Do you believe in love at first sight?" Gertie asked.

"No." I scooped the last handful of popcorn out of Gertie's bowl, and sat down next to her on the couch, avoiding the paw that reached out to bat at my hair.

"Why not?"

"You should get to know the guy before you fall head over heels for him."

"Don't you think you can meet someone and just know you're in love?"

"Absolutely not," I said, but then Mr. Sexy's face flashed in my mind. "Damn." I tried to push the strong jaw and the mischievous emerald green eyes away.

"What was that you said?" asked Gertie.

"I had some popcorn stuck." I cleared my throat to cover the lie.

"There's this guy who works in the library. He's a stacker," she said, and I swear I saw tiny little hearts fly out of her mouth and circle her head.

"He's a what?"

"A stacker. He stacks the periodicals and returns the books to their proper place so the graduate nerds can do their research. I'd like to get him behind the stacks."

"Gertie, that's not love, that's hormones!"

Gertie stood and stretched. "Haven't you ever met anyone that you wanted to jump his bones, then be together for all eternity?" she asked, folding a piece of gum into her mouth.

"No!" Mr. Sexy's face appeared again. At that precise moment, my necklace, which had lain dormant for five years, began to glow. The cat gave a low growl.

"Holy shit, you're glowing!" Gertie shouted, pointing at my neck.

"Oh my God, Gertie, I have to go outside." I bolted from the sofa, and ran out the back door. Gertie followed. I trampled across the garden. The door to the outhouse stood open, inviting me inside.

"What are you doing?" Gertie grabbed my arm, trying to stop me from entering the outhouse.

"I'm not sure," I said.

"You're not getting in that thing, are you?"

"Yes, I think I am." I shrugged off her grasp, took the final step and sat down. I gripped the two handles, whispered "Hanhepi," and prepared to be whisked away. Before the door could shut, Gertie took a flying leap into the outhouse. I shouted, "GERTIE, NOOOO!"

I felt my chest compress but not as badly as the last time. I flinched at the loud crack of thunder, and a screaming Gertie was projected from the outhouse right into the back of a man who was kneeling behind a bush.

Gertie, the man, and parts of the bush went tumbling down a small hill. I stepped out, shielding my eyes from the blinding sun. We were in a small patch of trees on top of rocky, red, dirt hills covered sparsely with cactus and other drought-tolerant plants. Similar hills surrounded us. Off in the distance, a small town sat nestled in the valley of the hills.

Inspecting my apparel, my heart sank—the vessel outfitted me in some kind of cowhand duds. I wore a cowboy hat, breeches, a western shirt over a tight top that squeezed my boobs up to my neck, and a holster. No gun, thank goodness.

I walked to where Gertie had landed. The man was facedown with Gertie lying on top of him, face to the sky.

As I approached, the man shouted, "Would ye please get yer arse off me, lassie!"

I stopped cold. It was him. Mr. Sexy. My heart began to pound, my blood began to boil, and any second, steam would shoot out of my ears.

"I'm trying," Gertie said as she struggled to stand. She was wearing a long brown dress with a high, cream-colored bib neck and black lace-up boots.

I grabbed Gertie by the hand, pulling her off Mr. Sexy.

"Jen, what happened?" She swayed slightly, and her voice was a little squeaky. I placed a hand on her forearm to steady her.

Mr. Sexy stood and brushed the red dust from his clothes. His jeans hugged the curves of a rather nice ass His white shirt, open halfway down the front exposed a tanned, muscular torso. The dark curls I remembered running my fingers through. They were shorter than before, but still curled around his collar.

As he turned, our eyes met, then his gaze dropped down to my chest. *You bastard, checking out my tits.* Then I realized around his neck he wore a necklace similar to mine, except his had a full sun with blazing rays.

"Oh no!" he shouted. "Oh, *bloody hell*, no! *You* are my transporter?"

"You are an asshole," I said, my face hot with rage. "You left me God knows where. How was I supposed to get home?"

"Why didnae ye tell me you were the transporter?" he asked.

"You two know each other?" Gertie asked, pointing to each of us, her voice stabilizing with curiosity.

"No!" we both said in unison.

"Yes!" Again, it was spoken simultaneously.

"Well, which is it?" Gertie eyed me suspiciously. "And what the hell am I wearing? Where are my clothes? Where am I?"

"Shut up!" Mr. Sexy and I both yelled.

"Don't you tell her to shut up! You left me," I said, my lip jutting out into an unpredictable pout.

"You didnae tell me you were my transporter." His voice calmed, regaining control.

"Well...I don't know what that is exactly, but you are a jerk, and I would be happy to transport you to Mars."

"You tell 'im, Jen!" Gertie stood beside me, her arms across her chest. I gave her a glare.

"OK," he said, running a hand through his dark, almost black hair. "Ye mean to tell me you don't know what you do? And who is this?" he nodded his head toward Gertie.

Gertie stepped forward. "For your information, I'm Jen's cousin, Gertrude."

"She sort of hopped in at the last minute," I added.

"You cannae bring a friend!" He stomped around. "This is naugh Disneyland!"

"Cousin," said Gertrude. "I'm family."

I didn't say anything, because he looked like he might be angry.

"Who's yer mentor?"

"My what?"

"The person who taught you aboot yer gift."

The confusion that I felt inside showed on my face and reflected the surprise in his voice.

"You mean...no one told you of yer gift?"

"Um, nope, the outhouse just got delivered one day after my aint died."

"Yer aunt?"

"No, aint. My *aint* left the outhouse to me in her will. I think she tried to see me before she died, but it just never happened."

"This is veery unfortunate." He scratched the stubble on his sexy chin. "Ah dinnae ken what to do aboot this situation."

"Why don't you start from the beginning so maybe I can understand what is going on."

"No crap," said Gertie.

"OK, ye have the gift of time travel. It's passed down from yer ancestors. Usually 'tis passed from a grandparent to a grandchild. But it can pass directly from parent to child. It seems to skip a generation more often than naugh."

"Oh, this is so cool," Gertie said excitedly. "We can go in the future and get the lotto numbers, I can see my true love, I can—"

"Gertie!" I said.

"No," Mr. Sexy said. "The vessel cannae travel into the future. We go back in time, and when we have made our capture, yer vessel takes us to Gitmo."

"Gitmo?" I asked.

"You mean Guantanamo Bay, Cuba?" Gertie asked. "I always wondered what they really did out there. You know you can't ever believe what you read in the papers."

"What do you mean by 'capture'?" I asked.

"I am a defender," he said. "There are others who can go back in time as well. Some are bad people. We call them brigands." He sighed, then walked over to my outhouse. "I come back to stop them, and you transport them to Gitmo. See, you have two seats, one, two." He pointed to the seats.

"Let me get this straight," Gertie said. "Y'all are like secret agents who go back in time and catch bad guys."

"Yes, sort of," Mr. Sexy said.

"Ain't that the shit. Wait till I tell Momma."

"No! Ye cannae tell anyone. YOU are not supposed to be here." He pointed at Gertie, then at me. "And YOU have already violated the code." We stood staring at each other. He looked as if he didn't know quite what to do or say.

He spoke at last. "It was veery careless of your mentor not to tell you this information."

"Well, she was about ninety years old and died before she could tell me."

"Ninety? Why was your grandmother so old?"

"I told you, she was my aunt. My great-aint Elma Jean Cloud, and she didn't have any children."

"Elma?"

"Yes, did you know her?"

He looked at me thoughtfully. "She waited a long time for you."

"You're tellin' me you have a gift that Aint Elma gave you, and I didn't get one?" Gertie stomped her foot.

"I didn't exactly ask for this to happen to me." I narrowed my eyes at her, then turned to him. "Can I get rid of it?"

"Cripes." Mr. Sexy pinched the bridge of his nose like he had a migraine headache coming on. "This has started off bad. We need to find a safe place to regroup, and I can try to help you understand."

"No shit, Sherlock," Gertie said.

"Well, an introduction might be a start," I said, hands on my hips.

"Oh right, I guess we didnae get aroond to discussing names before," Mr. Sexy said, with the corners of his mouth turning up in a sly smile.

"Caiyan McGregor." He extended his hand to me.

OK, handshake, right. "No, I guess *we* 'didnae get around to it before,'" I said mocking his thick Scottish brogue. "I'm Jennifer Cloud, and this is my cousin Gertrude."

"Call me Gertie." She shook his hand. "So, it's 'Cayenne,' like the smokin' hot pepper?" Gertie asked.

A cocky grin spread across Caiyan's face. "Well, 'tis spelled a little differ-ent, 'eh, but if the shoe fits…"

Geesh, what a conceited piece of work, I mentally smacked myself over the head for allowing him to be my first sexual encounter.

As we stared at each other, wondering what to do next, a strange sensa-tion burned the base of my neck. I reached up to touch my necklace, but it was gone.

"Oh no! I lost my necklace," I said, searching the ground for it.

"You cannae lose it," Caiyan said, worry creases appearing between his eyebrows. "It disappeared from your neck because a brigand has taken it from one that belongs to you."

"It disappeared?" I asked. "What do you mean one that belongs to me?"

"The necklace was taken from one of your ancestors. This is worse than I thought," he huffed.

"Worse than what?" Gertie asked.

"Yer necklace is a key. 'Tis the reason you are able to travel back in time."

"A key to what?" I asked.

"The key to your vessel. You must have it in order to travel in your, um…outhouse." Caiyan turned and looked down the hill at the small town.

"Where are we?" I asked, and Gertie leaned in to hear.

"'Tis a secret for now." His gaze drifted toward the town. He turned, motioning for us to follow him. "We need to get somewhere safe, and then I will explain everything to you. Follow me."

I looked behind me as we walked away, and my outhouse faded into thin air. Down the backside of the hill, I'll be damned if there wasn't a horse tied to a tree. What was up with this man and horses?

Caiyan had been camping at the base of the hill. He picked up a knap-sack and untied the horse, but instead of climbing aboard, he led the animal by the reins, and we walked. I couldn't help but wonder what or whom we needed to be safe from. Looking around, I saw nothing but rocks and trees. Maybe we were in Indian times, and he was hiding from an attack. I didn't think getting scalped would be a happy ending. I needed my key and some answers. This man had a lot of nerve being mad because I didn't know about my gift. I couldn't help it if my family had secrets they'd forgotten to share. I caught up with him, leaving Gertie trailing behind me.

"What happened to the accent ye had the last time I met you?" he asked me.

"I guess we all have secrets, yeah?" I caught a small smile tug at the corners of his mouth.

~

DOWN ABOUT A QUARTER MILE, we passed a small wooden sign that read, "Welcome to Presidio, Texas." I racked my brain to recall Texas geography. Where was Presidio?

Gertie piped up. "Some secret—the sign reads Presidio. We're down by the Mexican border."

"Is that true?" I asked.

"Aye," he grumbled. "We are in 1915."

Since Gertie was a history major, I imagined the wheels started turning inside her head.

"Isn't there trouble between Mexico and the United States in 1915?" she asked, cocking her head to the side like she was reading off an imaginary chalkboard. "I remember something about raids on the American people." She put her hands on her hips. "Isn't that right?"

Caiyan stopped walking and looked her straight in the eye. "Ye ask a lot of questions."

Gertie paused her inquiry for the moment, and we continued toward the town.

As we walked, Caiyan explained my key was specific to my vessel. I needed it to make my vessel take me back in time. Anyone who had the gift could use my key to drive my vessel. That was why we needed to keep the keys concealed. They would also need to identify my vessel to be able to summon it.

My inner voice began wringing her hands when my brain realized I would need my key to return home. I told her to calm down. Maybe Mr. Sexy, uh...Caiyan knew how to get me home without the key.

I was about to ask for more information, when I found myself entering a town that looked like every western movie I had ever seen. Dust kicked up around our feet as we ambled down the dirt road into the center of town.

A few people were milling about and turned to glance at the newcomers. Some tipped their hats to say hello, then they proceeded on with their business. Buildings lined either side of the makeshift street. Most of the buildings were single story and constructed of wood or stone. Occasionally there were taller buildings, like the saloon. I was able to identify this building not from watching Clint Eastwood movies, but because the sign above the door read "Saloon." The general store centered the middle of the town. Two men were sitting on a bench outside the store, and a metal sign above their heads advertised block ice for five cents.

Caiyan led his horse to a big trough in front of the store. The men gave admiring nods at Caiyan's horse, as if he were a sports car. Caiyan tied him to a post, then turned to us. "Wait here; dinnae talk to anyone."

He went in, leaving Gertie and me hanging around the horse parking lot. There was an iron pump at the end of the trough. The big brown stallion looked at me like, "Hey, chick, are you gonna give me a drink or what?" I gave the handle a pump, and water began streaming out of the pipe and into the trough. I swear the horse winked at me and began to drink.

"Amazing, how'd ya do that?" Gertie asked.

"I just lifted the handle, and the water came out."

"Not that, how did you get the pants off that gorgeous hunk of man without even knowing his name?" Gertie said with a smirk.

"I didn't get his pants off," I stammered.

"Oh, yes you did. I know that look. Don't even try to deny it. That's the same look the heifers get when they return from the bull's pen, a little shameful but completely satisfied." She wagged a finger at me. "It's so not like you at all, but I'm impressed."

I couldn't suppress the grin. "OK, I admit it. When I was eighteen, I had my first real journey back in time. I didn't know what was happening. Jake had just kissed me for the first time, and I ended up sitting in the outhouse. I had worn the necklace Aint Elma left me to my senior prom. The necklace started glowing. The next thing I knew, I was in Scotland, 'the year of our Lord 1568,'" I said, mocking Caiyan's Scottish accent and adding a few air quotes. "Caiyan was knocking some guy in the head with a big rock, and then there was the whole queen thing."

"He was knocking out gay people?" she asked, popping her gum.

"No, queen, like all hail the queen and queen mother, you know?" Gertie's eyes grew wide and she nodded her head several times.

"Fifteen sixty-eight is the year Mary, Queen of Scots, escaped from Loch Leven. Do you think you saw her?"

I did a shoulder shrug. Gertie bounced up and down, barely containing her excitement. Placing her hand over her chest as if the idea of seeing a queen meant the world to her, she said, "Do you realize what important events we could witness?" She grabbed my arm. "Jen, think of the people we could meet!"

I considered this for a moment. I wasn't sure I wanted to risk my life to see someone I could look up on the Internet. I had gone back in time twice, and both times I felt dazed and confused, not to mention I got the breath knocked out of me.

The horse swished his tail and continued to slurp the water. Gertie reached up, wiping a bead of sweat that had trickled down the side of her face, and blew an enormous bubble.

"Hey, where did you get the gum?"

"I had gum in my mouth when we left. Back on subject," Gertie directed. "So, when did you hook up with Caiyan?"

"It started to rain, and I got cold. We found a barn, and one thing led to another, then he was gone."

"You mean like *poof?*"

"No, I mean like I fell asleep in the hay and he left me before I woke up."

"The cad."

"Exactly."

"How was it?"

I was saved, because Caiyan appeared carrying a couple of bedrolls and a knapsack full of camping stuff. He told us there was no room at the inn, but we could camp about a mile outside town.

"Camp? *Oh my God!* I don't camp." I had a vision of the last time I had gone camping. My Girl Scout troop trip to the Ozarks. I set my hair on fire trying to cook a s'more.

Caiyan stared at me, and for the first time I realized his eyes were green —not just any green but a deep emerald green that made my heart do a backflip.

"Can't we just get back in our vessel thingy and go home tonight?" I asked turning my gaze away from his.

"Not withoot yer key. I'll explain but not here. Let's go, I need to see a man aboot a horse."

Remarkably Gertie had stayed quiet during this squabble, and as I glanced at her, she was grinning. I ignored Gertie and focused on our situation. This was how Mary and Joseph must have felt. Tonight, we wouldn't even get the barn. Dang.

At the edge of town, there was a small stable. A blacksmith pounded on a piece of metal. He glanced up as we entered his work area.

"Hey there, what can I do for ya?" he said as he laid his mallet to the side.

"Howdy. We need to purchase a horse," Caiyan answered in a near-perfect Texas accent.

"The Mattie Hobbs might have a few mares for sale. You from outta town?" He looked at us suspiciously.

"Yes," Caiyan said.

Gertie winked at the man and he blushed.

Clearing his throat, he pointed toward the road. "They live down at the end of the road there. I've shoed many of their horses. Take better care of the horses than the kids." We thanked the blacksmith and walked down the road with Caiyan leading the way.

CHAPTER 8

The term "down at the end of the road" was a bit of a stretch in my opinion. We had already walked at least a mile with no conversation and no sign of a house. Caiyan's horse decided he needed to relieve himself, and Gertie and I were hopping over giant mounds of horse turds.

"How does one horse poop so much?" Gertie asked.

"Good grass, I guess." I shrugged and gave Gertie a palms up.

"Where are we going?" I asked, moving up front to walk with Caiyan.

"Well, since there are now three of us, I need to acquire another horse." This was again spoken in perfect Texan.

"What happened to the Scottish accent?"

"I'm practicing. If you want to blend in, it is imperative you speak like the natives or as close as possible." He cut his eyes at me. "I assumed you knew this based on your stellar performance last time we met."

I cringed. "Are you really from Scotland?"

"Aye, lassie. Glasgow."

"Are you from the past?" Gertie inquired from behind us.

"It depends on what year you are from to determine the past."

"We're from 2013," Gertie blurted out, but I was curious too. It had occurred to me, he could be from a different time in the future.

"Aye, I am from 2013 as weel."

"We're from the same time." A heavy sigh escaped quicker than I had intended. I glanced his direction and a smile tugged at his lips.

"What a relief!" Gertie responded. "I would have hated for Jen to shack up with a really old dude."

I stopped in my tracks.

"Oops," Gertie said.

Caiyan lifted an eyebrow and eyed me with slight curiosity but proceeded on. We continued walking, leaving the town behind us.

"Why am I dressed like Laura Ingalls from *Little House on the Prairie,* but you get to be Bonnie and Clyde?" Gertie complained.

"The vessel determines your state of dress," Caiyan said.

"Well, I think I would have been a better Bonnie; Jennifer is all about style, and she wouldn't be caught dead in those boots."

She was right; so far, the "vessel" hadn't a clue about my shoe preference. The first time it had given me ugly loafers and now, dull, brown, round-toed cowboy boots with fringe down the sides. I envisioned buying my feet a new pair of Christian Louboutin pumps when I returned. The reality was it would use up my entire savings, but it was a nice daydream.

The road veered to the right, but Caiyan took a shortcut through the trees. The path narrowed and forced us into a single-file line. There was barely enough room for the horse to maneuver. I stayed in the front so I could speak to Caiyan. The horse followed, and Gertie brought up the rear.

"How long have you been here?" I asked Caiyan.

"I arrived yesterday."

"Where did you steal your horse from, or did you ride him back in time?" I cocked my head at Caiyan.

His mouth formed into a small, sexy smile, emphasizing the scar slicing through the top of his right upper lip. He moved the reins into his left hand and stroked the handsome beast on the neck.

"I won him in a card game last night while I was scouting for brigands."

"What's his name?" I asked.

"Dan."

"What kind of horse name is that?" Gertie asked. "He should have a name like Trigger or Silver."

I swear that horse lifted his tail, let out a big fart, and smiled.

"Lord have mercy." Gertie pinched her nostrils together.

"I think he was offended," Caiyan replied, fighting a grin.

The Hobbses' farmhouse sat back a ways from the road. The single-story clapboard house in need of a coat of paint had a small porch framed on either side by two small windows. The house was surrounded by pastures fenced and gated to hold the livestock.

We proceeded down the rutted dirt road toward the house. To the left a pasture housed a big longhorn steer chewing on some grass. His brownish-orange coat and long curved horns were magnificent against the backdrop of fall color. As we walked past him, he raised his head and looked at us like he was trying to decide what the heck we were doing here. I was trying to decide the same thing.

"You are going to be a famous mascot one day," I said to the steer. "Your head will be plastered all over our state." The longhorn huffed and blew snot out his nose, then continued with his chewing. Caiyan looked at me and shook his head.

To the right of the house and set back catty-corner was a big red barn. A couple of young boys were shoveling hay into a wagon in front of the barn. They spied us walking toward them. The older one came forward, pitchfork in hand.

"Can I help you with somethin'?"

"We need another horse. Is your father here?" Caiyan asked.

"Do ya hear that, Junior?" he said to the other boy, who was younger but their strong resemblance to each other left no doubt they were brothers.

"Yep, I heard it," Junior said, joining his brother. He held a wad of chewing tobacco in his cheek. He spit a big brown glob out of his mouth, and it landed next to my boot.

"Eeeyeew," I gagged, making a disgusted face and taking a step away from the boy.

"Well," said the first boy, "if you wants a horse, you gotta talk to Mamma, 'cause the only *father* we gots around these parts is the one at the church. Junior, go tell Mamma we gots comp'ny."

Junior headed off toward the house, and the teenager stood eyeing us like we were from child protective services. He was about Gertie's height, gangly but solid from all the manual labor I imagined he did on the farm. He had hair the color of straw that poked out from under his cowboy hat and a sprinkle of freckles across his nose. His teeth went every which way, and he wore a pair of overalls that had a hole in one knee.

A few minutes passed, and the screen door opened. Out came a woman with Junior at her heels. She was short and stout. Her housedress had small flowers all over it, and she carried a tin can in the crook of her arm. Behind her trailed three redheaded little girls. The oldest girl looked to be about ten, and she was carrying a toddler in a cloth diaper. The screen door slammed shut behind them, and they traipsed over to us.

THE SHOES COME FIRST

"I'm Mattie Hobbs." She introduced herself and spat into her tin can. One of the youngest girls clung to her leg. "What can I do fer you folks?" she asked with a big wad of chew in her jowl. At least this explained where Junior learned to spit.

"The blacksmith in town told us you might have a horse for sale," Caiyan said.

"I've got a few I might part with. How much you got to spend?" Her keen eyes searched us for signs of hidden wealth.

"We haven't any money, but we are willing to trade."

"No money?" the first boy spat. "That's horseshit."

"Clyde, you watch yer mouth, ya hear me, or I'll give you something to think about," Mattie Hobbs ordered. "Whatcha got to trade?"

"I have a nice pocket watch, real gold." Caiyan produced the antique timepiece and held it out to her.

Mrs. Hobbs took the watch and turned it over in her chubby hand.

"Clyde, go git that gray mare for the man."

Clyde gave a quick, snaggletoothed grin and set off to retrieve the horse. I had that queasy feeling in my stomach I get when something's not quite right.

"Where you folks from?" Mrs. Hobbs asked.

"Up north," said Caiyan.

"Mhm," she said. "We sure are getting lots of you visitors from up north. Just the other day a man came and bought three of my best horses. Said he was from up north, but he talked differ'nt than you."

"What did he look like?" Caiyan asked.

"Oh, 'bout yer height, dark hair, nice fella. Gave all the kids candy sticks. He was a smooth talker, yes sirree. I don't norm'ly trust those kinda men, seein' as I had one and he was good fer nothin' but knockin' me up with younguns and gettin' hisself killed."

Clyde led a big gray mare toward us. When she saw Dan, she flared her nostrils and bared her teeth. Her pearly gray coat melted into a dark flank with white spots sprinkled across her buttocks and down her legs.

"This here's Gypsy. She don't like you to get on her, but once you're there, she don't mind."

Caiyan eyed the horse, then brought Gertie and me into a huddle.

"I know this is a dumb question because I assume you would have told me before we walked all the way here, but can you ride a horse?" Caiyan asked Gertie.

"Of course we can," Gertie said matter-of-factly. "We're Texas girls."

She gave me a thumbs-up. I kept my mouth shut because Caiyan had already seen my expertise on a horse.

Caiyan told Mrs. Hobbs the sale was a go, and the boys brought Gypsy over to Gertie. She assessed the enormous horse, hiked up her dress, put a foot in the stirrups, and reached for the reins.

"Now, you hold still until I get up there," she commanded the horse. Gertie started to swing her leg over, and the horse did a slight two-step, swung her head around, and gave Gert a little nip on the rear.

"Owee," Gertie howled as she completed the feat. "You are a rude bitch!" Gypsy whinnied and shook her head.

The boys laughed at this, until Mrs. Hobbs gave them a glare.

Caiyan got on Dan, then turned to me. "What's it gonna be, me or Gertie?"

I looked over at Gertie. Her dress was wadded up around her thighs, and she was dancing around with Gypsy, telling her what a good horse she could be if she would just be still.

"You." I held my hand up for a boost.

We thanked the Hobbses, then rode off toward the trees. It was the first time I had been close to Caiyan since Scotland. I wrapped my arms around him, trying not to be too close because I was still put off by the one-night stand.

"You'd better hold on tighter, lassie, if you want to stay onboard. Dan can kick up the pace if he wants to show off for Gypsy."

I hugged tighter to his back and the warmth from his body enveloped me. Even in October it was still hot this far south, but the heat he generated was not from the sun. His body melted into mine and his manly scent of outside tinged with cinnamon had my hormones swimming downward. So much for self-control—if we didn't get to our destination soon, I was going to have an orgasm in the saddle.

As the trees began to thin out, a river sat off to the left following the line of trees. The water was flowing lazily downstream, and the wind was gently blowing, relieving some of the afternoon heat. A hawk spread his wings and swooped down toward the water, checking for a midday snack. Gypsy seemed content trotting along behind Dan. Gertie developed her riding legs and was able to maneuver the big gray horse along the trail. I loosened my grip on Caiyan because the heat we were generating between us was starting to make me sweat.

"It's the gift." Caiyan answered my unspoken question. "The connection between us generates a warmth, sometimes an extreme heat."

I pulled closer, and sure enough the heat intensified.

"Careful, lassie, I've been told I dinnae have good self-control, and you're making me veery warm."

I added a little space between us, but my inner voice gave me a high five for making him uncomfortable.

After riding for what my thighs screamed was too long, we came upon a clearing. In the middle of the space was a stone circle that looked as if it had been built for a campfire.

"This place is good to make camp," Caiyan said.

The river branched off to the right and formed a small stream. Caiyan tethered Dan to a tree near the stream, and the horse helped himself to a drink. Gertie tried to maneuver Gypsy in the same direction, but she stomped and snorted, then trotted sideways.

"This damn horse won't mind a bit." Then she gave Gypsy a good kick, and the horse freaked. She took off running, with Gertie screaming, "Shiii-iit! Stop! Halt! Brake, damn you!"

"Do something," I cried out, grabbing Caiyan's arm.

"What do ye want me to do?"

"I don't know, make it stop!"

Caiyan stepped forward and said in a very stern voice, "Whoa."

Gypsy came to a screeching stop, then lurched forward, sending Gertie sailing over the horse and landing in a grove of prickly-pear bushes.

"Well, that's one way to get off," Caiyan said and the corner of his lip pulled into a tight smirk.

I ran to the prickly bushes to check on Gertie. She was struggling to free herself. I gave her a hand out of the bushes and helped her pick the leaves out of her hair.

"Double damn, that hurt. Stupid horse wouldn't stop. What did Caiyan say to make her stop?"

"Whoa."

"I guess that would have been the obvious choice."

Gypsy sauntered over to Dan and started drinking from the stream. Caiyan snuck up next to her and secured her to the tree. Dan gave a snort, then decided he would see how things went.

The sun was starting to set in the sky, so I figured it must be around seven, give or take a few minutes or an hour. I never did understand the whole sundial thing in Girl Scouts. My stomach rumbled, and with no McDonald's to drive through, I would die of starvation if I didn't find my key. Home cooking was not my thing. Baking I could handle, but an entire meal? Not gonna happen.

"What are we going to eat?" I asked.

"I picked up a few things at the store," Caiyan said, opening his backpack. He unpacked plates and cups made of tin, a small cooking pot, and some utensils.

"If you ladies would help me find some wood, we can eat."

Gertie and I went in search of wood to burn. Caiyan set up a makeshift grill and made a fire. He cooked something that looked like beanie weenies, except the weenies were bigger.

Caiyan asked me to get the rest of the food from the backpack. I peered in to find bread and wine. *Well, at least I am getting Communion. If we all held hands and said a prayer, I could cut down on my Hail Marys for the month.*

CHAPTER 9

a thin veil of darkness blanketed the sky. I gazed at the full moon beaming back at me. There were so many stars here. An old oak tree had been uprooted and was lying on its side. I spread my bedroll out next to the tree, sat down, and leaned against it. I was exhausted from the ride.

"It's the time travel. Yer body needs time to repair. After you eat something ye weel feel better." Caiyan stirred the pot he had suspended over the fire.

I rested my head back against the tree and admired the clear night above. Caiyan handed me a plate of food and sat down next to me, balancing his plate on his knee. Gertie hiked up her dress and straddled a rock across from us.

"Thanks," I sighed. The aroma of the franks and beans made my stomach rumble, and I scooped a generous portion into my mouth.

Caiyan noticed my fascination with the stars. "You're missing aboot a hundred years of pollution."

"What?"

"That's why you can see so many stars." He pointed to the sky with his fork.

I glanced over at him. The dark hair that lay casually at his collar had become soaked with sweat during the ride and was drying in glorious curls around his neck. I wanted to reach out and run my fingers through it. He looked over at me, and our eyes met. He raised an eyebrow, and a slight smile tugged at his mouth. *Get a grip, Jen.* I told my inner slut to calm down.

"Are you going to tell me *aboot* my gift?" I asked him.

"Ye think you're real cute making fun of my accent?" he said. "Let me have a crack at yours then, lassie."

As we relaxed around the small campfire eating our meal, Caiyan explained in a perfect Texas drawl, "Y'all's gift was passed down through generations. Your aunt had given up and thought your family would no longer have the gift." He shifted his weight slightly and set his empty plate on the ground. "My grandfather told me if there are no children, the gift dies, or sometimes the gift just doesn't pass on to the grandchildren. I've never heard of it passing outside a direct line."

I looked over at Gertie and wondered why I was the one who inherited the gift instead of her. She was holding her plate at mouth level, scooping the last of the beanie weenies inside with a slice of bread. Go figure.

Caiyan continued. "The job we do is difficult, and the gift doesn't emerge until you hit puberty. When you put on the key, your gift can turn on the vessel. However, your mentor is supposed to protect your vessel until you are ready. It's kind of a built-in safeguard to protect you."

"Unless your mentor dies," I said. He pressed his lips together, nodded his head in agreement, and his eyes lowered. "But I didn't know I was going to be jetted back to the past."

"I can only tell you the story my grandfather told me. So far it's been true."

"OK, let her rip," Gertie said, hunkering down like she was about to hear a scary story.

"Legend has it that an ancient people, the Ancalites, had the gift of time travel. The gift was given to their king by the gods, and he was told the gift would be transferred through his bloodline."

"Oh come on, the gods?" I asked sarcastically. "As in Zeus and all that bull?"

"Do you want to hear the story or not?" he said, crinkling his brow.

"Sorry, go on," I said, trying to be more open-minded.

"The king's key was large, like the armor of a warrior. It fit around his neck and covered his entire chest. When his offspring inherited the gift, a piece of his armor would be removed, made into a necklace, and given to the new child. The armor was designed so each piece represented an element of the universe."

"So, I have—or *had*—the moon, and you have the sun." I realized that before we left the hill where we met Caiyan, he had buttoned his shirt, hiding the precious key.

"Yes."

"Who has the others?" Gertie asked.

"We have found several others. Searching for the remaining keys is our mission. The main key was made of titanium, which, by the way, wasn't even discovered until the seventeen-hundreds. Each element is formed from moonstone."

"Moonstone. I have read about that gemstone," said Gertie. "If you give your lover a moonstone when the moon is full, you will always have passion for each other."

"That's what I hear, but it also provides protection and healing powers," Caiyan said.

"Geesh, you don't really believe all that stuff, do you?" I asked.

"Maybe I should remind ye, lassie, we're sitting here in 1915."

"Good point." I wondered if he realized when he was annoyed, his accent returned. Mamma Bea always told me that everyone has a tell. When they are fibbing, there's always a sign that gives them away. She said it's good for poker and cheating husbands.

My tell was twisting a strand of my hair. My mom told me when I wound a piece of my hair around my finger, she knew I was lying. Gertie would bite her fingernails, and Jake would tuck his bottom lip under his front teeth. I'd bet money this was Caiyan's tell and stored it away for future use.

Caiyan continued. "When the king was young, he traveled back in time to help secure land for his tribe and make his tribe wealthy."

"You mean he went back in time and ripped people off," I said.

"I think he was more or less like Robin Hood. He only took what his people needed from those who had more than they deserved. He also went back to his ancient people and taught them how to grow crops and develop their culture, so they were progressively superior to the surrounding tribes. The advancement gave his people security."

Caiyan reached down and picked up a smooth rock from the ground. He rolled it around in his palms as he continued the story.

"The king's vessel was made of pure gold and was called the golden mountain because the king was rumored to be at least seven feet tall and built like Hercules."

"Now we're talkin'," Gertie added, doing a fist pump.

"During this time the king had many wives."

"Hold up," Gertie interrupted, holding her free hand in a "stop" position. "How many wives, like three or like twelve?"

"Many!" Caiyan said louder, glaring at Gertie. "The king had several daughters, and none of them had inherited his gift. He didn't understand because the gods had told him his bloodline would carry the gift.

When his only son reached sixteen years, he went through the ceremonial rite of passage celebrating his claim to be the next king. During this ceremony, the king placed his armor on the young prince, and it started to glow, revealing the gift. The king was ecstatic and had a piece of his key made into a necklace for his son.

He taught the prince how to use his vessel to travel through time to do good things and help their people become greater and wealthier.

As the king's son grew into a man, he fell in love with a girl he met while traveling back a few decades, and he wanted to marry her. The girl's name was Analia. She was from a poor tribe, the Mafusos. They were also an enemy of the Ancalites. The king would not allow the marriage."

"*Ooh*, very *Romeo and Juliet*," Gertie interjected.

"Aye," Caiyan said sternly, then continued. "One night the prince snuck off to marry Analia. He returned to the tribe hoping his father would accept his new bride, but the tribal king was not pleased. And because Analia had learned their secret of time travel, he sentenced the girl to death. The king also believed she had coerced his son into marrying her for his fortune.

The king traveled to the girl's time, secured the help of his trusted advisors from the Ancalite tribe he had assisted in the past, and held her captive. The king ordered her execution, but the prince snuck in and set her free."

"Why didn't the prince just stay with her in her time?" I asked.

"He could naugh, he didn't have enough time." Caiyan raked a hand through his dark hair, mussing it a little and making my toes tingle. "You see, the prince would only have a few years with Analia, and then he was to be born, and you cannae exist in a time when you are already living."

"What would happen if the prince was present in the time when he was born?" I asked.

"The grown prince would die. We have documented this before when a transporter tried to stay back in time. You just sort of vanish."

"That's kind of creepy," Gertie said.

"How do we know when to return?" I asked.

"Travel is based on the cycles of the moon. We go back when the moon is full. We have about three to five days to complete our task. When the moon begins to wane, we must return before it reaches the third quarter or half-moon appearance."

"What happens if we go back to a time when we were not alive and decide to stay?"

"When the moon reaches the final quarter, you get very...uncomfortable."

The way he said it made me uncomfortable. Maybe I didn't need to know all the details at once. Mamma Bea always said some things are better taken in small amounts, and I think this was one of those things. Mamma Bea was usually referring to liquor and men. Thankfully, Caiyan didn't expand on the details of the moon cycle.

"The prince was going to stay with Analia, knowing he would die."

"That's so romantic," Gertie said, placing her hand over her heart.

"Some of us that have the gift also have—How can I explain this? Let's just call them special abilities."

"What do you mean? Like superpowers?" I asked.

"Not exactly, but just imagine a few of us have extra gifts, and it's been told the king possessed every gift we have discovered so far."

"He was like a god, right?" Gertie asked.

"Sort of."

"Do you have a special gift?" I asked. "Do I?"

"I don't know what kind of gift you have, Jen," he said nonchalantly avoiding the first question. "Now where was I—oh yeah. The king controlled other travelers by causing a painful cramping sensation in all the muscles of the body simply by touching his key."

What if the brigands have this gift? I shuddered *What if they use it on me?*

"Oh my God, that is so awesome. Then what happened?" Gertie asked as if she were sitting front row at a Luke Bryan concert.

"The prince knew of his father's power, and he knew the king would never allow the prince to stay and die. The king was unaware Analia had been freed, so the prince secretly dressed in the girl's robes and took her place. The prince did not want to live without his beloved bride.

The next evening, the prisoner was taken to the great volcano to be sacrificed to the gods. As the prince was pushed into the volcano by his own guards, he removed the shroud, revealing his face. The tribe was in shock. Falling to his death, he shouted, 'I am sorry, Father, but my son shall live.'"

Caiyan paused for a moment and took a drink of wine from his cup. His eyes met mine as he sat his cup aside and proceeded with his story.

"The tribal king was so distraught at his son's death, he forbade all time travel. He returned to his own time and removed his key; with orders it was never to be used again. What the king didn't know was that although his daughters did not inherit the gift, some of his grandchildren would be blessed.

One day his favorite granddaughter found the key. As soon as she touched the key, it glowed. The king's wife was excited and showed the king the miracle; however, the king was angry, and frightened he might lose another child. He forbade anyone to wear the key. The wife disobeyed the king and divided the key into many necklaces. One for each grandchild who inherited the gift."

"So how did they travel without a vessel?" Gertie asked.

"We're not sure." Caiyan shrugged. "The legend says the tribe's witch doctor transferred the vessel's power into small stone discs with the symbol each child had on his or her key. These discs were placed onto their living huts, creating vessels of their own. They could travel without using the king's vessel. We think the magic can be transferred onto ordinary objects and this is where the common vessels originated."

"What happened next?" I asked, giving in to the magic of Caiyan's storytelling.

"When the moon was full, the tribal king went to the volcano to mourn his lost son, leaving the tribe alone. The tribe took this opportunity to travel back in time. The men would go back in time and get gold, grains, anything they needed, and then summon the women to come and collect the goods. That is the reason you are a transporter."

"Why are women the transporters?" I asked.

"Maybe because that was the way the tribe functioned. The men were the hunters, and the women were the gatherers."

Gertie let out a snort. "Figures, women always have to do the boring stuff."

I tried to take in all the information and sort it out to something I could comprehend, but I had so many questions that were still unanswered.

Caiyan was watching me intently. I think he must have realized my bewilderment, so he continued to explain. "I am not sure why the vessels of most men are only able to carry one person while the women can carry two or more." He shrugged. "Somewhere along the way, we lost the ability to transport objects."

"How do the brigands get their ill-gotten gains, so to speak, back to the present?"

Caiyan looked around as if someone in the bushes might be eavesdropping on this secret. "They bury it, or if it is not too far in the past, they may have secured a location they can retrieve the items from when they return.

"Like a hollow stump or a secret lair?" Gertie piped in.

Caiyan laughed his first big laugh since we had arrived. It made his eyes light up, and my toes curl a little. "No, Gertie, more like a post office box or the house of a relative. Cemetery crypts are also good hiding places."

"Crypts," I shuddered at the thought of having to search crypts for brigand booty. On the other hand, I didn't think Caiyan would mind disturbing the dead if it involved recovering a treasure. I leaned against the tree, and the bark on the tree trunk snagged my hair. I sat up and untangled it the best that I could and pulled my hair to the side so that it fell across my shoulder as I leaned back against the tree.

"Wait a minute, back up, what did the prince mean by his son shall live?" Gertie asked.

"Be patient—it's coming," he said, palming his stone in one hand and tugging playfully on a strand of my hair with his other hand.

I immediately pulled my hair out of his reach. He smiled and continued with his story.

"Many years had passed since the prince's death, and a girl mysteriously wandered into the Ancalite village. She was beautiful, with long, dark hair and mesmerizing dark eyes; it was difficult for any of the tribesman not to take notice. She lived with the tribe and won the king's favor. The king asked her to join him on his journey to the great volcano to mourn his son. As soon as he left, the gifted tribal members entered their vessels and transported. The remaining Ancalite tribe was invaded by the Mafusos, who overtook the small village, killing everyone who was left behind."

"That's so sad," Gertie said, pulling her knees to her chest and wrapping her arms around them.

"The beautiful woman seduced the king under the full moonlight, begging him to make love to her. The old king, being a fertile tribal leader, had no qualms about fulfilling her request. Afterward, the beautiful woman walked with the king to the edge of the volcano.

"'Do you know me?' she asked the king.

"'Have we met before?' the king asked, confused.

"'No,' she answered, 'but you knew my father.'

"'Who was he?' the king asked.

"'Your son,' the woman responded. The shocked king stumbled backward. The woman watched as the ground beneath him gave way and he fell into the volcano."

"Holy crap!" exclaimed Gertie. "This is some good shit—no wonder our family is so friggin' crazy."

Ignoring Gertie, Caiyan continued, "Apparently, Analia, the girl the king's son had married, was with child, and that was why the prince couldn't let her die. He wanted his son to live. However, the Mafuso tribe had learned of the prince's power and was behind the whole plot.

Analia gave birth to a daughter, not a son, and Analia was so distraught because she thought only a boy could inherit the gift. Feeling she had let down her people, Analia took her own life. The baby was named Jezebel and was raised by the wife of the Mafuso tribal king.

As Jezebel grew older, she began doing miraculous things. She was faster than the best boy in their tribe and smarter than any of the elders. She possessed gifts that made the Mafuso tribal king's wife curious if Jezebel had inherited the great powers. The evil Mafuso king plotted against the Ancalites by raising Jezebel to hate them. One night the Mafuso tribal king killed his wife, the only mother Jezebel had ever known. He told Jezebel the Ancalite king used his magic transporter to sneak into her chamber and kill her.

"Jezebel vowed she would seek him out and avenge her adopted mother's death. She waited until she was at an age when the king couldn't resist her and then went in search of him.

After she killed the king, she went for his key but couldn't find it or his vessel. She did, however, find keys the king's wife had hidden for the future Ancalites who had the gift."

"That is a very interesting story; however, I'm still confused about why I am here," I said.

"But the story gets better." Caiyan stood and began to pace as he continued his tale.

"Oh man, where is the popcorn?" Gertie asked glancing around like a popcorn vendor was going to materialize from the woods.

"The remaining tribe returned and found all their loved ones dead. Without a king, they took a vow. They would divide their wealth and separate from one another so this could never happen again. Many of the tribe members traveled to foreign lands, where they passed their gift down through their families. The subdivision of the Ancalite's tribe explains why we are from various backgrounds and cultures. They vowed only to time travel in search of the missing keys."

"Why didn't they just go back and stop the invasion?" I asked.

"They could not. The travelers were alive during the time of the invasion, and because the Ancalites were a peaceful tribe, they chose not to burden their descendants with the task of killing the Mafusos before they committed the crime." Caiyan paused. "Changing the past changes the future." He spoke the words with a hint of cynicism. It aroused more than my curiosity about this mysterious, sexy time traveler.

"That is so romantic and twisted," said Gertie.

"It doesn't explain us," I said. "What am I doing here?"

"Remember I told you the granddaughter seduced her grandfather?"

"Yes, sooo gross," Gertie said on the edge of her rock.

"She conceived a child," he said.

"Damn, this is a fertile family," Gertie said. "Jen, you'd better be careful. You'll be poppin' out those puppies like my cousin Bubba's rabbits."

"Me?" I questioned. "What about you? We are related, right?"

"I'm more from the poor Irish side of the family, obviously, since I didn't inherit any gift."

"Ladies, I am trying to explain the reason why Jen is here," Caiyan broke in. Gertie and I sat back and waited to hear my life's destiny.

"As I said, there was another child conceived, and this is where the bloodline for the brigands began. Filled with greed, they spent their time stealing and murdering. They had keys but no vessels, so they started tracking down Ancalites and taking their keys and vessels, which has filtered down to the pillaging we have today, I'm afraid."

In frustration, Caiyan tossed aside the small rock he had been caressing between his palms. "They are constantly trying to steal the keys and are in search of the king's vessel."

"So, are there others on our 'team,' I guess you would say?" I asked Caiyan.

"Yes, and you will meet them in time. Working for— our 'team' as you put it, is a very dangerous job; you could die."

"What happens if someone gets killed in the past?" I asked, uneasy.

"The traveler will die in both past and present time. If we are able, we transport the traveler back and make it look like an accident."

I gulped. "Is this what happened to my aunt?"

"I am not sure, lassie." But his eyes filled with regret, and his brogue thickened.

"How do I tell my vessel where to go?"

He pondered the question a moment. "For a transporter to travel back in time they must be summoned by a defender." He thought the idea over in his mind, then an amusing expression crossed his face. "You think of me."

"*What?*" I almost yelled it.

"Jennifer were you thinking of me when your key started to activate?" he asked with the corners of his mouth starting to turn up.

"No! Absolutely not," I stammered trying to get the words out.

"Yes you were!" Gertie blurted out. "Remember, you denied believing in love at first sight, and then I asked you about sleeping with a guy on the first date and..."

"OK, Gertie, we get it," I said, cutting her off. "I might have been reminiscing a little."

"When the moon is full, the brigands will go back. There is one family in particular who still carry the Mafuso name. They are after the king's vessel. Some brigands are still a part of the Mafuso family. Others have split away and go back to steal, change the past, and sometimes people die in the process."

"What about that guy in Scotland?" I asked, my ears turning a little pink with embarrassment from recalling our first encounter.

"Rogue is an independent brigand. He works for his own selfish gain."

"How do you know where these bad guys are going?" asked Gertie.

"We have ways to identify when brigands have taken the time passage. The defenders will travel back to catch them. To bring another defender or transporter back in time, I request the presence of a specific person, and that person will be summoned."

Caiyan sighed, then shook his head. "Normally, the transporter is the one being summoned, not the one who causes the time travel. Your gift is very strange. You can think about me, and your key will activate. We must have cross-connected. I was trying to decide whom I should summon for my transporter and imagine my surprise when my key started to glow. I wasn't sure what that meant. It has never happened before."

"Why is the Mafuso family after the king's key and vessel?" I asked.

"Remember, it's rumored to be pure gold, and it was the original, so possibly more powerful. Many believe if you have all the keys, you will have all the power, just like the king."

The flames on the fire were starting to die down as I digested my dinner and all the new information. I shivered as a slight breeze brought a chill in the air and caused the flames to lick up.

"Where are we exactly?" Gertie asked.

"We are in Presidio, Texas, in the year 1915," he said poking the fire. "I've been assigned to hunt down a member of the Mafuso family."

"How do you know where we are and what we are supposed to do?" I asked.

"Over time things became a little more civilized. We formed an alliance with the British Secret Service, which led to a pact with the CIA from the United States since many of the gifted are in your country. They gave us the name WTF."

"What the Fu—?"

"*Gertie!*" I interrupted her. Then we both started to laugh hysterically. I think we might have been suffering from post-traumatic stress caused by the unbelievable, but we laughed until our sides ached. Caiyan shook his head and chuckled at us.

"No, it stands for World Travel Federation. We are considered top-secret. Although there are some out there, like you, who don't recognize their gift right away or choose not to use the gift.

When the moon is full, we know the brigands will go back. The BSS works with the CIA to try to figure out where they will strike next. We have worldwide support because they know if we were to fall into the wrong hands, we could be used as a weapon."

"A weapon?" asked Gertie. "Whoa, that's heavy."

"Can you imagine what would happen if someone went back in time and murdered the Queen of England or one of your presidents?"

"Oh my gosh, you mean like Lincoln?" I imagined the ramifications of such an act was horrific.

"Yes, and Kennedy." He picked up the canteen of water and poured some into his cup. He took a drink and wiped his mouth with the back of his hand. "That is why Lee Harvey Oswald was killed so quickly. He was a brigand. Of course, his real name was Oswaldo Mafuso."

"What about Marilyn Monroe?" asked Gertie.

"No, she did that to herself. But there have been quite a few we couldn't save."

He ran a hand through his thick hair, making it stand up a little at the crown. Most men would look disheveled, but Caiyan only oozed more sex appeal with his tousled appearance. He hesitated like he was telling us too much and then proceeded on with the conversation.

"When we travel, we go with nothing. You can only return people through the transporter. That is why you are so valuable. We have to figure out what the brigands are after and then stop them before they muddle up history."

"Like in Scotland," I said. "You hit that guy with a rock, but how did you get him back if I am supposed to transport him?"

"Oh yes, Rogue," Caiyan sighed. "He is a clever bastard."

"You know him well?"

"Yes, he works alone. We have fought many times. He always seems to get away. He's a slippery one, that fellow."

"He got away?" I asked, alarmed. "I thought you catch them and put them in jail?"

"Sometimes they get away," he said casting his eyes downward.

"You're not very good at this hero stuff, are you?" Gertie said.

"It's not as easy as hitting them on the head with a rock. I got lucky I was able to stall him long enough for Mary Stuart to get away."

"Mary, Queen of Scots?" Gertie asked and put a finger to her lips, which she did when she was in deep thought. "But she never became the Queen of England, if my history serves me right."

"True, but Rogue was going to capture her; she had information on the location of one of the keys. It would have changed history if she did not escape to England."

"If you are lucky enough to catch these prisoners, I am supposed to pop back in time and take them to some place in Cuba, right?" I asked.

"We have a prison in Gitmo," he answered.

Looking wide-eyed, Gertie asked, "Why Guantanamo Bay?"

"Gitmo has a reputation. Prisoners don't want to go there, but really an underground prison exists to house these types of criminals.

In the past, our ancestors have traveled to save tragedy from happening in our present world. The problem is our society developed, and we couldn't just kill people and risk getting arrested and stuck rotting in a jail from the past. We decided we needed help from the government, and presto, the WTF was developed.

The prisoners stand trial for acts against the government, and then they are sent to prison. We have ways to force them to remove their keys, but it is almost impossible to find their vessels."

"What happens after they are sent to prison?" I asked.

"Some are rehabilitated and then released."

For a split second, I thought I saw Caiyan's key glow. But maybe it was a reflection from the fire. For the first time, I felt a longing well up inside me, like I was significant. I was needed for something besides deciding what type of shoe was going to be in style next spring. It made me feel special, and damn it, if people were counting on me to save someone, I was gonna do my best.

A noise pulled me out of my self–pep talk. It sounded like the drain in Mamma Bea's sink after she pulled out the stopper. The last of the water would go swirling 'round and form a tiny tornado, then it would get sucked out, creating a slurping sound.

"Wait here," Caiyan ordered as he rose slowly and eased through the trees.

"Are we gonna wait?" Gertie asked.

"No way!" We crept down to the trees at the base of the river and peeked through the bushes. A man was getting out of a bathtub. It was the old claw-foot type of tub, complete with a floral wraparound shower curtain.

I crouched down, and Gertie peeked over my shoulder. "Is that a bathtub?"

"Yes, hush, they will hear you."

Gertie scooted next to me and found her own spying spot.

Caiyan walked over to the man, and they shook hands like old school chums.

"Oh sweet Jesus!" exclaimed Gertie in her loud whisper voice that used to get us in trouble at church. "He looks like Keith Urban, the hot country singer."

I pushed a leafy branch out of my way to get a better view. I thought he looked more like Shaggy from the *Scooby-Doo* cartoon, but as I watched him walk, he definitely had a kind of swagger. He was dressed in brown pants and a dark-green button-down shirt with a brown leather vest and a strange-looking cowboy hat. It reminded me of Crocodile Dundee.

Caiyan and the man seemed to be having an intense conversation. He shrugged his shoulders and moved his hands in an "I don't know" manner as if Caiyan had asked him an important question he couldn't answer. I felt Gertie put a death grip on my leg.

"Here they come; let's get out of here," she said as she took off toward the camp. Her skirt brushed against the bushes, making a loud swishing noise.

I froze, hoping they wouldn't look in my direction. Easing backward, I turned to hightail it back to camp.

"Hold it, lassie." The stern words were from Caiyan. "I told ye to stay put." The two of them sauntered over to me. I turned around slowly, like I was caught with my hand in the cookie jar. They stood opposite me, arms across their chests. Both were eyeing me like I was an ill-mannered child.

I had my hands raised in the air in surrender.

"Should we put her in a time-out?" asked the new man as he looked me up and down approvingly.

"It wouldn't do any good, I'm afraid. She has a knack for getting into trouble."

I opened my mouth to refute this, but he spoke before I could get the words out.

"Put yer hands down, lassie, I'm not going to shoot ye." Caiyan grinned as he gestured to the new man. "This is Brodie; he's a defender from Australia."

"G'day, ma'am," Brodie said with a million-dollar smile, extending his hand. "I hear you're up to some trouble."

"Hi, I'm Jen, the new transporter, and I'm no trouble at all." I shook his hand, giving him my best smile in return.

"So McGregor tells me," Brodie said, barking laughter and slapping Caiyan on the back. "New Transporter, did ya say?"

I noticed Caiyan's grin disappear. I wasn't sure if it was because I mentioned I was the new transporter, or I because I said I didn't cause trouble. Go figure.

We walked to the camp, and there was Gertie, stretched out on her bedroll pretending to be asleep.

As we approached, she opened her eyes and yawned. "Guess I fell asleep." She looked up at us. "Oh, hello, who is this?" she asked, sitting and batting her eyelashes.

"Brodie," he responded as he stepped forward and offered his hand and pulled Gertie to her feet. "The boss man is not going to like the fact that a civilian is here. No sirree Bob." He sniffed the air and the pot of beans suspended over the campfire caught his attention. "What's on the barbie?"

Caiyan looked at Brodie, rolled his eyes, and said, "We've already eaten; help yourself." He turned back to us and said, "I have asked Brodie to come here and help me, since there seems to be a new student among us and another who shouldn't be here."

Great, I thought, *now all we need is a big brown dog and the Mystery Machine, and the gang's all here. Scooby-dooby-doo!*

"Let me get that for you," Gertie said and proceeded to fix Brodie a plate of beans.

Brodie sat down on the rock next to Gert and scrounged up some of the leftover bread. "What's our MO?"

"MO?" I asked.

"Modus operandi or method of operation," Caiyan answered.

"I haven't seen anyone, but I have a feeling Mortas is here," Caiyan said to Brodie.

"Not Mortas," Brodie groaned. "He is such an arrogant arsehole."

"Who is Mortas?" I asked.

"He is one of the craftier Mafusos," Caiyan explained. "He is the oldest grandson of the Mafuso family. He started traveling aboot the same time as Brodie."

"He's a real whacker. Been a pain in my arse ever since."

"What's a whacker?" Gertie asked.

"I shouldn't say in the presence of ladies, but a real dickhead." Brodie added, "The old Mafuso bastard only sends him on the more involved missions."

Caiyan stood and stretched. This time I saw his key glowed ever so slightly. What was this man up to? His jeans were sculpted around his taut leg muscles. *Focus,* I commanded myself. My cad sensors told me something was amiss. Caiyan excused himself to "stretch his legs."

Brodie finished his plate and began scraping the bottom of the beanie-weenie pot quite loudly, in search of seconds. I thought I heard a motor rumble in the distance. The can scraping got louder, and the horses started to whinny.

"I need to use the, um, bushes," I said. I stood and started toward the trees, making sure I went in the opposite direction as Caiyan.

Gertie jumped up. "Me too!" she said, following me into the trees.

"Do you always go at the same time?" Brodie asked, raising his eyebrows.

"It's a girl thing," Gertie responded, and I pulled her into the bushes.

I walked around the trees and then backtracked by the stream. The only source of light was the full moon, and I was trying to be careful not to fall over the tree roots that occasionally clambered over the path. What was Mr. Sexy was up to? The rumbling sound grew a louder. I headed in that direction. Gertie swooshed close behind me.

"Can't you keep your skirt quiet?" I asked.

"Hey, I'm sorry I didn't get the cool leather pants with the rawhide ties and the sexy chemise."

As we came to the top of a hill, I stopped. The rumbling noise was right in front of us. I crouched down behind a bush, pulling Gertie with me.

"Shit, that's sleek," Gertie whispered.

I followed her gaze. In the clearing was a shiny black Harley-Davidson motorcycle complete with a sidecar. It had chrome pipes and leather seats I could smell from where I was hidden. But the focus of my vision was the beautiful woman dismounting the bike.

She was tall and had mile-long legs that would have really worked a great pair of stilettos. She was fully clad in black leather, including the cowboy hat that hung low over her face. She removed the hat and let her shiny black hair fall to her waist. The tight bodice she wore accentuated her already perfect cleavage.

Caiyan stood next to her, offering his hand in assistance off the bike. My blood pressure rose a little. They moved away from the bike and farther away from us. They were having a conversation, but I couldn't hear over the noise from the exhaust pipes.

"Who is that?" Gertie asked. "Maybe it's Jezebel."

"Shhh," I responded. I didn't know who she was, but I knew *what* she was...a transporter.

Caiyan said something, and then he smiled. My blood pressure rose a little higher. *Calm down,* I told myself. *There is no use getting riled up. I don't even like him,* I lied to myself. *She is probably a relative.* Then she took her hand and laid it on his cheek, leaned over, and kissed him. It was definitely not a sisterly kiss. Gertie gasped behind me.

"Do you mates always go around spying on people?" Brodie popped up behind us. Gertie and I both jumped.

"Don't sneak up on us like that," Gertie said with her hand on her chest. "You'll give us a heart attack."

"Sorry, what are we lookin' at?" he asked, and then he peeked through the bushes. "Damn, hell must have frozen over."

"What do you mean?" I asked him.

"Well, the last time Satan's bitch saw Caiyan, she said she didn't want to see him again until hell froze over, so go figure."

"You know her?" I asked.

"Yep, 'fraid so. She's the Mafusos' little tattletale, and if McGregor finds us here, we are in deep kangaroo shit."

"You mean she's an informant?" Gertie asked.

Brodie nodded his head. "Good for us, not so good if she gets caught."

I pondered the idea of her getting caught, then Brodie added, "I don't know what McGregor has between those legs, but the women sure seem to like it."

That did it. My blood pressure began to rise, and I knew any minute steam would shoot out my ears, and I would whistle like a hot teakettle. My inner voice said, *I told you so,* and I took a few deep breaths to calm down.

The woman got back on the bike and then revved the engine and disappeared. We turned around and ran back to the camp. At least, Gertie and I ran. Brodie just ambled along like everything was hunky-dory.

"Why did you come looking for us?" I asked Brodie, trying to catch my breath after we returned to camp.

"You didn't take any paper," he said, holding up a roll of toilet paper.

Busted.

Then it hit me: I didn't know anything about Caiyan. He could have been married to that woman for all I knew. Boy, did I feel stupid. I had read too many fairy tales to think he might want a happily ever after with me. This was a job to him, and I had just happened to be an added bonus the last time. I didn't know where he lived or what he did for a living when he wasn't chasing bad guys; I didn't even know what kind of food he liked. I was stuck in the past fantasizing over a one-night stand.

I felt a panic attack coming on. I tried to slow my breathing. Bending over, I dropped my head between my knees, took a few slow, deep breaths and hoped this was a bad dream.

CHAPTER 10

*C*aiyan strolled back into camp. So much for bad dreams and the deep breathing—my blood pressure shot back up the minute I saw him. I tried to look away, but I caught the questioning look in his eyes.

Caiyan and Brodie went down to tend the horses and engaged in an intense conversation that apparently didn't include us. Gertie and I cleaned the dishes by washing them in the stream. I wondered how we were going to find the so-called bad guys. Maybe I would ask Brodie the next time he was alone. I could get information and the scoop on Satan's bitch.

"Unfortunately, all of the transporters are on assignments. I cannae get you back to your time tonight. We need to go into town and get friendly with the locals," Caiyan said to me as they returned from the horses.

"Good." I stood and brushed the dirt from my pants. "I could use something strong to drink." It didn't take us long to polish off the bottle of wine Caiyan had in his backpack.

"Not you, mate," Brodie replied, shaking his head at me. "We have to go scrounge up some coin."

"Brodie and I need to procure a card game, so we can win some money." Caiyan lifted the empty knapsack. "We also need more supplies."

"What if you don't win?" I asked.

"We always win," Brodie said matter-of-factly.

"Do you know how to use this?" Caiyan pulled a gun from the holster on his belt. It resembled the guns used in the movies when the actors played Russian roulette.

"Yep, sure thing," Gertie said. I hoped she knew how to use it, because I knew guns the same way I knew how to ride a horse.

"My grandpappy showed me how to use a six-shooter when I was young. But the real training came when my number-two stepdad taught me how to use the semiautomatics. He was into stealing things, and you never know when the owner might want a return, so he taught all us kids how to shoot in case we needed to cover him while he made a getaway."

The image of Gertie and her brothers covering her criminal stepdad while he ran for the getaway car was a little unsettling. *Oh man, what have I gotten myself into?*

All that self-righteous bullshit I'd conjured up earlier left like the morning train. Maybe I didn't want to fight the bad guys. Maybe I wanted to go home and put on my comfy pj's.

"Earth to Jen." Gertie waved a hand in front of my face.

"Sorry," I said. "I don't want to be left out here in BFE while y'all go into town and have fun."

"We are in Beefy?" Brodie scratched his goatee. "I thought this was Texas."

"No, she said BFE, which is the acronym for Bum-Fuck Egypt," Gertie answered.

Apparently, this was not a common term in Australia, because it sent Brodie into a fit of laughter. "She's a real beaut, Caiyan, and you're giving her a piece. Mate, you've got your hands full with this one. Let's go hit the piss."

"Oh, that's so disgusting," I said, still upset about being left behind.

"It means 'let's go drink some ale'—ye know, beer," Caiyan said as he placed the gun down next to Gertie.

"Do ya ladies not speak English?" Brodie huffed.

"I need the two of you to stay here." Caiyan motioned toward the ground. "Stay in the campsite and keep the fire going but keep it low. If ye hear anything, make sure you have the gun close. I am not expecting any trouble. I've not seen the Mafusos, and this is a veera docile town. Mostly farmers and cattle ranchers. There shouldnae be any trouble. Weel only be gone a short time."

Caiyan untied Dan from the tree, and Brodie attempted to mount Gypsy. He was almost ready to throw the other leg over when Gypsy did her little sidestep and bit Brodie right on the behind.

"Damn brumby bit me arse," he hollered.

Gertie and I couldn't help but laugh. Caiyan just shook his head. Brodie finally got hold of Gypsy. Caiyan gave me a warning "stay put" glare, and both men rode off into the night.

I turned to find Gertie staring at the gun lying next to her on the bedroll.

"Do you really know how to use it?" I asked.

"Well," she stammered, "I haven't ever shot a real gun at anybody, but I did shoot a BB gun at my cousin once."

"A BB gun!" I threw my hands in the air. "What happened to the semi-automatics...the number-two stepdad?"

"I do know how to hold one." She picked up the gun and pointed it as if she were one of Charlie's Angels.

Great, we are so dead. Maybe Caiyan was right and we would be just fine out here in nowheresville, but my sixth sense was telling me different. *I am just going to lie down and go to sleep, then when I wake up, it will be morning and maybe Caiyan and Brodie will have caught the bad guy and found my key. They will put him in my outhouse, and I can go home.* Kudos for positive thinking. I suddenly felt a little safer.

"I'm going to try and get some sleep. Keep your clothes on, in case we need to make a fast getaway."

"OK," Gertie agreed. She stoked the fire, ensuring it would last for a while, and we slipped into our bedrolls.

"Do you think Caiyan is in love with Satan's bitch?" I whispered to Gertie after we had settled ourselves.

"Naw," she said. "You should see the way he looks at you. Like he wants to do more but can't seem to find his nerve."

"I think he's got plenty of nerve. What if she's the reason he can't?"

"Well then, he will be the one missin' out," Gertie said mid-yawn. She turned over and began to snore softly.

I would be the one missing out, I thought. Then the fresh air took over, and I fell asleep.

I was dreaming Mr. Sexy was nuzzling my neck. A little kiss on the back of the ear, another on the curve of my jaw, and—wait, he was licking my face. That wasn't right. I opened my eyes and was staring face-to-face at beady black eyes surrounded by white-and-black fur. The animal was standing on my chest. At first, I thought, *what a cute cat,* and then I remembered where I was sleeping.

The fire had died down, and the cute cat was spotlighted by the afterglow. I let out a blood-curdling scream, which caused Gertie to jump up, grab the gun, and start shooting in all directions. The skunk turned, stuck its butt in the air, and ran, promptly spraying everything in its path.

"It's a skunk, it's a skunk," I yelled out, covering my head like that would protect me from the bullets. "Gertie, stop shooting!"

Gertie stopped and looked around. The animal was long gone, but we smelled like skunk spew.

"What's that smell?" she asked, covering her nose with her hand.

"I imagine it's that huge skunk you shot at, along with every tree and bush within a mile, not including me!" I scrambled out of my bedroll and surveyed the damage. Gertie had nicked a few trees, but everything else seemed fine.

"I hate skunks. The odor takes forever to go away."

"You mean 'forever' like a couple of hours or forever like ever and ever?"

"When Mamma Bea's poodle got sprayed, it took two weeks."

My eyes started to tear. "Two weeks?" I stomped around, flapping my arms in despair. "I have to go to work on Monday. I can't work smelling like skunk."

"Well, we could always get some tomato juice. It takes the smell out, a little."

I was wondering when tomato juice was invented. I was sure we were not going to walk into town for a can of V8. "How far was the town?"

"A few miles, I think." Just as we were contemplating the long walk, a horse snorted and the sound of someone coming through the trees cut into the night. *Good, the boys are back,* or so I thought.

A big black horse came slowly down the path. The rider appeared to be Mexican. He had a vest made of bullets that crossed in front of his shirt. He wore a black sombrero, a steely gaze, and held a shotgun aimed at my chest.

"*Hola,* senoritas, what are you doing out here shooting a gun all by your lonesome?" he asked with a thick accent.

I searched for the gun. Gertie had thrown it down after the skunk sprayed. It lay out of reach next to her bedroll.

"We were, um, l-l-l-lost," I stuttered. "We made camp until morning so we could find our way." I looked at Gertie, then eyeballed the gun.

Gertie made a slow move toward the edge of her bedroll.

"Don't even think about it, *chiquita,*" the man said. "I doubt you could hit me, but I am not going to let you try tonight."

I thought maybe a little friendly small talk might make him put down his gun.

"So, what brings you here to the, um, woods?" I asked the man.

Gertie rolled her eyes and whispered, "What are you trying to do, ask him out?"

I gave her a helpless shrug.

"I am on a mission for my people." He clicked his tongue and the horse moved closer to me.

A horse brayed in the distance, and I prayed we were about to be rescued. My hopes were deflated as more Mexican men on horseback came into view.

One of the men came up beside the first, gun drawn—of course—and said something in Spanish. They had a short conversation, keeping their guns on us. The second man shook his head as if in disagreement and rode his horse over to me. He had on a vest of bullets that crossed in the front, like the first man, and a big sombrero. One of his eyes wandered off in a different direction, so I couldn't tell if he was looking at me.

"Ayayayay," he said and held his nose, "*mofeta.*"

"Looks like the senoritas will be walking." The first man gave a nod toward the path.

"I don't think I can walk very far in these grandma shoes," Gertie said, lifting her leg and pointing at her high heel.

He cocked his rifle. Gertie and I both moved closer to each other.

"Wow, he looks just like Pancho Villa," Gertie said when she was near me.

"You have heard of me?" the man asked, sitting straight on his mount.

Holy crap! Gertie and I looked at each other.

"Yes." Gertie nodded wide-eyed. "Hasn't everyone heard of the great revolutionary leader Pancho Villa?"

"Are you a friend of my cause?" His dark eyes scanned us curiously.

"My dad's cousin Jorge was a Mexican," Gertie said. "He said Texas should be given back to the Mexicans because they had it in the first place. I think they are already on the takeover because there are so many of them moving in."

I did a mental head slap, but Gertie's words caused the Pancho man to scratch his head. He told the man on the horse next to him something in Spanish, and he rode over to me. He held his hand out and said, "Up!"

I shook my head. "No."

The man cocked his gun. I understood and accepted his hand. I put my foot in the stirrup and climbed behind him. I hoped an escape route would present itself later.

"You will ride with Paco," Mr. Villa explained. "I would not try to escape; Paco has not been with a woman in a very long time. Please do not give him a reason to end his abstinence."

The hair on my arms stood at attention.

Another man dismounted from his horse and picked up our gun. He gave it a look and said something in Spanish to the other men. Everyone laughed except Gertie and me. He put the gun in his pack and kicked dirt on our fire. He pointed at Gertie to get on the horse. Then he made a sour face and held his nose. More laughter. He and Gertie mounted his horse and proceeded down the path.

Villa led the way. My ride was second, followed by Gertie and the remaining bad guys. I had a strong feeling this was not part of Caiyan's plan.

After what felt like an hour, but in reality, was only about twenty minutes, my butt and legs became numb. I started to wiggle a little to increase my circulation.

"*Si*, senorita," said the guy saddled in front of me, then made a sound like "mmm, good."

Oh, gross! Some other time, buster. I remained still as a statue for the rest of the trip.

The sun illuminated the horizon, and I wondered if Caiyan and Brodie had discovered we were missing. My surroundings were coming to life as a small gray squirrel skirted in front of our path, barely missing the horse's hooves. The hills around us were beautiful colors of orange and green mixed in with large boulders that seemed to rise from the ground like miniature volcanos.

We rode through a heavy patch of cypress trees and crossed a small brook. The horses stopped for a drink, and we were allowed to dismount and stretch our legs. Gertie had to pee, but we'd left our toilet paper back at the camp. We asked Mr. Villa if he had any, but he laughed and said to use nature. Did poison ivy have three or four leaves? I knew I should have paid attention in Mrs. Dunham's biology class, but Jake and I always sat at the back and wrote notes to each other. Damn. I missed Jake, even if he did do the nasty with a girl named Bambi.

CHAPTER 11

*W*e proceeded with our ride, and a little while later we came upon a cattle ranch. We followed the barbed-wire fencing about two miles before we ever saw a sign of the house. Two six-foot walls made from Oklahoma stone flanked the entrance and reflected the rising sun.

The men stopped their horses to admire the different colors of the stones in front of a wide entrance framed in black iron. A curved iron sign emblazoned with a big *H* was centered between the two stone walls.

A brown wooden box that read "Hawkins"—most likely a mailbox—sat to the left and closer to the road. Two tidily done flower beds bordered with the same stone had been planted in front of the walls. Various wild-flowers filled the flower beds and offered a kind welcome to the Hawkins Ranch. This looked like a friendly place. I prayed we were going in as friends and not to kill the owner and take his cattle.

On our short rest stop, Gertie had filled me in on the details of the history of Pancho Villa. He was a Mexican rebel who fought against the government using men, women, and children to staff his army of pistoleros. And to confuse people, they were also called Villistas. He was also a cattle rustler, accused of various other crimes Gertie couldn't recall, and he was on the United States' most wanted list for something she couldn't remember, but she did know there was a famous general after him. The Mexican government also considered him dangerous, so he was indeed a wanted man.

Mr. Villa road his horse down a long, gravel road that I guess I would call a driveway. Each side was flanked by huge oak trees, creating a nice shady lane. Mr. Villa went first. I thought the head honcho always stayed in the back so if his men were killed, he could make a getaway. Not Pancho Villa. He led the way. I guess you had to respect that much about him.

As we came to the end of the lane, it opened, revealing the Hawkinses' homestead. The house was a two-story white frame house with green trim the color of the surrounding pine trees. The huge porch had several rocking chairs, and an old hound dog slouched in front of the door. He raised his head to check us out, then gave a sort of "ruff." Obviously deciding we weren't worth the trouble, he flopped back down on his belly and rested his head on his paw, indicating he had performed the extent of his guard-dog duty.

A tall, skinny man scrambled down the steps leading up to the porch. He seemed to be the owner and looked pleased at the arrival of Pancho Villa. Relief washed over me as Mr. Villa dismounted to shake hands with the man. He spoke in Spanish, and the man looked at us and something was said again in Spanish, and they laughed. The man went back into the house, and we dismounted our horses. Moments later the man returned and spoke in English, telling Villa there would not be a problem with the cleanup.

Gertie moved closer to me. "This house looks very familiar."

"Do you think you have been here before?" I asked.

"I don't think so, but I have that kind of déjà vu feeling."

Mr. Villa spoke with his thick Spanish accent. "This is Slim Hawkins; his wife will take you around back to wash. If you do not wish for Paco to watch, then I suggest you do not attempt to leave."

Paco gave me a little shove and led us around to the back of the house. A heavyset woman came out with a basket of ripe tomatoes balanced on her hip. She wore a floral housedress that hung down to her ankles. A white apron was tied around her plump waist, and she had her dark-brown hair pulled on the top of her head in a bun.

"Now I'm really having that feeling like I have seen these people somewhere," Gertie said.

"Maybe they look like someone you know," I suggested.

"Mmm, both of them?" she asked with a finger pressed to her lips. "Maybe."

"Howdy, girls, my name's Opal Hawkins. You can call me Mrs. Opal. Slim said y'all needed a tomater bath. Pee-yew!" She said as she waved her free hand under her nose. "Y'all sure do stink. That ole skunk must 'ave got you good."

"I'm Jennifer and this is Gertrude. Nice to meet you, and yes, it did," I said.

"Follow me this way." She motioned for us to come along as she waddled away from the house toward a small shed.

When we were out of earshot from Paco, I asked Mrs. Hawkins, "What do you know about this Pancho Villa dude?"

Opal looked at us kinda funny. Then she scrunched up her mouth like someone who was carefully choosing her words. "He's a hero to his people, not someone you'd wanna cross. He'll kill whoever gets in his way. Women, children, it don't matter."

I swallowed hard. I didn't want to be killed. I didn't want to stink like skunk. At least my priorities were in order.

"He's always been good to us on accounta he does business with my son."

"What kind of business?" I asked hesitantly.

"Oh, we're mule traders," she said proudly. "Mr. Villa uses the mules for hauling his, um, cargo. My son, Johnny, is on his way with the next shipment of mules. My Johnny raises the best jackasses in the entire state of Texas. That's why Mr. Villa trades with us."

"I remember reading about Pancho Villa," Gertie said. "He cut the soles off people's feet."

"You can read?" Mrs. Opal asked. "Must be why he wants ya. He don't read much."

We were standing in front of a square wooden building with a pointed tin roof. "Now, girls, go in that bathhouse and take off yer clothes."

The shed turned out to be a bathroom of sorts. A round metal washtub with a number three on the side sat in the middle of the room and an outhouse in the other half. Dried herbs were placed in jars around the room and surprisingly the small house didn't smell bad. She dumped the tomatoes in a bucket and began mashing them with a big metal hoe.

"You gals get on in the tub."

I looked at Gertie, and then we both looked at the small metal tub in front of us. The last time I had taken a bath with a friend I was five years old.

"Mrs. Opal, Jen wants to go first," Gertie said. She pointed at me like a first grader.

"No matter to me, first one in gets the fresh water," Mrs. Opal said, pounding the tomatoes to a pulp. We started ripping our clothes off, but the laces on the grandma boots hung Gertie up, and I got undressed first. I stepped into the tub as Mrs. Opal instructed.

The tub was small. I sat in the bottom and hugged my knees to my chest. Mrs. Opal poured the squashed tomatoes over my head, followed by a bucket of cold water.

After I screamed out loud from the shock of possible frostbite, she said, "Sorry 'bout that. Water's fresh from the well. Can't git the smell out with the warm water, and no time for heatin' now anyhow." She handed me a bar of soap that smelled good. I inhaled the sweet clean scent

"I make my soap outta lavender 'cause it smells so good and it calms your nerves," she said.

Sign me up for anything that would calm nerves. I was contemplating the state of my nerves and wondering if I should eat the soap when Mrs. Opal dumped more freezing water in my direction. I wanted to tell Mrs. Opal she had invented the first spa, but instead gritted my teeth and washed with the tomatoes and lavender in the cold water.

After the bath, I didn't smell as bad. I wrapped a towel around me as she repeated the process with Gertie. Mrs. Opal reached into her basket and gave us some clothes to wear.

"These belonged to my girls before they took the fever."

Gertie and I looked at each other and then at the neatly stacked clothes. Lord, I hoped my vaccinations held up in time travel. I didn't want the fever.

After we were washed, Mrs. Opal brushed and braided our hair. She insisted all the young girls were wearing their hair "plaited" like the French women. I tried to explain I could brush my own hair, but her face fell, and I relented.

"You have the most beautiful hair," she told me. "How lucky to have so many different colors."

I wasn't so lucky. It was ninety dollars worth of highlights by Blaine, but I didn't think Mrs. Opal would understand. Lucky for me young women wore bonnets. I tugged the hat over my freshly braided hair and felt about four years old. At least it disguised my hair. If the brigands turned up, I would fit right in. Hopefully...

While Mrs. Opal finished braiding Gertie's hair, I stepped outside to check for a way out of the place. Paco was leaning against the wall to the washroom, guarding the door. He licked his lips. I shivered and returned inside.

The house had an attached sleeping porch at the rear that extended across the width of the house. A long wooden table ran almost the entire length of the room. When we returned to the house, the men were sitting at the long table, being served food by several young Mexican women.

Everyone turned and looked at us as we entered, and I swear they sniffed the air and wrinkled their noses. They ignored the new aroma and continued to eat, so I guessed we weren't too offensive.

Mrs. Opal ushered us to the kitchen and demanded we help ourselves to some food. I must admit this was better than the canned food from the night before. There were scrambled eggs, pork sausage, pancakes, and homemade biscuits and gravy.

"Mrs. Opal, your breakfast looks scrumdiddelyumptious!" Gertie said.

Mrs. Opal arched an eyebrow at Gertie's word choice, but was summoned back into the dining room, so to speak, and left us standing with plates in our hands and drool forming in our mouths.

"Do you mind not using words from Charlie and the Chocolate factory before it was written?" I asked, placing a steaming biscuit on my plate.

"I think I have died and gone to heaven," Gertie said. "Do you know how long it's been since I had gravy?"

"Why has it been so long?" I asked, helping myself to a generous scoop of scrambled eggs.

"Do you know how many points gravy is? I don't even think it's in my diet book."

"Won't this gravy mess up your diet?" I was positive this food was made with real butter and whole milk. I doubted two percent had been invented, judging by the number of Mrs. Opal's chins.

"This is time-travel gravy. I bet I could eat whatever I want and then when we poof back to the twenty-first century, I'll be the same size as before."

I hoped she was right, and we were going to poof back. I was hoping it would be soon. One day had already transpired, and I didn't want to find out what happened if we were here for more than three days. The way Caiyan had avoided explaining the uncomfortable sensation that occurred when you exceeded the moon's waning cycle was disturbing.

Where was Caiyan? Surely he knew we were gone by now. Gertie and I ate in silence. She was savoring every moment of her gravy, and I was trying to figure out an escape plan. *Crap, I hated planning.* When I was younger, my mom planned everything. I just went along for the ride, not a care in the world. She told us where we were going, and we went, happy to be there. Now it was up to me, SuperJen, to find a way out of this mess.

My mantra from childhood began to play in my head but was disrupted by a commotion outside. The men remaining at the table stood and ambled outside. They stepped off the back porch and proceeded around the side of the house. Except for Paco, who kept one wandering eye on us. If we escaped, I was certain Paco would be next in line for the firing squad.

Gertie finished her Grand Slam breakfast, and we cut through the house to get a bead on what was happening outside. As we passed the living room, Pancho Villa was going over what looked like a map with some of his men.

Gertie and I stepped out onto the front porch. Mr. and Mrs. Hawkins were embracing a rail-thin young man who had dismounted from an equally skinny horse. I placed him in his early twenties. Mrs. Opal motioned us to come over.

"This is our son, Johnny," she said, her chest puffing up. "Johnny, this is Jennifer and Gertrude from up north." I was amazed how the words "up north" were enough information for these people. They didn't need specifics. They just didn't give a hoot. If you weren't from this part of Texas, you were from "up north."

We exchanged hellos, and Mrs. Opal told us Johnny was on a big mule drive. He was bringing down mules for Pancho Villa to buy. Apparently, Johnny lived "up north" in Fort Worth, a city located in north central Texas close to Dallas, and by the way she said it, you would have thought he lived in Alaska. He had ridden ahead to get the corral ready for the mules.

Johnny nodded politely at us and followed his parents inside to speak with Mr. Villa.

Paco watched us from the porch. He was getting to be a real annoyance. How were we going to escape if we were watched twenty-four seven? I was exhausted. After being sprayed by a skunk, becoming a hostage, and eating a full breakfast, I needed some sleep. Maybe if I could get a little shut-eye, I could figure out a way to find my key and summon my vessel.

"I think that Johnny is kinda cute," Gertie said.

"I thought you said Brodie was kinda cute."

"Well, he is, but they ditched us, and there's nothin' I hate worse than a man who don't stay around. My momma went through three husbands before she found one who would stay, and he ain't been around that long yet."

"I doubt they would really leave us in 1915. If Caiyan had known who I was in Scotland, he would never have left me."

"To see it is to believe it," she said, flipping her braid over her shoulder.

Johnny came out of the house drinking a glass of sweet tea.

"Sure is hot today," he said, wiping his mouth with the sleeve of his shirt.

Gertie nodded in agreement, then batted her lashes at him.

I rolled my eyes and silently asked the Lord to give me patience.

"Are y'all planning on going to Mexico with Mr. Villa?" he asked.

"No," I responded firmly. "We are definitely not going to Mexico."

"That's too bad; I'm riding as far as the border. I sure would enjoy your company," he said, his face turning a little red.

"Well, we might go to Mexico," Gertie replied.

"*No!*" I said loudly. "We are not going!"

Johnny shrugged and started to walk off. "Excuse me, I need to get started on the corral; the mules should be here by dusk."

"Why don't I come help you?" Gertie tagged along after him.

Johnny turned to look at Gertie. "That would be mighty fine, Miss Gertrude."

Gertie gave me a sly grin. *Oh brother, I'm exhausted, and Gertie is chasing around after the mule boy.* I returned to the house and asked Mrs. Opal if there was a room I could use to rest.

Mrs. Opal kept a tidy house. She called the front room, where Pancho Villa had taken court, the parlor. It resembled a living room to me, with a brown floral couch and two matching floral chairs. There was a yellow afghan folded and lying across the back of the sofa. A cherry coffee table stood in front of the sofa, and a matching side table split the two chairs. An old kerosene lamp sat on the side table, and I had a feeling of déjà vu. I shook off the chill that crept up my spine and reminded myself there was no way I had ever been here before.

To the right was a staircase that went straight up to the second floor. The kitchen was across the back of the house, and there was a bedroom off the kitchen.

Mrs. Opal took me upstairs, where two bedrooms split off the landing. The wood floors creaked below our feet as we entered the room to the left.

I took off the bonnet I was wearing and laid it on the dressing table. I loved the furniture. I would consider them antiques, but Mrs. Opal told me the furniture was delivered last week.

The double sized white wrought iron bed was centered in the room.

"It was a gift from Johnny, so when he come for a visit, he'd have a comfortable bed to sleep in," Mrs. Opal explained as I tried to hide a yawn. She told me she would wake me to help with supper and left the room.

The bed looked lumpy and was quite high off the floor. I guessed Johnny wouldn't mind if I stretched out on it for just a few minutes. I climbed into the bed and the softest mattress. swallowed my medium-sized frame. A crazy quilt was folded at the foot of the bed. I reached down and dragged it over my tired body. The warm breeze coasted in through the open windows and gently caressed me to sleep.

I was dreaming of Caiyan. Pancho Villa had a firing squad lined up, and Caiyan was one of the men he had positioned against a wall to be executed. Just as the order was given to fire, I threw myself in front of the bullet. I woke with a start, a scream stuck in my throat and my hands clutching the blanket around my chest. *Of all the stupid dreams, why would I risk my life to save a rat bastard rat who left me alone, again? Maybe he was trying to find me,* my subconscious argued. *Jeez, now I'm having an argument in my head.* Maybe the longer you stayed in the past, the crazier you became.

Shaking off the conflict in my mind, voices floated up through the floorboards. They were coming from the parlor directly below me. I recognized the harsh tones of Villa's voice and eavesdropped on the conversation.

"I do not trust the gringos," Villa said.

"Johnny said they came highly recommended," Mr. Hawkins replied. "I assure you the cargo will be with the mules." His voice was unsteady, and I bit my bottom lip as I listened

"If anything goes wrong, I will kill your entire family."

"But, Mr. Villa, we have done nothing but help you since you have traded with our Johnny," Mr. Hawkins pleaded.

I had a sick feeling in my stomach. We needed to find my key and get the hell out of here.

"After my mules and my weapons are safely loaded on the train, I will give them their precious package. It is not even gold; I do not see the value they place on it. However, your President Wilson has cut off all my other trade routes, so it leaves me no choice but to deal with the gringos. We will load the mules tonight after my men have been fed. I will deal only with the youngest male."

"But, Mr. Villa, Mortas is the leader; I'm sure he'll want to collect the payment himself." Mr. Hawkins tried to explain but Villa cut him off.

"No! Only the boy, or the deal is off."

"They'll be staying at the inn in town. I'm sure Mortas will wait there for his payment."

"See that he does," Villa replied.

"What about the girls?" Mr. Hawkins asked. "My wife has taken a liking to them and is concerned for their safety."

"I will take them to Mexico as a reward for my men. They have worked hard this trip, and although I do not prefer the white women, my men would enjoy them."

"But, Mr. Villa—" Mr. Hawkins started but was cut off midsentence.

"That is all, Mr. Hawkins."

Geesh, I am going to be some smelly Villista's sex slave. I felt a pain in my stomach and wished Caiyan would appear and get us out of here. My knees were shaking, and a bead of sweat trickled down my back. I didn't want to move for fear they would hear me.

"Tonight, we will have good food and drink before you leave for Mexico," Mr. Hawkins said, clearly trying to appease the outlaw.

"*Bueno.* I need to check on my men."

Footsteps shuffled across wood floor as the two men left the room.

I slowly climbed down from the feather bed. The floor creaked as I grabbed my bonnet and went outside to fetch Gertie.

I found her coming out of the barn with straw stuck in her hair.

"What have you been doing?" I demanded more than asked.

"Well, me and Johnny got a little caught up in the barn," she stammered.

"Gertie, please tell me you didn't do the nasty with him. For God's sake, he's from 1915. Caiyan said we have to be very careful what we do so we don't mess up anything in the future."

"Who are you, the sex police?" Gertie asked crossly. "For your information, Miss Nosy, I did not have sex with him. He's so skittish—I doubt he's ever been with a woman. Besides, Mr. Hawkins came lookin' for him, and he had to duck out. All I got was a short kiss. Not even any tongue."

"Thank goodness." I sighed with relief.

"You're probably right. Sex with me would be life changing." She laughed.

Opal came out of the house in a fit of excitement. "We're going to have a hoedown at our place tonight, and I'm gonna need your help to git everything ready."

Unlike Mr. Hawkins, Mrs. Opal didn't seem nervous. In fact, she acted like my mom when she was expecting company. My radar was telling me Mrs. Opal was being kept in the dark about the real cargo. She started listing off all the things she needed Gertie and me to do. "The Mexican women will help but I can't communicate with them."

"No problem," I replied. Maybe a chance for us to escape would present itself.

"Can you gals cook?" Mrs. Opal asked.

"I might know a few recipes," I said.

"Oh, Jen's mom is a..." I stopped Gertie in midsentence with a quick elbow to the ribs.

"Your ma is a what?" Opal asked, looking curious.

"She's a really good cook, and I might remember some of her recipes."

"Well, isn't that special. The Mexican women are the only ones who can cook for Mr. Villa, but we still need fixin's for everyone else. We're gonna have a good 'ole time tonight with Johnny bein' home an' all. In case you girls were wonderin', he's single," Mrs. Opal said with a gleam in her eye. "He ain't had nobody special since that Lowry girl, but she wasn't no good for him."

"I doubt she was the one that wasn't good," Gertie said under her breath.

Mrs. Opal continued chatting as we walked back to the house. "Johnny's considered a good catch, if you know what I mean. Especially now that he's makin' good money." Her chins jiggled as she spoke, and her voice heightened with enthusiasm. "He makes twenty dollars for each mule he sells."

Gertie and I looked at each other. I could tell she was doing the math in her head. I smiled politely and followed Mrs. Opal into the kitchen to figure out what dish I could create without a microwave.

CHAPTER 12

$\mathcal{T}$he Mexican women busied themselves preparing Pancho Villa's favorite dishes. He only allowed his people to prepare the food he ate. Homemade tortillas and something with corn were being hand rolled and wrapped in husks.

Mrs. Opal told us they had slaughtered a few heads of cattle in preparation for Mr. Villa's arrival and hung them in the smokehouse. She explained we would be having the beef and the chickens for the barbeque. My knees started to go weak. I was all for getting some protein in my diet, but I liked it processed and formed into patties.

Mrs. Opal assigned Gertie to catch the chickens since she had lived on a farm, once. I volunteered to make something sweet. Mrs. Opal told me if I needed anything, I should let her know, and she would see about it.

Checking the cupboards, I found the basics: flour, sugar, butter, and something in a ceramic jar that looked like real lard. Good grief, no wonder people died young in this decade—all this saturated fat. In the bottom cupboard, I found a few bags of beans, a big tin can of cocoa, and a bottle of pure vanilla. I decided to tackle a batch of brownies.

I realized the assigned tasks separated Gertie and me. Paco couldn't keep an eye on both of us. I nonchalantly slipped out the back door to check out the situation. Paco leaned against the porch post by the back door. Damn. I went back inside and tried the front door. My foot was on the bottom porch step when a voice from behind me caused the hair to stand up on my arms. "Where are you going, senorita?"

I turned to find Mr. Villa sitting in one of the rocking chairs. He was drinking a glass of lemonade and staring at me with those dark, sinister-looking eyes.

Double damn. "I'm going to the garden to pick herbs," I said and held my chin up in a defiant manner.

"The garden is that way," he said, pointing in the opposite direction. Then he sat back and twirled the end of his dark mustache.

"Oh, my bad," I said and started in the direction he indicated.

"Senorita, I have men scouting this entire farm; if you try to leave, I promise, you will not get very far, and I will have Paco remind you how close you need to stay." A shiver went down my spine. I turned away from him and followed the path to the garden.

I found it tucked to the left of a small barn. Ample sunlight and a rigged watering system sustained several rows of healthy vegetables. The herbs were planted toward the back, in a spot that took some shade. Lots of lavender, I assumed for Mrs. Opal's soaps.

There was mint, rosemary, and other herbs I didn't recognize. In the back row of the garden grew tall green plants with leaves shaped like stars. Now, that looks familiar. I recalled seeing this same plant grown in pots in Zane Miller's greenhouse.

Zane Miller was a total stoner in tenth grade. We would hang out sometimes after school. I would do his geometry homework, and he would teach me how to harvest the cannabis plant. Afterward, we would light up a doobie and eat a box of Twinkies.

The summer after tenth grade, I heard there was a raid at his house and his greenhouse went up in flames. Firefighters from three counties came to help put out the fire. Zane's greenhouse was about the size of a small tool shed. Go figure.

As I was examining the plant, the shattering of glass followed by a few choice curse words came from inside the small barn. I peeked in the door and discovered the barn was more of a potting shed. It was used for drying the herbs and storing flowerpots, compost, and other gardening materials. I found Johnny surrounded by glass from the Coke bottle he had been drinking.

"Hey," I said as I entered the shed.

"Oh, hi, J-J-Jennifer," he stammered. His face turned beet red when he realized I had heard the glass break.

"Yeah, that's me. Can I help you clean up?" I said, grabbing a broom that was leaning against the wall.

"I guess so. Sometimes I'm a little clumsy." He bent down to pick up the big pieces. There were several bushes of herbs hanging from the rafters of the small shed. The mixture of all the herbs smelled incredible, masking the remaining skunk stink emanating from my body. A bundle of dried cannabis was spread out on the table next to Johnny.

"What do you use this plant for?" I asked.

He eyed me curiously, then said, "We give it to the mules before we put them on the train. It helps calm them down a bit."

"The train?"

"Yeah, Mr. Villa transports all his animals in the train 'cause animals are more valuable than people."

Geez, that made me more determined to find a way out of here. The shrill tone of Mrs. Opal calling for Johnny had his shoulders slumping forward. "You go ahead; I'll clean this up," I told him. He nodded and hurried off to find his ma.

After I finished cleaning up the broken glass, I found a burlap sack and filled it with the dried cannabis. My inner voice was doing a victory dance in celebration that I had thought of an escape plan.

When I returned to the kitchen, I spied four large semisweet chocolate bars on the counter. Mrs. Opal was stirring something on the stove and keeping an eye on the Mexican girls.

"Mrs. Opal, what are you gonna do with all that chocolate?" I asked her.

"My Johnny always brings me chocolate from up north. There's a big chocolate factory in Dallas. It's harder to find down here."

"Do you mind if I use it for a dessert?"

"Help yourself; I never can eat all he brings, and I could stand to lose a few pounds," she replied, patting her round tummy.

I needed eggs. I opened the square wooden box Mrs. Opal called the ice box.

"Mrs. Opal, do you have any eggs?" I bent down searching for the familiar carton.

"Sure, honey, the basket's there by the door." I checked the basket. No eggs.

"Mrs. Opal, there's not any eggs in this basket."

"Well, for heaven's sake, girl. Go git 'em out of the hen house. Better to git 'em fresh daily—I don't like the taste of the ones we keep overnight in the icebox."

"You're kidding?" I asked. My mouth hung open in disbelief.

"Go on now and tell Gertie that Slim is ready for the chickens. We need to pluck the feathers off and take them out by the roasting pit."

"Yes ma'am," I answered back, grabbing the basket on my way out the back door. I gave Paco a salute as I passed by and decided I was getting more than a little irritated that Caiyan and Brodie had left us. Wasn't he supposed to know how to reach me? He was probably shacked up with Ms. Motorcycle Slut, not concerned with me at all.

I found Gertie in the chicken coop chasing a big white chicken.

"Come 'ere, you dad-burned bird," she yelled. The bird was running around clucking, then ducked under her legs. She twisted around and caught the bird by the neck.

"I gotcha now, bird." Then she started to swing it around like a yo-yo.

I stepped back a few feet from her. "Gertie, what are you doing?"

"I'm wringing this chicken's neck." At that moment the body of the chicken separated from its skinny little neck. Blood squirted up in the air.

I screamed as the headless chicken body went running around the pen, flopped over on one side, had a few convulsions, then settled.

Paco held his ribs as he laughed at me in the distance.

"Haven't you ever seen a chicken get slaughtered?" Gertie asked.

"No. I usually see chicken lying in a Styrofoam container covered in cellophane with the weight and expiration date stamped on it."

"How do you think it got there?"

"I try not to think about it." I shuddered as Gertie laid the chicken down next to its decapitated friends.

"Gertie, we need to get out of here. I have a bad feeling if we don't escape, we might find ourselves in Mexico. We only have a couple of days left."

"Are you...uncomfortable?" Gertie asked.

"No, I'm fine, but I don't want to find out what Caiyan meant by feeling uncomfortable. Mr. Villa said he has men everywhere, but I was thinking maybe tonight. I have a plan." Before I could make my plan known to Gertie, Mrs. Opal was hollering at us from the back porch.

"C'mon, girls, Slim needs those chickens."

I took the basket and speed-walked past the pile of lifeless chicken bodies to the wire mesh fence surrounding the chicken coop. Loud clucking noises sounded from inside the little chicken house. I guess if my friends were going to be dinner, I would be a little riled up too. The latch was left hanging open. Good grief, what if all the chickens got out? If Gertie thought catching one was hard, several would be a real workout.

The hen house was a small brown building with a slanted roof. It had a slatted wood door that opened to the inside. To the left of the door was a short, square opening with a long board slanting from the base of the opening down to the ground. One of the big white chickens was strutting her way down the board to the coop, volunteering to be Gertie's next victim. Lucky for her, Gertie was done wringing necks for the day.

I opened the door and ducked under the short doorway. As I entered, I had twenty sets of beady eyes daring me to take their precious possessions. The chickens nestled in two rows on each side of the hen house. They were stacked like bunk beds, each hen having her own little nest.

"OK, now you girls gotta give it up for Jen," I coaxed, moving a little closer to the hens. The clucking grew a little louder, like the birds were becoming nervous with my presence. There was a rustle, and the door swung shut. It wasn't my presence the chicks were nervous about; someone was behind the door. *Please, God, don't let it be Paco.*

I raised my basket above my head to throw at the intruder.

"What about me, lassie, can I give it up for ye?"

Shit...Caiyan. Now there's a neck I'd like to wring. "How did you get in here?" I lowered the basket and pressed my lips tightly together, trying to control my temper.

"I have my ways. Are ye not happy to see me?" Even though I was still a little pissed, I wanted to throw my arms around him with gratitude that he didn't leave us behind.

"Did you know we were taken by Pancho Villa?" I asked, expecting him to be at least a little worried.

"Aye, we learned of the deal at the saloon and figured we needed to infiltrate his camp, so good work."

"Good work!" I demanded, my voice rising an octave. "You mean to tell me I have been here, scared to death that we would be killed or raped, and you were delighted I was here?"

"Now, dinna fash yerself," he said gesturing with his hands out, palms toward me in a "calm down" motion.

I raised an eyebrow at his words.

"I mean, don't worry yerself. This is exactly where we need to be. Brodie is an excellent tracker, and he followed you here. We have been watching ye the whole time. I woudnae let anything bad happen to you."

"You wouldn't?" My knees went a little weak, but based on the intensity of his accent, I wasn't sure he was as confident as he suggested.

"No, I woudnae." He came forward and ran the back of his index finger down my cheek. I raised my eyes to meet his and was lost in the emerald seas staring down at me. He ran his hand around the back of my neck and brought his lips down to meet mine. A familiar heat flooded my body and my toes curled. Memories of the night we first met swirled around me, and I pulled away. We stood staring at each other, his arms grasping my shoulders. The look on his face had changed from lust and adventure to fear.

"What's that smell?" He leaned back, turning his nose away from me.

"I have no idea what you are referring to," I said my body tensing against his touch.

He released my arms and took a step back from me. "Villa will make contact with the Mafusos today."

"How do you know?"

"I have my ways, lassie."

I bet he did. She was tall and drove a Harley.

"Pancho Villa is known for hoarding treasure in a cave in Mexico. He may have come across yer key."

"How did the Mafusos find out Villa has the key?"

"The youngest of the Mafuso defenders came across a picture of Villa's wife in a textbook at school. She was wearing yer key."

"How is that possible? I would have known if I were related to Pancho Villa. Things like that are bragging rights in my family tree."

"I dinnae think she has the gift. I think he took it from someone, but I don't have the details."

I raised an eyebrow, suggesting maybe he was lacking in some capacity. Caiyan gave me a slight scowl.

"Villa is hard to find, but somehow they figured oot Johnny was trading mules with Villa." He ran his finger down my arm, and his green eyes turned dark. "Maybe we could become better acquainted this go-around."

My inner voice looked around for a place to get busy, and I slammed the door in her face.

"No you don't," I said, knocking his arm down. "Next time won't be so easy."

"Promise?" The corners of his mouth turned up in a mischievous smile. I moved away from him in case my defense system fell short. He converted back to serious mode.

"I want you to keep yer eyes and ears open for anything that might be useful. Try and make conversation with Pancho Villa. Maybe ye'll pick up a clue to where yer key is hidden."

My stomach curled at the idea of getting close to the evil man. I shuddered openly and Caiyan placed his arm around my shoulders.

"Don't worry, he needs you and Gertie for something, or he wouldn't have taken ye."

Yeah, I thought to myself, *to entertain his troops with my body.* The gate on the chicken yard creaked open. My eyes widened as Caiyan ducked behind the door just as Mr. Hawkins stuck his head in.

"What's keepin' you, girl?" he asked. "Mrs. Opal sent me to check on ya."

"Sorry, Mr. Hawkins, I'll get the eggs and be right out."

"You can call me Slim—everyone does." Mr. Hawkins watched me fill the basket with eggs. The chickens didn't seem to mind me sticking my hand under their feathered asses and confiscating the eggs. I guess it's all in a day's work.

As we left the hen house, I avoided looking in Caiyan's direction. I was afraid I might give him away, but as Slim pushed against the door to allow me to exit, Caiyan was already gone.

I entered the house to find Gertie and all the Mexican women plucking the chickens. Geesh, I didn't want to do that, so I gave Mrs. Opal the eggs, keeping a few for myself. I mixed the flour, sugar, eggs, cocoa, and butter. I added bits of the chocolate and the special ingredient I had found in the drying shed. I hoped the pointed plant had the same effect as it had in the back of Zane Miller's greenhouse.

I coated the pans with the lard. Since I didn't have a KitchenAid mixer, my arms burned from stirring until the batter was smooth and creamy. I carefully poured the mixture into a pan and looked around for an oven. I didn't think about the oven thing. What if Mrs. Opal didn't have one? Jeez, I could just smack myself. The lack of modern conveniences was starting to wear on me. To my right was the stove Mrs. Opal had used earlier. It was a huge black thing with a large pipe coming out the top and shooting up through the roof. There were two doors on the front.

"Mrs. Opal, do you have an oven?" I asked.

She stopped plucking the chicken and eyed me impatiently. "Girl, it's right there in front of you—open your eyes." I stared at the large appliance. I reached down and unlatched one of the doors. It resembled an oven, but I there weren't any heating elements. How did it cook the food? The walls were warm, but not hot enough to cook my brownies.

"Um, Mrs. Opal, I don't think the oven is hot enough," I said as I slid my brownie pan inside.

"Well, land sakes, girl, don't you know anything about cooking? You have to put the wood in first." She waddled over to where I was standing in front of the metal beast. She bent over, bumping me back a few steps, and grabbed some kindling from a basket on the floor. After she added the wood to an area on the side of the contraption, it heated up immediately.

The first batch burned right away, but once I got the hang of the oven, the brownies came out picture-perfect. I made four large batches. Martha Stewart would have been proud. I was surprised at how delectable they turned out. Even on my best day, I hadn't made such perfect brownies. Maybe it was the pure ingredients, not polluted with the preservatives of the future.

Mrs. Opal rounded the corner. "What smells so good?" she asked, breathing in the scrumptious aroma of my brownies.

"My secret recipe," I said, relieved my dessert had turned out so well.

She peeked in my pan and wrinkled her nose at the flat brown cake. "What is it?"

"Brownies," I said moving the pan out of her reach.

"Brownies?" her eyebrows furrowed, and she reached for a pan. "Never heard of such a thing, but these brownies are makin' my mouth water. Let me try one."

Red alert rang in my head. "Now, Mrs. Opal, they are for the party tonight. We wouldn't want to run out before the guests had some."

"Absolutely, dear," she turned hesitantly and left the kitchen with a backward glance at the brownies and mumbling about a man coming to take her picture. I placed the brownies on top of the wooden box Mrs. Opal had proudly announced was her brand-new icebox to cool.

CHAPTER 13

I carried a tray of sweet tea to the men on the front porch. Villa was holding court with his main Villistas. I handed each man a glass, and they nodded, indifferent to my presence. I offered a glass to Villa and he scowled as he took one. The men drank their tea and then dispersed. I sat down not too far from Mr. Villa.

Get your nerve up, Jen.

"So, Mr. Villa, how long are you planning to stay at the Hawkinses' ranch?"

He took a long drink of the sweet tea and narrowed his hooded eyes as he assessed me.

"Until the mules arrive tonight," he answered. "Then we will go by train to Mexico and return to my people."

"Well, I hope you have a safe trip," I said, standing and gathering the empty glasses.

He snickered. "You and your friend will be coming too."

I paused and tried not to let my face show the fear that flooded up inside me. I was pretty sure we were not going to Cancun to drink margaritas and hang out at Carlos and Charlie's Bar. Transporter or not, there was no way I was going to Mexico with this criminal. Gertie and I would be leaving tonight, come hell or high water.

My thoughts were interrupted by the sound of gravel crunching under hooves. A buggy pulled by a raggedy-looking mule plodded up the lane. A man in a bowler-style hat and a brown suit sat bent over in the driver's seat urging the poor creature to keep moving forward. The buggy bounced along, slinging the occasional rock here and there. The Villistas drew their guns.

"Lower your guns, my compadres," Villa said. "It is just the picture man coming to take my photo."

The man pulled the buggy to a stop and stepped down, greeting Mr. Villa with a tip of his hat. Pancho Villa descended the steps and spoke English to the man, pointing at a spot in front of the house.

The man shielded his eyes from the sun and searched the sky, then nodded. He began hauling his camera equipment out from the buggy to the agreed upon location. A stable boy came to take the horse and buggy.

The Villistas gathered in front of a large dogwood tree in front of the house, offering a beautiful backdrop for the pictures. Its white flowers had bloomed and gone, but pinkish-red fruit that resembled raspberries adorned the branches. The leaves were shades of purple, red, and yellow. I couldn't help but smile at the thought of all the fuss Pancho Villa was making about standing in front of the tree when the photographs from this time were black and white. *Go figure.*

The man in the brown suit scurried about, moving men around until Villa was standing in the middle and his main Villistas flanked him on either side. A row of men stood behind him. The photographer had arranged the tallest men directly behind Villa, but when Villa noticed, he had them moved instead toward the end of the row and had them squat to make themselves look shorter.

The camera guy ducked under a cover attached to the back of the camera. After poking his head out and then ducking back under several times, he held out a big stick with his right arm.

"On three." The picture man held up three fingers. "Uno, dos, *tres.*" The men mumbled. There was a *flash* of blinding light, followed by a loud *pop*, and a *poof* of dust clouded the air. All that work for one picture. I hoped it came out. I wouldn't want to be the photographer if the picture turned out fuzzy.

One of the Mexican men brought Villa's horse to him. The black stallion was regal, and although horses made me wary, this one gave stud a whole new meaning. After Villa sat astride his mount, he took his rifle and held it against his chest. The picture man scrambled under the cover again. After about five minutes, whoosh, another picture was made. Villa and his men had a few more pictures then retreated to the shade of the huge oak tree.

Gertie, Opal, and Slim had stepped out onto the front porch to watch the photo shoot.

"Oh, this is just grand!" Mrs. Opal clapped her hands then scurried down the steps, dragging Slim by the hand.

"Orville, thank you so much for comin' today," Mrs. Opal said to the photographer as she grabbed his hand and gave it a squeeze.

"Girls, come over here by Orville and tell me how I look when he makes the picture," Mrs. Opal said to Gertie and me.

"Mrs. Opal, you and Slim stand over there in front of the house," the photographer instructed.

Mrs. Opal moved to stand on the porch steps. She turned to straighten Slim's suit collar.

We did as told and watched as they prepared for their photo. Mrs. Opal looked pretty. She had applied rouge to her cheeks and done her hair up under a smart pillbox hat with a peacock feather sticking out the top. Slim was wearing a blue suit, wide tan cowboy hat, and his church shoes. I thought they made a nice-looking couple.

"One, two, three," said the photographer and, *flash, pop, poof,* followed by another cloud of blinding dust.

Gertie gasped beside me. She grabbed my arm to steady herself and fanned her face with her hand as if she was avoiding the urge to faint.

"What's wrong?" I asked.

"I have that picture on the table beside my bed," she stammered.

"What do you mean?"

"The picture Orville just took sits next to my bed at home." Her voice was shaking, and a bead of sweat was forming on her upper lip. "I'm a Jezebel."

"Are you telling me the Hawkins are your relatives?"

"That's exactly what I'm sayin'," she said, still holding on to me for support. "It just clicked when I saw him take the picture. They're my great-great-grandparents. Which means Johnny is my great-granddad."

"You didn't know he was your great-granddad?"

"No, Granny Azona's first husband was a Hawkins, but I think he was a junior. He was my ma's biological dad, but my ma always referred to him as John, because he died in the war when my ma was a baby. Then Granny Azona married Pawpaw Norton, and he adopted my ma. She always called him Daddy, but I am certain Johnny is the father of my granddad, John."

"Are you sure?" I placed a hand on her shoulder to steady her. "There are probably tons of people with the last name of Hawkins."

"Pretty sure," she shrugged. "After Granny married Pawpaw Norton, they had six more kids, so I guess it kinda got lost, but my ma always had that picture, and when she married stepdad number two, she gave it to me. I think she said he died of tuberculosis. I almost had relations with my great-granddad, just like Jezebel." Gertie covered her face with her hands.

"It doesn't count if you didn't know. Besides, all you did was kiss, no tongue, remember?"

"Well, there might have been a little tongue," Gertie said her face flushing slightly.

Crap.

Several of the Mexican women had come to watch Pancho Villa get his picture taken. They were laughing and pretending to pose for a picture. The noise level was escalating; Villa gave them a stern look, and they quieted. Johnny showed up and walked to stand next to his parents.

"Girls, get on over here." Mrs. Opal's voice rang out above the ruckus.

What now? I asked myself. How was I supposed to talk with Pancho Villa and get an escape route planned? Reluctantly, Gertie and I walked over to Mrs. Opal.

"You gals get on either side of Slim and me," she said, pointing an index finger indicating where we should stand.

"I don't think that's a good idea." I started backing away.

"*Nonsense!*" Mrs. Opal screeched. "Get in the picture. These picture people don't get around much, and Mr. Villa is payin' fer us to get a picture. Now git!"

I stood next to Slim, and he put his skinny arm around me. Johnny moved in next to Gertie. I glanced over at her. A perfect smile was frozen on her freckled face. She was in shock. Great, now I had to deal with a traumatized Gertie, organize an escape plan, and outsmart Pancho Villa. My list was growing long for my skill set. The photographer ducked under the cover and then popped out again. He told us to get closer together, bringing his hands from wide to narrow.

"It's as if my two girls were still alive," Mrs. Opal sniffed.

Slim placed his other arm around Opal. "Now, Ma, don't get all sentimental. Your face will be blotchy in the photo."

"Pa's right, Ma, these are happy times!" Johnny wrapped an arm around Gertie's back and squeezed her right buttocks.

Flash, pop, poof!

After the picture-taking experience, we went into the house to finish the preparations for the feast. There was plenty of food. How did the Hawkinses afford to feed all these people? I mean, how much money could be made selling mules? I needed some answers before I was carted off to Mexico.

Mrs. Opal assigned me to the potatoes and gave Gertie another task before she went to change out of her Sunday dress. The sound of hoof-beats on the gravel path that led to the house had me moving to peek out the front window.

Several cowboys on horseback were driving a herd of mules down the lane toward the back pasture. Three farm wagons each pulled by a team of horses followed the mules.

The wagons stopped at the entrance to the back pasture. Villa left his post on the front porch and went out to inspect the contents of the wagons. The men driving the wagons were heavily armed. *That's a lot of protection for mules,* but what did I know? I leaned closer to the window and angled myself for a better view. *I wonder what else they are hauling?*

Following the wagons was a man on a chestnut horse. He sat tall in the saddle. His dark hair was tucked under a black cowboy hat. Behind him riding a dapple-gray mare was—I couldn't believe it—the Satan bitch. What was she doing here?

Riding next to her was a younger male. From the way he was slouched in the saddle, I surmised his age to be somewhere between fourteen and sixteen. He must be the Mafuso Caiyan was referring to earlier. The one who discovered my key. Good, at least there was one Mafuso my size. I might even be able to take him down if necessary.

The man in the black hat dismounted and shook hands with Villa. They turned to inspect the contents of the wagons. There were a few nods. Satan's bitch and the younger boy got off their mounts, and a stable hand took the horses to the barn. There was more hand shaking, and they turned to come into the house.

Not good. I rushed down the hallway in search of Gertie. She was sitting at the kitchen table snapping green beans and singing "Achy Breaky Heart."

"Gertie, snap out of it." I gave her shoulder a light shove.

"Easy for you to say," she said. "You didn't almost have relations with your grandpa."

"The Mafusos are here and Satan's bitch is with them."

"I knew she was trouble the minute I laid eyes on her." Gertie placed her hands on her hips.

"We have to pretend we belong here." I said, desperately trying to think up a plan. "We can't let them know we are from the future."

"Girls." Mrs. Opal's voice came down the hallway. "Come in here, would ya? We have more guests from up north."

Gertie and I glanced at each other with an apprehensive stare and moved slowly into the front parlor room. Villa sat in one of the chairs next to the small side table. To his right sat the man in black. He had removed his cowboy hat, revealing an angled jawline, dark hair trimmed close, and his deep-set, almost black eyes bore into me as I stood in the center of the room.

Satan's bitch and the younger boy were standing, sipping some sweet tea. The boy's gaze stopped at my tits and held. Satan's bitch didn't give me a second glance. Instead, she focused on her manicure. *A time without nail salons, oh, how did she manage?*

"Gertie and Jennifer, this is Mortas, Mahlia, and Mitchell Mafuso." Slim gave the introductions.

Three Ms, how cute. "Hello," I said.

Gertie responded with a "Howdy, nice to meet you."

"Where are you from...up north?" Mahlia asked with a slight New York accent. She raised an eyebrow in Gertie's direction.

"Amarillo," I said, but Gertie replied, "Vermont," at the same time.

"Well, we are originally from Amarillo, Texas, but we are currently living in Vermont." I tried to explain.

"Interesting," purred the bitch. "I have never been to Vermont; you will have to tell me all about it."

"Sure, um, maybe later. We need to get the food ready. Nice to meet everyone." I gave them a finger wave and backed out of the room with Gertie in tow. When we were out of earshot, I turned to Gertie. "Vermont? What were you thinking?"

"It's the farthest Northern state I could think of," she said, shrugging her shoulders.

"I've never been to Vermont, have you?"

She shook her head as we entered the kitchen, sat down at the table, and returned to snapping green beans.

"What am I going to tell Satan's bitch if she asks me questions about Vermont?" I asked Gertie.

"Tell her it's cold, and people ski there."

"I don't know if people ski there in 1915!" I didn't even know if there were any ski resorts. I slept through history class, but I was pretty sure World War I was around the corner and the Depression right behind it. Skiing almost certainly wasn't high on anyone's list in this time. Ski resorts probably didn't even exist.

I grabbed the tea jug to refill the glasses. I needed to hear what was going on in that room. The door leading to the parlor was closed. Damn. I contemplated going back upstairs to the bedroom I had napped in. Villa's men were standing—or slouching—guard at the stairs. Double damn.

There was a small cupboard built into the wall adjacent to the parlor. I opened the door and squeezed in next to the shelves of canned mason jars filled with fruit and veggies. I reached for one of the empty glass jars and turned it, open end to the wall, then put my ear against it. Girl Scouts training 101. I could hear Villa talking about his cargo.

"The train will be here at dusk; we will load the cargo and the mules I'm purchasing and return to Mexico."

"Do you have the necklace?" asked Mortas.

"It's in a safe place. After I load the cargo, I'll give it to young Mitchell."

"Very well, Mitchell will accompany you tonight." Mortas paused, considered, and said, "If he does not return with the necklace, I will come for you myself."

The rustle of a gun drawn from its holster and the small cock of a pistol made me cringe as Villa said, "How dare you insinuate I do not keep my word?"

"I don't take anything for granted, my friend," Mortas replied.

"And what about the one who gave you the key?" Mahlia asked.

"The young girl is well cared for by my wife. She has a special fondness for taking care of women in her condition. My wife did not want to give up your necklace but did so to spare the life of the young girl."

Whomever Villa had taken the key from was alive. This was good news for me. Maybe my family tree was still intact. I assumed Villa had the key on his person. Something so valuable to the Mafusos wouldn't be left in the care of his men or Johnny Hawkins.

The cupboard door opened, and Mrs. Opal shrieked, "There you are!"

I jumped three feet, spilling tea on my dress, and holding up the empty mason jar. "I was looking for glasses to take tea outside to the men. I figured they were thirsty."

"What a nice thought," Mrs. Opal said as she bustled inside the tight space and searched the shelves of canned goods. "They probably would like my sweet tea instead of their rusty canteens filled with water." She chose a can and took the jug of tea from me.

I gathered half a dozen mason jars and followed her out of the cupboard.

We joined Gertie in the kitchen. Mrs. Opal refilled the tea jug and arranged the glasses in a basket for me to carry them. Gertie grabbed the jug of tea and followed me out the back door. Paco watched me from under the big shade tree. His good eye constantly tracked my every move.

"Where am I gonna go?" I shouted.

Gertie stuck her tongue out at him, and we didn't offer him any tea.

We walked past the barn and the chicken house. I kept an eye out for Caiyan, but there had been no sign of him since this morning.

As we walked through the pasture, I felt Paco easing his way slowly behind us. Since he was out of earshot, I confided with Gertie, "I don't understand how we ended up here with your relatives, but we must leave tonight. Pancho Villa is planning on taking us to Mexico on the train."

"Are you sure?" she asked.

"Yes, he told me himself. But I overheard him tell the Mafusos he has my key." I shifted the weight of the basket to my opposite hip. "Maybe we can outfox Paco."

"What are we gonna do?"

"I have a plan," I told her as we approached the back pasture. "After we make sure Johnny is busy, let's check out what's in those wagons."

A large corral ringed a herd of sad-looking mules. I hadn't noticed earlier, but most of them were skinny and looked like they wouldn't do a day's work if you hung a carrot in front of them. I couldn't believe Pancho Villa was going to buy such a sad lot. A stake-and-rider fence formed the large corral. Johnny squatted by one of the posts, checking the fence for breaks.

"What's up?" I asked.

Johnny lifted his head, and as soon as he saw Gertie, his face went beet red.

"Up where?" He cocked his head at me.

"I mean, what are you doing?" I asked. "Why are you way back here?"

"Oh, I like to keep the mules away from the house," he said. A pleased grin threatened the corners of his mouth.

Johnny had two corrals, and the animals were divided evenly between them.

"Why do you keep the mules in separate pens; are they different sexes?" I asked Johnny.

He looked over at the animals. "These mules here are Mr. Villa's," he said, pointing to the nearest pen. "Them over yonder belong to Mrs. Hobbs. She lives down the road a piece and likes a good trade."

"Yeah, we bought a horse from her," I said.

He smiled big. His crooked teeth, stained from sweet tea and tobacco, lit up his face in a boyish grin.

"She sold you Gypsy. I saw her in the barn."

"Why is that so funny?" I asked.

"Outsiders buy her and, in a day or more, return her. Mrs. Hobbs keeps the money on account of she has a no-return policy, and she still gits her horse back."

Caiyan had been swindled by the chaw-spitting, housedress-wearing memaw. I couldn't help but smile.

"Would you like some tea?" Gertie asked, trying to stay as far away as possible.

"Sure, Miss Gertie." Johnny reached into my basket and retrieved a glass. He held the glass out in front of Gertie, but she didn't move. I gave her a gentle nudge and she poured Johnny the tea. He downed it in one gulp and wiped his mouth with the back of his shirt sleeve.

"Hot out here," he explained. "Thanks for the tea." He handed Gertie the glass and knelt to stir a white, fizzy liquid he had in a metal bucket.

"What's that bubbling stuff?" Gertie asked Johnny.

"It's a special tonic for the mules. It makes them stronger."

I hoped it worked like spinach did for Popeye, because those mules needed a dose of supervitamins.

Gertie moved in for a closer look. "Why, that's Alka-Seltzer."

"Alka-what?" Johnny scratched his head.

"Johnny, are you giving these mules sodium bicarbonate to make them swell up?" Gertie asked propping the tea jug on her hip.

Johnny looked sheepishly at Gertie. "By the time it wears off, they'll be back in Mexico."

"Johnny, you're dealing with Pancho Villa; he will kill you, and then he will kill your family," I said.

"*No!*" Johnny stood, fists clenched. "I have it figured out. Mr. Villa is a wanted man. My friends told me President Wilson is sending General Pershing to capture Villa, so he won't be coming back to Texas after this trade. Besides, he's got plenty more important things to worry about in Mexico "

"Are you referring to your friends that arrived earlier?" I asked. "The Mafusos?"

Johnny's face turned red, and a bead of sweat ran down the side of his face. "I have already sold the land and the house. As soon as we finish our business and Mr. Villa crosses into Mexico tonight, I'm moving my family to Mount Pleasant. I bought us a real nice house and we have family there. Even if Mr. Villa came after me, it's too far north for him to travel."

I had a sick feeling in my stomach. Villa was dangerous, and I didn't want anything bad to happen to the Hawkins family. If something happened to Johnny, it might affect Gertie's future.

Johnny took a step back and his features softened.

"Maybe we could get together for a ride tonight, Miss. Gertie, before we leave with Mr. Villa."

Gertie started shaking her head and mumbled, "Eeuuww."

I immediately stepped between them with my back to Johnny. "Say yes," I mouthed.

Gertie stiffened and plastered a fake smile on her face. "Sorry, I thought I saw a spider. I'd love to go for a ride with you."

"After I conduct my business with Mr. Mafuso, I'm sure Mr. Villa will let you accompany me on a ride."

"What business do you have with Mortas?" I asked Johnny.

"Um, Mr. Mafuso is buying the supplies I brought from Dallas and trading them to Mr. Villa to help fight the bad people who are taking over Mexico. Mr. Villa told us if we don't help him, the bad people will come to Texas and kill our family."

"That is such a bunch of horseshit," Gertie said.

Both Johnny and I stared at her with our mouths hanging open.

"I mean...," she searched for the words, "Pancho Villa probably won't let them get to Texas. He's a great revolutionary."

"You're right about him, Ms. Gertie," Johnny said. "He's a cruel man, but no one messes with me anymore because they know we have business with him."

"Johnny, what sort of supplies are you selling Mr. Villa and Mr. Mafuso?" I asked.

Johnny's face turned red again, not because he was sweet on Gertie but because he had revealed a secret. "You girls had better get on to the house;

Mamma don't like it when she has to do all the work. You can hear her yellin' in the next town." His mouth drew up in a wide smile, and Gertie and I took the hint. Whatever was in those wagons, Johnny was keeping to himself.

We walked back toward the farm, and I saw the back of one of the wagons peeking out from behind the barn. The horses had been unhitched and were being fed and watered

One of the cowboys was leaning against the wagon wheel. He was tall and lean, and his skin was weathered from work. He had on a pair of chaps over his jeans and a brown cowboy hat pulled down low on his brow. He was slowly chewing on a long piece of grass and eyeing us as we approached.

"Would you like some sweet tea?" I asked, batting my lashes.

"Sure." He pushed himself away from the wheel and moved toward us with a sly smile. "I never turn down a pretty lady."

Gertie poured him a glass. He took a long drink, savoring the copper liquid.

"Oohwee, that's good," he said. "Which one of you young ladies made this fine tea?"

"I did," I lied.

Two of Villa's men were guarding the wagons. They had their rifles lying across their laps as they sat on the back of the wagon.

Gertie walked around and held up the tea jug, indicating she would give them some. Since they didn't speak English, they both nodded their heads, and she filled up a couple of mason jars for them.

I looked around for Paco, and sure enough, there he was, standing in the shade next to the barn. At least the barn blocked his view of the wagon, so maybe if I created a diversion, Gertie could check the wagons.

"Gosh, it sure is hot out here," I said and began to fan myself. I took a hankie out of my pocket and began to dab my face a little. "I'd better set these glasses down; I feel kinda faint."

I sat the basket of mason jars down on the step of the wagon and proceeded to fan myself. The two Mexicans and Gertie had come around to see what all the commotion was about. I raised an eyebrow at Gertie. She took the hint and slowly stepped backward toward the wagon.

"I think my top is cutting off my circulation; I need to loosen these ties. Do you mind helping me?" I turned around so the cowboy could loosen the ties on my top. I grabbed the neck of my dress and pulled it down a bit, revealing the mounds of flesh pushed up by the corset. My breasts threatened to pop right out of the dress, and I moved forward slightly to keep their attention focused on me.

"Maybe you better sit down a spell," the cowboy said, speaking directly to my bursting boobs.

"I should probably have something cool to drink."

"Here, drink this," he said giving me his tea.

I took the glass of tea and put it to my forehead. "Oh, that feels good... it's cool."

I slowly ran the glass down my throat and across my bosom.

Just as I was about to bring the glass to my lips for the most sensuous drink, a loud crack sounded from the trees on the other side of the wagons. The Mexicans sprang to attention from where they were observing me and ran around to discover what caused the noise. The cowboy and I followed them.

Out of the corner of my eye, I saw Gertie crouching down in the wagon. The men were pointing their guns at a body lying spread eagle on the ground. A man had fallen out of the tree and landed face up in leaves. I peered around the cowboy to see the man.

Crap, it was Brodie. The Mexicans cocked their rifles and held him at gunpoint until Paco joined them. He grabbed Brodie by the shirt, pulling him to his feet.

"Easy now there, pardner," Brodie said. "I'm just lookin' for work."

His eyes trailed behind the cowboy and I knew Gertie was sneaking down from the wagon.

"This is the Hawkinses' farm," I said, drawing the attention to Brodie, and treating him like a stranger.

Gertie stepped in behind Paco. "Yeah, you should ask Mr. Hawkins about a job."

Paco said something in Spanish to the other two men, and one of them took off toward the house. After a few minutes, Pancho Villa returned with Mr. Hawkins, Mahlia, and Mitchell.

I saw Mahlia roll her eyes. Mitchell looked on suspiciously. There was no sign of Mortas.

"What have we here?" Pancho Villa asked, "Another gringo?"

"Hey, mate, I'm just lookin' for work." Brodie's accent kicked up a notch.

Villa took the butt end of his rifle and hit Brodie across the jaw, knocking him to his knees.

Gertie and I shrieked in unison.

"Fucking A, kick his ass!" Mitchell taunted. Mahlia put her hand on his shoulder and gave him a definite "shut up" squeeze.

I knew I didn't like that little prick. The men looked at Mitchell, who slunk back with a sneer.

"Now, Mr. Villa," Slim said. "The man was just looking for work; there's no need to be cruel."

"He was in the tree," Villa responded. "A spy for the Mexican government."

"No, I'm from Australia; I sleep in the trees, mate," Brodie replied, wiping the blood trickling down his face with the back of his shirt sleeve.

"Tie him up in the barn. Tomorrow Hawkins can deal with you after we are gone," Villa said, pushing Brodie to the ground.

Villa's men took Brodie to the barn. I grabbed the basket of glasses and tried not to run to the house. Gertie followed behind me.

When we made it to the kitchen, Gertie told me about the guns she had seen in the wagon.

"What are we gonna do?" she wailed. "Where's Caiyan?"

"Shh," I said as Mahlia entered the kitchen. She eyed me curiously.

"Your accent doesn't sound like Vermont—maybe a little more Southern," she said.

"Like I said, our parents were from Amarillo. It's the reason we came back to Texas," I snipped.

"I thought you were from Vermont." She crossed her arms over her chest.

"We only lived there a short time," Gertie said.

"Mmm," was all she said as she left the kitchen.

I grabbed a cloth and a basin of water and told Gertie I was going to check on Brodie. Maybe they would let me clean his face.

Two of Villa's men were stationed at the barn door. I walked toward them, looking around for Paco. For the first time, the slimeball wasn't lurking in the shadows. I motioned to one of the men that I wanted to clean the prisoner's face. He looked at the other Mexican, and he shrugged. I guess they didn't think one woman with a water basin was a big threat.

I opened the door and walked inside. The barn door swung closed behind me, and metal clanged as they latched the door. There were four empty horse stalls to my right. A straight ladder led up to a loft above the stalls. Hay bales were stacked to the left, and Brodie was tied to a chair in front of them.

His head was hung down as if he was unconscious. How had this happened? Villa only hit him once. I ran over to him, sloshing water on the way. I set the basin at his feet and lifted his head. Blood oozed out of the cuts on his face. It looked like he had been whipped across the face. He opened one swollen eye.

"What happened?" I asked him.

His eye focused behind me, and a creepy sneer echoed in the barn.

I turned to find Paco. He smiled at me as he slapped a leather strap across his palm.

"You?" I lost my cool. "You asshole!" I walked toward him. "What gives you the right to beat him like this?"

Paco raised the strap to hit me. My arms flew up to protect my face. A flash of metal, and a shiny blade came across his throat. His good eye bugged out in horror as Caiyan dropped from the loft above and cut his throat. Blood ran down his neck, and he collapsed on the ground.

Caiyan grabbed me as I stifled a scream. "It's OK; I've got you, lassie." I let my weight lean into him as he led me away from Paco's body. He sat me gently on the ground next to Brodie. He wiped the blood from his knife on his pants and replaced it into a small holster on his calf.

Caiyan tucked his finger under my chin and lifted it until my eyes met his. A wave of warmth spread from his fingers across my cheek. His deep green eyes held concern instead of the sharp irritation or the smoldering lust I had become accustomed to.

"I've got to get rid of the body before his buddies come back. Can you cut Brodie loose?" Caiyan asked, holding a pocketknife out for me.

I nodded my head yes. Then with shaking hands I began to work the knots binding Brodie to the chair.

"It's not as bad as it looks, mate," Brodie said as I cut away the rope. After he was free, I helped him wash his face with the water.

Caiyan pulled Paco's body to the back of the barn, covered it with hay and several sacks of feed. He took my rag and washed the blood from his hands. Grabbing the pitchfork from the wall next to the horse stalls, he began spreading fresh hay over the bloody area on the barn floor. Villa's men would assume any blood was Brodie's, at least for a short time until they found the body.

The latch on the barn squeaked. Someone was coming, and there was nowhere to hide.

"Go back and pretend to be tied up, 'tis better to surprise them." Caiyan said to Brodie.

Brodie sat down in the chair, and I pulled the rope around him. As I knelt to pick up the washrag, the barn door swung open, and Mahlia sauntered in.

She stopped when she saw me with the washbasin.

"I should have known she would be one of your women, Brodie. Did you get her on the ride over? Or did you win her in a game of cards?"

I felt my jaw tighten, and I held back the urge to claw her eyes out.

"They tried to tell me they were from Vermont, of all places." Mahlia said, flipping her manicured hand nonchalantly in the air.

I started to respond, but Brodie grabbed my hand and held it. "Yep, Texas has such sweet young things, I couldn't help myself."

"Where is Caiyan?" She circled around the barn like a cat searching for the rat in the haystack. "I can't believe he would miss all this fun."

"You're right," Caiyan said, swinging down from the loft. The rat appeared.

"So, the other one must be yours, although she's really not your type." Mahlia flipped her long brown hair over her shoulder and eyed Caiyan. "Who is transporting for you?"

"Weel, I wouldnae want to spoil the surprise. And ye shouldnae talk aboot it in front of the locals." He jerked his thumb in my direction, but I wan't sure she bought it.

"Remember our deal, Caiyan. No member of my family is to be hurt or arrested." Mahlia spoke as if her words were above my level of knowledge, with no regard for spilling any secrets, the same way Caiyan spilled blood.

"I remember, Mahlia," Caiyan said. "Now, ye lassies go start some trouble outside, so Brodie and I can get oot of here."

I was dumbfounded. Not only was Caiyan sneaking away again, but now he was leaving behind a dead body.

Brodie bent down like he was giving me a kiss on the cheek. "We'll return for ya tonight," he whispered. His rough stubble scraped against my face. I nodded my head slightly and stood, cutting my eyes at Caiyan as I exited. An amused expression crossed his face, and I felt a hot flush of anger cover mine.

Mahlia and I exited the barn. We needed to cause a distraction

"I saw the cute Australian guy first, so you keep your hands off," I snapped, then reached out and gave her a good hard push. She stumbled sideways, giving me some much-needed satisfaction. But I didn't expect her retaliation.

She gave me a harder shove to the shoulder. "I will have him for myself."

I lost my balance and fell to the ground. The water basin flew out of my hands. My bonnet fell off my head, exposing my Toni & Guy hair. She turned on her heel with a smirk and went into the house.

The two Mexicans looked at each other and shook their heads. One went to pick up my water basin, and the other came over to help me. I saw Brodie and Caiyan leave the barn behind them. I grabbed my backside and cried out in pain. Both men came closer to examine my rear end as the real pain in my ass snuck away into the trees.

CHAPTER 14

$\mathcal{I}$ limped a little on the way back to the house just for show. The harsh rays of the October sun had mellowed with the help of a few white, fluffy clouds. A soft breeze floated the smell of roasting chicken and smoked beef through the air.

When I returned to the house, the Mexican women were in a frenzy trying to get things ready for the feast. I wove my way through the small kitchen and retrieved my brownie pans from the top of the icebox to cut them into squares. One of the pans had a generous piece missing.

"I couldn't resist," Mrs. Opal said and then suffocated a giggle. "Jen, those brownies are scrumdiddelyumptious!"

I bit my lip. Mrs. Opal sat at the kitchen table staring at the fading wallpaper. "I swear those flowers are dancing. Don't you see them, Jen?" At least I knew the brownies would work when the time came. I patted her shoulder, then cut the brownies and hid them behind a large sack of flour.

I found out Mortas had returned to the town. *Good,* I thought, *at least he didn't see Brodie.* If he had seen Brodie, he probably wouldn't have gone back to town so easily. Apparently, Brodie had never met Mitchell, or the little weasel would have snitched. At least Mahlia kept her mouth shut. She was currently holed up in the parlor discussing strategy with Mitchell.

Mahlia was giving information to Caiyan to protect her family from being arrested and taken to Gitmo. Caiyan might have promised, but I didn't. She wouldn't be too happy when she found out I was the transporter. I wasn't sure exactly what that meant, but I intended to find out. And why did Brodie and Caiyan want Mahlia to think I was Brodie's girl? Unless Caiyan didn't want Mahlia to know he had kissed me in the hen house...that two-timing snake. As I contemplated the reason why men are so irritating, I walked out through the enclosed dining area and out the back porch, letting the screen door bang closed behind me.

The porch steps provided a beautiful view of the setting sun. Hues of orange and pink stroked the sky like a watercolor masterpiece. I remembered the time I sat with Jake on his rooftop patio in downtown Dallas watching the sun create magic against the skyline. Holy crap, I had forgotten about Jake again. What would I tell him when I returned? *Hey, Jake, I can travel through time, and, by the way, I know you are seeing other people; well, now so am I. Sort of.* OK, that didn't sound mature. It sounded ridiculous. And who was the two-timing reptile now?

"Hello, earth to Jen." Gertie waved her hands in front of my face. "You were a thousand miles away."

"Try a century." I continued down the porch steps, and I explained to her what had gone down in the barn.

"Jen, Caiyan killed a man. How do you feel about that?"

"He was a bad man," I answered, but the shock of Caiyan's actions weighed heavy on my mind.

"Do you think they have discovered Brodie is missing?"

We stepped away from the porch for a better view of the layout of Villa's men. Guards were stationed at all the exits to the front of the house and the road out of here. Villa was sitting in the shade under a tree, surrounded by several Mexican women.

"I don't think they care," Gertie said. The moonshine was flowing. A few of the Mexican men were strumming guitars—a snappy tune I'd heard the mariachi band play at my favorite Mexican restaurant. Some of the Villistas began to sing. The cowboys and the Villistas were dancing, drinking, and eating.

Gertie and I made our way to the food table and filled our plates. We would need fuel if we were going to make a run for it later. I didn't want to be lost in the woods and hungry. We ate sitting on the porch steps so I could keep an eye on the outlaw.

When bellies were full, and the moonshine was empty, Villa began checking his watch. The cowboys had left to hitch the wagons. The women had become bored and were dancing with one another and any available male they could recruit. Slim was dancing with Mrs. Opal to a tune with words I couldn't comprehend.

Most of Villa's men were leaning against a fence and watching the women, occasionally giving a few catcalls. But they always looked ready. Ready for battle, their pistols strapped in their holsters and their shotguns within an arm's reach. My gut was topsy-turvy, and I couldn't stomach much of the food.

"You'd better start handing out those brownies, so we can get outta here," Gertie said, stuffing the last bite of chicken in her mouth.

"I can't believe you can eat that chicken after you killed them."

"I'm hungry, and they were happy to help out."

I made a face at her as we went to retrieve our secret weapon.

Gertie grabbed a plate full of brownies, and I got the second one. "You go offer the guards a brownie, and I'll take some to the men around Villa." Gertie gave me a nod and headed off toward the nearest Villista.

The sun was turning in for the night. A small wedge of light reflected off the horizon, casting shadows as I walked out into the backyard. Metal lanterns hung on wires from the big shade tree and illuminated the area under it.

The women were sashaying around in a circle. I knew it wouldn't be long now. We had to make sure Villa gave Mitchell the key, and then we could grab him and get the heck out of here.

Most of the Mexican people were sampling the brownies Gertie offered. Johnny and Mitchell joined the cowboys to prepare the cargo for transport. Mahlia sat at a picnic table sipping tea and watching every move I made. I ignored her, took the plate over to Villa, and offered him one.

"No," he said.

"But I made them special," I said, doing my best pouty-lip impression. I used it to sell Girl Scout cookies when I was ten, and it worked like a charm.

A well-endowed Mexican woman sitting next to Villa helped herself to a large brownie. She took a bite and licked her lips, then said something to him in Spanish, which made him smile. I offered the plate to him again, and he cooperated and took a small one. He took a bite as he slid a hand up Ms. Boobs's leg, and I backed away. *Jeez, what about his wife in Mexico?* I guess even his big deal with the Mafusos didn't stop a man's penis from being *numero uno*.

Johnny returned to the fiesta looking a little downtrodden. I offered him a brownie, and he shook his head no. "Mr. Villa has requested I stay here instead of riding with the train."

"Isn't that better, considering the, um, state of health of the mules?" I asked, remembering the Alka-Seltzer potion Gertie had referred to earlier.

He shrugged. "I didn't want to leave you and Miss Gertie without an escort." This sweet boy was going to risk his life to save us from the Villistas and sex slavery. It was more than I could say for Caiyan. He was nowhere to be seen. Brodie said they would return, but my time was running out.

A shrill train whistle sounded off in the distance, and Villa became excited. He jumped to his feet and motioned for Johnny to move the wagons down to the train.

The Villistas began packing up, and Mrs. Opal was wringing her hands. "I don't know why Mr. Villa has to take these nice girls with him," she said to Mr. Hawkins. "It's so dangerous in Mexico, with that crazy President Carranza and his band of Carranzistas after Mr. Villa."

"The Carranzistas won't catch Mr. Villa. I'm sure he needs the girls to, um, help with the mules," Mr. Hawkins said.

Help with the mules, my ass. He knew exactly what Villa had in store for us but was too afraid to help us. I guess I could understand. Pancho Villa was a scary dude.

I stood watching and waiting. Mitchell and Mahlia were getting their horses ready. There was no sign of Caiyan or Brodie. I thought it odd no one had noticed Paco was missing. I guess he wasn't really liked all that much. Then it happened—an ear-piercing scream came from inside the barn. One of the Mexican girls clung to the barn door screaming and pointing inside. The Villistas went running to the barn. This would have been a great chance to get away, but I still didn't have my key. So I waited.

Villa came out, gun in hand. The two Mexican men who had been guarding the barn spoke to Villa and pointed to Mahlia and me. My heart skipped a beat, and I thought now would be a great time for Caiyan to rescue me. Where was the knight in shining armor when I needed one?

"The gringo has gone to report to the Carranzistas of our return. We leave now!" Villa yelled out to his men and women.

He pointed the gun at me and Gertie. "Let's go." This would have been a fine plan, except most of the Mexicans were stumbling around and giggling.

"What did you do to my people?" he said, aiming his gun at Mitchell. Mahlia stepped between them.

145

"We did nothing. Why don't you ask the whores?" she said, pointing to me.

Bitch.

"You stay here." Villa pointed to Mahlia.

"We're not whores!" Gertie shouted, stalking toward Mahlia. I grabbed her arm, holding her back. "You Hells Angel slut thief!"

This got Mahlia's attention. She had that "I know what you are" look on her face, but it was directed at Gertie.

Villa looked at me and huffed. He grabbed my arm and forced me up on a horse with one of his men. He did the same with Gertie. I glanced behind me as we made our way out through the back pasture, Mitchell riding close on our heels. Mrs. Opal was standing at the back gate waving good-bye.

Now I understood why the Hawkins ranch made such a good rendezvous. The railroad ran at the back of their property. There was a steam engine train with a passenger car and two cargo cars for transporting the waiting animals. The mules were being loaded inside, and the cowboys were cussing at the stubborn beasts trying to get them inside the train car. The other cargo had apparently been transferred from the wagons, which now sat empty at the side of the train.

Villa and his henchman took Gertie and me to the side of the train car.

"*Up!*" he demanded, pointing to the top.

"Oh no, I'm not gettin' up there. I have acrophobia." Gertie shuffled backward. "How do you say fear of heights in Spanish?" One of Villa's henchman poked her in the back with his gun.

"Let's go, Gert," I said and began to climb up. My inner voice was also questioning the whereabouts of my rescue team. If Caiyan let Villa take me to Mexico, I was moving him to the top of my ten most hated list.

At the top of the train car, large sandbags were arranged around the perimeter. My guess was the sandbags were to keep us from falling out. One of Villa's men pulled me over and Gertie tumbled in after me.

There were six men and five women on top of the train car. Most were armed with rifles. All were smiling. They had enjoyed my brownies. I scrambled to the side and peered over. Some of Villa's men were still on horseback. I guess they were planning to ride back to Mexico. Villa and Mitchell were standing next to the train beneath me. I strained to hear what they were saying.

"We have done our part, Villa," Mitchell said. His words stuttered as he tried to negotiate with Villa.

"Very well, gringo." He pulled a small bag out of his pocket, then tossed it to Mitchell. Villa motioned for the train to go and entered the passenger car in front of mine. Mitchell opened the bag. He reached inside and lifted my key from the pouch. The gleam of blue diamonds glistened in the last slice of light. He looked up at me and an evil smile snaked across his face. As the train begin to lurch forward, adrenaline took over.

"Gertie, we have to jump," I whispered.

The band of men on horses rode to the front of the train. This was our chance.

"No way in hell am I jumping off the top of a train," Gertie stammered, "Did you see how high it was? Nope, no way. Not today, no how. Never."

"It's never. When I say go, grab for the big willow tree branches coming up on the side of the train."

The train started to pick up a little speed. The flowing branches of the tree hung over the train, petting each car gently as it chugged along.

"Now!" I hollered as our train car went under the tree, and I dove for the nearest branch. I felt Gertie jump after me.

"SHIIIIIIIIIIIT!" she yelled as we slid down the tree's limbs and landed, splat, on the ground. I'm sure I caught the words "crazy bitches" shouted in Spanish as we leaped to freedom. Darkness had finally taken over, but the Mexicans were shooting anyway. I ducked under the row of willow trees pulling Gertie by my side.

My last vision of the train was Pancho Villa hanging off the side of the car, pistol in hand, taking a shot at me. He was shouting in Spanish to his men, but his orders were drowned out by the train engine.

"I think I sprained my ankle," Gertie said.

"Can you walk?" I asked, helping her up. I had skinned my knee, and my left arm was aching.

We cut through dense brush and hobbled back toward the house. About halfway there a small stream cut through our path. The water was knee deep, but we managed to make it across. We struggled up a hill, then found our way through the back pasture.

The glow from the lanterns still lighting the area behind the house welcomed us as we ran as fast as our injuries would allow. We came out of the trees just in time to witness Caiyan take Mitchell down. He was holding him face to the ground in a wrestler's pose.

"Get the key," Caiyan commanded. I ran to where Caiyan had Mitchell pinned and grabbed the pouch from his pocket.

"Where the hell were you?" I stood over the two men, one hand on my hip, the other holding my precious key. "We were almost taken to Mexico."

"Now is not a good time, lassie." Caiyan tightened his grip on Mitchell, who was struggling fiercely. With both hands securing the younger man, Caiyan could not reach his gun.

"You were supposed to rescue us." I kicked some dirt with my boot.

"Yeah, we had to jump off the top of the train. I sprained my ankle." Gertie held her boot-clad foot up for Caiyan.

He looked up at the two of us and huffed. "What do ye think I'm doing?"

It looked to me like he had been saving the key before trying to rescue us, but considering the situation, I decided to keep it to myself.

Caiyan managed to drag Mitchell to his feet. He was a skinny little thing but continued to struggle.

"Where's Brodie?" I asked Caiyan.

"He's keeping Mortas company. I didnae want any surprises."

The cock of a rifle halted the conversation. "Let him go, Caiyan." Mahlia came into the light. Caiyan's shoulders sagged. His spy had turned on him. I bet that was a surprise.

"Criminy," Caiyan mumbled, then released Mitchell.

"About time, sis," Mitchell scoffed at Mahlia. He came over and jerked the pouch out of my hands. "Sorry, honey, but that's ours." The musicality of his New York accent was revealed in its full intensity.

He walked over and handed the pouch to Mahlia. She didn't take her eyes or her gun off Caiyan. Mitchell pulled a small revolver out of his holster and waved it around in the air as he came and stood between me and Caiyan.

"Mahlia—" Caiyan started to say.

"Keep your hands up." She moved her aim from Caiyan's chest to right below the belt. I saw Caiyan's eyes widen. "I know you are with her. I don't know why, but they are from our time. This means she must be your new transporter." Mahlia cut her eyes at Gertie, who was still recovering from the jump off the train.

"Mahlia, dinnae be ridiculous. We just picked them up on the way here."

Never call a scorned woman ridiculous. I grimaced. Mahlia shot him in the leg. Caiyan went down but took Mitchell with him. I lunged at Mahlia. The gun went off in the air. Gertie stood frozen, and the screen door of the house slammed against clapboard as the owners came running out of their house.

"What's going on?" Opal's shrill voice had us turning toward the back porch. Slim, Opal, and Johnny stood, mouths open, surveying the scene.

About then all hell broke loose. The Villistas had come back to claim the white women. They were shooting haphazardly in all directions. If only I had a box of Twinkies; the brownie effect was at its peak, and they would have dropped their guns immediately.

Opal and Slim ran back inside. I dove for cover under the porch. Caiyan had retrieved the gun from his boot and had it on Mitchell. I searched for Mahlia, but she was gone. I also couldn't find Gertie.

Mr. Hawkins and Johnny, armed with shotguns, came back out on the porch and started picking off the Mexicans. I guess Villa had gotten what he'd come for, because he wasn't among the men. He had sent his Villistas but kept the train going full steam back to Mexico. They could catch up later, with or without us.

"Where's Gertie?" I shouted to Caiyan as I peeked out from my safe haven under the porch.

Two of Villa's men came sneaking around the side of the barn. They were dripping wet and must have fallen into the stream while pursuing us. One of the Villistas had a six-shooter and sent a bullet toward Johnny. Luckily, it went wide taking a chunk off the porch timber.

As Mr. Hawkins got off a shot, Brodie came around the side of the house driving a wagon pulled by Gypsy.

"You people all right?" Mr. Hawkins asked. "Those damn Villistas fell in the creek. Their backsides are sopping wet. Maybe it'll slow 'em down."

Brodie stopped the wagon and surveyed the scene. He hopped off and beckoned toward Caiyan. "You alright there mate?"

Caiyan nodded and motioned toward Mitchell. "Get him in the wagon."

"We need to be going now, mate. Cover me while we get our guest in the wagon," Brodie said to Mr. Hawkins. Johnny came down from the porch and helped Brodie load Mitchell into the back of the wagon.

"Are you OK?" I asked, belly-crawling over to Caiyan. A dark red stain covered his jeans about midthigh.

"Jest a flesh wound, lassie."

I ripped a section from the bottom of my dress and wrapped it around his thigh.

"I'm sorry I yelled at you." I pulled the cloth tight around his muscular thigh, making a makeshift tourniquet.

His green eyes held mine for a moment. "Stay here and keep yer head down." He stood and limped over to Brodie. I disobeyed the order and scurried over behind the wagon too.

He rolled his eyes at me, then focused on the more important problem at hand.

CHAPTER 15

$\mathcal{M}$r. Hawkins and Johnny provided protection while Caiyan helped Brodie secure Mitchell in the back of the wagon. Brodie had Mitchell bound and gagged and ready to be transported, but I still didn't have my key, and there was no sign of Gertie.

Mrs. Opal came out onto the porch, sawed-off shotgun in hand. She blasted a round off at a Mexican who had moved toward the bathhouse. He dropped his gun and went down, clutching his arm. They were starting to flank out and surround us.

"She took her," Mrs. Opal said. "I was coverin' the front in case one of 'em rascals got through the trees. The gal with the long hair took Gertie off on her motorized horse." Mrs. Opal blinked twice. The uncertainty of her words showed on her face.

"Oh my God, they took Gertie!" Tears pricked at my eyes, and I couldn't stop them from leaking down my face. This was all my fault. What if they killed Gertie because they thought she was the transporter? The air felt thin, and I couldn't breathe. Caiyan pulled me to him and wiped away my tears.

"They willnae kill her. They need something to use to negotiate the freedom of Mitchell. As long as we have him, they won't hurt her."

"You swear?" I sniffed, wiping my nose on my sleeve.

"Aye, we have to get oot of here before we spend eternity in nineteen fifteen." Caiyan began barking orders. "Brodie summon Ace and have him meet ye at the Hobbs farm. If Villa returns, he willnae think to look for ye there. Jen, go with Brodie, and I weel hold them off long enough for you to get back to the town."

"I can't leave you here by yourself." Another shot clipped the wagon next to me, and all three of us ducked for cover behind the wagon. Brodie leaned in next to me.

"C'mon, darlin', we need to make a fair go of it," Brodie said. His eyes begged me to be reasonable. Caiyan scooped me up and plopped me down in the bed of the wagon next to Mitchell. He didn't look happy about the company, and he gave me a good kick in the leg to show his disapproval. Considering his hands were bound behind him and his feet were tied together, this was a pretty good feat.

Caiyan pointed his Colt .45 revolver straight at Mitchell's head and cocked the hammer.

"I can't kill you, but if ye touch her again, I'll have Slim Hawkins kill you, and then I weel drop yer dead body on Daddy's doorstep."

Mitchell's eyes got wide, and he scooted as far away from me as possible.

Mrs. Opal came running down the porch steps and I reached a hand down to meet hers. "Godspeed to you, dear. We'll hold them off, and don't worry about your fella," she glanced over at Caiyan. "Our ranch hands are coming up behind them Mexicans. It won't be long now."

"Get oota here," Caiyan said to Brodie.

Brodie gave the reins a swish. Gypsy barreled through the trees and down the gravel driveway toward town.

I watched Caiyan take cover behind the shed, giving him a view of any Villistas who might sneak in from behind. Bumping down the path toward the exit from the Hawkins ranch, we passed Dan, securely tied to a tree. The wagon took a turn behind a hill, and Caiyan was gone from sight. Guns fired in the distance, but we continued our frantic pace to the neighbor's farm.

I looked over at Mitchell. He had his back turned to me, and he was curled into a ball. I assumed since this was his first trip and he had gotten himself captured, he wouldn't be high on the Mafusos' list of promising young time thieves.

More gunshots echoed behind us. My heart beat hard and fast and felt like it was caught in my throat. Swallowing my anxiety, I assessed my situation. I was worried about Gertie and afraid for Caiyan's life. My dress was torn at the bottom from the bandage I had made for Caiyan, and I had a big rip down the right side of the bodice, probably from the leap off the train. The bonnet that hid my highlighted hair was history. I couldn't remember losing it, but it must have come off in the rush to return to the Hawkins farm.

My life had taken a turn. At my last job, the only difficult decision I made involved choosing which shoes would be the fashion trend for next year. My life seemed insignificant compared to these people. Would they allow me to become one of them? Did I want to become one of them? I wasn't sure I could stomach the danger.

What I did know was I wanted to find Gertie. I wanted her safe and back home telling me she forgot to go grocery shopping. And I wanted to feel Caiyan's finger stroke my cheek. I buried my face in my hands and tried hard not to cry...again.

The full moon shone bright in a cloudless sky, providing enough light to find our way, but the well-worn road was difficult to navigate, and Brodie was not making any rest stops. We turned onto the long, dirt road that led to the Hobbs farm. Brodie slowed Gypsy down to a trot.

"Aren't we endangering the family by hiding out here?" I asked Brodie.

"I'll tell you the details later, mate," he answered, jerking his head toward Mitchell.

We rambled alongside the pasture with the longhorn chewing his grass. He didn't look surprised to see us back so soon. When we pulled up in front of the small farmhouse, Mrs. Hobbs came out, coffee can in the crook of her arm. Following her were her two sons, Clyde and Junior. The younger of the two carried a kerosene lantern, which gave off a small amount of light that illuminated their faces horror-movie style.

"We need a place to hide," Brodie said and opened the collar of his shirt, exposing his key.

Mrs. Hobbs's eyes looked weary, but she said, "In the barn with you."

"Aw, Momma, I knew they was up to no good. Why are we lettin' them hide here?" Junior whined.

"Shut yer mouth, Junior. You're not old enough to understand, yet."

Brodie steered the horse toward the barn. Mrs. Hobbs's boys opened the double barn doors and Brodie coaxed Gypsy inside.

As the wagon came to a stop, the older boy, Clyde, helped me down from the wagon. We both looked at Mitchell.

"Leave him there for now, mate. His ride will be along in a moment."

Junior began unhooking Gypsy from the wagon, and when he was out of earshot, Clyde ask Brodie, "What's it like?"

Brodie's eyes met mine, and I understood. Clyde had the gift. He looked to be about fifteen, but wasn't wearing a key.

"It's an adventure, mate, but it's also dangerous and sometimes scary, like tonight."

"Is he one of them?" Clyde pointed toward the wagon.

"Yes, and we are taking him to jail."

"Why don't you just slaughter the murdering sack of shit right now?" Clyde asked, clearly upset Brodie wasn't taking more action.

I didn't understand why he was so angry. He didn't know what the Mafusos had been up to.

"He's young, mate, and we don't do that anymore. We have a way to control them now."

"Seems to me like y'all are a bunch of pussies in the future," Clyde said, spitting a wad of tobacco on the ground.

"Maybe," Brodie paused. "But it seems to work out better for everyone involved."

"Ma won't let me have the key. She keeps it hidden, says I'm not old enough yet, but I know I am, and when I find it, I'm gonna get them bastards and they won't live to see the next day." He walked around the wagon and looked in. "Besides, I'm as old as he is," Clyde said, pointing a thumb toward Mitchell.

"And he got himself captured," Brodie responded.

"Boys!" Mrs. Hobbs shouted as she came through the barn door. "Git your butts out here, now!" The boys scampered toward her.

She came around and looked in the wagon. Mitchell gave her a glare. "He's a puny one. Are they gettin' smaller?"

"Nope, he's only sixteen," Brodie said.

"Sixteen!" She put her hand over her heart. "Next thing ya know, they'll have the toddlers out stealing and killing. It's pathetic." She spit a wad of chew into her can.

We walked Mrs. Hobbs outside.

"Thanks for the use of your barn," Brodie said. "We won't be here long."

"If there's trouble, I can't promise I can help. My family's gotta come first."

"We understand." I spoke for the first time in the conversation.

Mrs. Hobbs looked me up and down. "What are you?"

"I'm a...a transporter," I said my chest puffing up a little.

"Where's your key?" she asked, poking a chubby finger at my neck.

"Pancho Villa took it from one of my ancestors and sold it to the brigands."

Her eyes got wide at the mention of Villa's name. I assumed she was mentally counting every available weapon she owned in case the Villistas came calling.

"Yer better off without it." She turned and headed out of the barn. "Boys, come." And that was that. The boys followed behind her. Clyde glanced back at Brodie like he had a million questions. His questions went unanswered for now.

After they left, I looked over at Brodie. He knew I was also full of questions.

"I'm not sure how much I'm supposed to tell ya since you haven't formally been inducted into the WTF."

"Spill it," I demanded.

"Mattie Hobbs's husband was the best defender of his time. He saved over three hundred people in a battle that was created by the brigands."

"Where is he?" I asked.

"He didn't make it out alive."

"How sad for Mrs. Hobbs to have to raise the children alone."

Brodie looked at me through green eyes flecked with brown and gold. He put a hand on my shoulder in a comforting gesture.

"Ya see, mate, it's serious business, what we do, so if you decide to join, you have to be committed. I have to know you can back me up if I need ya."

"Right," I agreed, but my knees were knocking together.

Brodie's words cleared my vision. He was no longer one of the Scooby-Doo gang. Working for the WTF meant saving our world as we know it. He had substance under the rough exterior. I knew he would be there to back me up, so I wasn't going to let him or Caiyan down. I had a job to do, and I was going to be brave and do my best. Well, after I found my key so I could actually do my job.

"What are we going to do now?" I asked.

"We're waiting on Ace to transport Mitchell back to headquarters. Hopefully, he'll be here soon."

"Who is Ace?"

"Ace is my transporter." Brodie let out a long sigh.

"How is Ace a transporter? I thought all the men were defenders. Isn't he a man?"

155

"Well, sorta," Brodie said. He paused then shook his head. "I'm going outside to keep watch."

Brodie stayed outside to keep a lookout for Ace, Caiyan, or any trouble that might present itself. I was inside keeping an eye on our captive. Every now and then, he would try to holler a curse word at me, but it was muffled by the gag. I would respond by poking him in the ass with the end of a hoe.

Outside there was a noise that sounded like a whoosh of wind, accompanied by a flash of lightning. I poked my head out the barn door. "What was that?"

Brodie was leaning against the barn wall staring at the patch of trees in front of us.

"Ace." Brodie's jaw clenched.

And then I saw him. About five-ten, slightly muscular, dressed in tight, bright-blue spandex pants, a sparkly gold-sequined top, and a feather boa. He had on a pair of Via Spiga black leather over-the-knee boots. I was green with envy. I wanted those boots, but looking at the size of his feet, I knew there would not be any swapping.

He was coming from the direction of a carnival photo booth—the kind you get in with a friend, and you pull the curtain closed, then it spits out a strip of four black-and-white photos. The gold shirt was open to the navel, revealing skinny but firm abs, and around his neck was a key in the shape of a lightning bolt.

He sauntered over to Brodie. "Heeey, Brodie baby, what's up?" This was kind of like a crocodile meeting up with Tinkerbell.

"What took you so long, mate?" Brodie grimaced and shifted uncomfortably.

"I had curlers in, hon; I can't travel with me 'air a mess." He gave his long brown waves a toss, and then he noticed me.

"Well, what do we have here, another conquest from the past?" His clipped British accent was laced with cynicism as he circled around me.

"Excuse us, sweetie." He pulled Bodie to the side and spoke in a low tone, but the concern in his voice escalated, and I could hear every word. "I mean, really, Brodie, it's not like you have a magic wand that can erase a memory with the flash of a red light. You really are being careless with the locals. She saw my ride and everything."

"No, she's one of us," Brodie said.

Ace paused, considered, and moved closer to me. "Nice hair."

"Nice boots," I replied.

"You like? I got 'em on clearance at Neiman's, fifty percent off, girl, can you believe it?"

"No way?"

"Um," Brodie interrupted. "This is Jennifer Cloud. She is our newest transporter, and we have a bad guy to transport."

"Why doesn't she do it?" Ace asked, pointing my way.

"The Mafusos have taken her key," Brodie said.

"And my cousin, Gertie."

"Damn thieves. Show me where he is, and I'll get 'im out of here."

As we walked back to the barn, Ace in the lead, I whispered to Brodie, "How come he isn't in western clothes like us?"

"We can't figure that one out. The vessel can't seem to overpower Ace's clothing. He always comes dressed as is...and sometimes it's a little scary."

"I heard that!" came Ace's voice from inside the barn.

We walked together toward the wagon. Ace peered over the edge and got a glimpse of Mitchell. "Oh, he's just a little thief. Come on over here to Ace, darlin'."

This sent Mitchell into a kicking fit. "Woo, and feisty too! I like 'em with a little spunk."

Brodie got up in the wagon and pushed Mitchell to the edge. Mitchell tried to squirm, but Ace had him in a death grip. Brodie gave him a thunk on the head with the butt of his gun, and Mitchell was out for the count. Ace picked him up and threw him over his shoulder. "We need to blindfold him. Can't have him waking up and gettin' a look at my ride now, can we?"

Brodie found a feed sack in the barn and secured it over Mitchell's head.

"That will do. How is Miss Priss here gettin' back?"

"I'm waiting for Caiyan," I said.

Ace paused, then looked me up and down. "Of course you are. Call me, Brodie, hon, if I need to return, but make it quick; I've got a date with a rock star."

We walked outside, and Ace said something in a language I didn't understand. His photo booth appeared in front of us with a windy gust. He loaded Mitchell inside.

He gave me a wink and said, "Say cheese, baby!" There was a flash of light, and they were gone.

Brodie and I sat in the barn on a bale of hay. He told me stories of Australia and his family's farm. He worked there in between time travels, and I was glad to finally meet a partner who also had to earn his living by working the old-fashioned way instead of through trust funds and family money.

I told him about my boss getting arrested and about my new job at the chiropractic office. In the middle of our stories, we would pause and listen for any noises outside the barn.

A little later Mrs. Hobbs brought us some stew and cornbread. She hadn't heard of any trouble, yet. Brodie assured me Caiyan would summon him when he was ready for help. I kept wondering, *What if he can't? How long do we wait?* But Brodie's cool exterior had me curling up in a ball, covered with a handmade quilt, and falling into a restless sleep on the hay in a barn, once again.

I was jostled awake by Brodie the next morning. "Let's go, mate."

"Where to?"

"We're going after Caiyan."

"Did he summon you?" I asked, rubbing the sleep out of my eyes.

"No, and it's been too long. I don't want to risk Villa or his Villistas coming after the Hobbs family. They've had enough loss. Caiyan gave me orders to have Ace transport you back, but I may need help if Caiyan's been captured." Brodie frowned as he adjusted the saddle on Gypsy. "Besides, I can't risk Ace walking around looking like hooker Barbie in this time."

We prepared to leave. Brodie led Gypsy out of the barn, leaving the wagon behind. She didn't look happy about departing the comfortable barn. Brodie climbed on, avoiding the bite we both knew was coming.

He motioned for me to climb up on a stack of hay. I did as he suggested, and he pulled Gypsy up next to me and I climbed aboard. We rode down the dirt road past the longhorn, who I think was sleeping, but since he was still standing, it was hard to tell. Brodie kept the horse at a slow pace, pausing occasionally to stare at bits of upturned earth. When we made it back to the main road, Brodie got off and knelt on the ground.

"Caiyan came through here all right but headed toward the town. He was being followed by about eight horses, maybe more."

"Why doesn't he just call his vessel?"

"Maybe he didn't have enough time. He was being chased. When you summon your vessel, ya have to make absolutely sure you have about ten minutes of safe time. If ya don't, you may not make it back to where you came from."

"If you don't return to your time, where do you go?"

"I dunno, maybe lost in time."

I stored this information for future reference, because I didn't want to be lost in time. Brodie moved to the front of the tracks.

"Bugger me! This is Villa's horse. He must have stopped the train to get his horse off."

"Why would he come back when he got what he came for?" I asked.

"I don't know."

"Maybe one of his Villistas is riding his horse," I suggested.

Brodie looked at me, doubtful. "Let's ride toward the town."

CHAPTER 16

e followed Caiyan's trail into the small town, keeping close to the trees. As we approached, we saw smoke. Brodie pulled Gypsy into the shadows of the piney woods, and we crept in for a closer look.

Flames licked the walls of the saloon. The Villistas were riding up and down the street, shooting out windows, and raising hell. The townsfolk were lingering outside the buildings and watching the production. A few brave souls were throwing buckets of water on the saloon.

I spotted Villa astride his horse stopped in the center of town. Brodie was right—he wouldn't allow two girls to get the best of him, and because of our escape, I've caused an entire town to suffer.

Villa shouted to the crowd, "I know you are here, worthless gringo. If you do not show yourself, I will slaughter everyone in this town." He paused. "Starting with the women and children." People started to scamper inside the buildings, but a few heads peered out the windows. A person just couldn't resist a good gunfight.

"This is bad," Brodie said.

"What can we do?" I scanned the area for Caiyan.

Villa turned his horse in a circle. His Villistas lined the dust-covered road. "My men have told me of the dark-haired stranger who helps the Australian gringo." He scouted the tops of the buildings. A few of his men were there shaking their heads to indicate there was no sign of either gringo.

At the opposite end of the town, Caiyan rode Dan out from the cover of the woods.

"Villa," he shouted. Villa turned his horse in Caiyan's direction but waved his hand in a downward motion, indicating to his Villistas to hold their fire.

"Mortas double-crossed you," Caiyan yelled, riding toward the outlaw "He works for President Carranza. The Carranzistas. They will be waiting to capture you when you return to Mexico."

"I don't believe you. You work for the Carranzistas," Villa tightened his hold on his horse's reins. "Why would Mortas sell me guns if he was not on my side?"

"He wanted the necklace. He knew the Carranzistas would be waiting when you return. I am after Mortas and his accomplices. The necklace belongs to me."

"Why does everyone want the necklace?" Villa asked. "It is not gold, and the stone is not valuable."

"It's a family heirloom."

"All of this for a family bauble?" Villa shook his head in disbelief. "I think, gringo, there is more to the story. That is why I got off the train." He shifted in his saddle. "You may consider me a fool, but you would be wrong."

Caiyan no longer had to yell to be heard by Villa. He had ridden Dan front and center. He was within arm's length of the nearest Villista as they closed in around him.

"What's he doing?" I asked Brodie. "He's riding right into the middle of it."

"Damn, he's summoning me." Brodie's key glowed briefly under his shirt.

I looked in Caiyan's direction, and sure enough he had his hand on his key. "What? Why would he do that? You'll be in danger too."

"I believe he's going to do a magic trick," Brodie said. A faint tug at the corner of his mouth formed a half smile.

"Magic? What are you talking about? What should we do?"

"I guess we make ourselves available." Brodie gave Gypsy a small tap with his heel and we rode slowly toward Caiyan, keeping within our hiding place among the shadows.

Villa's men formed a half circle behind their leader. Some of the curious townsfolk had come outside to see why the shooting had stopped, and a crowd was starting to form. As Brodie and I grew closer to the end of our cover, Caiyan spotted us. His face darkened with irritation as he saw me. All eyes were fixed on Caiyan, including mine. I didn't like the hard, cold glare I received from him.

Brodie let me off at the edge of the road, forced his pistol in my hand, and told me to blend in with the townspeople. He turned Gypsy and rode her out of the tree shadows and toward the mayhem.

The sound of shotguns arming indicated the Villistas had finally seen Brodie. Villa told his men to hold their fire. Brodie joined Caiyan in the center of the road. Villa pointed his gun at Brodie. I made my way amongst the spectators, moving close enough to hear the conversation.

"I see your worthless compadre has joined you for the execution. This man works for the Carranzistas. He was caught spying on us."

"No, he works with me," Caiyan said. "He was watching the Mafusos."

"How do I know what you say is true?" Villa said.

"Mortas told me of your plans to invade Camp Furlong near Columbus, New Mexico," Caiyan said. The townspeople gasped and moved farther away from Villa and his men. Villa shook his head in disbelief.

"I have a deal to make with you, Villa," Caiyan said.

"I make no deal with you, gringo."

"Ahh, but this deal involves magic."

"What kind of magic?" Villa asked raising a bushy dark eyebrow.

"I can make a man disappear," Caiyan announced to the crowd.

The Villistas laughed, and a few townspeople let out stressful groans in disbelief.

I bit my lip. *What was the guy up to now?* My inner voice covered her eyes with her hands but left her fingers open to see through them.

"I bet you I can make this chap disappear," Caiyan said, pointing to Brodie.

"And if I can't, you may execute me however you like, but if I make him vanish, you leave the people of this town and never return here."

"As you must know, I am a man of my word," Villa replied, stroking his mustache and contemplating the wager in his mind. "I will make this bet with you, and if this is true, you will show me how."

Caiyan and Brodie dismounted. I moved closer to a large man wearing a lead apron. It was the blacksmith we had met previously. I fell into his shadow, staying out of sight of the Villistas.

"Why is she still here?" Caiyan asked Brodie through clenched teeth.

Brodie shrugged in his outback way. "Dunno, mate, I thought she could help."

"Cripes, has everyone gone mad?"

"OK, folks, everyone stand back," Caiyan said raising his voice and using his hands to shoo the crowd backwards. "I must first summon my disappearing machine."

A murmured laugh spread through the crowd, followed by a few skeptical remarks, but they moved back a few feet. Villa was still on his horse in front of Caiyan, his gun pointed to Caiyan's chest. Brodie faced Caiyan with his back to Villa and the Villistas.

Caiyan gave Brodie a slight nod.

As Brodie touched his key and mumbled something, Caiyan spread out his hands like Moses parting the Red Sea and drew Villa's attention.

There was a crack of thunder, and Brodie's bathtub appeared in front of Caiyan. The crowd cried out with astonishment. Villa raised a hand, and there was a sudden silence.

"Parlor tricks," Villa claimed. "I have seen them at the traveling circus. You have managed to make a washtub appear in front of us."

Some of the townspeople nodded their heads in agreement. Others stared in awe.

"Now I will have my partner get in the magic machine, and I will make him disappear right before your eyes."

I remembered David Copperfield making an elephant disappear at one of his Vegas shows. Maybe David Copperfield was one of us.

Caiyan saw me standing next to the blacksmith. He cut his eyes to the right. I followed and saw Dan lingering next to the water trough. Gradually I made my way over to him and hoisted myself into the saddle. Brodie stepped into the bathtub. All eyes were focused on him.

"Good luck, mate, see you back at the office." Caiyan clapped Brodie on the shoulder, and they did the arm-hold thing that I equate to a guy hug. Caiyan moved back and raised his arms in the air.

There was a loud gurgle, and Brodie was gone. The crowd shrieked in amazement. Villa walked his horse to the spot Brodie had just occupied.

"I want to know how you do your tricks, gringo."

"A good magician never tells his secrets," Caiyan said.

"I am a man of my word. I will leave this town." A few people cheered. Villa raised his gun, and they cowered back.

"But I did not agree you would go free." Villa motioned toward Caiyan.

You will accompany us to Mexico, I will learn your secret magicks, and then..." Villa shrugged.

My heart sank. He was going to kill Caiyan anyway. My inner voice was scouting the area trying to come up with a plan to save Caiyan.

The sound of pounding hooves interrupted my scheming. At the crest of the hill, Mr. and Mrs. Hawkins, Johnny, the oldest Hobbs boy, and all the cowhands who worked on the ranch were driving the herd of hopped-up mules toward us.

Villa turned his horse to view the stampede. The Villistas scattered. In the moment of chaos, Caiyan fled toward me.

"That's our queue, sunshine, we're oota here." Caiyan jumped up behind me on Dan. He encircled me with his arms taking the reins in his hands. He gave Dan a kick, and we galloped off.

Villa and the Villistas were after us, shooting their guns. Luckily the mules had slowed down their pursuit.

"Why didn't ye go back with Ace?" Caiyan asked. His voice tinged with anger.

"I was worried about you."

"Shite," was his only response.

The sound of beating hooves and gunfire echoed behind me. We rode Dan through a break in the trees and a loud crack had me shrinking down in the saddle. In the center of the clearing, sparkling with the reflection of the morning light, stood a red phone booth. The crown of England was imprinted above the door.

Caiyan, being a defender, couldn't take me with him. My heart leaped into my throat. Was he going to leave me for Villa? He pulled on Dan's reins, and the horse came to a halt. Dan was breathing hard, but I felt like I was going to hyperventilate. Caiyan slid down from the horse then helped me dismount.

"Thanks, Dan." Caiyan gave him a pat on the behind, and he wandered off into the trees.

"Where should I go?" I asked, trying to control the panic flooding up from my chest.

"With me, lassie." Caiyan grabbed my hand and led me into the phone booth.

"But you're a defender. You can't transport two people. We could get lost in time." I tried to step out of the booth, but he pulled me in tight and closed the door.

"Aye, then I hope this works."

Villa's horse cut through the trees and I saw the surprised expression on Villa's face. He raised his gun in our direction and fired. A bullet pinged off the phone booth. Caiyan said something I couldn't hear over the gunfire, then put his mouth to mine, and we disappeared.

CHAPTER 17

*C*aiyan's kiss was mesmerizing. An intense heat poured through me and down into the inner sanctum of my body. The forces of the time travel swirled around me as if I were protected inside a ravaging tornado. When the vessel stopped, our lips parted. It worked. I was still in one piece. My hands were resting on his firm chest, and his arms were wrapped tightly around me. I pulled away from him, and his dark lashes fluttered open, revealing a look of relief in his emerald-green eyes.

"I'm alive," I said, my knees giving out beneath me. He gathered me in his arms and kissed me again. A ball of fire formed in my gut and seemed to explode out my fingertips. When we parted, he must have felt the same connection because his eyes bore into mine, searching my soul for an answer.

Then I felt the other sets of eyes staring at me. I turned to face three men in suits standing with hands on hips, glaring at us through the glass door of the phone booth.

Caiyan reached for the knob and pushed the door open.

"Welcome to Gitmo. Lassies first." He gestured with a palms-up movement toward the men.

I was standing on a small platform about two feet high. "Um, hello." I gave the men a finger wave. One of the men came forward and assisted me as I stepped down from the platform.

From behind the men, footsteps echoed into the room. A voice of authority rang out. "Where the hell have you been?"

The wall of men parted, and Jake came front and center.

"Oh shit!" we both said simultaneously.

Caiyan stepped forward. "Meet our fearless leader," he said with a hint of sarcasm.

"Jennifer, what the hell?" Jake tried again.

"You two have met, yeah?" Caiyan said, stepping aside. He backed up to lean against the wall and crossed his arms over his chest. His western wear had changed into a worn pair of Levi's, a tight-fitting, black T-shirt, and black Doc Martens. I looked him up and down, and he raised an eyebrow at me. "Not exactly what I expected," he said, the corners of his mouth turning up.

I looked down and realized I was in the dreadful smiley-face scrubs from the clinic. Damn.

"Um, these are my work clothes."

"Nice boots," Brodie added, joining the group.

I took in my surroundings. It was a big empty space that reminded me of an underground airplane hangar, no windows. There were twelve square platforms lined up in four rows. Each platform was about ten square yards, providing plenty of room to land a vessel. Brodie's bathtub sat on the next platform.

"Agent McCoy, should we take the...um...passenger to the debriefing room?" asked the suit on the right.

"No, I'll talk to her first. McGregor, go to the infirmary and get checked by a medic. Everyone else, go directly to the blue room. I'll be in shortly."

The blood had seeped through Caiyan's pant leg and left a large stain. He pushed away from the wall and sauntered off down a long hall to the right, followed by the three suits and Brodie.

Jake grabbed my upper arm and ushered me down a long corridor. He was walking at top speed and dragging me with him. It felt like a trip to the principal's office.

"Slow down," I muttered as we turned left and went into a small room. He released his grip on my arm and shut the door behind me.

His desk held a laptop surrounded by stacks of files, a black leather office chair, a gray metal file cabinet to the right of the desk, and a black upholstered metal chair in front of the desk, which Jake motioned toward.

"Sit," he commanded as he took a seat at the desk and closed the laptop.

I'm no dog, but I sat anyway, because I sensed a fight coming on. Growing up, Jake and I had butted heads a few times, so I knew when he was about to blow. He looked at me, started to say something, then shut his mouth, obviously trying to find the right words. He picked up a blue ball-point pen and clicked the cap a few times.

"What are you doing here?" he finally asked.

"I am a transporter," I replied smugly. "What are you doing here?"

"This is my top-secret assignment, babysitting the time travelers." He stared at me with chocolate-brown eyes that made my heart melt. Avoiding his gaze, I checked out his office.

Several maps were tacked to the walls. Some of them dated back to the seventeen-hundreds. There wasn't a name plate on his desk, or a potted plant placed near a window. There wasn't a window. The room reeked of hand-sanitizer and coffee. Jake tapped his pen on the desk.

"How did Caiyan take you?"

On a bed of straw was my first thought, then I realized Jake was asking how I ended up here. I quickly explained that Aint Elma had left me her key and reminded him about the time the outhouse threw him into the yard. This drew a small smile out of him.

"Yeah, that explains a lot about the outhouse. It was pretty funny, but what we do here isn't fun." The storm cloud returned.

"I understand the danger. Hell, I have experienced the danger. Besides, Caiyan and Brodie have given me a brief synopsis."

"When did you start traveling?" Jake put the pen down and interlocked his fingers. It was his way of controlling his anger. If his fingers were locked together maybe he wouldn't strangle me.

"Well, my first trip," I paused, remembering it was our prom night. The first night Jake kissed me, and the first time Caiyan kissed me. Skipping the exact date, I continued, "I was eighteen...but I didn't know what was happening to me. This would be my second trip."

"Where did you meet McGregor?"

"In Scotland, the year of our Lord 1568," I told Jake, mocking Caiyan's Scottish brogue.

"Did you sleep with him?"

"Well, I don't think that has anything to do with the WTF."

Jake rose out of his chair, came over, and put both hands on the arms of my chair. He leaned down and looked me directly in the eyes. "*Did you sleep with him?*"

"Maybe..."

THE SHOES COME FIRST

"Shit, Jen." Jake pulled back and paced around the room. "Have you been traveling around the world having sex with him the whole time we dated?"

"No." Then I went into a brief synopsis about my traveling experience.

"Jen, he's not a good person. He kills people. The only reason he's not behind bars is because we need him to work with the WTF."

"He only kills bad people," I said in Caiyan's defense.

"Yes, but sometimes good people get killed in the process." He put both hands on his hips. "I'll not allow you to do this."

"*No!*" I jumped to my feet. The metal chair scraped on the floor in my haste. "You can't make me quit. It's my gift. If I get my key back, I don't need your permission." I crossed my arms over my chest and held my ground.

"Where is your key?" Jake seemed alarmed.

"The Mafusos took it."

He huffed. "I run this operation. If I say you don't travel, you don't travel." He planted both feet firmly, squaring me off like he was prepping for a gunfight. We'd had many disagreements in our long friendship. We were both hardheaded, determined people, and we had battled like this before over much less serious issues.

We stared at each other, not saying a word for a full minute. Damn, I felt my heart beating frantically in desperation. My eyes started to fill with tears of defeat. He looked away and then back at me again, and his eyes softened.

"Your key is gone," he said gently. "I'll arrange for transportation home."

"Jake, please don't take this away from me. I finally have a job, the right job." I gave him my saddest bleeding-heart, tear-filled eyes.

"Don't use those baby blues on me; it won't work."

Moving around next to him, I placed my hand over his. "I know it's dangerous, but I can make a difference."

The landline on his desk rang, distracting him from our intense conversation. He informed whomever we would be there shortly and slowly replaced the phone in the cradle. He turned and looked at me again.

"Jen, you can't."

"Yes, I can," I said, interrupting. "Besides, they took Gertie, and I have to help her."

"God, this just keeps getting better and better. Does Gertie have the gift too?"

"No, she sort of hitched a ride with me."

Jake ran his hand through his hair. "I'm needed in the blue room for the debriefing. You have to come too. I need to hear everyone's story."

"Thanks, Jake."

"This discussion isn't over, but I have a job to do. Follow me." He picked up a file from his desk and walked past me. "Christ," he mumbled as we set off to the debriefing room.

We walked down another long hall in silence. "How did you know I had sex with Caiyan?" I asked Jake.

"He sleeps with everyone."

Ouch, that hit hard. After the kiss in the vessel, I was looking forward to more, but maybe I needed to keep a working relationship.

"I thought we were sleeping together?" Jake stopped and waited for me to answer.

"Did you sleep with Bambi?" I threw back at him.

He looked momentarily confused, and then reality set in. Busted.

We entered a room decorated with dusty-blue wallpaper halfway down the wall and dark mahogany paneling from the chair rail to the floor. A long executive meeting table ran front to back, and a projection screen hung to the right of the table. Black chairs lined each side of the table, and a large high-back executive chair captained the end. Caiyan and Brodie sat across from each other, drinking coffee out of Styrofoam cups.

Caiyan gave me a concerned smile as I entered the room. I grabbed the seat next to Brodie. Keeping my distance from Caiyan might be a wise decision considering Jake's foul mood. The three suits gathered at the far end of the table.

I sat down, and Jake placed a cup of coffee in front of me. Black, two sugars.

"Hmm..." Caiyan remarked under his breath.

I avoided looking in his direction and focused on what Jake was saying.

"I already have Ace's dramatic revelation of what his part involved. We have Mitchell Mafuso with a partial concussion in a holding cell. Now I need to hear your story." Jake sat down in the chair at the end of the table. He flipped open the file he was carrying and wrote something down.

One of the suits put a small recording device on the table and nodded his head toward Jake.

Caiyan began explaining how he was unaware I was his transporter when we met in Scotland, thankfully skipping the part about the barn. He continued through the entire trip to 1915, with Brodie and me adding our parts in as well. When we were done, Jake asked if we had any ideas on how to locate Gertie and the key.

"We need to find the Mafusos," I said.

"We know exactly where they are. Don't we, McGregor?" Jake asked. The bite to his words left me feeling like I had missed a piece of the puzzle.

Caiyan's gaze met mine. "The Mafusos run the Staten Island portion of the Mafia."

"The Mafia!" I stood, shouting. "No one told me they were the friggin' *Mafia*!"

"Still want to be a transporter?" Jake asked me.

I sat down and collected myself.

Caiyan continued. "Old man Mafuso still runs the show, but I've heard he's training Mortas to take over."

"Mortas does almost all the traveling; I haven't seen the old man go back in years," Brodie added.

"They'll want Mitchell with his key intact for the trade. But I doubt they will trade Gertie and Jen's key. It will be one or the other," Jake said.

That doesn't seem fair," I added.

"The Mafusos don't deal in fair," Brodie said.

"What about our inside help?" Jake turned his attention toward Caiyan.

"I'm afraid that has come to an end." He smiled at me, leaned back in his chair and chewed on a coffee straw.

Jake glared at Caiyan.

I huffed. "If you know where they live, why don't you just sneak in there, free Gertie, then steal my key back?"

"Jen, this isn't James Bond. We cannot just sneak into someone's very-well-guarded house," Jake said.

"Haven't ya ever seen *The Godfather*?" Brodie asked. "Breaking into the Mafia is like askin' for a death wish. They tend to get even."

How were we going to rescue Gertie? My inner voice began biting her nails.

"I need to go over a few details about the WTF with Jen," Jake said. "You guys go home—get some rest. We'll meet back here tomorrow at 0800 hours."

"Roger that, Cap'n." Brodie stood and saluted.

Jake rolled his eyes.

"Before you go, Brodie, summon Ace," Jake ordered.

"Man! Not two times in the same day. He's goin' to be a mite pissed; he had a date with a rock star."

"Summon him here. *Now!*"

Brodie sighed, put his hand on his key, shut his eyes, and mumbled something.

Caiyan looked at me and smiled. "See ye later, sunshine." They both stood and left me with an annoyed Jake.

Jake glanced at me. I knew the look. The furrowed brow, the hard jawline, and the tiny vein in his temple that stood out when he was determined to complete a task. The task was me.

I gave him a confident nod. I wasn't going to cave in. He was going to let me continue with the WTF or else. *Or else what?* My inner voice asked. *Oh, shut up!*

"Let's go someplace we can talk." Jake got to his feet, and I followed him down the long hall to a set of elevators. We entered the elevator, and Jake inserted a key fob into the slot on the elevator panel. He pushed the level-one button.

"The WTF operates covertly underground at Gitmo," Jake explained. "The bottom floor is ours. The WTF prisoners are held in cells on the same floor. The first and second floors house the maximum-security prisoners for Camp 6, which is where we are now. The staff, prisoners, and any visitors have no idea we even exist below them."

He paused then continued. "The elite Gitmo staff knows there is a top-secret base but do not have access. The camp forms a rectangle and is monitored by computers. The main control access to Gitmo is here. There are many other camps at Gitmo. Some are maximum security like this one; others are medium. There are no minimal-security prisons here. Only myself and members of the WTF enters Level B."

"What's the *B* stand for...basement?" I asked.

"Bottom," he said with a sad tone that tugged on my heartstrings. It was as if all his time and training ended with him here, among the bottom dwellers of the CIA. I thought being involved in a top-secret project should have been exciting, but I knew Jake, and he would have wanted to be the one with the gun, capturing the bad guys, not the one pushing the paperwork.

The elevator doors opened to a large room. Jake walked us through an X-ray unit not unlike the ones found at the airport, complete with big scary security guards. We crossed what seemed to be an intake area for prisoners, then exited out the front door.

Jake used his key to open the security gate outside the main door. We walked through; the door slammed shut behind us, trapping us between two large gates. A loud buzz made me jump, and then the gate in front of us opened. A sidewalk snaked between the buildings, leaving the Camp 6 building secured with high electrical fencing and razor-wire tops behind us.

A military jeep driven by a young private was waiting for us. He motored through another large, heavily guarded gate, and we drove around a small town. As we passed a McDonald's, I looked curiously at Jake.

"The military personnel have to live here. There's a school, bowling alley, and movie theater. It's not Sunnyside, but it provides a temporary life for the people on base."

We turned a corner and came up to a large chain-link gate minus the razor wire Afro. A guardhouse was positioned to the left with two men in uniform manning the gate. When we stopped, Jake produced his identification and a piece of paper explaining my presence, and they waved us through.

"These buildings are the military base of Gitmo," Jake said. Several multistory cement buildings were scattered throughout the complex.

The jeep pulled up to a long, white, three-story building.

"Thanks, man," Jake said to the young driver.

Jake key-fobbed us through the front of the first building. We took the stairs up two flights, and he used a different key fob to enter one of the doors—Jake's new apartment.

His décor consisted of military-issue furniture: basic brown couch and chair, plain side table, and coffee table. But it smelled like Jake. He had worn Abercrombie cologne since high school. Sometimes I would nag him for not trying a new fragrance, but truthfully, when I smelled it, a warm, comfortable sensation would surround me like an electric blanket set on just the right temperature.

When Jake was away at college, I would go into the store to smell the cologne and relish in that comfortable high. Safety. A feeling I had missed since I began the trip to 1915.

Jake dropped his keys on the small breakfront in the dining area inside the door. He turned and pulled me into his arms.

"I thought you were mad at me," I said.

"I am, but you're still the most important person in my life."

I rested my head against his chest.

"If anything happened to you, I'd blame myself for allowing you to be a part of this warped mess."

I pulled away. "Jake, I am supposed to be a part of this. I can't describe in words how frightened I've been these last few days, but it feels like my destiny."

Jake drew his lips into a tight line. "Are you hungry?"

He'd changed the subject, but I was too tired for a fight. "Yeah, I guess maybe I am. I can't remember the last time I ate."

"How about a couple of subs? There's a deli on the roof. Let me get out of this jacket, and we can go grab something."

"On the roof?" I asked, walking around his sparse apartment. No pictures, nothing personal on the counters. Very different from his cool apartment in Dallas.

He called to me from the bedroom. "The roof has the best view, so the dining area is up there."

I avoided going into his bedroom. That was a complication I didn't need at the moment.

Jake reappeared without the jacket, sleeves rolled up and shirt partially unbuttoned, revealing his top few sexy chest hairs.

"Can you walk around without wearing your official jacket?" I asked.

"I'm on my time now, and the base is pretty casual. Since we're so isolated, it's not likely the president is going to pop in for a surprise visit."

"Jake, you've met the president? Of the United States?"

"That's classified." He smiled, and his dimples winked at me.

We took another couple of flights up to the roof. Jake was right—the view was amazing. Blue ocean as far as the eyes could see.

I gaged the temperature at about eighty-five degrees, and a nice breeze was coming in off the bay. Several tables with umbrellas were scattered about. A walk-up deli was to the right, with a canopy of the same red, white, and blue stripes as the umbrellas.

Jake walked over to the deli counter. A man who looked a lot like Ricky Ricardo was behind the counter and smiled wide as Jake approached.

"Good afternoon, Agent McCoy and his lovely lady friend, who is so happy today."

Geesh. Stupid smiley-face scrubs.

"Hey, Rubén. Two turkey subs with chips, tea for me, and a beer."

"Comin' right up."

Jake paid, and we walked over to one of the tables that overlooked the ocean. I took a deep breath of the salty air. "This is a nice view."

"Looking out that direction is nice," he said. Grabbing my hand, he led me to the other side of the roof. "This direction is a different experience altogether."

Tall electric fences with the razor-wire tops circled the perimeter like a barbed eel ready to strike anyone who dared to touch its sharp skin. Jake pointed out the Cuban border.

"I see your point."

We walked back around to the table and sat down. Rubén brought us our sandwiches and two big bags of potato chips.

"I didn't realize how hungry I was." I devoured my lunch. Jake picked at his sandwich.

"It's one of the side effects of time travel. Since your body thinks it was gone many days, and since you return into the same time, give or take a few hours, your internal clock gets confused. Usually there's increased hunger, fatigue, and sometimes severe headaches. The beer will help the side effects."

"I don't have a headache, but I would really like to get out of these clothes; I feel ridiculous smiling at everyone."

The corners of Jake's mouth turned up. "I could help you with that."

The old Jake was back. I laughed but didn't offer any encouragement. I had more important things to deal with than the men in my life.

"So, tell me how I learn to become a good transporter." I took a big swig of my beer. It was a dark beer, not what I was used to, but it had a deep, full flavor and quenched my dry throat. Jake shifted uneasily in his chair.

"I can give you history, but you'll need training. Intense training that includes learning fighting skills, linguistic studies, weapons training, and drills so intense, some people couldn't complete it."

Something to look forward to. My inner voice pulled out her memo pad and began taking notes.

"Caiyan told me the history of the gift," I said.

Jake sighed. "The World Travel Federation was created in December 1963 by President Johnson. The assassination of JFK by a brigand led to the capture of a defender, Jack Ruby. He was ultimately taken into custody but died in prison before his transporter could rescue him. An alliance was made with the government to assist the time travelers and give them protection from being captured in a past time."

"Why Gitmo?" I asked, helping myself to a handful of Jake's chips.

"Guantanamo Bay was the best place to hide the covert operation because of its isolated location and the amount of military protection already in place.

"This alliance, formed by the time travelers, the British Secret Service, and the US Department of Defense, gave more control over what went on in the traveling by establishing a set of rules and giving the time travelers a place to imprison the brigands."

"Caiyan told me the Mafuso family are brigands and that there are other brigands as well."

The mention of Caiyan's name caused Jake to wince slightly. "The Mafusos are a threat, but they respect the code of time travel. There are others who do not."

"What is the code?"

"There are rules, such as, rule number one, you can't intentionally disrupt events that happened in the past because you can cause a change in the future. For example, if you killed the mother of the future US president, it could severely change life the way we know it."

"Caiyan mentioned that, but it didn't keep him from killing Paco."

"Yes, I'm aware of his inability to follow orders. McGregor plays by his own rules, which makes him dangerous." Jake paused. "Jen, killing's in his blood."

"He killed Paco to save me."

"Why didn't he just knock him out and restrain him?"

I pondered this for a moment. *Why didn't Caiyan just hit him on the head and knock him out? We could have tied him up and left him. Maybe he was afraid Villa would find him before we could escape.* The main reason tore at my gut: he was more interested in capturing brigands and retaining the keys than saving our lives. Jake watched me as I came to the conclusion. I decided a simple explanation would do for now, until I could talk to Caiyan.

I took a long pull on my beer and said, "I think the others would have heard the commotion and come to help Paco."

"Maybe. But many times when Caiyan returns, I have to research the bastard he took down to find out how to fix any problems he might have created."

"How do you find the problems?"

"We have a computer program that is designed to locate the ripple effects left by the time travelers." He took my beer and finished it off. That was probably a violation during work hours, but Jake looked like he needed more than a swig of beer.

"Was Paco the father of the next US president?" I asked.

Jake grimaced. "No, he was killed March 9, 1916—he and five hundred

Villistas attacked the Thirteenth US Cavalry at Camp Furlong near Columbus, New Mexico, using the guns supplied to them by Mortas."

I remembered Caiyan mentioning Camp Furlong to Pancho Villa. "No family?"

"No."

"Then we're OK, right?"

"It doesn't make it right, and we have to research every person Paco might have killed from the moment McGregor killed him to his original death and all their ancestors."

"Were there many?" I asked uneasily.

Jake rolled his eyes and avoided my question. "Rule number two is you can't tell anyone, which you have already broken by not only telling Gertie but also taking her back with you."

Thinking of Gertie gave me a sick feeling in the pit of my stomach. "I didn't tell her; she hopped in, and then she found out."

"Rule three, you must *never* let a brigand set eyes on your vessel. It makes it easier for the brigands to use your key if they know what your vessel looks like and can find it." Jake was ticking off the rules using his fingers.

"I think I got it."

Jake eyed me and kept on talking. "Rule four, you cannot force a brigand to remove their key. You will not be able to remove it, and no other person can remove yours. We have tried cutting them off, burning them off, and other means, but with no luck. Unless the person is dead, or he takes the key off himself, it stays on."

"OK, let me get this straight. So far, the Mafusos have respected our present-day relationship. All our conflicts take place in the past, not here." I held up my fingers as I listed the rules. "You can't tell anyone, which I have already violated." Jake frowned at me, but I continued anyway. "You can't let anyone catch sight of your vessel. I broke that one too." I should have listed the rules that I hadn't broken first. My inner voice gave me a kick in the shins. "You can't kill anyone because it might screw up the future, and you can't take off another traveler's key."

"Very good," Jake said.

"Unless you go back and take it from an ancestor," I added.

"Yeah, there's that. When you travel to the past, it is forbidden to force a traveler to remove his key. You cannot leave him running amuck in the past, screwing with the future."

"But the Mafusos took my key."

"Not really, they went back and bought the key from someone who took it from your ancestor in her own time, therefore you never received it. They found a loophole to the rule." Jake leaned forward. "The brigands don't always obey our rules; that's why we are always pursuing them, and until we have all the keys, it won't stop."

"Why don't the brigands just kill us and take our keys?'

"That's the most important thing you should understand about your gift." He paused, took a deep breath, and released it slowly. "If you kill another traveler, you die."

My mind went numb for a second. "Die?"

Jake looked me straight in the eye, "Yes, die."

"What if it's an accident?"

"There can't be any accidents."

Jake took a bite of his hardly touched sandwich and offered me the other half. I had practically inhaled mine, so I accepted. We both chewed on the prior information as we chewed on the sandwich. I decided not to dwell on the parts of my gift I had no control over. I wasn't planning to kill anyone, anyway. I *was* just the transporter, right?

"What happens next?" I asked.

"My operations manager is drawing up paperwork for you to sign. Sort of a business contract between the WTF and you."

"I hate paperwork."

"I know, I remember doing several papers for you in high school. The contract will explain what you can and cannot do concerning time travel. For example, you cannot go back in time for personal gain."

"Right."

"Your friends Caiyan and Brodie also have a problem with this part of the contract."

I didn't understand what he meant by this, but I had a gut feeling it had something to do with the little episode between Caiyan and me during my first trip. I decided some questions were better left unanswered.

After lunch I was leaning against the railing looking out at the ocean. Jake disposed of our trash and came to stand beside me.

"I'm going to ask, no, beg you not to get involved with these people."

"I am already involved." I avoided his big brown eyes. "Besides, I have to help find Gertie."

Jake's cell phone rang, and when he disconnected, he said, "They're ready for you."

"Who is?"

"The WTF."

"I thought you were the WTF?"

"No, I am an agent of the CIA who works with the WTF."

Lunch was over. We returned to his apartment, and he grabbed his jacket. Jake seemed defeated as he ushered me back downstairs. Another jeep was waiting to take us back to Camp 6. We went back through all the security gates and the X-ray to the elevator that took us down to Level B.

Jake led me down the long corridor to a large office outfitted with an expensive mahogany desk and several leather executive chairs. Seated at the desk was a gruff-looking man. His gray hair and steely gray eyes made him look like all the military generals I had ever seen portrayed on film.

"Jen, this is Major General Potts." The general shook my hand. "He's the military commander in charge at Gitmo and over the WTF."

"Glad to have you on board, Miss Cloud."

To his right was a man dressed in a navy suit. "This is Agent Geoff Grant. He's with the BSS. He oversees the European division of the WTF," Jake said.

I shook hands with Agent Grant. I assumed he was Caiyan's boss and the reason why Jake had little control over Caiyan.

"Please sit down, Miss Cloud." Agent Grant indicated a seat next to him. Everyone sat down, and we began the meeting that would change my life.

A pretty woman about my age in a white military button-down shirt and navy pencil skirt brought us coffee, and tea for Mr. Grant. She politely asked if I preferred cream, then she winked at Jake. His face turned red, and he glanced in my direction. The pressure of his front teeth biting down on his bottom lip turned the skin pink. His tell. What he had been doing with his free time just became clear.

It didn't take long for Jake to replace me after he left Dallas. My mission just became clearer. I needed to make this decision for myself. I needed independence and self-fulfillment. I had to start making my own way.

General Potts presented a contract to me that listed all the "rules" of time travel.

I never had enough patience to reading documents thoroughly. I made a C minus in my business law class, and I hated reading contracts or any kind of instructions. This usually meant spending several extra hours assembling a project. But that's how I roll, and when I'm done with my project, I have self-satisfaction and a few "extra" pieces.

179

Grabbing the pen, I signed my codependent life away without further hesitation.

"Don't you want to read it first?" Jake asked. General Potts cleared his throat, and although Agent Grant was beside me, I could feel him shake his head no at Jake.

"Well, what I meant was...if you want to," Jake stammered.

"Nope, I know what I'm doing," I said firmly, confidently. I was ready for the new me.

"Thank you, Miss Cloud," General Potts said as he hastily stuffed my contract away in a file.

"How do we get Gertie back?" My first official inquiry.

"We're waiting on the Mafusos' demands. In the meantime, we are interrogating the little bastard—um, excuse my language," General Potts said, glancing my way. He coughed slightly. "This one might just crack."

Although I thought Mitchell was a little weasel, I didn't want him tortured. He was only a teenage boy. Weren't they prone to making bad decisions? And what if they hurt Gertie because we hurt Mitchell?

"Do you have to crack him?" I asked.

Jake nudged me with his knee.

"Miss Cloud, you'll soon become accustomed to our ways here. If not...." The General let his conversation die, but I got the picture.

"Ace is going to take Jennifer home to change clothes and rest, then we're meeting back here tomorrow at 0800 hours," Jake informed the men.

We were dismissed. Jake and I walked down the long hall.

"Are you sure they won't hurt Gertie?" I asked.

"Pretty sure," Jake said.

"Are you pretty sure like when I asked you in fifth grade if herpes was a type of weed because I overheard my sister's friend Vanessa say she had herpes in her patch of grass?"

"Um, yeah, pretty sure." He grinned at the reference.

"That's what I'm afraid of."

We turned down a hallway that seemed to be a dead end. A camera was mounted in the corner, but I had seen several of them in the building.

"What are we doing here?"

"Now that you're an official transporter for the WTF, you have access to top-secret information," Jake said as he walked to a panel on the wall and used his key fob. The panel slid open, revealing a keypad. Jake punched in a number, leaned in toward a metal object with a hole in the center, then placed his chin on a little stand.

"Retinal scan." He stared straight ahead, and the machine made a click. A large door materialized in the wall to the left of the panel and, just like Star Trek, slid open without a sound.

"Welcome to the travel lab," Jake said, extending his right arm out in an "after you" gesture.

"Cool," I said as we walked into a giant room filled with computers and flat-screen monitors. Three large projection screens hung on the wall opposite me. Images of maps with red dots blinking on them illuminated the screens. The technology gave NASA a run for its money.

"This is where we monitor the time travel," Jake said. There were two people in the room. An older gentleman who was either Charles Darwin or Father Time monitored one of the big screens. "This is Albert. He watches you when you go back in time, then he performs the follow-up on everyone to make sure there were no changes to the future."

"Hey there, little lady. Just call me Al." He walked slightly bent over as he came around to shake my hand.

"I'm Jen, the—"

Al cut me off. "I know who you are—been watching you for days."

"Me?"

"Well, we didn't know who exactly, but we caught your wave when you appeared in 1915. I knew I had seen that blip before but didn't put two and two together until you came back this time."

"You saw me in 1568? In Scotland?"

"Yep, you blipped on my screen but then disappeared. I tried to tell them there was someone new flying about in Elma's vessel, but they didn't believe me. Now here you are."

"I don't understand. You can see us?" I was so confused.

"Jen, when anyone travels back through the time gateway, their vessel gives off an exhaust, so to speak. We analyzed this and came up with a titanium and phosphorous emission. We can track where you go and keep an eye on your location," Jake said.

"So you knew about my aint Elma?" I asked.

Jake took a deep breath. "Yes. The WTF has been watching your family for years. The gift has never transferred outside a direct line. Elma didn't have any children, so we assumed the gift died when she died. We couldn't find her key. She must have known you had the gift and made arrangements to get the key to you if she passed. I'm glad a brigand doesn't have the key." It was the first positive thing Jake had said about my gift.

"She told me when I was nine, but I didn't understand. I thought she was just a crazy old lady." I sighed regretfully. "Just goes to show, you should listen to your elders."

"My sentiments exactly!" Al chimed in and gestured toward the screen. "Observe the blinking dots. Those are the people you left back in Presidio. We can watch until the portal closes. Probably a few more hours.

"Are the Hawkins OK? Did they move their ranch?" I asked Al.

"Looks like they are heading north." He pointed toward a few red blips on the screen.

"And Villa?"

"Back in Mexico with his Villistas."

"Good." I felt better knowing the Hawkins family was safe from Pancho Villa.

Al smiled, then returned to his desk. Jake directed me toward the right side of the room, where a man sat in a circular desk surrounded by computer screens. He wore a Mighty Mouse T-shirt, and his key hung from a leather necklace. The smooth stone had an image of a tornado embedded in it. His eyes lit up as we approached, and I thought he resembled a cross between Bob Marley and Will Smith.

"Jake, my mon, is dis the lovely creature stirring up so much trouble wit our tribe?"

"Yes. Pickles, this is Jennifer Cloud."

"What do you mean 'trouble'?" I asked, shaking hands with the man, and digging his accent. It was totally island. Maybe the Bahamas or Jamaica.

"Ya nuh see it? So far you 'ave caused a disruption in de travel portal, disconnection from our contact wit de Mafuso family, revealed our secret to an ungifted, who was captured, by de way, dispelled de notion de gift can come only through a direct line, and not to mention traveled in de dafender's vessel, subjecting him ta possibly getting las' in the time continuum." Pickles crossed his arms over Mighty Mouse.

"Well, there's that," I said.

"Pickles is a defender with a special gift," Jake explained.

Pickles motioned for me to have a look at his screens. As I moved around from behind the computers, I saw Pickles was wearing Bermuda shorts and in a wheelchair.

"He can envision where the brigands travel right before the travel takes place when they engage their vessel. Everyone must be ready to go when the full moon starts to cycle. Pickles gets the coordinates, and then we decide who goes after the brigands. The WTF show up on the screens as blue dots, and the brigands as black dots."

"Sort of like ESP but with flair," Pickles added.

"How do you know?" I asked, watching the dots bounce around on the screen.

"When a gifted decides to travel, there is an increase in the consciousness surrounding that person," Jake explained. "Have you ever seen *The Butterfly Effect*?"

I nodded.

"Similar to dat, and it comes to me like a dream." He waved spirit fingers in the air above his head. "The problem is dat there are many traveling when de moon is full, so I have to pinpoint de ones who are going to mess around versus de ones who are going to cause disaster."

"But if we know who they are, can't we stop them before they go back?"

"No, not enough time, only a few minutes to spare. I can't tell exactly who dey are, only dat a brigand is going back to a certain time. It works de same with the WTF too; I can perceive everyone's choice of where dey are going unless dey change at de last minute, which is what Miss Fancy Pants did." He raised his eyebrows in my direction.

"But I didn't know where I was going."

"Mmm." He scratched his dreadlock-covered head. "Caiyan didn't summon you, and you didn't know where you was going?"

"Well, I was sort of thinking about him," I said, keeping my eyes lowered and avoiding Jake's stare.

This brought a deep laugh from Pickles. "Well, wouldn't it be somethin' if she could summon our Scottish philanderer for a change." He laughed again.

Jake scowled. "I need to have Jen transported back home; we are meeting tomorrow morning, 0800 hours. See that you are present."

"Don't go gettin' in any trouble now, ya hear?" Pickles wagged a finger at me as we left the secret room.

We returned to the large room that held the vessels. Caiyan's and Brodie's vessels were no longer on their platforms, leaving the room completely empty.

"Damn, where is that guy?" Jake checked his watch.

No sooner had he spoken than there was a crack of thunder and a lightning flash, or in this case a camera flash, and Ace's photo booth appeared on platform three. The purple curtain pulled back, and Ace exited his vessel.

Stepping down from the platform, he strolled over wearing a white Vera Wang gown and a sparkling tiara on top of a long, wavy red wig. Jake didn't seem surprised at Ace's appearance.

"Where have you been? Brodie summoned you two hours ago."

"Well, 'ello to you too, handsome." Ace pulled off his long white dinner gloves. "I told the boys I had an important date tonight, and now you've made me late."

"I need you to take Jennifer home to rest and change clothes, then have her back here at 0800 hours."

"Eight a.m.—are you nuts? I need my beauty sleep. Besides, I might be out late tonight, or maybe *all night long* if I'm lucky."

"I agree with the first part, but you'll have her back here at eight a.m., or you will have an unpleasant consequence." Jake's voice was stern and promising.

"Ooh, I hate unpleasant consequences." Ace shuddered and motioned for me to follow him. "Let's go, hotcakes."

CHAPTER 18

$\mathcal{A}$s I entered Ace's vessel, I noticed two things. One, the seat was padded in purple velvet, and two, the walls displayed photos of every brigand he had transported to Gitmo, and there were many. Riding with Ace was an amazing experience. Instead of the swift, forceful ride I had in my vessel or the smooth ride with Caiyan, Ace's vessel sort of rocked. Swirling colors flashed around me giving me the sensation I was inside a lava lamp. As we traveled, I swear I heard music.

When the music stopped, the colors disappeared. I stepped out into the gray drizzle of the Saturday I'd left behind.

"Was that the Beatles?" I asked.

"I like to add my own personal touch when traveling. It makes me more comfortable." He stopped and looked around, taking in his surroundings. "This weather is going to frizz my hair, doll. Let's get inside."

I opened the sliding-glass door and took Ace inside. Gertie's empty popcorn bowl was sitting on the coffee table. I said a silent prayer for her safety. The demon cat was lazily stretched across the back of the couch.

"Hello, little kitty," Ace said.

"He's got issues—I wouldn't get too close."

"I like cats, but they don't respect me. Besides, it would shed all over my Vera Wang, and we can't have that, now can we?" Ace moved away from the cat.

Gertie's Brando movie had restarted, and the opening credits were running, waiting for the play button to be pressed.

"*Ooooh*, I love this one!" Ace said. "Marlon Brando is so sexy."

"Um, yeah," I agreed. I bent down to pick up the remote from the coffee table to turn off the movie and knocked Gertie's gum wrapper on the floor. "Hey, that reminds me—Gertie had gum in her mouth when we transported back to 1915. I thought we couldn't take anything back."

He pinched the silver piece of foil with his red manicured nails and took it from me. "If you put something in your mouth, it can go back with you."

"Really?" I thought about the possibilities of this statement. "What, like maybe a small knife, or some other weapon we could use for protection?"

Ace's freshly glossed cherry lips curved into a cunning smile. "Or maybe a condom."

OK, not the type of protection I had in mind, but it resolved some of my unanswered questions.

Ace moved around the room and flopped down in an easy chair. "These shoes are murder on my feet." He pulled off his pumps, revealing big hairy toes painted red to match his hair and nails.

"Yep, we had a defender come back with the clap after he had been visiting 1965. Those hippies like to get it on with everyone and everything."

"I thought we weren't supposed to go back for our own pleasure."

"Girl, there are rules that are meant to be broken. Sometimes our job may take a while, and let's just say you run into James Dean while he's filming *Rebel Without a Cause*. You gonna pass up that piece of meat?"

"Mmhmm, how did you figure out you could transport objects in your mouth?"

"Caiyan figured it out. Blimey, talk about a piece a meat—that boy is finer than frog hair split three ways. From what I gathered, he was a teenager when he first started travelin'. You know how the hormones rage at that age. Anyhow, girls in the past, or the present for that matter, couldn't take their hands off 'im. His transporter had to save his cute derrière many times so he wouldn't get shot by an irate daddy or beheaded for deflowering the Queen of England."

Crap, I could have lived all day without that information.

"Now that you're his sexy new transporter, you'd better watch that tight little butt of yours, or 'e'll eat you for lunch."

I guess my face said it all.

"Uh-oh, looks like he already conquered that territory." Ace came over and put an arm around me. "Don't worry, doll, men are just shit."

"You're a man."

"Yes, but I am a man on estrogen, so I've got your back."

"It's complicated, and it's in the past anyway."

"Always is, sugar. Why don't I go upstairs and help you put together an outfit that will make him wish he treated you better."

"I thought you had a date?"

"Always better to make 'em wait."

We climbed the stairs, and I showed Ace my closet. "Have at it," I offered.

Ace rambled around in my closet for a while. I went to my bedroom, plopped down in my comfy chair, and put my feet on the matching footstool. While working at Steve Stone Shoes, I used my discount to redecorate my room. I had found a Ralph Lauren chair at a boutique on Knox Henderson, a street with trendy shops, and coordinated my duvet for my bed.

As Ace entered my room, he observed my décor and nodded. "*Trés chic*, sort of Mary Poppins meets Versace." He laid out a few tops on my bed, then went to my dresser to search for jewelry.

I had forgotten about the picture I kept on my dresser of Jake and me at the prom. I jumped up and grabbed the frame. Ace snatched it out of my hands.

"Well, well, well, looks like you and the boss man go way back." Ace tapped on the glass as he examined the photo.

"We grew up together. He's been my best friend since fourth grade, a little more than that these last few years."

"He was sexy back then too. I loooove the Zac Efron hair. Met 'im at the Oscars, you know."

"Jake?" I asked.

"No, Zac Efron, right after *High School Musical Three*. He's totally gorgeous," Ace said, returning the frame to my dresser. "I found a few good pieces in your closet, but you know, girl, the shoes have got to come first."

Finally, a girl—or guy, I guess—after my own heart. I opened the slider closet in my room, revealing floor-to-ceiling shelves of designer shoes.

"Be still, my heart," Ace said, dramatically grabbing his chest. "Where did you get all these precious babies?"

"I worked as a shoe buyer, and I got a great discount."

"Honey, these Manolo Blahniks are gonna make his tongue roll clean out of his mouth. I think with this Marc Jacobs top and that rockin' miniskirt," he said, holding up the red low-back top. "In fact, there may just be a war between the WTF and the CIA."

"I don't care about the clothes. My only concern is to find Gertie and my key."

"We will. Those boys will figure out something. I should be goin'; my date awaits."

"Thanks, Ace."

"No problem, sugar. Get a good night's sleep. I'll be back to pick you up at 0700 hours—that way we can stop off at La Marmount for breakfast."

"I don't think there's one around here," I said as I walked Ace down to his vessel.

"Of course not, silly, the only La Marmount is in Paris."

"Paris? As in Paris, France? How do we get to Paris?"

"Lateral travel, hon, didn't you read your contract?"

"Well, um..."

"Honey, you gotta read before you sign. They'll have you doin' all the dirty work and not havin' any fun. Page three, paragraph eighteen, line seven says if we are not engaged in working for the WTF, we are free to travel inconspicuously as we please."

"I thought there had to be a full moon?"

"Not for lateral travel. Anytime, day or night."

I had my hand over my heart in disbelief. "You mean we can just pop over to Paris and go shopping?"

"Absolutely, but you have to be discreet, because it makes General Poopy Potts grumpy."

I envisioned myself strolling down the Champs-Élysées carrying bags of Prada and Sephora. "I'm in!"

"Of course you are. See ya tomorrow, doll." Ace gave me a wave, and he was gone.

I was pretty sure stopping off for breakfast in Paris was breaking a rule. I returned to my room and relaxed against the big pillows on my bed, thinking about everything that had happened over the last couple of days, at least time traveling–wise. Based on the present time, we had returned approximately four and a half hours after I left, and that included my stop at Gitmo. I felt exhausted, when in reality only a few hours had passed. Time traveling was going to take some getting used to.

There had to be some way to rescue Gertie and get my key back. I

THE SHOES COME FIRST

wanted to prove to Jake I wasn't some dumb blonde who couldn't be trusted to protect my key and do my job as a transporter.

A ringing noise jostled me back to reality. My cell phone was on the table next to my bed. I checked the caller ID. Perfect...Cousin Trish. What was I going to tell her? Sorry, your daughter hitched a ride back to 1915 and then was kidnapped by the bad guys, who turned out to be the Mafia. Maybe Gertie's stepdad, Vinnie the Fish, knew this Mafia family and could ask them to release Gertie. I decided to answer.

"Jen," came Trish's sultry voice. I always thought she sounded like Cher and looked like Kristin Chenoweth. "It's cousin Trish. I was trying to get hold of Gertie; is she there?"

"Um, no, not at the moment." It wasn't a total lie.

"She's probably got her nose in some book at the library. Could you tell her Vinnie's family is coming to New York for the weekend? And I thought it might be nice if my kids came for a visit. Ya know, those Ferraris are so highfalutin'—I want some of my kin here too."

"Sure. Uh, Trish, do you know a family by the name of Mafuso?"

"Well, doesn't everybody this side of Manhattan? Bunch of gamblin', no-good thieves. Always jammin' up the port authority so my sweet Vinnie-pie can't get his fish shipments."

I guess they are not on such good terms after all.

"Tell Gertie I'm e-mailing her a plane ticket for next weekend. The twins are coming too. Gonna cost me extra since they take up two seats each on the plane. I keep tellin' Vinnie we should buy our own jet. The Ferraris have their own jet. You remember Vinnie's nephew Marco, don'tcha? He's always showing up in fancy places all over the world. One day London, then the next day he's in Rome. Disgusting, the way they flash their money."

"*Trish*," I interrupted. "I'll tell Gertie next time I see her."

"Oh, OK, thanks a bunch, sweetie. Give your dad a kiss for me. Bye now."

I fell back against the pillows. Now I was truly exhausted. I let my mind wander and remembered the last time I had seen Marco. I was sixteen.

CHAPTER 19

July 2004

*A*s spring turned into summer, Texas began her early ascent into triple-digit temperatures. It was ninety degrees in the shade when we received the invitation to Cousin Trish's wedding.

I was at the kitchen table struggling my way through my algebra homework. Dad was in the den, sitting in his favorite chair, and Mom was in the laundry room on the other side of our townhouse. I overheard Mom telling Dad she couldn't believe Trish was having an outdoor wedding in the month of July.

"July Fourth, can you believe it?" echoed Mom's voice from inside the dryer. "She wants to have fireworks at the wedding. What's going to be next, an elephant parade?"

"I'm sure whatever happens will be fine, dear," Dad called to her from behind his newspaper. "The rumor is the lucky groom is a wealthy businessman from New York. Maybe he's from your neck of the woods."

"Unlikely." She passed me carrying an armful of clean laundry.

"It's nice cousin Trish has found love," I said, following her into the den.

"Cousin Trish has found love twice before," Dad said with a chuckle.

"Gertie needs a father figure," I said. "Her dad doesn't visit very often."

"Mmhmm," was Mom's only response.

When Aint Elma passed away, she gave me an outhouse and gave Cousin Trish her little white house in Mount Vernon. Gertie's family moved out of the trailer house and into the small white frame house with the beautiful garden.

Knowing her family, and more importantly her friends, could not afford to fly to New York, Cousin Trish decided to marry her wealthy New York businessman in the hundred-degree heat in the backyard of the Mount Vernon home

When July fourth arrived, we piled into the car to drive the two hours to the country. Since Melody was away at college, Eli and I each got the privilege of a window seat. Everyone had on his Sunday best. Eli kept trying to loosen the tie around his neck.

"I swear, when I get a job, I'm not wearing a stinkin' tie," Eli complained. My inner voice was holding him hangman style by his necktie.

"Your tie looks nice, dear," Mom said, turning around in her seat.

"But, Mom, it's friggin' one hundred degrees outside."

"Eli, please do not say *frigging*; it's not polite," she said, licking her finger and smoothing down a hair trying to curl up on Dad's temple.

"Well, it sucks," he mumbled under his breath.

"We could play slug bug," I made a fist and slugged my brother in the arm.

"Ouch!" Eli balled up his fist and reared back to slug me.

"Oh, no you don't!" Mom scolded again. "The last time you played that game, Jen ended up with bruises all down her arm. She's wearing a sundress, for crying out loud."

"But, Mom, that's the whole point of the game—when you spot a Volkswagen Beetle, you are supposed to slug the other person."

"No, and that's final," she said through clenched teeth and turned back around to the front.

No more words were spoken except the mumble of "that sucks" from Eli.

We traveled the rest of the way in peace. Eli and I were listening to music on our iPods. Mom was talking to herself as she edited Paula Dean's latest cookbook, and Dad was humming along to George Jones. Thank God for headphones.

Dad turned off the main road and entered the tree tunnel. I loved the way the light filtered through the branches. Even though the weather was warm, I thought an outdoor wedding was romantic.

We turned into Aint Elma's driveway. I guess it would be Cousin Trish's driveway now. Instead of a chaotic parking lot, there were two men in black tuxedos, sweating profusely, waiting to take our car. Dad put the car in park and rolled down the window.

"Howdy."

"Hey there, yous wantin' your car parked?" asked the big guy, mopping his forehead with a handkerchief.

"Sure thing," Dad said, turning off the ignition and handing over the keys. A smaller guy with dark, curly hair and wing-tip shoes came around and opened the doors for Mom and me.

Everyone climbed out, and the smaller guy offered his hand to my dad. "I'm Sid, Vinnie's cousin, and this here's Anthony." He jerked his thumb toward the big man who had placed himself in the driver's seat.

"Yo." I guess that means hello in Anthony language.

We made introductions. Sid slammed the driver's door and banged twice on the hood. Anthony took off in the car to God knows where—probably the chop shop.

I scanned the yard that I played in as a child. The tire swing was gone, and a coat of white paint had been recently applied to the house. Several rosebushes were growing in the flower beds, and an artificial flowering garland had been woven around the banister on the front porch. Papier-mâché wedding bells hung above the door.

As we entered, I swear the same old people from the family reunion were seated in exactly the same places. Aunt Mable clapped as we entered, and I dodged the hug. I didn't want to be in the middle of that again. For one, I was bigger, and two, so was she. The extra weight slowed her ascent out of the easy chair. Lucky for me, I had more time to get away.

The wedding was to take place in the backyard. There were about fifty white folding chairs set up under the old oak tree. A long red carpet had been rolled out, dividing the chairs in half, and forming an aisle for the bride to walk down. A white arch decorated with flowers was at the end of the carpet.

The sun hung low in the sky, and two of the junior bridesmaids were lighting candles on either side of the arch. I milled around listening to Eli talk to a group of girls. He flirted awkwardly, which made me want to barf, so I went in search of my parents.

I found them surrounded by relatives.

Mamma Bea had named all her children after famous people. I had an uncle Buster Keaton and an aunt Loretta Lynn. Uncle Buster and

Aunt Loretta's husband, Wayne, were flanking my dad. He was telling them a story, and they were all laughing. Dad was a master storyteller, probably because most of his stories were true, thanks to his crazy family. He claimed he never told a lie, but we knew he embellished a little.

"What's up, pretty lady?" I turned to find a boy a little taller than me with his hair slicked back like John Travolta in the movie *Grease*. He had a cherry Blow Pop in his hand that went in his mouth after he spoke to me.

"Um..." was all I could say.

"Cat got your tongue?" he said after popping the sucker out of his mouth. "I know, I have that effect on women. I'm Joey, Vinnie's cousin." He held out his lollipop-free hand for me to shake.

Eeew. I grudgingly stuck my hand in his. "I'm Jennifer, second cousin of the bride." He grabbed my hand and kissed it with his Blow Pop–red lips. I hastily snatched it back.

"Nice to meecha."

"How many of Vinnie's cousins are here? I met Anthony and Sid."

"Sid's my brother. Anthony, he ain't no cousin, but he's part of the family, if ya catch my drift?" He popped the sucker back in his mouth and winked at me.

I could tell Sid and Joey were brothers; they both had slicked-back hair and made my skin crawl.

I felt a shadow fall over me. "This little weasel botherin' you?" I looked up to find Billy Ray and Bobby Ray, Gertie's half-brothers. They couldn't have been more than thirteen. *What in the world are they feeding the kids down here?* Both were at least six feet tall. They had matching Afros, and when they smiled, both of their front teeth were missing.

"Where are your teeth?" was the first thing that popped out of my mouth.

"We got them knocked out kickboxin'," one of them answered, but I couldn't tell who was who.

"Yo, buzz off, kids...Me and the lady are havin' a chat." Slick Joey shooed his fingers at the twins.

"Bobby Ray and Billy Ray, this is Joey, Vinnie's cousin," I said, trying to subdue an impending fight.

"Yeah, we know him; he's supposed to help us usher the guests in. Mamma Bea sent us over here to drag his skinny Yankee ass back to the usherin'."

"Well, let's go," I said, looping my arm through Joey's and angling him toward the chairs. "You can usher me to a seat." Lord knows I didn't want a brawl to start so early in the ceremony.

Joey gave the twins a smirk, then popped the sucker back in his Yankee mouth and strutted me down the aisle to my seat.

I sat down next to my mother. We were each given a fan on a stick. I flipped it over and laughed at the picture of Cousin Trish with her groom. She was all boobs and teeth, while the groom, dark in comparison to her light features, had a menacing look on his face. My mother put a finger to her lips, more to subdue a snicker than to hush me. We sat fanning ourselves, waiting for the magical moment when the bride would appear.

A three-string quartet playing classical music was assembled next to the archway, and a soft melody swam through the air. Aint Elma's siblings began to enter and take their places in the front two rows assigned to the immediate family of the wedding party—family and friends of the bride on the left side and the groom on the right side.

Since Aint Mable was too large for the folding white chairs, they brought an extra-big chair out for her to sit in comfortably. It creaked under the strain as she sat down.

Her husband, Uncle Earl, sat next to her. They were truly the Jack Sprat nursery rhyme come to life. Uncle Earl tugged on his clerical collar, trying to let in some air. I had never seen him without the collar, although he had been retired for many years.

Uncle Durr, Aint Elma's baby brother, came strolling down the aisle, unescorted, in a big, black cowboy hat and tails. He was dressed for the occasion by his own personal stylist, Willie Nelson. Last but not least, Mamma Bea, representing my grandfather, John Wolfe Cloud, took her seat in the front row next to the chair decorated for Aint Azona, mother of the bride.

The music changed to a slow country song I recognized, and Aint Azona was escorted to her seat on the left in the front row. She was a short, sturdy woman with dyed-red hair that almost matched her beaded purple suit.

Slick Joey escorted an elderly lady to her seat on the right in the front row. I assumed it was the groom's mother. She was dressed in black, as were all the guests from New York. It must be a tradition in the Northeast to wear black to weddings. In the South we only wear black to funerals and bank robberies.

That completed all the living children of Mahalo Jane, the Native American woman, and Jeremiah Cloud, the half-Cherokee cattle rancher.

Missing were my grandfather, John Wolfe Cloud, who had passed away when my dad was young, Aint Elma, God rest her soul, and Uncle Ruppert, Aint Elma's oldest brother, who died in prison. The family gossip was he accidentally (on purpose) killed his wife.

A man in white robes, whom I recognized as the local Baptist preacher, took his place at the front, followed by two very robust men dressed in black tuxedos. They were both red-faced and kept dabbing at the beads of sweat running down the sides of their faces with the backs of their suit sleeves.

Mom leaned over and told me they were the brothers of the groom. I wondered if they were real brothers or just "in the family" like Anthony.

Soon a shorter man in a tuxedo appeared. His hair was also slicked back. *Jeez, what's with all the grease?* I recognized his face from the picture on the back of the fan. The groom. He looked sort of like Al Pacino and Sylvester Stallone rolled into one. His mouth was set in a firm line across his face. Eli wore the same look when my mom took him to the dentist.

A young girl with long dark hair came down the aisle flinging rose petals in the air and at the guests.

Next up was Gertie. She looked pretty in a dress, but pink was not her color. She was taller than I remembered but still a little plump. Her hair was darker but orange, nonetheless.

She caught me looking at her out of the corner of her eye. Pulling her bouquet up toward her face, she stuck her tongue out at me. A shiny metal stud glinted light off her tongue. She had her tongue pierced. *Ouch!*

The groom cleared his throat. Gertie straightened and took her place at the front. She was followed by Aint Loretta Lynn, the matron of honor. The music changed, and the wedding march began to play.

Everyone stood for the entrance of the bride. Cousin Trish sashayed down the red carpet. Since Aint Azona's husband had long ago flown the coop and it was Trish's wedding, she decided to float down the aisle by herself.

Trish wore a snow-white wedding dress. *Seriously?* The plunging neckline pushed her generous boobs up for display. White lace followed her curves, belling out as it reached the ground, and a long, flirty train trailed behind her. The dress matched her personality. Vinnie had commissioned Carolina Herrera to design her gown. A bit over the top for my taste, but what I really wanted to see were the shoes.

Just as Trish passed me, she hooked her four-inch stiletto on the carpet and started to teeter backward. I got a great view of the strappy heel. Stuart

Weitzman, no doubt. They were fabulous. There was a gasp from the crowd, then she steadied herself and proceeded on down the aisle.

Vinnie offered Trish his hand. She slipped her hand into his and the couple stepped under the arch.

Aint Loretta went around straightening Trish's train; grabbing the ends, she popped it like a freshly laundered sheet, revealing that Cousin Trish had decided to go commando under her white wedding gown.

The audience made another gasp. Vinnie turned around, eyeballing the crowd, and everyone hushed. The wedding proceeded without further ado.

After the preacher announced the union of Mr. and Mrs. Vincent Gambino, everyone stood as the happy couple walked down the aisle and exited toward the reception. The crowd followed the happy couple, and Aint Mable dabbed her eyes with a tissue.

"I just loooove weddings, don't you, Earl?" she asked her husband as she pushed past me to the buffet.

"Eh, pearl? No, I think he gave her a diamond ring, not pearl," he said, tagging along behind her.

A giant white canopy tent was erected for the reception, and box fans rotated the air inside the tent bringing the temperature from sweltering to slightly miserable. A long table with a tented sign marked "wedding party" was centered against the far wall and ran the length of the tent. Tables covered with white linen cloths and white folding chairs were positioned underneath the tent separating the head table from the food table.

I was sure Vincent must have lots of money, because the food was catered. There wasn't a casserole in sight. Instead there were silver warming trays filled with meatballs and little chicken strips. Mounds of cocktail shrimp heaped over silver platters, with a giant ice sculpture erupting from the center shaped like a fish. How in the hell were they keeping that thing frozen in the hundred-degree heat?

Gertie found me and promptly cut in line. The toothless twins shouted complaints from behind me.

"Kiss my ass!" she called back to them.

"We'd be here all night!" they responded in unison.

"Hey, Jen, what a wedding, huh?" Gertie said. "Can you believe it? Number four."

"What I can't believe is Trish let you get your tongue pierced."

"You saw, huh? Drives my new stepdad crazy."

"Why do you want to drive him crazy?" I scooped a few of the plump shrimp on my plate next to the fruit kabob.

"You know he works with the Mafia," she said, lowering her voice as she piled her plate full of chicken.

"You're kidding?"

"Nope, see that fish?" Gertie pointed at the sculpture. "Vinnie's nickname is Vinnie the Fish."

"Why?" I asked, wide-eyed. "Does he like to fish?"

"No, silly, one of his companies imports fish, but I've heard a rumor many of his business partners end up down at the docks with the discarded fish."

"That's sort of creepy."

"Tell me about it." She piled her plate high with meatballs. "I'm on a special diet; you can only eat meat."

Gertie explained to me that she had to sit at the head table since she was in the wedding party, but she would come find me later. I carried my plate toward the round tables. Centered on each table were two glass fish dancing around a votive candle. Gertie's story about the fish made me shiver.

I found Eli at the Gambino girls' table. They were swarming around him like honeybees, saying things like, "Oh, Eli, I love your accent," and "Eli, your blue eyes are so dreamy." *Yuck!* I located my parents and sat between my dad and Uncle Earl.

"Hello there, youngun," said Uncle Earl.

"Hi, how are you?" I glanced up at him. The amount of wax caked in his ear canal gave me second thoughts on the caramelized pineapples in my fruit kabob.

"Wha'd she say?" he asked Aint Mable, who sat to his left.

"She asked how you are," Mable hollered into his good ear.

"Oh...I'm better than a fat kid in a candy store."

Wow, OK, great, I thought as I smiled politely and looked to my mom to help me out with this conversation.

"Uncle Earl, are you ninety-two or ninety-three?" my mom asked, leaning toward Uncle Earl.

"Climb a tree?" he answered. "Naw, I can't climb a tree, but I can sure chop one down."

Good grief. Conversation with Uncle Earl was more work than I was into at sixteen. I finished my food without any further conversation.

"Can I be excused?" I prayed my parents would have mercy. In our house, it was understood you had to ask permission to leave the table. Dad would look at Mom. Mom would either nod her head, which meant we could go, or she would purse her lips, which meant we needed to finish something on our plates. I looked over for the sign. Head nod. Great.

"Go ahead," Dad said, but I was already gone.

After dinner the sun was a light crease on the horizon. Clear twinkle lights strung through the trees and miniature lanterns hung from the branches created a warm romantic atmosphere.

A band began to play, and several people strolled toward the temporary dance floor laid out on the lawn. Joey patrolled along the edge of the dance floor scanning the area. I made a beeline in the other direction.

Making my way to the back of the yard, I ached to walk through the beautiful gardens and return to the old willow tree. The hedges of Photinias were overgrown and unkempt compared to the last time I was here. Pushing back the branches, I found the old white gate. Aint Elma's sign still hung in the same spot. Darkness enveloped the gardens lingering beyond the gate. I squinted trying to see past the shadows, wishing I could conjure up a flashlight.

"Need one of these?" A male voice startled me. I pulled my head out of the bushes and observed the cute boy standing next to me holding out a small light attached to a key chain. I didn't recall seeing him at the wedding.

He appeared a little older than me, with blond hair that curled around his boyish face and a big dimple in his chin. The relationship to Vinnie the fish was obvious. They had the same deep-set eyes. Unlike Vinnie, who's dark eyes watched every movement, this boy's eyes were ice-blue and tinted with a sadness that made my heart melt.

"Um, no, I thought I saw a cat." The lie was simple, and if he'd go away, I could find the secret garden.

He raised a dark eyebrow, which sharply contrasted with his blond hair, reached around me, and pulled back the bushes, exposing the gate. Busted.

"I caught a reflection off the sign when I was looking around earlier. Let's go check it out," he said, leading the way.

I hesitated. I mean, he wasn't family; was I supposed to take a stranger into the garden? It was too late to think about it, since he was through the gate and holding it open for me to enter. I shrugged and followed him into the darkness.

We slowly wound our way around the bushes, and although I could only glimpse fractions of the remaining gardens, my stomach knotted up like a fist ready to throw a punch. What were once beautiful flowers and green bushes had turned brown and lifeless.

"Looks like someone used to have a garden back here...must have dried up. I'm Marco, by the way."

"Jen. Are you a cousin?"

"No, I'm a nephew." He laughed. "Are you a cousin?"

I laughed, thinking my question must have sounded dumb. "As a matter of fact...I'm a second cousin."

We continued to walk and came upon the vegetable garden. Rotten watermelons lay wasted on the ground. Gone were the orderly rows Aint Elma had created. I held my breath as we passed the brown stalks of corn and turned the corner. The willow tree sat in the back. Its branches still wept like a waterfall.

"Could you shine the light on that tree?" I asked. Marco pointed his flashlight toward the willow.

The tree looked tired, almost depressed. My heart ached. Marco must have felt my anguish, because he put a hand on my shoulder. A sleeve of warmth trickled down my arm. He immediately withdrew his hand.

"The garden was so beautiful. I can't believe Trish didn't take care of it."

"Let's go back," he urged. "The fireworks are starting soon."

We made our way out of the garden, or what was left of it. As we walked toward the side yard, people were gathered in groups waiting for the fireworks show. Some sat in chairs, others stood sipping drinks and catching up with family members.

I spotted Gertie standing next to Joey. I marched up to her, grabbed her by the arm, and jerked her around to face me.

"What happened to the garden?" I demanded more than asked.

"Ow." Gertie looked surprised at my question, then, jerking her arm free, she said, "We watered almost every day, but as soon as the outhouse was taken away, everything started to die." She lowered her voice. "I always thought that thing was haunted."

I suddenly realized why my backyard was becoming a green wonderland. The outhouse was my fertilizer.

Marco had been stopped by a family member but had finally caught up with me. I introduced him to Gertie, and I found it funny they had never met.

Gertie explained Vinnie's family was huge and there were several relatives who couldn't even make it to the wedding. I listened as Gertie, Joey, and Marco made small talk about certain cousins they had seen lately. The outhouse kept coming back to my mind. Was it haunted like Gertie suggested?

The fireworks started exploding overhead. I could hear the oohs and aahs of my family and the wows of the Italians

I raised my eyes, and the fireworks were magnificent. I had overheard my mom say Trish had hired a professional fireworks company for the wedding. Everyone seemed to be enchanted with the display. My mom and dad had arms around each other and were gazing upward. Even Uncle Earl had pulled a chair up next to Aint Mable and was whispering in her ear.

"Let's lie down on the grass so we'll have a better view," Gertie suggested.

We joined friends and family on blankets spread out across the lawn and watched the fireworks light up the sky. After a short time, Marco eased his hand next to mine and I interlocked my hand with his. My fingers began to tingle, and we watched, linked together. After a few minutes, a warm sensation spread slowly up my arm.

He propped up on one elbow and ran his hand up my arm, caressing my shoulder. The warmth seemed to be coming from his fingertips. Using his index finger, he followed the outline of my collarbone, pausing at the shallow in the base of my throat.

I turned my face toward him, and he leaned over and kissed me. My first kiss. Fire shot through my body like a bottle rocket. I parted my lips, and when our tongues met the heat went straight to my boy-howdy.

My sister had told me Diane Valdez down the street had gone to third base with her boyfriend. If first base was this good, I was definitely going to steal home.

Marco pulled away.

"Wow, that was pretty amazing," he said.

I put my hand to his chest and followed his shirt up to his throat. Along the way, my hand passed over something hard, a necklace. I pulled the corner of his shirt back to reveal a familiar piece of metal. Mother Earth was formed out of a pale stone. The stone gave off a small sparkle and I leaned closer, but Marco pulled my hand away, then buttoned up his shirt.

"I'm sorry," I said, coming to a sitting position. "I was admiring your necklace."

"Yeah," he said, now completely sitting, hands resting on his knees. "It was a gift from my grandfather."

"Is your grandfather at the wedding too?"

"No, he died recently." He said it with such sorrow, I couldn't find the words to offer condolences to this boy I had just met.

With the fireworks in full on finale mode, Marco turned to me. "I should go, but maybe I'll see you at the next family function." He leaned in and gave me a quick kiss on the cheek.

"Um, OK. See you 'round."

He stood, stared down at me as if he had more to say, turned and left.

The fireworks ended, and I stood, along with Gertie and Joey.

"So, you like Marco?" Gertie gave me a smirk.

"I barely know him."

"Ya know, his father owns Ferrari," Joey said.

"Like the car?" I asked.

"Yep, thatta be the one."

"What does your father own?" Gertie asked Joey.

"A funeral home."

"Geesh."

CHAPTER 20

October 2013

Holy crap! The realization of what was around Marco's neck woke me from my daydream. A key. Maybe he could help me rescue Gertie and my key.

I hurried downstairs to use the computer, which sat on the desk adjacent to the bookshelves that housed Gertie's collection of biographies. I logged on to the Internet and googled Marco Ferrari. Seconds later my screen filled with clips about car races and brought up a picture of Marco Ferrari and the last Formula One car race he'd won. I didn't know he raced cars, but I never was a fan of the sport.

I scrolled through a few articles and studied the photos of him. After each race, the articles had pictures of Marco celebrating his victory. Marco with a gorgeous girl, Marco drinking champagne, Marco holding a trophy and, in each photo, he was wearing the key.

I came across a few pictures of him out publicly. He was quite the catch according to the magazine link. He was voted last year's most eligible bachelor from *People* magazine, *Men's Fitness* had an article about him, and he was pictured in various other publicity magazines. The gossip columns were full of what Marco was doing and whom he was dating or wasn't dating anymore.

Thinking back, I remembered he was cute when I first met him, but he had certainly filled out his Levis, based on the pics I was seeing. He was only wearing the key in the race photos, never in the social ones.

The last clip was from the Formula One website, stating Marco would begin training for the Grand Prix next weekend. There was a link to the local gossip guru's website. I clicked on the link, and in the "Gossip of the Week" box was a blip about the marriage of pop star Liv Regalado to Marco's team member Enzio Tortino at the home of Wheelen Motorsports' number one sponsor, Mafuso Motors. I went slack-jawed. Could Marco be one of the Mafusos? He just didn't seem as smarmy as the others, but things could change in ten years.

I needed to get to New York. Even if Marco did work with the Mafusos, maybe he would still help me, or at least swap me for Gertie. I debated calling Jake. No, he would never let me swap places with Gertie.

I came across an old article about the death of Marco's grandfather. There was a family photo taken three weeks before the death. The caption under the photo explained that Giorgio Ferrari, pictured standing in the back row, left, tycoon and founder of Ferrari Motors, was murdered Friday night at his office.

I scrolled back up and enlarged the picture. The grandfather was a handsome, silver-haired man with a long face, dimpled chin, and sophisticated features. Next to him stood a short Italian woman with a partial frown on her face. Seated in front of them was Marco's father. He was similar in features to the older Ferrari, except his hair was dark and he wore the Italian woman's scowl. He had the same dimple in his chin.

Marco's mother, seated next to his father, was a beautiful blond woman with blue eyes and a slight smile. That explained Marco's blond hair. Marco stood next to his mother. He looked about eighteen in the picture and wore a mischievous grin, which accentuated his adorable family dimple. A younger girl, who looked about fifteen, stood in front of Marco. He had his hand on her shoulder, typical of family photos.

Marco wore a black suit, as did all the men in the photo. But where his father and grandfather had on ties, Marco had his shirt open at the neck, and peeking out between the V in his collar was the Mother Earth I remembered from the wedding. The article went on to explain Marco's grandfather Giorgio Ferrari was found dead at his office. All information surrounding the death was under investigation.

I scrolled through a few more articles and found one that said the death of Giorgio Ferrari was determined to be a homicide. The murder weapon was never located, and an investigation was pending. I couldn't find any more information regarding any suspects or arrests made concerning the crime. The picture was taken a few months before Cousin Trish's wedding. Marco's grandfather died around the same time as Aint Elma.

I decided a change of clothes was needed. Ace wouldn't like the fact I exchanged the rockin' miniskirt and the stilettos for a white cashmere sweater, black Dior pants, and black leather Marc Jacobs boots, but New York was cold this time of year. When Ace arrived the next morning, we would be going to *breakfast at Tiffany's*.

I spent the rest of the night tossing and turning, worrying about Gertie and finding Marco. My dreams took me to my first kiss with Marco and the incredible heat that engulfed my body then disappeared as quickly as it had appeared. My dream transformed from the dark night and fireworks to the dusty barn where Caiyan first showed me what sex was all *aboot*. The incredible heat surged through my body, then came the moment when he took me over the edge, and I exploded.

I woke suddenly, drenched in sweat. Exasperated. *How can Caiyan have that effect on me even in my dreams?* I looked at the clock: 4:30 a.m. *Geesh!* My hormones were overloading my brain. I took a hot shower and contemplated the events that had taken place since I met Marco. I hoped he would remember me from the wedding. Almost ten years had passed since my first kiss.

At promptly 7:00 a.m. a swoosh came from my backyard. I had just finished my second cup of coffee and hoped the surge of caffeine would give me the courage to ask Ace to take me to New York instead of Gitmo. I unlocked the sliding door, allowing Ace to enter. I was mildly shocked; he was wearing red leather pants and a white Guess button-down with a multicolored T-shirt layered underneath. His hair was dark and curly to his shoulders, and he had on a kick-ass pair of cowboy boots. Basically, he looked like a tired rock star.

"Good morning, love." He kissed me on both cheeks, then looked me up and down. "Where's the sexy outfit I picked out for you?"

"I'm thinking there might be a change of plans."

Removing his designer sunglasses, he looked down his nose at me, then wandered into the kitchen. "Got any java?"

"Um, yeah, there is still half a pot left." I opened the top cupboard and presented him with my yellow "Have a nice day" coffee mug, complete with a big smiley face imprinted on the front.

He frowned at the mug. "What gives with the smileys, hon?"

I poured the coffee. "They gravitate to me, I guess. Dressing down today?"

"Orders from the chief. I'm supposed to be as manly as possible today. I am also ordered to take you directly to Gitmo, no side trips. I swear that man has ESP. How did he know I had an exceptional breakfast planned at a sidewalk cafe in Paree?" He poured some vanilla-flavored creamer in his coffee, no sugar.

"What happens if we don't follow orders?"

"*Ooh*, girl, don't even think about it. They ground you."

"They what?" I asked.

"They make you remove your key, and they lock it up. You can't lateral-travel, which means no fun. In fact, the last time I was grounded until the next full moon, and you know what they say: all work and no play..."

"Damn, I really need to go to New York City."

He lowered his mug and looked at me quizzically out of his bloodshot hazel eyes. "What is in New York?"

"I have an acquaintance who lives there that has the gift and might help us."

"Brilliant! Who is this person?"

"Marco Ferrari."

Ace threw his head back and laughed. "Why do you think Marco is going to 'elp you?"

"Because he's related to Gertie." *Sort of.* "Do you know him?"

"Girl, someone needs to sit down and tell you about our dirty little past. Marco doesn't travel."

"Why not?"

"After his grandfather was killed, he took off his key and hasn't transported since. The WTF has tried to claim him, and so 'ave the Mafusos. He works for neither. It's a shame, really, because Marco has a great gift. Even his grandfather didn't 'ave the gift like Marco."

"What can he do?"

"I'm not allowed to say. It's classified. Your super-secret agent McCoy will have to tell you, or Marco himself."

"How do you know about Marco's gift?" I narrowed my eyes at him.

"I've seen him in action. Mmm." Ace licked his lips. "My grandfather would take me to train with Marco. Back when your Aint Elma was Giorgio Ferrari's transporter."

"What?" I didn't understand.

"OK, I'm probably not supposed to tell you this either, but since it was never stamped confidential...Your great-aunt and Marco's grandfather were lovers."

"No way."

"Yes, and I know this because when I first became a transporter, my grandfather was beside himself. He was a defender and came from a long line of defenders, but it was obvious when I inherited the gift, transporting was me gig." He sipped his coffee and sat down at the breakfast table, crossing his legs, and finished his story.

"Anyhow, my grandfather consulted Giorgio. They were friends from the old country. We met at the cute white frame house in the country. It needed a decorating overhaul, those curtains and that couch—"

"Elma's house," I said. Ace nodded then continued.

"My grandfather thought it was the safest place. While they were discussing my so-called tragedy, she was there. I remember her twinkling cornflower blue eyes and the way she smiled when she took me into her kitchen and gave me cookies. I was barely sixteen, had terrible acne, and my hormones were completely out of control. My grandfather couldn't figure out why I didn't want to shag females. He thought it was confusing my gift, and if he could fix it, I would miraculously change into a defender. Honestly, I didn't know what I wanted to shag. I call those my swinging-door years."

"Anyhow, Elma told me it didn't matter what I was, I should always be true to myself and to 'ell with what other people thought. She was a strong woman, and I remember Giorgio coming into the kitchen and placing an arm around her, and she kissed him."

"But wasn't he married?"

"Yes, but according to some, his wife was a bitter woman. He was from the old country, an arranged marriage."

That explains his wife's scowl in the family picture. I poured Ace more coffee and topped mine off.

"When you pass the key, you no longer travel. You are supposed to train the younger generation to take over. When Elma was in trouble, Giorgio forced Marco to give 'im the key, and he went back to help her. They were both killed." Ace put a hand over his mouth. "Oops, that was confidential, I'm sure of it."

The year I turned sixteen, I thought to myself, *and the same year the picture of Marco's family was in the paper and Cousin Trish got married.*

"If you could convince Marco to come work with us, we would get major brownie points from Agent Hot Buns." Ace tapped a well-manicured finger on the table as he contemplated the situation.

I gathered the mugs. My heart raced waiting for his decision.

"Let's do it. But we'll have to make a pit stop."

My hands shook slightly as I rinsed our coffee mugs in the sink. "You mean for weapons?"

"Absolutely, I 'aven't seen Marco in a while and I need a jacket to go with these pants. Looks can kill...you know."

I couldn't control the wide grin that spread across my face as he trotted off toward the backyard. Excitement and fear were fighting for position on my ladder of emotions. I chose excitement, and my inner voice crushed fear with the spike of her stiletto.

I followed Ace outside. My outhouse sat looking forlorn in the shadow of Ace's photo booth. I couldn't help feeling responsible for Gertie and my inability to travel in my own vessel. *I'll get them back.*

I stepped into Ace's vessel, rolled my slouching shoulders back, pushed my chest out, and braced myself for the mystical ride. Ace pulled me close to him and pressed his cheek next to mine as we stared into the mirror in front of us.

"Smile, hon." He made a kissy face at the mirror.

"What?" I started to say, then a light flashed. Orange and purple swirls formed in front of my eyes. The Rolling Stones sang "I Can't Get No Satisfaction," and we landed with a quick rock back and forth.

The lights blinked on. Ace pulled back the purple curtain and jumped out while I waited for my eyes to focus.

"Let's have a look at our photo," he said, doing a disco spin. He picked up a strip of black-and-white photos from the little slot in the front of the booth.

"*Oosh*, honey, you gotta relax."

I stepped out and looked at the photo. My mouth hung open, my eyes were squinting, and a "what the hell" expression contorted my face.

"You could have warned me you were taking my picture." I frowned.

Ace shrugged and tucked the photo strip into his shirt pocket. We landed in a park. A large tree partially camouflaged our arrival, but we were not too far from a hot-dog vendor whose cart was positioned on the stone walkway. He didn't question how we had materialized from thin air.

"Didn't he see us pop in?" I motioned toward the vendor.

"No, the landing of an experienced traveler is so subtle; we sort of glide in, and people just don't notice. Besides, people believe what they want to believe."

The vendor was busy stacking his buns and barely gave us a second thought.

"So, where are we?"

"Central Park, baby." Ace swished his hips and started walking. I sped up to match his pace. I recognized the park from movies and the Tv show *Friends*.

We walked through the park, passing a large fountain. A few joggers ran around us. People were out for morning strolls, walking their dogs, and picking up the dogs' poop with plastic bags. Men and women in suits and coats rushed by us on their way to work with a coffee clasp in one hand and a briefcase in the other hand.

"Why didn't Jake tell me about Aint Elma and Marco's grandfather?" I asked.

"Agent McCoy is new, and I am sure the boss upstairs said you are on a need-to-know basis."

"But he's my friend."

"Not when it comes to General Potts. All work and no play, that one. He most likely has something to do with making sure you are with the WTF and not the Mafusos."

"Why would I work with the Mafusos?"

"Oh, power, money, fame...what most people who live in Manhattan are striving for."

"But the Mafusos are bad."

"Easy to turn the other cheek when your pockets are lined with gold." Ace put his hand on my shoulder and gently nudged me to the right, gesturing for us to turn off the path.

"Why don't you work for the Mafusos?"

"Doll, I do this for my family. It's expected, and I like the perks of lateral travel. If my family thought for one minute I was working for anyone but the WTF, they would rip the key right off me British neck."

"But you would have to be dead for that to happen, right?"

"Exactly. Besides, in between transporting the bad guys, I can be in Rome or Greece doing as I please."

"How do you afford to go to these places? I mean, I understand how you travel there, but where does the money come from to hang out?"

"Trust fund, baby." Ace grinned widely.

"I don't have one of those."

"It makes traveling a little more difficult, but there are several of us that hold down regular jobs in between travels."

"Like Caiyan?" I asked and felt my face flush. I was dying to know what the guy did for a living, but the opportunity to ask had never presented itself while escaping from Pancho Villa.

Ace laughed. "Caiyan owns things. He flits around the world buying art and real estate. If you need a place to stay, he would be the one to contact, because he has 'connections' in every major city."

"Figures." I shrugged off the news that Caiyan was out of my league, but my inner voice pulled out a tissue.

"The Mafusos, of course, have a family business," Ace said. "They practically run Staten Island."

"That's what Cousin Trish said."

"Who?"

"Gertie's mom. She's married to Vinnie the Fish."

Ace froze. "Blimey, are you kidding?"

"No, why?" I paused, shielding my eyes from the sun to look at him directly.

"Because everyone knows the Gambinos and the Mafusos are archenemies unless they are working together evading the law."

"Aren't we the law?"

"Exactly."

"I thought the WTF would have known all about my family tree."

"After Elma died, they assumed the ability to travel was lost, and stopped monitoring. They do a periodic check of the *dead* families," he said, making air quotes.

"But what if they miss finding a traveler, like they did with me, and the Mafusos recruit them?"

"Trust me, you are the exception." He smiled and placed a gentle hand on my shoulder. "If you were from a family that has a strong gene lineage, your grandparents would have been slapping that key on you from the moment you got your first pimple."

As we walked through the park, I gawked at the tops of the tall buildings that peeked out above the treetops.

"First time in New York?"

"Yes, I can hardly wait to see the city," I said.

We passed a beautiful fountain I recognized from several movies and the Central Park Zoo. "Next time when you're 'ere for fun, I'll take you to all the cool spots," he promised, but his mouth held a sly grin. "Today we work."

As we left Central Park, the tall buildings sprang up around us. We strolled down Madison Avenue. Many of the shops were open thanks to the time change between Texas and New York.

Ace popped into Armani and picked out a terrific jacket. It cost my entire month's salary. The sales associate spoke to Ace with a degree of familiarity. He obviously shopped here often enough for the jacket to be added to his "account."

I could get used to this new lifestyle. My inner voice checked my bank account and shook her head sadly.

Ace had decided the best place to look for Marco would be his penthouse. He reassured me it would be better to catch Marco midmorning than to wake him up, so shopping was a good diversion.

I was beginning to like Ace and all his eccentricities. We cut back to Fifth Avenue, and I ogled at Tiffany's and Gucci. After an hour of satisfying browsing, we set our sights on finding Marco.

Ace stopped at the corner and looked up and down the street. "Marco lives in SoHo. We should catch a cab."

"Why don't we ride in one of those?" I said, pointing to the pedicab that was waiting curbside. The bicycle-driven cart was missing its driver.

"You're kidding, right?" Ace scowled at the pedicab.

"C'mon, I want to see the city, and it looks like fun."

"Girl, you got a weird definition of fun, but if you want to risk your life, I'm game." He gestured to the group of guys clustered around another bike, and a lanky, young man came over to help us.

We climbed aboard a rickety, pale-blue pedicab, and our driver welcomed us with a big white smile that glowed in contrast to his dark skin. He told us his name was J'rule and he was from South Africa.

"Newlyweds, yes?" J'rule peered over his shoulder at us huddled together in the pedicab.

"No offense, love, but 'ell no," Ace responded.

J'rule wove through traffic and took us down Seventh Avenue, right through the middle of Times Square. It was amazing. The lights of the billboards blinked at us, and people rushed around on their way to wherever. The huge flashing marquees displayed ads, the latest musicals, and showed the most up-to-date news.

J'rule talked us through the garment district, avoiding a large red double-decker tourist bus by mere inches. Ace shrieked and grabbed my hand.

"Do not fear, good people, you are in safe hands with J'rule," our driver said.

"If we get through this alive, transporting should be a cakewalk," Ace said, cutting off the circulation in my fingers with his death grip.

"Haven't you ever ridden in one of these before?"

"I can thankfully say never, and this will definitely be the last time."

As we Fred Flintstoned down Seventh Avenue, the traffic eased up, and Ace took a deep breath. The spindle top of the Empire State Building was to the left, and the smells of the local pizzerias preparing their dough infused the air. My stomach growled, and I realized I didn't have any money. How were we going to buy food, or pay for this ride?

"So, how are we going to pay for this cab tour?" My eyebrows knitted together as a vision of Ace knocking out the friendly driver flashed across my mind.

"Rule number one: when you lateral-travel, make sure you take your driver's license and credit card. Stealing in the twenty-first century is much harder than while traveling back in time. People don't leave their doors unlocked, and almost everyone has an alarm system. If you go back to 1955, you can hot-wire a car in ten seconds. No alarms, no fuss, and most of the time, the keys are left in the ignition." Ace sighed. "The good old days when people trusted each other."

I laughed. "Maybe if you didn't steal their cars, the alarm system would never have been invented."

"Hmm, something to consider." He looked at me over the top of his sunglasses.

"So, you put your credit card in your mouth and hope you don't choke to death?"

Ace laughed. "Lateral travel is different. You can put things in your pockets. Cell phones, credit cards, money. You keep the same clothes, so you keep the contents of your pockets. But for some reason you can't take luggage, purses, and such. One transporter tried to take some Prada luggage home, and the thing ended up shredded. Such a loss, but it was so last season anyway."

J'rule turned left down Houston Street, and cute little shops representing the artsy nature of SoHo welcomed us. He took a right on Mercer and stopped short in front of a tall, brick building laced with intricate scrollwork on the outside.

Ace and I lunged forward, trying not to get thrown from our seats. After Ace offered a few thank yous to the lord above for our safe arrival, we stepped out, and he paid the driver.

"See you later, honeymooners." J'rule smiled as he rode off.

Ace growled, "Get a real job, damn wanker."

The building had several buzzers outside the door.

"Marco lives here?"

"You expected something fancier?"

"Well, yeah, I thought being the son of a multimillionaire and a famous race car driver, he would at least live in a building with a doorman."

"Marco likes to keep things simple." Ace began pressing all the buttons.

"What are you doing?" I asked.

"You don't actually think he's going to buzz us up, do you?"

"Well yes, why wouldn't he?"

"Because to 'im, we are the enemy."

Several voices came over the speaker asking who's out there. One sounded like the Chinese guy who owned the Superclean where I took my dry-cleaning. Ace spouted off something back, and the door buzzed open.

"You speak his language?"

"I told him I was a delivery boy." He did a shoulder shrug and pocketed his sunglasses. "Just wait, the WTF will have you speaking six languages and shooting an Uzi."

"A machine gun, really?" My voice squeaked up an octave.

He looked at me out of the corner of his eye. "Well, maybe they 'ill give you a slingshot."

"It worked for David against Goliath."

"Somehow, doll, with your gumption, I think you would 'ave the same result." Ace waved me through, holding the door for me. Inside, we walked down a short hall, passed mailboxes, a door marked "stairs," and ended at a single elevator.

We rode the elevator to the top floor. It opened out to a long hallway. There was a door at the end opposite us. I followed Ace to the door, passing a large gilt-framed mirror. I caught a glimpse of my reflection and shuddered.

Jeez, my hair was a mess. How was I supposed to convince Marco to help us if I looked like Barbie on acid? I stopped and smoothed down a few flyaway pieces of hair, then bit my lips to give them a little color. Ace turned around and came to stand beside me. We looked at each other in the mirror.

"Don't fuss; you have natural beauty that even Christie Brinkley would die for. No makeup needed."

I stared at my reflection, wide-eyed. No one had ever told me I was a natural beauty.

"Trust me; I'm a professional when it comes to appearances." He pressed his lips against his first two fingers and planted them on my reflection in the mirror.

True, he did have good taste in his designers.

Ace and I rang the bell, but no one answered. *He's probably not home,* I thought. *Now what?*

Ace put his hand on the knob and turned it. The door slid open. "Well, a trustworthy soul does exist."

"What are you doing?" I put my hand on his arm, stopping his progression into Marco's apartment. "We can't go in. That's trespassing."

"Do you want to find your cousin or what?"

I removed my hand and followed Ace into the apartment. There was a small entry hall with a long mahogany side table positioned against the right wall. The entry opened into a living room that held a comfy-looking leather sectional opposite a flat-screen TV. The remote and the sports section of the *New York Times* were lying on the glass coffee table. The news was blaring over the TV about today's stock market expectations.

"*Yoo-hoo,* anyone home?" Ace called out.

"This is today's paper; maybe he just left," I said doubtfully, since the TV was on. My brother was always leaving the house and forgetting to turn the TV off, so I was still hopeful we wouldn't be arrested for B and E.

"You're good at this spy stuff; maybe you should ask for a raise when we return," Ace joked. "Let's split up and search for clues as to where he might be today."

I went down the long hall to the right, and Ace took the kitchen and study. I entered an exercise room. I walked by a top-of-the-line treadmill, exercise bike, and a set of free weights. Mirrors lined the entire wall in front of the treadmill, giving me another horrified look at my messy hair.

I left the workout room and wandered into the master bedroom. The king-sized bed sat against the far wall. The brown satin sheets were twisted across the bed, looking like Marco had recently crawled out of them. A dresser sat across from the bed.

I checked out the contents lying on top of his dresser. Black leather wallet, Tagheuser watch, tray with various coins, and a ticket stub from the opera. *He likes the opera. So cool for a guy to like opera,* I thought, or maybe a girlfriend dragged him there. I picked up a bottle of Versace and sniffed. He had been wearing the same cologne the night he kissed me. I remembered how wonderful he smelled, and parts south of the border started to tingle.

The sound of running water pulled me out of my daydream. Was the water running when I entered the room? I didn't think it was. The door next to the dresser was shut. Should I knock? Maybe he was in the shower and wouldn't hear me. I debated getting Ace, but maybe a quick peek to confirm it was Marco before I pulled Ace away from his search was a better idea. Besides, if he was in the shower, I could be quiet as a mouse, and he would never know I was there.

I slowly turned the knob and inched the door open. Steam escaped through the open slit in the door. I poked my head in and saw the shower going. *Should I go in?* I asked myself. Well, we did share a kiss, and based on the photos from the Internet, I was not passing up a chance to see that body.

I couldn't make out a figure through the frosted glass. I slowly eased into the room closing the door softly behind me. The steam was so thick, I could hardly see my hand in front of my face. *Should I call out? No, maybe I should try to get a closer look to make sure it's really him.* I stepped closer, but the steam had fogged over the glass door. Just a peek to confirm. I reached up to rub some steam away, and a voice startled me.

"See something you like?"

I jumped about three feet, then turned to find Marco standing behind me with a white towel wrapped around his waist. He was taller than I expected and had obviously used his exercise equipment extensively since our last meeting. His skin was a deep tan; his wet blond hair was cut shorter but still curled around his face in an early Paul Walker sort of way. The big dimple in his chin was covered with a five o'clock shadow.

"Marco, shit, you scared me," I said with my hand on my chest.

"I scared you?" His right eyebrow rose in question, then recognition glinted in his eyes.

"Jennifer Cloud."

"You remember me?" I asked, averting my eyes from his glistening body.

"I wondered how long it would take you to figure out what we had in common."

"You knew even then?" I tried to hide the disappointment in my voice.

"When I kissed you, I knew for sure. No one heats up like that unless she has the gift."

"Why didn't you tell me what I was?"

"It wasn't my place to tell."

I pondered this for a minute, then my eyes trailed over his biceps, and I lost my train of thought. He laughed, then walked behind me to turn off the shower. "Good thing I forgot my razor, or you would have caught me in the shower."

"Yeah, good thing," I said.

As we were leaving the bathroom, Ace came blowing in. "I can't find a single thing..." he stammered.

"Ace," Marco said.

"Marco," Ace said, eyeballing Marco's chest. His gaze drifting down to the tiny towel.

"Um, let's wait out in the living room until Marco can talk to us," I suggested, pushing Ace out the door before his drool hit the floor.

Ace and I sat on the sectional waiting for Marco. "Did you get a load of that body?" Ace asked me. "Yum."

"Puh-lease control yourself, we are trying to convince him to help us." I chose a magazine off the coffee table and thumbed through the ads.

"Don't tell me you didn't notice how yummy he was?" Ace leaned back and crossed his arms over his chest.

OK, maybe I did notice. I gave Ace an eye roll.

Ace smirked. A buzzing noise sounded from his pants pocket. He reached in and pulled out a cell phone.

Checking his phone, he grimaced. "We better hurry. The boss man is wanting to know our ETA."

"Tell him I wasn't ready."

"It's your heinie, sugar," he replied as he typed in a response.

Marco entered the room smooth-shaved and completely clothed in ripped jeans and a white T-shirt. He sat with one hip on the arm of the sofa.

"Why are you here?" he motioned toward Ace. "I take it since he's here, you're one of them?"

"I sort of just got inducted."

"Congratulations," he said. His voice tinged with a touch of sarcasm. "Where's your key?" He pointed to my empty neck.

"Where is yours?" I asked back.

"Mine is safely tucked away so the likes of the people you work with and others don't end up killing me."

"Now, Marco, you know the WTF didn't have anything to do with your granddaddy's death," Ace said.

Marco's blue eyes clouded, and I could see a wall start to form.

"Ace, we are here about Gertie, remember?"

"What's wrong with Gertie?" Marco asked.

"The Mafusos took 'er," Ace said.

Marco's eyebrows shot up, but he listened as I described my trip back to 1915 and how we grabbed Mitchell, and how Mahlia took Gertie, thinking she belonged to the key.

"Since you have connections with the Mafusos, we thought maybe you could help us," I said.

"I'm sure Ace explained I don't travel anymore."

"Don't you care what might happen to Gertie or to us if they continue taking our keys?"

"Not my problem, and I have a wedding to attend today." He stood and tapped the face of his Tag watch.

"We know about the wedding; I was hoping to go with you. Gertie might be held captive at the house."

"I dunno," Marco said.

"I guess since you retired your key, winning races doesn't come so easy?" Ace asked. "And how does your transporter feel about her destiny being taken away?"

Marco didn't seem to like the insinuation Ace was making. "I will do what's necessary to protect my family."

I sat looking confused. "I'm not sure what y'all are talking about, but Gertie is my family, and I have to help her."

Marco looked at Ace. "You didn't tell her?"

"I can't—it's classified." Ace pouted.

"They classified me?" This brought a smile to Marco's face, but the smile faded quickly as he pointed at Ace's key. "Ace, you're glowing."

"Oh bollucks, I forgot to watch the time." He held up a watchless wrist and did a palms up. "Now they will all come to find out why Jennifer is 'ere."

"Who is 'all'?" asked Marco.

"Oh, Caiyan, Brodie, some WTF agents. It's going to become pretty crowded in here."

"No, you don't. Don't bring all those bastards here. Get out, now." Marco pointed toward the door.

Ace grabbed his chest and doubled over in pain. I rushed to his side. "What's wrong?"

"I'm being summoned, quite painfully, I might add," he said, clutching his side.

"How can Brodie do that?" I asked Ace.

"Not Brodie...Caiyan," Marco answered. "One of the many so-called gifts he inherited. He loved to use it on us when we were kids."

"C'mon, Ace, let's get you outta here before those bastards invade my space and McGregor decides to use his other gifts." Marco and I helped Ace stand.

I couldn't believe Caiyan would do that to his own teammate. Physical pain. I was beginning to discover a side of him I didn't understand.

Marco took us out to the rooftop. There were four walls surrounding what resembled an enormous garage. It ran the width of the entire building and could easily hold a fleet of cars. The only thing in the garage was Marco's race car. It was spectacular—red with the Ferrari emblem on each side of the body. Across the hood various sponsors were displayed. The race car sat low to the ground with wings that spread out in front and a big spoiler on the back plastered with the Mafuso Motors insignia.

We helped Ace across the garage to an empty space.

"Call your vessel," Marco ordered. Ace whispered a word I couldn't comprehend, and his photo booth magically appeared. He scowled at me, and I stood grounded. "I can't go back until I find Gertie."

Ace grabbed his back in pain, then lunged into his vessel, and he was gone with a flash.

Marco and I stared at each other. "You should have gone with him. They're going to come here."

"Maybe not. How do they know where I am?" I touched the empty hollow of my neck. "I don't have my key, so they can't summon me, and I'm not in my vessel, so they can't locate me."

"Maybe," Marco said, but he didn't look convinced.

"So, is this your vessel?" I asked, running my finger along the rear spoiler of the race car.

"You know it is."

"It's nice, way cooler than mine. But I would still like to have the use of mine back."

"So, this is not all about saving Gertie. It's about getting your key back."

"Look, Marco," I said, moving closer to him. "I know you still use your key, maybe only to drive in your races, but I have seen it in photos."

He sighed. "I'm not going to deny anything, but I am not going back to time travel." He took a step toward me and ran his hand along the side of his car. "We probably only have about ten minutes before we are invaded by the WTF assholes. I can help you get into the wedding tonight, but that's it. I can't help you find your key."

"Gertie is my main priority. Marco, what happened to you?" I held his gaze for a moment.

His eyes clouded over, and he started to turn away from me. I reached out to grab his arm, and as soon as I made contact, a sharp bolt of heat ran up my arm. He turned toward me, and I leaned into him.

The heat consumed me like a fire bursting from within the core of my body. Marco brought his lips down on mine, and there was a loud drumming in my head as if I were underwater. I didn't pull back this time but responded with all the pent-up frustration I had been reserving for Caiyan. He slid his hand down my back and pulled me in tighter. His tongue ran over mine, and I knew sparks were leaping out at each touch. I felt the ground shake, and then I thought I heard a crack of thunder. Everything in my body was humming like a finely tuned aircraft.

Caiyan's voice interrupted the drumming. "Um, that would make me want to come to work every mornin', yeah?"

Marco and I broke apart. Caiyan stared at us from across the garage. His arms crossed. Guilt washed over my face, followed by anger that I was feeling guilty when the man standing in front of me had a reputation of being a player.

"Marco and I are old friends," I said, wiping the kiss from my mouth with the back of my hand.

"Aye, seems so," said Caiyan with a slight grimace.

Marco looked at me and then at Caiyan. "Jen, you didn't hook up with him, did you?" He ran his hands through his hair. "Don't you know—"

"Yes, I know." I stopped Marco in midsentence. Just as Caiyan was about to make some witty remark, there was a flash and a whoosh. Jake jumped out of the photo booth and ran to grab me in a bear hug.

"What's wrong? When you didn't show this morning, I was worried about you."

"I'm fine," I answered, avoiding the raised eyebrows from Caiyan and Marco. Ace followed behind Jake. And to make it extra crowded, Brodie's bathtub appeared, gurgling in the middle of it all. Jake stepped back and tried to compose himself.

"Woo," Ace said, fanning himself. "The testosterone in here is off the charts. You know, hon, they won't buy the cow if you give the milk for free."

"Did you just call me a cow?" I lifted an eyebrow at Ace.

"Figuratively speaking, darling." He came and slung an arm around my neck.

"Are you all right?" I asked him.

"Fine now, hon," Ace said, glaring at Caiyan, who shrugged his shoulders. "I'm sorry to give away your location, but I wasn't given a choice."

"No worries," I told Ace while giving Caiyan the evil eye.

Caiyan dropped his head like a misbehaved schoolboy.

Ace made introductions. "Marco, this is Agent McCoy, the new pit boss and past romancer of our good friend Jennifer Cloud." I rolled my eyes.

Caiyan's head shot up at the last remark, and a wily smile creased his face.

Jake put forth a hand, but Marco refused to shake it. Instead he kept his arms folded across his chest.

"I told Jen I would help her gain access to the Mafuso mansion tonight, but that's all I have to offer," Marco said.

"Well, that's aboot as good a place to start as any," Caiyan said. "Let's go inside and make a plan."

Marco led everyone inside, and as Caiyan passed me, I spoke in a hushed tone. "The next time you use force on someone who is doing me a favor, I'm coming after you."

"Promise?" He nodded a head toward Jake. "Just following orders." Now I had Jake and Caiyan to blame for Ace's forceful summons.

We sat around Marco's living room while he explained the wedding was a masquerade theme and a costume would be required. He clarified the Mafusos were a very generous sponsor to his racing team, hence the relationship.

"Most likely a ploy to lure you to their side," Brodie said.

"Hasn't worked so far, but I'll take their money for my team," Marco said.

Jake decided Marco should take Ace as his date instead of me.

"I'm not taking a dude as my date," Marco sputtered.

"Well, then think of him as a good friend," Jake said.

"No."

"Look, gorgeous, when I get all fixed up, there's not a *dude* in here who can tell the difference."

"He's right there, mate," Brodie said. "I thought he was a chick for the first week. Until that stint in Afghanistan."

"Hey, I had to pee, and there are not a lot of options in the desert."

"Why can't I go instead of Ace?" I asked.

"No, the risk is too dangerous; the Mafusos might recognize you," Jake said. "I need my people to go in separately to avoid detection. The Mafusos know we're trying to rescue Gertie. They assume she's the transporter, and if we don't get to her soon, they'll find out she's not."

I frowned, but I was outnumbered and if the Mafusos found out Gertie wasn't the transporter they could kill her.

Jake walked around the room as he plotted. "I will go to headquarters here in the city and secure a van, where we can monitor from the outside. After Marco and Ace arrive, we need to position Caiyan and Brodie on the inside."

"Not a problem for me; I have my own invitation," Caiyan said.

Yeah, I knew how he got it, and why did I care if Caiyan was trading information with the enemy? Because now I knew he could cause unprecedented pain to his friends and didn't mind doing it. There was something else I couldn't put my finger on. *The way he felt when I touched him.*

Jeez, there I was, lost in my own thoughts, and I wasn't paying attention to what was being said. Exactly like high school. I snapped back to attention, noticing Caiyan was watching me with a curious expression. I deduced the plan was for Jake to leave for headquarters, Caiyan and Brodie were going to the flat Caiyan had somewhere in the city, and I was to go with Ace to help him find a costume for tonight's shindig.

Jake gave us strict orders to keep a low profile in case the Mafusos were out and about. We would meet back at Marco's at 1600 hours. I felt like I should be on an episode of *Get Smart*. If Jake started talking into his shoe, I was going to raid Marco's medicine cabinet for some Valium.

Caiyan and Brodie left for Caiyan's flat. I pictured something deep and dark, like Dracula's lair or the Batcave.

Ace and I stood outside Marco's building. The sun was shining, but a cool wind had the trees dropping leaves on the sidewalk, and I shivered.

"You know the best thing about today?" Ace asked.

I did a palms up. "No idea."

"Today we are working for the WTF, that means we can turn our receipts in for reimbursement."

"Really?"

"Yes, and you know what else?"

I shook my head.

"You don't 'ave to worry about *me* trying to get in your pants." I laughed. Ace grabbed my hand and yelled, "TAXI!"

Ace and I were seated in the taxi. I studied the driver's ID, because my mom always warned me the taxi drivers were crooked, and if I ever went to New York, to be sure I knew who was driving me around. His identification stated his name was Bob, but he looked more like an Abdul or Osama to me. Ace told him to take us to West Thirty-Fourth and Broadway, then patted my knee.

"Don't worry, sometimes the foreign folks take on an American name to make life a little easier."

"Oh, like in the nail salons back home—my manicurist goes by Nicky, but she is from Vietnam and always asks if I 'like nail.'"

Ace laughed at my impression of Nicky.

"Let me ask you something." I turned to Ace.

"Shoot, sweetheart."

"When I touch Marco, there is this huge amount of heat that makes me feel like I'm going to explode."

"Well, I would too; he's hot."

"No, I'm serious, and when I'm with Caiyan, the heat is there, but it's different, subtle, more like a humming, but when we kiss, just as powerful."

"Hmm." Ace thought. "All travelers give out heat when they connect with each other, but most of us stabilize as we reach adulthood."

"When I touch you, I don't feel a zap of heat."

"Give me your hand." Ace held out his open palm for me.

I placed my hand in his. "Now concentrate; how do I feel?"

"Your hand is warm but in a comfortable way."

"No, hon, how do you feel inside? Concentrate."

I sat for a minute, then closed my eyes, and a mellow sensation washed over me. "I feel kind of happy but with a little fear." I explained this to Ace.

"I think you're a reader. You can sense emotion, you know, like read people's feelings. I've heard of others who have similar gifts."

"Why is Marco on fire when we touch?"

"Probably Marco has a lot of pent-up hostility, and he doesn't know how to control 'imself like our cool cat Caiyan, who's had years of practice hiding his real feelings from the world."

"Why does Caiyan hide his feelings?"

"Who knows, but maybe you could solve the mystery and give all of us a break."

The cab pulled over, and the driver said, "Here we are. That will be ten fifty."

I peered out the window and a wave of excitement washed over me. "Ace, this isn't a costume shop—this is Macy's."

"You need a coat, and I might need a few things." He winked at the cab driver. "Don't forget the receipt."

CHAPTER 21

 t 1500 hours, after shopping and eating a fabulous lunch at Sardi's, where Ace knew just about everyone, we returned to Marco's apartment. I didn't think we were keeping such a low profile, but we had fun. Ace and I stood at the stoop surrounded by our packages. Where else were we supposed to get ready? We buzzed Marco, but no response. He was probably hoping we would go away. Ace hit all the buttons until someone let us in. I wondered how many serial killers had been buzzed in before us. We took the elevator up to the top, and Marco opened his door dressed in full racing gear except for his helmet.

"Nice, very original," Ace said. "No one will ever guess it's you."

"You didn't expect me to go out and rent a stupid costume, did ya?" Marco stepped aside to let us enter.

"You could at least throw a mask on," Ace said.

"I'm wearing my lucky racing baseball cap." He grinned, plopping a red cap adorned with his sponsors' logos on his head.

"I need to borrow a shower, and Jen needs to freshen up a little."

Marco sighed and pointed toward a hallway. "You can use the guest bath down the hall on the right."

"I just need something warm to drink," I said. "It's cold outside."

"Must be that thin Texas blood running through your veins."

"Was that a dig at my home state?"

"No, that was a dig at your bloodline." He scowled at me and went into the kitchen to operate a state-of-the-art espresso maker like a pro.

"He's just jealous, hon, because unlike our avaricious ancestors, yours actually tried to find the missing keys and took nothing for themselves." Ace swished off toward Marco's shower.

"I guess that's why you guys have trust funds and I work for my brother." I envisioned Marco's grandfather carrying chests of gold while Aint Elma hoed her homegrown vegetables.

Marco handed me an espresso, and I slid onto a barstool at his kitchen counter.

Marco leaned against the dark granite counter of his immaculate kitchen. "Having to work for what you have is not a bad thing. It builds character. You value what you have, and you don't take things for granted."

"You sound like my mother." I sipped my espresso. "Is that why you live here in SoHo and not Park Avenue?"

"I like the people here. They work during the day and keep to themselves at night. No one asks questions. I own the building, so I can keep my vessel safe. I don't like being in the public eye. But I do like racing."

"Does your key help you win races?"

Marco straightened, avoiding my question. "You can use my room to change, if you like." He reached for my empty espresso cup and set it in the sink.

I made him uncomfortable, so the key must have played a role, which meant he had it close. I gathered my purchases, compliments of the WTF, and paused for a moment before I went to his room.

"Marco, why is there so much heat exchanged between us when we touch?"

He shrugged, and then an evil smile kicked up the corners of his mouth. "I'm not sure, but I bet the sex would be unbelievable."

"Um." I looked down and kicked some imaginary dirt around on his hardwood floors.

"Don't worry, I can tell you have some confusion rambling around in that head of yours. I'll try to keep my distance, at least for today."

I smiled. "Deal, and thanks for helping us."

He frowned. "I'm helping you and Gertie."

"Right, well, thanks anyway." I turned and power walked down the hall. Part of me hoped he might change his mind, and the other part kept aching for Caiyan. I didn't know where I factored Jake into the whole scheme. Thinking about it made my head hurt. *Is it possible to love three men at the same time?*

At precisely 1600 hours, Caiyan and Brodie appeared at Marco's door. Caiyan was dressed entirely in black, with a black fedora-style hat pulled down low over one eye. He had a rose tucked between his teeth.

"Who am I?" he asked through clenched teeth.

"Let me guess, Don Juan." Suited him perfectly.

He removed the rose. "Aye. Right on the money. I hoped it might take a few tries. I thought for sure you would go with Zorro."

Seriously?

Brodie had a briefcase with him. He sat it down on the coffee table, and after he fiddled with a combination lock, the top flipped open. Inside were several types of listening devices, headsets, and gadgets I didn't recognize. Mission Impossible was right on target.

"Where is Ace?" Brodie looked around the room. "I need to fit him for a mic."

"Right here, love." He was in the hallway leaning against the far wall, right hand behind his head and the other hand resting on his hip in a sexy pose. He looked great. An exact duplicate of Marilyn Monroe. White halter dress with a flared skirt, mole on the left cheek and short, sexy blond wig. We stood slack-jawed staring at Ace. I walked over to him.

"Amazing. How did you get your eyelashes so long? They are exquisite."

"They're Eyelets," he said, batting his luxurious lashes at me.

"Whatlets?"

"Eyelets, individual lashes that glue on. It does take a while, but you can't even tell they're fake. The only problem was the store sold out of my normal superhold glue, so I had to buy the cheaper kind. I'm not sure it holds as good."

"Well, they look one hundred percent real," I said.

Marco scowled at him from across the room.

He smiled and walked over to Marco, "Whatcha think, big boy?"

"I think we need to have a no-contact policy at the wedding."

"You're no fun. Who's going to believe I'm your date?"

Marco backed up a few paces from Ace.

Brodie fitted each of us with an undetectable earpiece and microphone. In order to activate the microphone, I pressed the pearl brooch he attached to my sweater.

I wondered why I needed a communication device since I wasn't going on the inside, but Brodie explained Jake wanted everyone outfitted in case we got separated. Marco refused.

"I'm only getting Ace in the place, that's it," Marco insisted.

After we were all communication ready and tested, Brodie's cell phone rang. A brief conversation ended with a concerned look from our Australian defender. He explained to us that Jake had to wait for the van, and I should ride in the limousine with Caiyan and him. Thank God Brodie would be there too. Being alone with Caiyan for a two-hour ride outside New York City was not what I needed right now.

Ace and Marco would go in Marco's car and arrive at the wedding first. The limo would drop me and Brodie off at the rendezvous with Jake. Caiyan would arrive at the wedding ten minutes later, hopefully distracting the Mafusos to make them keep an eye on him, allowing Ace to snoop around.

We followed Marco into the elevator and took it down to a basement garage, where most of the occupants of the apartment housed their vehicles.

"Oh, baby, I love your toys!" Ace clapped his hands together as he stood in front of a shining red Enzo Ferrari. Marco also had a black Ducati Desmosedici motorcycle in the next space. Caiyan and Brodie circled the machines like they were doing a lust-filled tribal dance.

"I didn't know these bikes came in black, yeah?" Caiyan said as if experienced in the world of motorcycles. Meanwhile Brodie's tongue practically hung out of his mouth as he ran his hand down the car.

"They don't," Marco answered proudly. "It was a birthday gift from my mother. She had it custom painted for me." They bobbed their heads in male bonding approval. Geesh, I felt like Jimmy Kimmel would be coming around the corner to hand out man cards any second.

"Guys, we need to get a move on. Wedding, remember?" I broke up the summit, and heads bobbed in agreement.

A long black limousine waited out in the street. Marco and Ace hopped in the Ferrari while Caiyan, Brodie, and I took the stairs out of the garage and climbed into the limo.

In all the excitement over the boy toys, Ace had accidentally pushed his microphone, and it was stuck in the on position, because we could hear the conversation between Marco and Ace. Apparently, the device worked walkie-talkie fashion, because I tried to tell him he was stuck on, but he didn't respond.

"How fast can she go?" Ace asked Marco.

"Oh, I've gone up to one hundred and sixty miles per hour on the highway, but she should max at two hundred and twenty-five mph, no problem."

We heard the deep growl of the Ferrari's engine as Marco revved the motor, making it come to life.

"It's stuffy in here," Ace said. "When was the last time you drove this thing?"

"Damn, Ace, you're so high maintenance. I drove it about a month ago; I usually ride the bike in the city. Here's the air."

There was a click as Marco turned on the air, and Ace shrieked, "Not the air!"

Caiyan, Brodie, and I looked at each other.

Pretty soon Ace's voice came over his transmitter: "Base, we have a problem."

The limo circled the block, and we returned to the garage, where Marco and Ace were both standing outside the car yelling at each other.

"What's wrong?" I asked as I ran toward them.

Marco shrugged. "How was I supposed to know the air was on high?"

I looked over at Ace. His once beautiful, luxurious eyelashes were now stuck individually all over his face. His blond wig was hanging haphazardly on his head, and he had broken a nail trying to fight the air vent.

"Bullocks," Caiyan said, coming up behind me.

"No shit," Brodie stated. "Should I call Agent McCoy and tell him we will be late?"

"We can't be late. It's a wedding!" I said. "How would it look if we sauntered down the aisle *after* the bride?"

"She's right; it would attract too much attention. We need to arrive with the other guests," Caiyan added.

"It will take at least an hour to redo my makeup," said Ace.

"Let me change clothes with Ace. I'll go in with Marco," I said.

Three simultaneous nos sounded as one.

"It's our only choice, mate," Brodie said matter-of-factly. "We need more than one operative on the inside. I don't have a costume, and I'm not wearing that dress. I'm not telling our boss, because he'll nix the whole plan, and we need to make our move tonight. The longer we wait, the more time they have to find Jen's vessel and hurt Gertie."

Ace and I returned upstairs to Marco's apartment. Brodie, Caiyan, and Marco stayed downstairs to salivate over the motorcycle and probably talk about all the ways to keep me out of trouble.

In ten minutes tops, I was in Ace's dress, and he had added some blush and blue eye shadow to my makeup, put extra mascara on my eyelashes, and glued the fake mole to my cheek. The dress was longer on me but looked good enough.

Everything fit except the shoes, and luckily, I had purchased a pair of white Fendi strappy heels while we were out shopping. I thought Jake owed me a pair of shoes for not telling me about lateral travel. Besides, they matched the white cashmere coat I purchased perfectly. I mean, what's a girl to do? It was cold outside.

We returned to the garage and headed out to the wedding.

We took the on-ramp to the Long Island Expressway. There was only one way out to the Mafusos' mansion in the Hamptons. Marco and I followed the limo, leaving the famous city's skyline behind us. When we reached a stretch of highway with lighter traffic, Marco zoomed past the limo and showed me how fast his car accelerated. I tuned out Caiyan growling objections in my earpiece.

Riding in the Ferrari was exhilarating. The powerful sound of the engine, the smell of the leather seats, and the smooth ride felt like we were going 40 miles per hour, but the speedometer read differently.

"Wahoo!" I held my hands up in roller-coaster fashion as we came flying down a hill. Marco laughed at me and shook his head. He slowed the car and allowed the limo to catch up.

I had so many questions about my gift, and I knew Marco could answer some of them for me. I wasn't sure how to approach him, knowing he was hesitant to talk about his gift. I decided to dive in and see what happened.

"I never really knew my aint Elma."

Silence.

"Um, why don't you tell me what happened the night your grandfather died? Maybe it would clear up a few things for me."

More silence. He kept his eyes on the road, and for a minute I thought he wasn't going to answer.

"He came to my race in Monte Carlo. I thought he was coming to watch me. My grandfather loved the Grand Prix races. He began racing as a young man and never intended to build street cars."

"I'm glad he changed his mind; this car is fabulous," I said, running my hand over the soft-as-butter leather.

Marco nodded in agreement, then continued with his story. "After the test runs on the first day, he told me he needed my key. I told him no. I was using my vessel to race. My nonno, that's what I called him, wouldn't take no for an answer. He told me Elma had gone back and was in trouble. One of the other defenders, McGregor, actually, had been on a mission. He came back in bad shape, three broken bones in his hand and arm. Broken leg. He also had a severe concussion and was in a drug-induced coma until the swelling around his brain was reduced."

"Why was Caiyan with Elma?" I asked.

"After my nonno retired, she became Caiyan's transporter. He was new, and the WTF wanted someone with experience. You should have heard him bitch about how old she was, but I know that lady was tough as nails. My grandfather urged her to retire, but she said there was no one, and her legacy would die when she did. Then she found you."

I was fuming. Caiyan had known my aint Elma very well and never said a word. Rat-bastard-rat.

"You knew about me?"

"When it was discovered that I was a defender, my grandfather was so proud. He took me everywhere to teach me. One day we went to the white house in the country."

"Aint Elma's house."

"Yes, I had recently turned sixteen, and the WTF wasn't ready to let me go on a mission yet. My nonno wanted to introduce me to his transporter. She was like no one I had ever met. Strong but pretty in a Katharine Hepburn kind of way. I could tell by the way he looked at her, they were more than just friends. I overheard Elma say it wouldn't be long until you were of age, and you could be my transporter."

"But I'm Caiyan's transporter. Is that because you're not traveling? Was I supposed to be with you all this time?"

"No. You are not meant to be my transporter. There's someone else."

"Who?"

"It's complicated. I can't tell you, because she doesn't know what she is, and I don't want her involved in this mess."

"She must be very special if you want to protect her, but don't you think she has the right to make her own decision?"

"*No!*" His response was abrupt, so I didn't push for more information about his transporter.

Marco's grip tightened on the steering wheel like he was trying to deal with conflicting emotions. I reached out and laid my hand on his shoulder. The warmth trickled into my fingertips. "Your secret is safe with me," I said. He relaxed and continued his story.

"My grandfather explained Caiyan couldn't go back to save Elma. I was young and stupid. I hated her for having an affair with him. My nonna and I are close. My parents were never around much. They were always off at some charity function or promoting the company. I was raised by my nonna. She's a kind woman but very stern.

My grandparents were married in Italy before they came to America. Old school, old rules—you marry for life. At least that's what Nonna always told me. I don't know if she knew about Elma, but I had a feeling she knew there was someone else."

"I'm sure that was difficult for her," I said sympathetically.

"I finally caved in and gave him my key. My car was in the racing garage waiting for the race the following day. He transported right out of the garage. Do you know how dangerous it is to use your vessel in an enclosed space?"

I nodded. Jake told me we needed an open space with a safety net of ten square feet.

Marco continued. "I stepped out back for a smoke."

"You smoke?"

"Only when I'm stressed out. What can I say, I'm Italian; my whole family smokes. Are you going to lecture me, or do you want me to finish my story?"

"Sorry, you just don't look like a smoker."

"Jen."

"Sorry, go on."

"It seemed like he was only gone about five minutes when the car returned under a big tree behind the garage...empty. A few minutes later, the outhouse appeared. Elma had my grandfather; he had been shot. I helped her lay him down on the ground. He opened his eyes and told me they had found it. He died in my arms."

"I'm sorry," I said. "What happened to Elma?"

"Elma was injured, but instead of traveling to Gitmo she sent her vessel away. She removed the key from around my grandfather's neck and told me to take my car back to the racing garage. I didn't want to leave, but she said I must protect the gift. She took off her key and told me to make sure I gave it to you. In fact, she made me promise. I was so shaken up by my nonno's death, I did what she told me to do."

He swallowed hard, and I knew it was a difficult story for him to tell.

"After I returned my car, I went back to help, and they were both dead. Elma had been strangled. She rested against the tree with my grandfather's head in her lap. From a distance it looked like two lovers relaxing under a tree together. I should have known someone was coming after them. Why else would she have taken off her key? I was stupid."

I laid my hand over his hand resting on the gearshift. "You didn't know. You were only eighteen years old, right?"

"I remembered there was the faint scent of garlic in the air. Someone had been there in the short time I was gone. It had to be a brigand. No one else could have been there so quickly." He pounded his fist on the steering wheel.

"Garlic?"

"Yeah, the phosphorous emission from the vessel sorta smells like garlic."

"What did your grandfather find?"

"I'm not sure, the king's vessel, maybe. But I never got the chance to ask him. I summoned the WTF. They took the bodies. My grandfather's body they took back to his office, made it look like a crime scene. I found out Elma's was set up as an accident. After the police came, they interrogated everyone in my family. I hid my key and haven't traveled since."

"Wait, you sent me the key?"

"Yes, and the vessel. I thought it would be safe with you because you didn't understand the gift. I never suspected you would figure it out on your own."

"Is that why you came to Cousin Trish's wedding?"

"It's funny how life comes full circle. Uncle Vinnie met Trish at my grandfather's funeral. He's buried in Anacapri, a city on the island of Capri in Italy. Trish was visiting with a potential husband and met Vinnie at the hotel bar. The way he tells the story, it was love at first sight. Neither Trish nor Vinnie knows about the gift or the WTF. I came to the wedding to meet you. I needed to find out if you really had the gift. There is no record of it passing from outside a direct line."

"Yeah, that's what everyone tells me." I looked behind me and watched the lights disappear as we headed north, away from the city.

The scenery changed from skyscrapers to farmland. I didn't realize New York had farms. I'd always thought of it as one big city with tall buildings, incredible shopping, gangsters, and lots of traffic. We slowed as we entered South Hampton.

"How much longer?" I asked Marco.

"The Mafusos' place is on the other side of East Hampton. Just a little farther up the road."

We passed several large houses characteristic of the beach style: three-story wood-framed houses the Hamptons are so well-known for.

Driving through Bridgehampton, I noticed the cute town had high-end stores lining the main street. I made a mental note for future shopping adventures. Marco was drumming his finger in time with a Maroon 5 song on the radio. I sat back and tried to relax, even though the closer we got to the Mafusos, the harder my heart started to pound.

I jolted when Caiyan's sexy voice hummed in my earpiece. His thick Scottish accent made my thighs tingle.

"Things are good, yeah?" he asked.

I responded by pressing my brooch and with an unsteady voice said, "Um, we're fine." Marco raised an eyebrow at me.

"Ye dinnae have to do this if you are feeling scared."

"I'm fine. Over and out," I said firmly. I needed to be confident. I needed to prove I could be a team player.

Marco grinned. "If you say breaker, breaker one-nine, they will take away your transporter card and put you behind a desk."

"I just feel like I should say good-bye; it seems rude to disconnect without an ending, sort of like hanging up on someone."

Ace's voice came over my earpiece. "Darlin', we are twenty minutes from base, over and out." *Thanks, Ace.* He always had my back.

Jake had acquired a communication device, and his voice echoed in my ear telling us he was in position. Caiyan told him there was a minor problem and we had made an adjustment. I figured I was the adjustment, and I needed to get inside before Jake found out and changed my plans. Caiyan told Jake not to worry; they would arrive at the rendezvous soon.

We passed lovely houses tucked back into quaint neighborhoods. As we drove further into East Hampton, the homes sat back from the road and were hidden by the lush landscape.

There was a clicking noise in my ear and the sound of a van door opening resonated through my headset. Jake began cussing and then all hell broke loose. Ace's microphone was stuck in the on position again, and I could hear him trying to explain the situation.

"What can I say, accidents do happen," Ace replied.

"Jen, you do not go into that wedding," Jake demanded.

He was shouting orders in my ear. I pressed my pretty lapel pin, then tapped my fingers on the top. "Sorry, come again? I am getting static. I can't hear you."

Marco laughed. "You're sneaky—no wonder Jake worries about you.

So, which one is it?" he asked, gesturing with his palm. "The cool superagent or the bad-boy defender?"

"Neither," I replied, listening to Jake complain in my ear. "They both seem to end up with other women, so I am currently off men."

"Maybe I can change your mind."

"What about the no-contact policy you had with Ace?"

"Babe, that only applies with Ace. You are full contact."

Yikes!

We pulled through tall, black iron gates into the circle drive of a huge stone mansion. A valet dressed as a monkey helped me out of the car. As we started toward the front door, a photographer jumped out of the bushes and snapped a picture. I threw my hands over my face in surprise. A big burly man dressed head to toe in black came and grabbed the photographer.

"No paparazzi. This here's a private party."

"Who is she, Marco?" the photographer yelled. "Is it the French princess or the Greek tycoon's daughter?"

Marco tucked his hand in mine and ushered me inside.

"Sorry about that," he said, sulking.

"Well, sounds like you have your fair share of women too," I said.

Marco was about to respond when a lovely girl dressed as Alice in Wonderland came up and gave him a big smack right on the lips. I smirked at him.

"Marco, where have you been hiding?" she asked, grinning ear to ear. "Mother said you haven't called in over a week."

"I've been out of town. I just returned late last night."

"You could have at least worn a costume." She pressed two full, pouty lips together. "Everyone will recognize you in your racing gear."

Marco shrugged, then the girl noticed me standing next to him.

"Hi! I'm sorry, I am being completely rude. I don't know if I have ever met you with the costume and all. Who is this, Marco?"

"Sorry, Jen. This is my sister, Evangeline."

His sister! I exhaled, not realizing I was holding my breath. This got a smile from Marco.

"Nice to meet you." I extended my hand, which she took, and then she pulled me to her and kissed my cheek.

"Everyone calls me Angel," she explained. "Ooh, your hands are so warm." I felt a zing of warmth run up my arm. Marco eyed me curiously and abruptly drew his sister away.

"C'mon, you can sit next to me and Mother. She will be so excited to see Marco." Angel locked elbows with Marco and me, then escorted us into the evil lair.

We came through the foyer, which opened into a huge entry with an enormous Scarlet O'Hara staircase. It ascended a story, then split into two staircases that continued in opposing directions. Red velvet brocade carpeting covered the stair treads.

Centered on the landing at the top of the first set of steps was an arbor decorated with a variety of roses in a rainbow of color. As we moved farther into the hall, the red carpeting transitioned from the stairs and began creating a wide aisle. White chairs were set up on either side of the red-carpet runner. My shoes clicked on the Italian marble tile as we made our way to the chairs.

Ushers were seating people, and a harpist was playing in the corner. Everything looked like a normal wedding except for the fact that everyone was in costume and the court jester was making his way over to seat us.

"Yous with the bride or groom?" he asked.

I remembered him from Trish's wedding. He was a cousin or something to Vinnie.

"Joey, you're so funny." Angel gave him a punch on his skinny bicep. "You know we are with the groom. Seat us next to Mother."

"I knows, but I'm sposed to ask; it's the rules. Hey, Marco, nice costume, very original. Who's the dame?"

Marco grabbed my hand and said curtly, "A friend." I smiled apologetically.

"OK. Jeez, I get it. She's an actor or someone famous. Yous knows I can keep a secret. Ya know, Enzio is my cousin on my mother's side. That's why I'm usherin'."

He offered an arm for Angel. Marco and I followed her down the aisle. Joey dropped us off at seats about halfway up, where a gorgeous blonde sat in a white Chanel suit. She had the same nose as Marco and Angel and smiled politely when Marco introduced us. She was holding a mask on a stick.

"Who are you supposed to be?" Marco asked his mother.

"I am myself in a mask," she responded with a slight accent. "I think these things are silly. A wedding should be done in a church before God, not at a costume party."

Dang, I couldn't remember the last time I had gone to church. My palms started to sweat, and I began mentally making a list for confession. I looked over my shoulder and caught Caiyan coming in unushered. He chose a seat toward the back.

Not too far behind him entered a woman dressed as a showgirl. Her headdress spanned the doorway with feathers molting to the floor as she walked. She was arguing with Joey about having to sit in the back because people couldn't see over her costume. After a few words, I realized it was Cousin Trish. I took in a quick breath and grabbed Marco's arm. He turned to see what caught my attention. Vinnie had come up behind her, not really in any form of costume.

"What are they doing here?" I asked. "I thought they were Mafia enemies."

"Enzio is related to Vinnie, which means common ground during the wedding. Don't worry, they probably won't recognize you in the wig."

My heart rate escalated a couple of notches. How could Mortas hold Gertie captive in this house while her mom and stepdad were guests? I was in awe at the criminal world. Things didn't make sense. The bad guys were all mixed up with the good guys. Finally, Cousin Trish compromised by taking off the feather headpiece, and they were seated closer to the front on the groom's side.

The ushers finished seating everyone, and I recognized several of the guests as actors I had read about in *People* magazine or seen on TMZ. Their costumes didn't disguise them well enough to hide their identity, which was precisely the point. The joker was present, but with a sparsely painted face, allowing me to place him as a cast member of a TV sitcom. Looking at it from a famous person's perspective, I realized there was no point in attending a function if you didn't get the notoriety that came along with it.

A band appeared from I don't know where and began to play. The mother of the bride was escorted in wearing an *I Dream of Jeannie* costume. Not bad abs for a woman her age.

I was contemplating starting an exercise program when Marco whispered, "There's the Mafuso elder, Gian-Carlo Mafuso." A silver-haired man walked down the aisle and took a seat next to the mother of the bride. He was either not in costume or dressed as a mortician; I couldn't decide but opted for the former.

"Is he a brigand?" I asked.

"Yes and no. Rumor is he flew in from Italy tonight." Marco's breath was warm on my neck and made the hair on my arms, among other things, stand at attention. I looked over at him, and the wicked grin had reappeared on his gorgeous face. He knew exactly what kind of effect he had on me and was totally playing it up. *Men, geesh!*

"What do you mean yes and no?"

"He has already passed his key to Mortas. He only directs the show now. His grandchildren have the starring roles."

"How many of his grandchildren have the gift?"

"So far as I know, the three Mafusos you have met, who are Gian-Carlo's son Dominic's kids."

Marco pointed to a stocky man with dark hair and a round face. "That's Guido his other son. He has two children, but I don't know if they have the gift. It doesn't matter because they are out of keys."

"No wonder they want mine."

"They can't do anything without the vessel."

The music changed to trumpets played by three knights. Their costumes clanked as they moved into their places at the side of the big hall.

A priest appeared under the arch dressed as himself. The Catholic church most likely frowned on a costumed master of ceremonies. Three groomsmen, fully clad as lords, came down the stairs on the right to stand on the groom's side of the arch. One at a time, each bridesmaid came flouncing down the aisle until three bridesmaids, dressed like tavern wenches from medieval times, were standing opposite the groomsmen. I realized the second wench was Mahlia. Perfect outfit.

A young girl dressed as a peasant walked gracefully down the aisle and took her place with the wedding party. She was followed by a young boy in a squire's costume. He carried in his chubby hands a purple satin pillow with a ring sparkling in the center. Halfway down the aisle, he stumbled and tilted the pillow. The ring slid off and rolled under my chair.

I jumped up, and the boy scrambled to find it. The kid was crawling under my chair as the guests stared at me. Marco tried to bend down, but the seats were too close together to allow him to search under the chair. The boy announced rather loudly that he had located the missing ring. He backed out from the chair, and accidentally stood up under my skirt.

"*Oops,*" he said.

In my haste I inadvertently pressed my brooch and said, "Get out from under there, you little shit."

Jake's voice returned in my ear. "Who is under where? What's Marco doing? I'll kill him."

I couldn't deal with the voice in my ear or the child under my dress, who was pulling the fabric down instead of up—my boobs were starting to come out the top. I looked up, frantic, and saw Mahlia staring at me. Recognition came over her face, and anger lit up her eyes. Marco leaned over and pushed the kid's head down until he was out from under my dress. An applause sounded from the crowd and a few boos, mostly from the men.

The ring bearer, red-faced and scowling, looked up at me. "Jeez, lady, don't you wear any underwear?"

I sat down fast and didn't look up until he reached the wedding party.

Caiyan's voice purred in my ear. "Lucky lad."

Jake replied harshly, "Stifle it, McGregor, or your ass is mine."

Marco had a wide, wicked grin on his face. *Damn, I shouldn't have worn the new Victoria's Secret thong Ace made me buy.*

The band changed tunes again, and a very Italian-looking man dressed as a prince came down the right staircase and joined the groomsmen.

I didn't recognize Mortas, but maybe he was in costume. The music changed again, and a brass section played Madonna's "Like a Virgin."

I looked over at Marco. "Are you kidding me?"

He smiled and draped an arm around the back of my chair, stroking the back of my neck with his fingers. I could feel things heat up down south, so I clamped my legs together to extinguish the flames.

The bride flowed in from the left staircase, dressed in a princess gown and tall, pointed hat with matching veil. I could feel Mahlia's eyes on me throughout the ceremony, but I avoided looking at her. I didn't want to screw up Gertie's rescue.

The ceremony concluded with the bride singing a solo and all members of the royal wedding party providing backup. The guests were asked to move to the grand ballroom so photographs of the wedding party could be taken. Fine by me—I needed a drink.

Marco took my elbow and led me down a hall on the right, which opened to a huge ballroom. Polished wood floors gleamed under my feet, and huge gilt-framed paintings adorned the walls, giving me the impression I had walked into the Louvre. At the far end was a stage, where another band was set up and already playing. A long table extended down one side of the room for the wedding party.

Several guests were making their way to the round tables scattered about the room and to additional tables on the patio outside. Each table had a small glass centerpiece shaped into a pumpkin surrounded by colorful fall leaves. Candles glowed from the center, and napkins printed with the couple's names were placed next to a place setting of antique china. The chandeliers were dimmed, making me feel a little less conspic-uous about being discovered. Marco grabbed two flutes of champagne off a passing tray carried by Lurch from *The Addams Family*.

"Thanks," I said as he handed me the glass. We stood next to a Cezanne painting entitled *Temptation of St. Anthony* as we sipped the champagne and watched other guests enter the room. I didn't see any sign of the Mafu-sos. I assumed Satan's bitch would have her picture taken with the rest of the wedding party.

I spotted Marco's mother across the ballroom in deep conversation with Vinnie and Cousin Trish, then she pointed in Marco's direction, and they headed our way. I grabbed Marco's arm. He saw them approaching as well.

"What should I do?"

"Dance." We dumped our champagne glasses on a passing tray, and he swung me out onto the dance floor. I tried to protest because I wasn't a very good dancer. The music was a slow swing, which I managed without stumbling.

"You are a good dancer, Mr. Ferrari," I said to Marco.

"My mother made me take lessons, which have turned out to my advantage since I am always attending some kind of charity function." I spotted Trish and saw Marco's mom make an "oh well" sort of gesture. They chose flutes of champagne and headed off toward the patio.

He spun me around again. "So, what is the gift you have that no one can talk about?" I asked off the cuff.

"Well..." He smiled. "I'm not supposed to tell you, but I can show you." He waved his hand in the air not unlike he was performing a Jedi mind trick, and the entire room seem to slow down like a warped record. Time had slowed for everyone except for us. Marco spun me in tight. Then everyone clicked back up to speed. The effect was only for a few seconds, and no one in the room seemed to notice. Well, almost no one. Caiyan tapped Marco on the shoulder.

"Mind if I cut in, lad?"

"Be my guest; my work here is done. Later, Jen." And Marco was gone, leaving me with the Scottish Don Juan. The music slowed, and Caiyan pulled me in tight. I pushed against him, trying to put a little distance between us.

"Marco should naugh have done that—the Mafusos could have been in the room," he said, drawing me to him.

"But they weren't, so no harm done." I pushed away.

"Mmhmm," was Caiyan's response as he pulled me to him and nuzzled my neck. He smelled really good, and the mask was putting my hormones in overdrive.

"I thought we were supposed to keep a distance from one another?"

"Aye, but Mahlia has already spotted me, and your display with the ring bearer certainly caught her attention."

"That wasn't my fault. He lost the ring, for Pete's sake."

"The boy's name is Francisco, nephew of the groom." Caiyan said.

"It's a phrase, like crying out loud," was all I could muster as a response.

As we danced, Caiyan told me we needed to split up and look around. I was to stay on this level, because it would be easier to explain that I was a lost guest. He would go upstairs and check things oot.

When the music ended, we strolled outside, and he left me on the patio overlooking the gardens. I gave him a minute, then I wandered back inside, keeping a lookout for family members. The bride and groom were making their entrance. It was the perfect time to duck out.

I turned around, and Julia Child offered me an hors d'oeuvre. I refused and asked where the ladies' room was located.

"Down the hall on the right," Julia replied in a very deep voice. I wondered if maybe he knew Ace.

I meandered in the direction he pointed, bypassed the bathroom, and slipped into the room at the end of the hall. I found myself in a large study. Floor-to-ceiling mahogany bookshelves lined the walls to my right. To my left were wood-paneled walls with strategically placed artwork of dogs hunting a fox.

An enormous floor-to-ceiling stone fireplace encompassed the far wall. I was in awe. A fire burned steadily in the hearth. The Mafuso family crest was engraved in a stone block about halfway up the fireplace. A thick piece of wood formed the mantel, which held a large black marble urn and two brass candlesticks. I suddenly had a vision from the old Clue game...*She was killed in the study with the candlestick by Professor Plum...*

"Jen, where are you?" Jake's voice jarred me out of my hallucination.

I pressed my brooch. "I'm in the study."

"Tell me what you see."

A huge mahogany desk hovered in the middle of the room. A computer, a cordless phone, a tray filled with papers, and an expensive marble pencil holder were neatly placed on the desk. I relayed this to Jake.

"Look through the desk and tell me what you find."

I thumbed through the papers on the desk. Nothing exciting—a few bills, a racing program, and a couple of purchase orders. I powered up the computer, but there was a password. I shut down the computer and dug through the drawers. Nothing. No secret files. No hidden panels with ancient scrolls, and definitely no Gertie. I told Jake I would get back to him and listened as Caiyan reported in. He was probing around the second floor.

A spiral staircase snaked up to the right of the stone fireplace. I went up the stairs, which opened to a cozy library. A comfortable couch and chair sat on the wide landing. There were three bookcases, containing a respectable collection of old books.

The door to the study opened, and footsteps clacked across the marble below. I peeked over the banister and saw Mortas and Mahlia enter the room.

"I tell you, it's the other one," Mahlia said with fisted hands.

"Calm down, Mahlia," Mortas said. "You knew they would come here looking for the transporter."

"She's not the one," Mahlia said. "We have tried several times, and she refuses to call the vessel. The key doesn't light up on her neck."

"Just because the key doesn't glow does not mean she is not the one. Powers are deceptive. We still don't know all that exist."

Mortas crossed the room to the fireplace and turned one of the candlesticks. The fire extinguished, and the interior wall of the fireplace opened. The two of them entered. I leaned over to get a better look. Mahlia, the last to walk through the fireplace, turned quickly, looking up in my direction.

I jerked back, hoping she didn't see me. She frowned, then told her brother she would be down momentarily. The clacking of her heels on the marble floor echoed as she crossed the room and begin climbing the stairs.

Panic. Mahlia was coming after me. I had to tell Caiyan about the secret room. I knew that's where they were holding Gertie, but I was afraid Mahlia would hear me if I spoke into my brooch.

I scanned my surroundings. The three bookcases ran parallel to the back of the room. I scurried behind the last row of shelves. Luck was with me: there was a door to the right of the last bookshelf, which I hastily went through, trying to be as quiet as possible. I found myself in a long hallway. There were two rooms to the right. I chose one and ducked inside.

It was a small den. A leather sofa was situated in front of several flatscreens. I looked around—nowhere to hide in here. The den connected to a bedroom that had a balcony overlooking the Olympic-sized pool.

Several guests had ambled out and were indulging in before-dinner drinks around the pool.

I checked the dresser. Keys, valet stub from the 40/40 Club, and spare change were in an oval metal dish. Nothing. I went into the bathroom and snooped through a closet the size of a small house and found several men's suits. The bedroom door creaked open and shoes shuffled across the hardwood floor. I squeezed back between Armani and Ralph Lauren. *Damn.* Mahlia had found me.

Jake's voice in my ear startled me as he requested the status of my location. I pressed the microphone and whispered for him to hang on. I recited my mantra: "I'm spunky and I'm fierce and I'm smarter than most men. Bad guys run and hide 'cause here comes SuperJen."

The door to the bathroom opened, and footsteps crossed the marble floor. The hinged doors of the closet opened, and someone entered the closet. I got ready to attack if necessary. I was about to jump out and surprise Satan's bitch when two hands reached in and parted the suits in one quick swoop.

Caiyan was laughing. I was shaking. He reached over and removed my hand, which had been pressed against my brooch since Jake had asked my location. Upon its release, laughter sounded from various voices.

Caiyan helped me out of the closet. "SuperJen, naugh bad. I thought of you more as Sexy Jen, but I'll call ye whatever you like, yeah?"

"Oh, shut up. It's just a rhyme I made up as a kid." I pushed the mic. "If y'all would kindly quit giggling like schoolgirls, I'll tell you where they are keeping Gertie."

Everyone gave me their undivided attention, and I explained about the fireplace. Caiyan agreed it was worth checking out. Jake ordered us to go back to the wedding reception and wait for Mortas and Mahlia to turn up, then we could make our move.

We returned to the reception in time to hear the inebriated groom serenading the bride in sloppy Italian. Most of the guests had helped themselves to the monstrous buffet and were seated at the round tables eating and listening to the groom belt out "That's Amore."

Caiyan and I entered separately to avoid any suspicions. I searched the room for Marco. He was sitting at a table with his family, absent-mindedly twisting the olive in his martini. I didn't spot Mahlia or Mortas, so I grabbed a passing glass of champagne from one of the servers and plopped down next to him.

"No luck?" he asked, his blue eyes driving into me like an ice pick.

"Not yet. Do you know where Mortas is?"

"Why?"

"I thought you didn't care?" I raised an eyebrow.

"I don't care, and no, I haven't seen him," Marco said stubbornly.

The music stopped and the toasts were beginning. Mahlia and Mortas appeared as if by magic. Mahlia returned to her seat at the head table, and Mortas sat at a table with his grandfather, Gian-Carlo.

This was our opportunity; they were all present and accounted for.

Caiyan buzzed in and said he was going in.

"I'm coming too," I said.

Five simultaneous nos sounded in my ear.

"What's with you guys? Caiyan may need me. What if there are armed men down there?"

"Look, Jen," came Brodie's voice. "Caiyan needs someone to tell him if the Mafusos leave the reception. You are the only one there with a mic."

I felt like this was a dig at Marco, but I agreed. I explained to Caiyan how to turn the candlestick and enter the fireplace.

"Who are you talking to?" Angel looked at me with big eyes.

I had forgotten there were other people sitting at my table. Marco was distracting his mother with conversation about her charity work, and Angel was waiting for an answer.

"Um, sometimes I just talk to myself," I stuttered.

"Oh, my cousin Griselda does that, and then she takes a pill."

Fantastic, now Angel thinks I'm schizophrenic.

Mahlia was scanning the room, searching for me. I wasn't sure if she had positively identified me. I pretended not to notice her and leaned into Marco. He raised his eyebrows at me.

"Sorry, I need a cover." I bent over and kissed him. I'm not sure if I really needed to use him for cover or if I was curious about our connection. But I swear there was a sizzle when our lips met. He pulled me into him, and the temperature started to rise. Our tongues met and began an ancient exploration of mouth and mortal soul. He ran his hand up my leg and under my dress. *Whoa.* I placed my hands on his chest and pushed back, meeting his eyes and stalling the advance. The corners of his mouth turned up in a grin.

Marco's mother and sister both sat staring at us slack-jawed. My face turned red, and I excused myself to go to the ladies' room. I hoped Mahlia had disregarded me as one of Marco's bimbo girlfriends. She was engaged in conversation with the maid of honor as I left the room.

When I made it to the restroom, there was a plump lady dressed as Oprah washing her hands. Maybe it was Oprah; I didn't have time to ponder the meeting. I put on some lipstick and fluffed my blond wig until she left, then I checked under the stall for feet. Empty.

I ducked in a stall and asked for status. Caiyan was not answering and did not report in. I was listening to Jake trying to reach Caiyan, and my heart was beating like a hummingbird on crack. Why wasn't Caiyan answering? I told myself to take a few deep breaths, and I mentally recited my mantra, sans the microphone, for good measure.

Jake told me to go back to Marco and stay with him, and that Brodie and Ace were coming in over the east wall. Which way was east? My sense of direction sucked. Caiyan needed my help, but Jake told me to stay put.

As I sat on the toilet contemplating my choices, the bathroom door opened, and a tapping of heels sounded on the marble floor. I waited until the guest went into the stall next to me, just in case it was one of the few people who could identify me. I returned to the ballroom. Marco was still seated at the table, and he was still grinning.

I sat down and asked, "Where are your mom and sister?"

"They went to watch the wedding couple cut the cake." He pointed in the direction of a large crowd of people. I remembered seeing the five-tiered wedding cake when we had arrived earlier.

The crowd was gathered around the cake, so the only thing visible was the top tier complete with a hand-painted bride and groom. Marco's mom had told me earlier the cake topper was an exact replica of the happy couple.

This was my opportunity to go check on Caiyan. The wedding party was all present and accounted for; I just needed a little help with the surveillance.

"I know you don't want to be involved, but could you please take my brooch and earpiece and tell them if the Mafusos leave this room?"

"What do I get if I do?" He smiled an evil smile.

Jeez. Men, they are so predictable. "Fine. I can offer second base, but that's it."

"Jen, I'm not in grade school. I almost had second base at the table. Go do what you need to do; I'll spy for you."

"Thanks." I gave him a quick, steaming peck on the cheek as he inserted the small earpiece into his right ear and tucked my microphone brooch in his pocket.

I passed the restroom and returned to the study. As I was about to turn the candlestick, I realized I didn't have a weapon. Searching the room, I found a silver letter opener with a black marble handle. Better than nothing. I grasped the letter opener tightly in my hand, then turned the candlestick. The fire extinguished as before, and the wall slid open into blackness.

I crossed the secret threshold. The wall slid closed behind me, leaving me in the pitch black. *Damn, why couldn't I have a Maglite for a weapon? At least I could use the light.*

I inched along the wall, feeling my way with my right hand and holding on securely to my poor excuse for a weapon. When I returned to Gitmo, I would make sure Jake taught me how to use a gun. Maybe not a gun, maybe a knife...no, maybe some nunchakus—*what was I, the Karate Kid?* I contemplated which weapon I would most likely be able to use in a battle. My palms were sweaty, and my stomach felt queasy.

I slowly moved forward, putting one foot in front of the other. My focus was to find Gertie. The wall changed from a solid surface to what felt like stone or rock. The air became cool, making goosebumps stand up on my arms.

On my next step, I couldn't find the floor. I felt around with the toe of my shoe and I realized I was at the top of a staircase. *Jeez, I can't believe they have all this money, and they didn't install lights.* I eased down each step until I reached the bottom.

I made the turn at the base of the stairs and ran into a solid object coming up fast. Something hard and male connected with me, then I tumbled backward. As I flailed my arms to save myself, my left hand, holding the letter opener, hit flesh. I heard a curse that wasn't mine. As I went down, I grabbed out with my free hand and found a fistful of material, the fabric ripped, another uttered curse and the male shape fell on top of me.

I was winded, and my head was ringing from hitting the stair tread. Even stunned in the dark, I recognized the cinnamon and soap scent of Caiyan.

"Bloody hell, Jen, are you hurt?"

A certain area of Caiyan was pressed very intimately between my legs and seemed to be getting heavier.

"Get off me," I finally managed to say.

He moved to the side and popped on a small flashlight. He was shining it at me, checking for any injuries, but I could see I had torn his shirt, and he had a gash on the side of his neck. He had removed his mask and hat.

My annoyance dissolved instantly into concern. "*Oh my God*, did I do that?" I asked, peeling the remains of his shirt away from his neck and leaving his key exposed.

"Aye, lassie, I wouldnae want to get in a brawl with ye, now would I?"

His leg was still intertwined with mine, and his movement was starting to send signals to parts of my body I didn't want throbbing. I pulled out from under him and tried to stop the bleeding on his neck with the remnants of his shirt.

"We're in a cave under the house they've converted into a storage area. I was coming back up because my mic stopped working down here." He shined the small light toward my chest. "Jen, where's your mic?"

"I left it with Marco so he could tell us if the Mafusos left the reception. I thought you had been captured."

"So ye were worried aboot me then, yeah?"

"Don't flatter yourself. I'm worried about Gertie."

"Let's go...SuperJen." He helped me to my feet, and we made our way down a long passage. There was a ninety-degree turn, and a beam of light reflected off the walls.

Caiyan extinguished his flashlight, and we peeked around the corner. One of the Mafusos' henchmen sat on a stool smoking a cigarette. A guard. He leaned against a metal door. My guess was I'd find Gertie on the other side of that door.

Caiyan looked at me and whispered, "Give me your ring." He was referring to the big, fake diamond ring Ace had bought for the Marilyn Monroe costume. Ace had said when the gig was done, I could keep it, since I was having ring envy.

"No, Ace gave it to me."

"Dinnae be disagreeable, sweetheart—I need to distract him."

"Fine," I said, pulling the pretty ring off my finger. "I'm not your sweetheart, and why are you always taking my stuff?"

"Cripes," Caiyan said, then tossed my ring down the hall. "Act like you're tipsy when he comes to investigate, yeah?"

The man tossed his smoke aside and walked down the hall toward us. "Who's there?" he questioned sternly.

Caiyan looked me up and down and then yanked the front of my dress lower, making my cleavage pop out the top. I frowned, and he spun me around and gave me a shove forward, out into the light. I stumbled forward and froze. The man jerked his head in my direction.

"Oopsy." I put my hand over my mouth and giggled.

The man pointed his gun at me and said, "What the fu—?"

"Uh, uh, uh." I shook my finger at him and slurred, "Or I will habe to wash your mouth out wuth soop."

He lowered his gun. "Lady, you're loaded. How did you get all the way down here?"

"I lost my wittle wing," I said, holding up my finger, keeping my other hand, clenching the letter opener, hidden in the folds of my dress. He looked around and spotted the diamond ring. When he bent over to pick it up, Caiyan grabbed him in a choke hold. In an instant the man went unconscious, and Caiyan lowered him to the floor.

"Did you kill him?" I asked, trying to control my panic-stricken voice.

"No, just turned oot the lights for a minute. We need to bind him and gag him." Caiyan eyed me.

"I'm all out of accessories, sorry." We dragged him down another passage, which dead-ended. Caiyan removed the man's socks and shoes. He handed them to me, telling me to take out the laces. He removed the man's shirt, replacing his torn one. After binding the guy's hands behind his back with his own shoelaces, Caiyan stuck a sock in his mouth. I had to giggle at the thought of the poor guy waking up shirtless and barefoot. Caiyan picked the man's gun up off the floor, where it had landed in the scuffle, and tucked it in the back of his pants waistband.

We returned to the door. This door was heavy metal. The Mafusos were hiding something important. I hoped that something was five foot five and had freckles.

Caiyan reached for the door latch, and I grabbed his forearm.

"You're not going to walk right in, are you?"

"How else are we going to see what's behind door number one?"

"What if there are bad guys in there?"

"Then we weel have to change our plans."

Caiyan started to pull the latch on the door.

"Wait!" I said.

"C'mon, lassie, be brave. We cannae just sit oot here. If a bad guy is inside, pretend he's Royal Mail delivery bringing you the post and slice 'em with your lethal letter opener."

"If I'd known it was you on the stairway, I'd've put more force behind it."

"There's my girl. Now let's find out what these buggers are hiding," he said, pulling the door open.

The room was the size of a warehouse, and the fluorescent lights blinded us as we made our way inside. The Mafusos had taken great care to build a basement of sorts in the underground cave. Several rows of metal shelves ran horizontally across the room. Brown boxes with shipping labels on the sides were stacked chest high on each shelf.

"Give me your opener."

I handed it to Caiyan, happy my weapon had come into use. He opened one of the boxes, revealing stacks of US currency.

"Counterfeit?" I checked the bill. It looked genuine enough to me.

"Most likely," he replied. "This is Mafia country. They are into many different illegal ventures. It's not why we're here but could come in handy." He grabbed a stack of neatly bundled bills and put it in his back pocket. I raised an eyebrow.

"Evidence." Caiyan closed the box and returned it to its original place.

The center aisle emptied us into the end of the room. To our right a bank of overhead doors ran the length of the wall. Now we knew how the boxes came in. To our left was a small loading area. A lightbulb hung from a single wire in the middle of the room. A chair sat under the wire. On the far wall was a big picture window that was blackened with a film. Next to this stood a single door secured by a deadbolt. My heart did a summersault, and I had a gut feeling this was where I'd find Gertie.

"They're keeping Gertie here," I said.

"Aye, I agree. 'Tis the perfect setup for a hostage."

As we approached the black window, the latch on the door clicked open.

"Someone's coming," I said. We ducked behind the stack of shelves just as Mortas, Mahlia, and the older Mafuso entered the room.

"I told you she is not the one," Mahlia said. Her lips pressed together in a tight irritated line. "There was another girl as well. Neither one wore a key."

The men ignored Mahlia's protesting.

"Is this the right time? We have a house full of guests, and where the hell is Dante? He was supposed to be guarding the door." She looked around suspiciously, making sure everything seemed to be in order.

"Mahlia, I am only here for a short time. I need to see the girl tonight." The old man held up his hands and used a coaxing, gentle voice when speaking to Mahlia. I had a hard time believing he was a notorious criminal.

"Why would the WTF allow her to travel to 1915 if she weren't a transporter?" Mortas argued. "She has to be the one. We are running out of time, especially if the WTF are here tonight."

"Relax, you two," the older man said. "Dante is perhaps outside smoking as usual. Bring me the girl."

Mortas frowned, then walked to the door and unlocked it. He went inside, and it sounded like he was struggling to move something. A few minutes later, he appeared, dragging Gertie, who was putting up a humdinger of a fight.

She was blindfolded, her hands were tied behind her back, and there was a gag in her mouth. Mortas plopped her down in the chair and turned on the light above her head.

Mahlia moved to turn off the overhead lights. We were plunged into darkness, except for the small light emitted by the bulb hanging from the ceiling over Gertie's head. The darkness allowed us to move closer without being detected. We crouched behind the last shelf, where we could get a full view of Gertie.

Mortas removed the blindfold and gag, explaining she could scream at the top of her lungs, the room was soundproof, and no one would hear.

"So, you told me before," Gertie said, shielding her eyes from the bright light. "Y'all can question me until the cows come home. Dragnet me all you want; I told you people; I don't know anything."

"How did you get to 1915?" Mortas asked.

"Like I said before, the cute Australian guy met me in a bar and offered me a ride in his bathtub."

Way to go, Gertie. She was telling a lie to cover for me. My eyes teared up and I wiped away the tear that escaped down my cheek. However, she had just revealed Brodie's vessel to the enemy.

"She's lying," Mahlia said. "The WTF wouldn't be so stupid to allow a common person to travel. It's forbidden. She would have died traveling with a defender anyhow."

"Is that you *Satan's Bitch*? I wondered when we would meet again."

"Answer the question," Mortas demanded. "How did you get to 1915?"

"As I said before, we had a few drinks at the bar, then we left, and I had some of my granddaddy's secret recipe stashed in my car. My granddaddy's moonshine is pretty stout. After Brodie and I drank a pint, he was all bragging about his flyin' tub. I didn't believe a word of it, but he sweet-talked me into taking a ride."

"Who is your grandfather?" asked the older man.

"Well, on my daddy's side, it was Papa O'Malley. He made the moonshine and owned pubs back in Ireland. But I never met him. My daddy passed down the secret recipe before he split."

"And your mother's side?"

"I never met my mom's dad. He died before I was born. And I'm tired of answerin' all these dumb questions."

"See what I mean?" Mahlia asked. Her words filled with sarcasm. She waved her hand in the air toward Gertie "There is no way this dimwit could be a transporter."

I saw red. Mahlia was being cruel to Gertie. Caiyan rested a warning hand on my arm. Gertie sat straight in her chair and looked Mahlia right in the eye.

"You forgot to ask me who my stepfather is," she said.

"OK, who is he, Huckleberry Finn?" Mahlia and Mortas both snickered.

"For your information, Huckleberry Finn is an important character in one of the great American novels. My stepdad, however, is better known to you people as Vinnie the Fish."

The Mafusos froze. After a few seconds, the thaw began.

"Oh jeez, Grandfather, I didn't know Vinnie was her stepfather," Mortas spat out first.

"So, not only have you brought me the wrong girl, but she also belongs to Vinnie. Schmuck!" he said, slapping Mortas upside the head. "This is not a complication I need right now. If Vinnie finds out I have kidnapped his stepdaughter, he could make my business deals very difficult."

Mahlia remained silent as the old man circled around the room, tapping his finger to his mouth. "Still, is it possible Vinnie knows something I do not?" He pondered this idea for a minute.

"Open the door and try the key again," Gian-Carlo commanded. Mortas moved to the big steel overhead door. He flipped a switch, and the door opened, revealing a dock somewhere around the back of the mansion. The moonlight enveloped the room, casting shadows on the stone walls. I realized even if Gertie were able to call a vessel, it couldn't materialize inside the basement. There wasn't enough room with the shelving and the boxes. We needed to be outside.

The wind swept into the room, bringing in the smell of sand and saltwater. The swift breeze against the overhead door created a whistling noise that masked any accidental noise Caiyan and I might make.

Mahlia held a small wooden box. She opened the lid and removed my key. My heart started to pound louder. I was a few feet from my key.

"My key," I whispered.

Caiyan held steady with his grip on me.

"I dunno why y'all keep making me put that damn thing around my neck," Gertie complained.

Mortas unbound Gertie's hands. Mahlia handed the key to Gertie. "Put it on."

Caiyan shook his head, stifling a laugh. "They're idiots. They want the vessel so badly; they didn't even try to take the key off themselves. They would have known immediately simply by being able to remove the key."

Mortas pulled Gertie to her feet and moved her chair closer to the open door. He sat Gertie back down with a loud thump and secured her to the chair.

"Just in case your vessel does come, I wouldn't want you to make a run for it," he said.

"Speak the word that calls your vessel." Gian-Carlo folded his arms across his chest as he waited patiently for Gertie to call the vessel. The others hovered near her. Their impatience made me uneasy.

"Oh, vessely poo, come out, come out, wherever you are." Gertie laughed.

The old man nodded his head toward Mortas, who went forward and slapped Gertie across the face. I started to jump forward, and Caiyan put his hand on my arm, holding me steady. I looked at him with disgust. How could he allow them to be so cruel to Gertie?

"Do not make fun of something that is sacred," Gian-Carlo said to Gertie.

Gertie's lip began to swell. The old man walked around her. "I do not believe your story. It is impossible for a defender to carry another person. Therefore, you are either lying about the way you time traveled or the Australian defender. Now, which is it?"

Gertie just sat there eyeing him. Gian-Carlo nodded to Mortas, and Caiyan dropped his head on his arm and said, "Shite."

Mortas pulled back to give Gertie another whack, and I jumped forward.

"Stop!" I screamed, running at Mortas with my letter opener. I sliced through his upraised arm before he could hit Gertie. He howled in pain and grabbed me around the neck.

Caiyan stepped out with a gun in his hand. Mahlia also had her gun drawn and pointing at Caiyan.

"What have we here?" Gian-Carlo's eyes focused on Caiyan.

"Just give us the girl and the key, and we will go aboot our business," Caiyan said.

"McGregor. I should have known you'd be lurking around," the old man said.

"Drop the gun, McGregor, or the girl gets it." Mortas sneered as he jammed his gun into my ribcage.

"Let's see, if Mortas shoots Jen, and I shoot you, old man, then Mahlia shoots me. You, Jen, Mahlia, Mortas, and I will die either by bullet or for killing their own kind. That leaves Gertie, whom we are here to rescue in the first place. So, all is good, yeah?"

Everyone looked at Gertie.

"So, if Gertie is the transporter, why doesn't the key work for her?" Gian-Carlo asked, waving a hand in her direction.

"She is not what you seek," Caiyan said.

"What, are you pretending to be some kind of Jedi knight?' Mortas asked. "She is not the one you seek. Would ya get a load of this guy?"

Gian-Carlo gave Mortas an angry glare. "Mahlia has told me you needed the key for your transporter to return home."

I cut my eyes toward Caiyan, and he looked away, regretfully. *The dumb shit*, I thought to myself. *Did he honestly think she would just hand it over to him?*

"And Mortas has told me this is the key the old woman was wearing when the king's vessel was discovered."

"That's right, Grandfather. I heard Giorgio say they had found it," Mortas said. His hold on me tightened as he relished in the attention from his grandfather.

"The true holder of the king's vessel has still naugh been recovered." Caiyan kept a steady hand on his gun as he spoke.

"How do I know you are speaking the truth?" Gian-Carlo asked Caiyan.

"Do ye think I would be sitting here if I had access to the king's vessel?" Caiyan asked.

The old man laughed.

"You are like your grandfather, Caiyan. Always seeking more riches. I do not know why you pretend to work for the WTF when it is just a means to supply you with past treasure. I could help you, without all the work."

"If it wasn't for you and the other brigands running amuck, I wouldn't have to work," Caiyan said.

"Your other friend does not wear her key." Gian-Carlo looked directly at my bare neck. "Has she become disillusioned with us like young

Marco?" I realized they didn't have a clue the key they took belonged to me.

"Yes, I'm exactly like Marco," I lied. "I'm not going to travel again."

"Such a waste. I was good friends with his grandfather, you know? Like brothers we were, back in the old country. We had many adventures together and gained great wealth." He sighed. "Then he met that woman and she changed him. Made him turn against his own family. Pity Mortas disposed of them before we could get the information we needed."

Mortas's head snapped up and directed an accusatory glare at his grandfather.

"Elma was trying to stop us from getting to the king's vessel," Mortas said to his grandfather. "I told you it was an accident. My hired hand was worthless...The gun went off by mistake. We had to take Elma out too— she knew too much."

"You killed Aint Elma?" Gertie's bottom lip began to quiver, and then big crocodile tears started pouring down her face.

"Not personally." Mortas shrugged.

"Aunt?" Mahlia asked.

"Yes, she was our great-aunt. A sweet little old lady who never harmed a soul, and you murdered her, you bastard!" I directed my anger at Gian-Carlo. Mortas tightened his grip on me. Caiyan grimaced and I knew I had revealed too much.

"I assure you, the sweet little old lady you refer to did in fact kill in cold blood." Gian-Carlo paced back and forth as he spoke. "I have many battle wounds inflicted by that aunt of yours."

"But still, it's not a direct line," Mahlia said.

"The gift never surprises me in its idiosyncrasies." The old man stopped in front of me. "You resemble her." He looked distant for a moment, then asked, "Is it possible we have the key around the wrong neck?"

All eyes shifted to my neck.

Gian-Carlo huffed. "Did anyone try to remove the key from the girl's neck?"

Silence filled the room as Gian-Carlo moved toward Gertie and removed the key. He raised a hand to stop Mortas as he tried to make excuses for his stupidity. "Seems like Vinnie's stepdaughter is no longer of use to me. Maybe a gift to him would loosen his reins on the port authority. All eyes turned to Gertie.

"Kill her," Gian-Carlo ordered.

I looked at Caiyan for answers. He placed his hand to his key, and I saw his mouth move. Mortas dropped to his knees, clutching his side in pain.

I threw my arms around Gertie as Mahlia fired the gun at her. The whole room stopped in time, and the bullet seemed to slow down. I couldn't move, but I saw a flash of color out of the corner of my eye. Marco was there, pushing Gertie and me out of the bullet's path. It was over the split second it took for Marco to move us, saving our lives. But he didn't have time to disarm Mahlia.

She fired another shot, but before he could wave his hand and slow down time, the bullet hit him in the chest. Marco went down at the same time Brodie, Ace, and Jake entered through the overhead door with their guns drawn. The three Mafusos were swiftly disarmed and detained.

"Just taking back what you took from us, mate," Brodie replied, tossing Caiyan his knife. Caiyan cut Gertie free from the chair. She marched over and yanked the key from Gian-Carlo's grasp.

I was down on my hands and knees putting pressure on Marco's chest. He moved in and out of consciousness, and his breathing was labored.

Mahlia was white as a sheet. When he died, would she just disappear? I didn't know how it worked.

Brodie came and looked at the wound. "We have to move him, mate."

"He needs an ambulance," I protested.

"It doesn't work that way; we have to get him to headquarters and they will take care of him there."

"I'm on it." Ace called his vessel, and we put Marco inside. Ace left in a flash.

While I was helping Marco, Jake ordered the Mafusos locked in the room where Gertie had previously been held captive.

After they were secured in the room, Jake hugged me close. "Are you OK?" he asked.

"Yes, I'm fine," I said, but my knees were shaking, and my lip was quivering. "Maybe a little more training might help."

"Soon, I promise. We need to get everyone out of here in case the police show up. People may have heard the gunshots and called it in. The WTF investigation team will be here shortly to sort this mess out." Jake ran his tongue across his front teeth as he assessed Gertie. "Gertie, if you don't want to ride home with Ace, I can put you on a plane back home."

"Don't bother," I said. Gertie had her arm linked with mine and held on with a death grip. I squeezed her hand. "Cousin Trish sent you a ticket to come here tomorrow. She knew there would be family in town for the Mafusos' big party and wanted her family here afterward."

"I'll take her to Trish's house and debrief her on the way," Jake replied. "Ace can pick me up me later."

Gertie gave me a hug. "Thanks for coming after me. I knew you would."

"We're blood, right?" Gertie smiled. She opened her palm and presented my key to me. It glowed softly as I closed my fingers around the stone and pressed it to my chest. She waved to the others as Jake escorted her out.

"Jen, we have to take this key back to the past owner," Caiyan said.

"I know, I need to return the key to my ancestor, but how will I find her?"

"You'll have to wait for the next moon cycle," Brodie said, looking up at the pearly glow of the half moon.

"Ye should wear it until then," Caiyan said, lifting the key from my palm and placing it around my neck. His warm hands brushed against my bare skin, causing goosebumps to rise on my arms. My key began to glow, and my outhouse appeared in front of me.

A soft voice began singing a lullaby.

"I can hear a voice singing," I said tapping the side of my head.

"What the bloody hell?" Brodie asked. He and Caiyan looked at each other, then at me.

"Can you hear it?" I asked them

They shook their heads.

"Other than lateral travel, have ya ever heard tale of anyone who could travel between moon cycles, mate?" Brodie asked Caiyan.

"No' in three thousand years."

"I think the key wants to go home." I walked toward my outhouse.

"Sorry, lassie, you're not going withoot me."

"Suit yourself," I said, climbing into my vessel. Caiyan sat down next to me. Brodie give us a concerned wave as I shut the door. I concentrated on the year 1915 as the soft song played in my head. I recited the ancient word, "Hanhepi," and we took off.

CHAPTER 22

$\mathcal{M}$y outhouse came to a screeching halt. Neither Caiyan nor I was vaulted from the vessel. This was good; I was finally starting to gain a little control over my vessel. I stepped out but didn't recognize my surroundings. Caiyan stood by my side and surveyed the area.

"I should have gone to the WTF and checked on Marco," I said to Caiyan.

"Marco weel recover. His thick racing suit slowed the bullet, and I dinnae think it hit any major organs."

"Is that why Mahlia is still alive? Because she only injured Marco?"

"Aye. The doctors at Gitmo weel take care of him there in the infirmary. They're veera good, patched me up a time or two."

I recalled Marco's story of Caiyan's injuries after the mission with Elma. He'd almost died. I was curious how many other times Caiyan had been "patched up."

"After he is stabilized, the WTF creates a fictitious cause of injury. They'll move him to a local hospital, where he weel get a lot of unneeded press to increase his already enormous popularity."

I smiled at the picture Caiyan painted, knowing Marco would hate the attention but appreciate the publicity for his racing team.

Mountains surrounded us on all sides. I inhaled the heady scent of clean air, rusty earth, and fresh pine. The full moon shone brightly in the night sky.

"Caiyan, the moon is still full here. Tonight, in this time."

He looked up, nodding his head in agreement. "Maybe 'tis the reason you could travel."

On another night it would have been intoxicating, but tonight with the lullaby growing louder in my head, I needed answers.

"Where are we?" I asked him

"I dinnae. Maybe close to Villa's home." He scanned the scenery. We landed at the mouth of a large cave. The vessel had changed our dress once again to the western wear from before. A soft wind ruffled the hair at Caiyan's collar. He sported a gash on the side of his neck, reminding me of our meeting in the dark staircase.

"I'm sorry about your neck. I hope it doesn't scar."

"I have many scars, lassie, and none of them were as exciting to receive as this one, yeah?"

My face heated, but Caiyan's words were quickly ignored as the singing in my head grew louder. "Do you think we're supposed to go into the cave?"

"Won't know unless we try."

Caiyan interlocked his fingers with mine and led the way. I knew if Gertie were here, she could probably tell us some historical fact about these mountains. Caiyan walked through the mouth of the cave with me in tow.

Not too far inside, a large rock blocked the path.

"Open Sesame." I waved a hand at the large rock.

"Funny." Caiyan cocked a grin at me. "If it had moved, I would have raced ye inside to find the magic lamp." Caiyan pushed, and the rock rolled out of the way surprisingly easily.

"'Tis not real stone, most likely a man-made camouflage."

Beyond the mouth of the cave, light and air were filtered in from a small opening in the roof. The full moon beamed through the gap.

Further into the cave a lighting system had been strung along the ceiling, providing a lighted walkway, and tracks from an old coal mine ran parallel to the far wall. The convenience made me uneasy. Was Villa waiting at the end of the tunnel?

Caiyan led the way. I held his hand in a death grip as the singing grew louder. The tunnel emptied into a room containing empty cages. A prison. In the last one, a girl huddled into the back of the cage singing softly to herself. Once she spotted us the singing stopped.

I slowly approached the cage and asked her if she was OK. She looked at me with huge, frightened brown eyes, then a hopeful look came over her face. She struggled to stand, hesitantly coming over to the cell door.

I blinked twice, because in the dim cave light she looked exactly like my sister Melody, except she was extremely pregnant. She wore a simple cotton dress, and her feet were covered in moccasins.

"We're going to get you out of here," I said. I put my hand to the cell door and pulled, but it wouldn't open.

"Villa has the only key," she said sadly.

Caiyan smiled and put his hand on the lock. It tumbled open.

"You are one with us?" she asked him.

"Aye," Caiyan said. "Is this the secret cave where Pancho Villa is rumored to keep his treasures?"

"Yes," she explained. "This is the Sierra Madre Mountains. Down that tunnel is an old mine shaft. At the bottom is a vast treasure collected by Villa and his hombres." She shuddered and pointed toward the mine.

"I was not supposed to travel in my condition, but the mountains are the only place where I can find a special vine that helps with my pregnancy. I was so sick after the first baby, I wanted to make sure this time would be different. That's when Villa snagged me. He saw my key and thought he could sell it. I gave it to him so he wouldn't harm me and the baby."

I opened the neck of my western shirt, revealing the key. Her eyes glistened with fresh tears. I removed the key and placed it around her neck. The key began to glow, and my identical key reappeared around my neck. Amazing.

Her eyes grew wide when she saw my key "You are family?

"Yes," I said. She reached out and pulled me into her arms.

"We should go now," Caiyan said. We walked out of the cave in time to see a whirlwind develop in front of us.

The girl giggled. "My husband. He is coming to rescue me."

A large teepee materialized. Paintings of wolves and Indian hunters with spears adorned each of the sides. Out stepped a man with straight black hair pulled back in a ponytail. He was wearing faded jeans and a plaid shirt. His complexion was lighter than the girl's skin, but the Native American characteristics were undeniable.

He looked at us apprehensively at first, but the girl ran toward him. He swept her off her feet in a big hug.

"I'm sorry, I didn't know what to do with our baby boy. I had a day's ride on horseback to the neighbor's ranch and asked them to keep him. Are you well?"

"I'm fine, and thanks to these good people, I have my key."

He came forward and shook our hands.

"I am Jeremiah Cloud, and I'm grateful to you for saving my wife."

"That means you're Mahalo Jane," I said.

"Yes. These people are from our future family," she said to Jeremiah.

"Just me," I said. "I'm Jennifer Cloud, and this is Caiyan McGregor, my defender." Caiyan looked down at me and smiled. I was overwhelmed by the fact that I was standing in front of my great-grandparents and they were so young and happy.

"What's a defender?" Jeremiah cocked his head toward Caiyan.

"Um, nothing for ye to worry aboot in yer time."

Jeremiah shrugged.

"I'm glad to know our gift has passed on to our descendants." Mahalo Jane smiled at us.

"Let's go, my love, before Villa comes back to get you for himself," Jeremiah said.

Mahalo Jane laughed. "Even Villa didn't want me in this condition," she said, patting her big belly.

"Dinnae you want to get the gold?" Caiyan asked, pointing toward the mine.

"No. Taking what doesn't belong to you only leads to trouble. Villa will get his in the end," Jeremiah said, wrapping a protective arm around his wife. "Besides, I already have my treasure."

"Thank you again, and many safe travels to you." She smiled, then followed her husband to his teepee. Just as she was about to enter, she turned and looked at us thoughtfully.

"What do I name this one?" she asked, rubbing her tummy.

"You name her Elma, Elma Jean."

"Elma Jean," she replied cheerfully. "A girl. I was hoping for one." Then she turned and entered the teepee. She tilted her head upward to Jeremiah, and he placed his mouth over hers. The wind whipped up around us, there was a loud crack, and they were gone.

I looked at Caiyan, and he was grinning down at me. "I think I know how ye got your gift. Yeah?"

"My great-grandfather and great-grandmother both had the gift. But wouldn't that have at least made my grandfather or my father a defender?"

"'Tis true, one of them should have inherited the gift, but that was before the WTF. I haven't heard anything aboot either of them, and Elma never mentioned it."

"Ya know, I have seen that teepee somewhere." I tried to remember, because I was sure I had seen it before.

"Let's go, lassie. More adventures are waiting." He eyed the cave, mulling over right and wrong. I could tell he was struggling to keep from helping himself to some of Villa's riches.

"We should probably go before Villa returns." I motioned toward the clearing where Jeremiah's teepee had disappeared and called for my vessel.

"Aye, ye come from a good stock of people."

I smiled as we entered my vessel, and in the next instant, I was back in my garden at home.

Caiyan stepped out and extended his hand to me.

"So, this is where ye live?"

"Yep, probably not as exciting as your many homes."

"Let's have a look." He pulled my sliding-glass door open, wagging a finger and tsking at me for leaving it unlocked. He looked around, nodding his head in approval of my home. The big gray cat raised his head as we entered; he yawned, then kept one eye on Caiyan, who moved into the kitchen to make a call.

I grabbed two bottles of water from the fridge, handed one to Caiyan, and listened intently.

Jake's voice projected from the phone. I searched the pantry for a snack, coming up empty handed as Caiyan spoke to him. He gave them the info on what had gone down in 1915 and got information on the Mafusos' arrest.

He put the phone on speaker so I could hear the update on Marco. He was recovering from a slight concussion, broken rib, and collapsed lung. The bullet had been slowed by his suit and deflected by the rib. The broken rib had punctured a lung. He had hit his head when he fell but should recover nicely. They had him sedated and said I could visit him tomorrow.

After Caiyan got off the phone, I asked him, "Did the WTF arrest all the Mafusos?"

"Not exactly. Gian-Carlo offered up Mortas in prison for three years in exchange for Mitchell."

"Three years? That's it? You mean Mahlia gets off for shooting Marco? And the old man doesn't even get arrested?" I stomped around. "It's so wrong, so...so...*unfair*!"

"True, but this way we have made an arrest for the murder of Marco's grandfather. The crime was reported in the news and needed to be solved. It will appear to the public that Mortas is getting life imprisonment, but he will be lost in the system and released after three years. Mahlia has been a spy for us for the past year, which goes to her credit. Mitchell is harmless right now, and we have his key, so that puts one vessel out of commission."

"What about all the counterfeit money?"

"Your CIA is allowing Gian-Carlo to make it disappear."

"Well, that sucks. If this is what our tax dollars are paying for, then we had better do something to make things better." I sulked.

"Lassie, you might make a fair transporter after all."

"Really?" I asked. "Is that why you travel? To make things better, not to steal?"

Caiyan put his arms around me and pulled me close, feeling my hesitation.

"You cannae always believe what other people say."

"You're telling me you don't go back in time and sleep with random women?"

"I didnae say that, but people can change."

"Are you going to change?"

"Whit's fur ye'll no' go past ye."

"What does that mean?" I asked, looking up into his deep green eyes.

"'Tis Gaelic for 'what weel happen weel happen.'"

My heart was racing, and my insides were turning to mush. I wanted him badly, even though I knew the risk. This was the new me, Jennifer Cloud, transporter, agent for the WTF, fearless risk taker, chiropractic assistant, and horny lassie.

Caiyan swept me into his arms and carried me upstairs. He took me into Gertie's room and laid me gently down onto the queen-sized bed.

"This is Gertie's room," I said.

"It's pink," he said, looking around and pulling his shirt off. His hard body was cut to perfection, making me all too eager to run my hands over his torso. Lying there in my white Marilyn Monroe dress, I removed the pearl earrings as he stood watching me. I turned to set them on Gertie's nightstand and gasped.

"What is it?" He moved on the bed close to me, concerned.

I picked up the framed photo that sat on the table next to Gertie's alarm clock. In the picture were Slim and Opal Hawkins, their son, Johnny, and Gertie and me smiling back.

"Bloody hell," Caiyan said taking the photo from me. He placed the picture frame back on the nightstand.

"Whit's fur ye'll no' go past ye," I said in my best lassie voice.

"Ye know what else?"

"What?" I crossed my legs and admired my new Fendi strappy heels.

He ran a hand down my leg and pulled off my shoes.

"The shoes come first," he said as he tossed my new babies to the floor and turned out the light.

~

DID you enjoy The Shoes Come First? Here's a quick link back to The Shoes Come First to leave a review! (http://www.amazon.com/dp/B00TQHULKME) Every review helps other readers take a chance on falling in love with Jennifer Cloud! Thank you for reading! I hope you're looking forward to Jennifer Cloud's next adventure.

~

Turn the page to read the first chapter of *Dress 2 Impress (Book 2 in the Jennifer Cloud Novels)*

Scotland 1602

I WAS SITTING with my forehead resting on my knees, cursing Caiyan for leaving me here alone. My body ached from two days of riding on horseback around the Scottish countryside, looking for our mark. The mud oozed around me, stuck to my tartan skirt, and slipped inside my loafers. The icy rain drizzled down around me, and I wondered how much longer we were going to lie in this pigpen, waiting on our bad guy to appear. *Damn him for leaving me here to wait.*

I moved deeper into my shelter and sighed, reminding myself that I, Jennifer Cloud, had chosen to be part of this. Well, I'd chosen to continue to be part of the WTF, or World Travel Federation. When I was eighteen, I discovered I had the gift of time travel. Apparently, I inherited some special gene that allows me to travel through time. Great-Aint Elma Jean Cloud left me her time machine. The WTF refers to it as my time vessel. I call it a smelly old outhouse that scares the crap out of me every time I travel in it. I smiled at the memory of the argument my parents always had about the word *aint*. My dad is from the backwoods of East Texas, and everyone down there has aints, not aunts, as my East Coast parochial school mom would have corrected.

The friendly and much-wrinkled face of Aint Elma flashed to my mind. The vision of the little old lady with eyes the color of a summer sky, clapping with excitement over my gift, surfaced from my memories. When I met her at the age of nine, I didn't understand what was in store for me. A warm tingle caressed the skin above my heart. I reached up to touch the other gift Aint Elma had left me—her key. A medallion made from moonstone hung from a dainty but inviolable titanium chain around my neck. The unique medallion lay flat on my chest, hidden under the high-necked blouse with the plaid buttons. Carved in the moonstone was a crescent moon surrounded by tiny blue diamonds that sparkled like they had been freshly polished. I could feel a slight hum from the key, almost as if it were alive. In order for my outhouse to take me back in time, I have to wear the key and say a magic word. Sometimes I feel like I fell out of a Disney story.

I pulled the wool coat closer, trying to keep the wind at my back. My hair was secured under an ugly brown toboggan that matched my equally ugly wool coat. But I could feel the tendrils of my blond hair brush against my neck as they made their escape from the cap. One of the rules of the WTF was no hair dye. This rule was just in case I was sent back to a time when hair dye was obsolete. I think that might be the Stone Age, in which case, the locals wouldn't give a hoot what color my hair was as long as they could grab it and drag me to their cave. I put my foot down about going back to the dishwater blond from my childhood and finally compromised on a Marilyn Monroe blond. No highlights, no lowlights. Other rules included no tattoos, no fake fingernails, no body piercings (too late for that one—I had my ears pierced when I was five), and above all no implants. A prior transporter was injured back in time, and the local doctors operated on her, revealing her breast implants. The doctors promptly removed them, and she remained under arrest until the WTF could rescue her and convince the authorities the "water balloons" were not some kind of secret smuggling device. Thankfully, I inherited my mom's slim hips and voluptuous bustline.

The rain was tap-dancing above me on the small troll bridge that provided my shelter. How much longer was I going to wait? I had my limits. Caiyan had disappeared into the twilight, telling me to, *"Wait here, lassie."* I should have known the important question was "How long?" Instead, I just shook my head and smiled up into his gorgeous green eyes. The thoughts of last night's passion-filled frolic still embedded in my mind clouded my judgment. Caiyan is a defender. He works for the WTF and is sent back in time to capture the bad guys, or what the WTF calls brigands.

I am a transporter. The defenders can't haul the bad guys around, so it's up to me to come back and transport any brigands that Caiyan may catch back to headquarters. I am also his backup. Well, at least his backup in training. Since I am new to the WTF, Caiyan had to pull a few strings to allow me to assist him on this mission.

Before I left on this assignment, I was given a history lesson by my boss, Jake, on seventeenth-century Scotland. Jake was my childhood friend, and we had history together. I was as surprised as he was when our paths met again after a long on-again, off-again love affair. He took a job with the CIA, and I discovered how to time travel. Mamma Bea used to say, "Things happen for a reason, sugarplum." Those things keep happening to me like flies drawn to a cow pie. The reasons remain unknown.

Jake speed-tutored me for this trip, even though he didn't want me to travel until I was better trained. He threw all the customs and rituals of the very poor to the upper elite at me like darts at a dartboard. If only I could have unscrewed my head and poured the information in like cake batter, I might have recollection of them. Right now, all the information was a jumbled mess. Maybe Jake was right; I needed more training. The main brigand Caiyan usually followed was a smarmy guy named Rogue. Our mission was to capture him and bring him into custody at the WTF. I had helped capture Rogue on our first adventure together, but sadly, he escaped.

Rogue is after the missing key, allegedly owned by Mary Stuart, the queen of Scots. Although she didn't have the gift—that we can prove—we have a picture of her wearing the key. It was one of the few oils painted of her while Queen Elizabeth I imprisoned her. Although they were cousins, we believe Queen Elizabeth I was in cahoots with Lord Byron Mafuso, a known brigand. Rumors say they were responsible for the death of Mary's second husband, Lord Darnley. Blown up...

Rogue knows she gave the key to her lady's maid for safekeeping before she was beheaded on drummed-up charges of betraying Queen Elizabeth I. The trail is lost there until we get to 1746, when the key appears in a painting around Flora MacDonald's neck.

The MacDonalds are known for having the gift. We assume she used the key to transport Charles Edward Stuart, better known as Bonnie Prince Charlie, to safety during the Scottish rebellion. Rogue has attempted many times to retrieve the key before it gets to Flora.

There is some confusion as to what happens to the key after that, but Caiyan assures me the key is safe, and we need to keep it that way.

~

THE BOGGY SCENT of decaying vegetation rose up from the river bottoms. Huge naked trees hugged the sides of the riverbank and extended their branches like skeletal hands intertwined in prayer. I sighed as a small mud-covered frog leaped over my loafer. Jeez, the inhabitants of the river that ran under the bridge were starting to come after me. What was probably a beautiful babbling brook in the summer had turned into a raging river in November. The water below me swooshed and churned as I watched a tree branch float by at maximum velocity. I pulled tight on my coat and carefully exited my hidey-hole into the cool rain.

"Going somewhere, lassie?" Caiyan asked from above me. He was leaning casually on the railing of the bridge, staring down at me. Water dripped from the brim of his hat and cascaded down the shoulders of his black riding coat. The green plaid of his kilt matched the color of his eyes.

"How long have you been up there?"

"Only a minute. I rode back toward the village, and I saw Rogue stop at the inn."

"So is he coming?"

"Aye, I think Rogue will come this way after he has rested a bit. It's not an easy journey to cross the Minch by boat this time of year. He is most likely tired and hungry, but he knows he is out of time."

The rain had slowed to a light sprinkle and tickled as it hit my face. I scrunched my nose as I looked up at him. His silhouette was dark against the full moon over his left shoulder. A murky gray sky had hidden the sun all day, and the remaining light was waiting for the night to pull its cover over her.

"We should get under the bridge. It may be an hour or more before he passes here."

I grumbled at the thought but crawled back into the alcove. My feet squished in the mud as I moved over to allow Caiyan room in the space.

"Are ye cold?" He moved closer and drew me into his arms. It is impossible to carry anything with us when we go back in time. Money, food, and weapons are all things we have to acquire once we travel. We have the clothes on our backs and the keys around our necks. The only place items can be smuggled from present day is in our mouths. Before he met me, Caiyan would sneak condoms on his travels, in case he needed to sacrifice his body for the greater good. This random act of kindness would not have met with approval from our superiors. If the boss found out we'd brought an item from the present back in time, he would ground us. This meant our key would be locked up, and we could not lateral travel, which is the best perk about having this gift. I can go anywhere, anytime in the present, in the blink of an eye. I can also carry things in my pockets like money and cell phones. Last weekend I was in Paris buying *macarons* at Ladurée and dining at Le Soufflé.

"What's wrong?" he asked, removing his hat and placing it on the ground next to him.

"Nothing," I said.

"Ye huffed."

"No, I didn't."

"Aye, ye did."

Maybe I did. "I'm tired and cold and wet. Why can't we just go catch Rogue in a dry place?"

"Aye, today is *dreich*. Fetching the bad guys is not always done under sunny skies." I arched an eyebrow at him, and he snuggled in closer to me.

"Did your contact tell you this is the best place to get him before he gets the key?" I asked with a hint of sarcasm.

The last time we had to catch a brigand, Caiyan's contact was his past lover. She looked like she belonged on the cover of a fashion magazine, with a body like Jennifer Lopez and hair like spun silk. I knew that even if there was a contact, he wasn't going to divulge that information. Last time I found out by accident, actually by spying on him, but that's beside the point.

"No contact this time, lass." His face was inches from mine, and his green eyes seemed to glow in the shadows of the troll bridge. "I'm afraid we have to sit and wait this one out," he said, moving closer. He started to run his nose up the inside of my neck. Hot flashes nipped at my jaw and ran straight to my boy howdy. I turned my head and pressed my lips gently to his. A muffled, "Jeez," rumbled from deep inside his throat, and he kissed me hard. I intertwined my fingers through the back of his thick, dark hair. He moved slightly and ran his hand up my thigh and under my skirt. I was working the buttons on his wool coat when the sound of horse hooves beat overhead.

"*Shite!*" He scrambled from under the bridge. I made it out just in time to see Caiyan run up the hill and take a flying leap onto the back of Rogue's unsuspecting horse. The horse reared up and threw both men to the ground. I recognized Rogue from our previous meeting, when I was eighteen and had time traveled by mistake. Our first encounter was from

266

a distance, so I was surprised when he spoke with a strong Russian accent.

"Not this time, McGregor. You are not getting me before I recover that key."

"I am afraid so, my friend. Ye cannae have what doesn't belong to ye."

"You are no friend of mine, Scottish bastard." Rogue lunged at Caiyan, grabbing him around the middle. He was shorter than Caiyan but quite stocky, and his bulk knocked Caiyan off his feet and to the ground. Fists were flying, kilts were ripping, and curses were being yelled out in five languages. One loud crack and Caiyan was knocked out cold. Rogue pushed himself to his feet with a satisfied smile on his face. His knuckles were oozing blood, and he was rubbing his hand. I panicked and ran forward to help Caiyan. Rogue's head snapped up, making me realize he hadn't seen me behind the crest of the hill.

He sneered at me. "What is this?"

I stopped and tried to channel the local accent. "I am a friend of Caiyan's. We just met in the Highlands."

"I think not." He walked toward me, cutting off my path to Caiyan.

"I know who you are, little lady." He pointed a stubby, bloody finger at me. "You are the transporter, and as you can see, I will not be going on a ride with you today. In fact, I am going to make sure you don't take anyone anywhere, ever again!" He closed in on me, and I turned to run, but there was nowhere to go except the river. He caught me at the top of the embankment. Grabbing the collar on the back of my coat, he threw me to the ground. I quickly got to my feet, and we struggled. I was trying to remember the lessons my boss and ex-boyfriend, Jake, had given me on self-defense, but the only thing I could recall was to make it count. I reared back and sent my knee straight up into his groin. He released me, and I fell backward, landing with a hard thud onto my butt. His face paled with shock, and a Russian profanity (I am sure of it) escaped as a whisper from between his lips. He curled into a ball, rolled head over ass down the hill, and plopped into the raging water. I saw his head surface as he went bobbing down the river and out of sight.

As I stood to climb up the knoll and check on Caiyan, my shoes slipped on the muddy surface, and I began sliding down toward the river. My arms flailed in the air, and as I started my descent, a firm hand grabbed around my wrist, pulling me to safety.

"Now where do ye think ye are going, lassie?" Caiyan, thank God. He dragged me to the top of the hill, and we both collapsed, faces to the sky, panting from the physical effort. My adrenaline spike wore off, and the aftershock caused my entire body to shiver. He wrapped his arms around me until I settled.

"Are you hurt?" I asked him, trying to check his face for cuts in the dimming light.

"I think I might have broken a finger or two, but I'm used to the battle scars."

"We didn't get Rogue," I said, thankful that it was now too dark to see the disappointment in his eyes.

"Nay, but he will remember ye fer the next few days while he's icing his manhood." He chuckled and stood up, holding out his uninjured hand to help me to my feet. "We should go. Call your vessel."

"Don't you think we should try to track him? What if he comes back and takes the key?"

"The way that river is moving, I would say he will be lucky if he gets out before he hits the Atlantic Ocean. Besides, we dinnae have much time left."

I agreed with that. We only had about three to five days of the full-moon cycle before we had to return, and we had already spent a day in England and two days on horseback trekking around looking for the smarmy bastard. I didn't want to take any chances of getting stuck in the past because we missed our window of time. We stood in a clearing about thirty feet from the troll bridge, and I summoned my vessel. There was a crack of thunder, and presto, my outhouse appeared about ten feet in front of us. Weathered gray wood stood tall like a soldier waiting for the next assignment. The symbol of my key was carved above the door. A few seconds later, Caiyan's bright-red phone booth materialized next to my vessel.

"Don't you want to ride with me again?" I asked.

"Darlin'," he said, mocking my Texas accent, "I have seen you drive."

"Fine, you go first," I told him.

"Are ye afraid to face the boss man alone?" Caiyan asked, raising a dark eyebrow and crossing his arms over his chest.

"I just want to make sure you aren't going to stay behind for another shot at Rogue."

"I wouldnae dream of having all that fun without ye."

"OK, let's go at the same time."

A wisp of wind blew a stray lock of my hair across my face. Caiyan reached out and tucked it into my cap. His eyes stayed on mine, and I felt the long stare of contemplation piercing the back of my mind.

Caiyan leaned forward and kissed me good-bye. I entered my vessel and watched him enter his. I gave him a finger wave and sat there for a minute, going through the events of the past three days and trying to decide what to tell Jake.

ABOUT THE AUTHOR

Janet Leigh is a full-time chiropractor and acupuncturist. The Shoes Come First is her debut novel in the Jennifer Cloud series. She lives in Texas, where she splits her time between seeing patients and working on her next Jennifer Cloud adventure.

VISIT JANETLEIGHBOOKS.COM
FOR UPDATES, EXCERPTS, AND ALL THAT EXTRA STUFF

The Jennifer Cloud Novels
The Shoes Come First
Dress 2 Impress
3 Ways to Wear Red
In Style 4 Now